DECLARED HOSTILE

DECLARED HOSTILE

CAPT Kevin P. Miller USN (Ret.)

Aura Libertatis Spirat

DECLARED HOSTILE

Braveship Books
www.braveshipbooks.com

This book was edited by Linda Wasserman,
owner of Pelican Press Pensacola:

Pelican Press Pensacola
P.O. Box 15131
Pensacola, FL 32514
850-206-4608

www.pelicanpresspensacola.com

Cover Design by Asser Elnagar, 99Designs

Back cover photo courtesy of *Splash!* Magazine

Map courtesy of Central Intelligence Agency (Public Domain Resources)

ISBN-13: 978-1-939398-73-4
Printed in the United States of America

*To my mother, Margaret, who taught us
how to forgive, and how to be forgiven*

ACKNOWLEDGMENTS

No sooner was *Raven One* published when both my editor and publisher said I needed to write another one.

The warm reception my first novel has received is gratifying, and I'm told readers appreciate the authenticity of the action and especially the inside politics of squadron life with real people, all of them flawed, as all of us are.

Declared Hostile will also pull back the curtain of my former world as we explore another theater of operations, this one in our own hemisphere, and no less important to our national defense than the actions taking place in the Central Command Area of Responsibility in the Middle East.

I am in debt to those who helped me research the geostrategic situation of the area in which this novel takes place and suggest improvements to the rough manuscript. My War College classmate Rear Admiral Vince Atkins, U.S. Coast Guard, was instrumental to my understanding of the region and the pol/mil interplay of the many and diverse state and non-state actors involved. My trusted shipmate Captain Will Dossel, USN (Ret.) provided valuable story edits and detailed knowledge of threat systems that serve to enhance the realism of a plausible future scenario. Captain Kevin Hutcheson, USN (Ret.), a loyal friend since flight school, freely shared his thoughts on the moral aspects of warfare, the subject of his remarkable and well-researched doctoral thesis. A friend and squadronmate for almost as long, Captain Bill Johnson, USN (Ret.), contributed numerous edits that forced me to reassess the meanings of my passages and tighten them down for greater impact. Admiral Tim Keating, USN (Ret.), another trusted shipmate and friend, provided fascinating insights into the exercise of national power and high level command and control. Captain John Stevenson, USN (Ret.), my flight lead and mentor of many years, offered his thoughtful suggestions on leadership topics and kind encouragement to keep going and tell a story that needs to be told.

Fellow author and friend Kevin Lacz, a former Navy Special Operator, was free with his time and most helpful on how Special Operating Forces could play into scenarios I was contemplating. Shipmates, thank you for your assistance and friendship.

Two trusted agents, Chandler and Count, were key to my ability to insert the cockpit realism of today's naval aircraft into the flying scenarios when my experiences from the last century fell short. Thanks guys.

My superb editor and faithful friend Linda Wasserman of Pelican Press Pensacola did another outstanding job in editing this novel. Her love of and devotion to the English language is evident, and that coupled with her extraordinary attention to detail is a winning combination. *Declared Hostile* is Linda's second "deployment" with me, and, as with my other shipmates, it is an honor and privilege to serve alongside a true professional. Linda, well done!

The genius of Jeff Edwards and his micro publishing labels Stealth Books (and the newly-launched Braveship Books) was not completely evident to me when I joined his stable of authors. An outstanding and accomplished writer, Jeff saw the possibilities of the digital revolution where an independent author could succeed while writing the book he or she wants. If you like naval genre fiction, Jeff's USS *Towers* trilogy is a must, and readers of military action adventure and cutting edge science fiction should check out the offerings of Braveship Books and Stealth Books. Both imprints specialize in smart books for smart readers.

My family, led by Terry, has been supportive of my hours of solitary toil spent writing and editing. This is the same love and devotion she gave me during my years in uniform, allowing me to serve as I did. Without question Terry and spouses like her that kept the home fires burning served/serve our country and society. To paraphrase another noted naval aviation novelist, *where do we get such women?*

Military leaders seek responsibility and take ownership. Flaws found in *Declared Hostile* are 100% my responsibility.

CAPT Kevin Miller USN (Ret.)
Summer 2016

Glossary of Jargon and Acronyms

1MC — ship's public address system

5MC — flight deck loudspeaker system

20mm — Twenty millimeter cannon round, the size of an FA-18 and CIWS bullet, also known as "twenty mike-mike."

AAA — Anti-Aircraft-Artillery; Pronounced "Triple-A."

Afterburner — FA-18 engine setting that provides extra power by igniting raw fuel creating a controlled overpressure. Also known as "burner," "blower," "max," or "light the cans."

Air Boss — Officer in Primary Flight Control (ship's control tower) responsible for aircraft operations on deck out to five miles from ship.

AMRAAM — Advanced Medium Range Air-to-Air Missile (AIM-120)

AMV — *Aviación Militar Nacional Bolivariana de Venezuela* (current name of the Venezuelan Air Force).

Angels — altitude in thousands of feet. "Angels six" = 6,000 feet

ARG — Amphibious Ready Group

ATFLIR — Advanced Targeting Forward Looking Infrared. IR targeting sensor placed on fuselage mounted missile station.

AWACS — Airborne Warning and Control System; aka E-3 *Sentry* aircraft

Bandit — confirmed enemy airborne contact; also known as "'hostile."

Bingo — emergency fuel state divert from ship to shore base.

Bogey — unknown airborne contact

Bolter — tailhook flies past or skips over arresting wires, requiring a go-around for another attempt.

BRA — Bearing, Range, Altitude

CAG — Carrier Air Wing Commander; formerly Commander, Air Group

CAP — Combat Air Patrol

Cat — catapult

CDC — Combat Decision Center

CG	—	Guided Missile Cruiser
CIWS	—	Close-in Weapon System; surface ship 20mm gun primarily for terminal airborne threats.
CO	—	Commanding Officer; in aviation squadrons known as "skipper;" on ships, "Captain."
COD	—	Carrier On-Board Delivery. The C-2 *Greyhound* logistics aircraft is known as "the COD."
CPA	—	Closest Point of Approach
CVIC	—	Aircraft Carrier Intelligence Center
CVW	—	Carrier Air Wing
DCAG	—	Deputy Carrier Air Wing Commander
DDG	—	Guided Missile Destroyer
EP-3	—	signals reconnaissance variant of P-3 Orion aircraft, aka *Aires.*
FAV	—	*Fuerza Aérea Venezolana* (former name of the Venezuelan Air Force).
Fire Scout	—	popular name of MQ-8C unmanned helicopter.
Flag officer	—	admirals *or* generals…but typically a navy term for admiral.
Flanker	—	NATO code name for Su-27 series aircraft, to include the Su-30.
FLIR	—	Forward Looking Infra-Red. Targeting pod that detects heat contrasts. Aka ATFLIR.
Fox	—	radio call associated with firing of air-to-air missile with type. "Fox-2" = *Sidewinder*.
Fragged	—	as planned or previously assigned. "Proceed as fragged."
Fulcrum	—	NATO code name for MiG-29 series aircraft.
g	—	the force of gravity. "4 g's" is four times the force of gravity.
GPS	—	Global Positioning System
Growler	—	popular name of EA-18G Airborne Electronic Attack aircraft, a *Super Hornet* variant.
Gunner	—	squadron ordnance officer; typically a Chief Warrant Officer specially trained in weapons handling and loading.
HARM	—	High Speed Anti-Radiation Missile (AGM-88) used to home in on radar energy.
Hawkeye	—	popular name for E-2C Early Warning aircraft, also known as the *Hummer*.

Hellfire	—	popular name for AGM-114 air-to-surface missile.
Helo	—	helicopter
Hornet	—	popular name for FA-18C Strike Fighter.
HS	—	Helicopter Anti-Submarine Squadron
HSC	—	Helicopter Combat Support Squadron
HUD	—	Head-Up Display. Glass display in front of FA-18 pilot that depicts aircraft and weapons delivery information.
ICS	—	Inter Cockpit Communication System
IP	—	Initial Point
ISR	—	Intelligence, Surveillance, and Reconnaissance
JO	—	Junior Officer - lieutenant (O-3) and below.
JTAC	—	Joint Tactical Air Controller (formerly FAC – Forward Air Controller).
Knot	—	nautical mile per hour. One nautical mile is 2,000 yards or 6,000 feet.
LCS	—	Littoral Combat Ship
LEX	—	Leading Edge Extension. Narrow part of FA-18 wing leading to the nose of the aircraft.
LSO	—	Landing Signal Officer, also known as "Paddles."
MANPAD	—	Man Portable Air Defense System. ("Hand-held" SAM)
MIDS	—	Multifunctional Information Distribution System; displays linked information from other aircraft to build situational awareness.
Mk-76	—	25 lb. practice bomb, aka "blue death."
Mother	—	radio reference for the aircraft carrier.
Ninety-Nine	—	radio broadcast call used to gain attention; i.e. "listen up."
NORTHCOM	—	U. S. Northern Command
Nugget	—	first cruise pilot
NVGs	—	Night Vision Goggles
OPSO	—	Operations Officer
PLAT	—	Pilot Landing Aid Television; closed circuit video picture of flight deck operations.
Plug	—	take fuel from tanker.
Rhino	—	slang name for FA-18E/F *Super Hornet*.

ROE	—	Rules of Engagement
RPG	—	Rocket Propelled Grenade
RTB	—	Return to Base
SAM	—	Surface-to-air missile
SAR	—	Search and Rescue (CSAR is *Combat* Search and Rescue).
Seahawk	—	popular name for MH-60 series multi-mission helicopter.
Sidewinder	—	popular name for AIM-9 infrared heat seeking air-to-air missile.
Sierra	—	slang name for MH-60S *Seahawk*.
SLAM-ER	—	Standoff Land Attack Missile – Expanded Response.
SOF	—	Special Operating Forces
SOUTHCOM	—	U.S. Southern Command
Strike	—	tactical airspace controller/coordinator in vicinity of ship.
Super Hornet	—	popular name for upgraded FA-18E/F single seat or two-place Strike Fighter with increased range and payload; also known as "*Rhino.*"
Texaco	—	nickname for a tanker aircraft, typically S-3B.
TLAM	—	Tomahawk Land Attack Missile; long range cruise missile launched from surface ships and submarines.
TOPGUN	—	Navy Fighter Weapons School, Fallon, NV
Trap	—	arrested landing
VAQ	—	Fixed Wing Electronic Attack squadron
VAW	—	Fixed Wing Early Warning squadron
VFA	—	Fixed Wing Fighter Attack squadron
VID	—	visual identification
Viper	—	slang name for F-16 *Fighting Falcon*.
VLS	—	Vertical Launch System; missile launchers found on cruisers and destroyers.
Winchester	—	out of ordnance
Wire	—	A 1.25" diameter steel cable stretched across carrier landing area to arrest tailhook aircraft, also known as "the cable" or "cross deck pendant."
XO	—	Executive Officer

CVW-6 "Broadsword" call letters AE "Alpha Echo"

Squadron	Nickname	side number	Callsign	type aircraft	ready room #
VFA-23	Blue Lancers	(100)	"*Raider*"	FA-18F	RR 7
VFA-54	Hells Angels	(200)	"*Hobo*"	FA-18E	RR 6
VFA-16	Firebirds	(300)	"*Ridgeline*"	FA-18C	RR 5
VFA-62	Hunters	(400)	"*Arrow*"	FA-18E	RR 8
VAQ-144	Gremlins	(500)	"*Comet*"	EA-18G	RR 1
VAW-129	Sea Shadows	(600)	"*Condor*"	E-2C	RR 2
HSC-18	Rustlers	(610)	"*Flintlock*"	MH-60S	RR 4
HSM-76	Whalers	(700)	"*Harpoon*"	MH-60R	RR 3

Strike-Fighter Squadron SIXTEEN (VFA-16) Officers

CDR Jim Wilson	Commanding Officer	*Flip*
CDR Jennifer Schofield	Executive Officer	*Annie*
LCDR Ted Armstrong	Operations Officer	*Stretch*
LCDR Sam Cutter	Maintenance Officer	*Blade*
LCDR Rich Freeman	Administrative Officer	*Ripper*
LCDR Kristin Teel	Safety Officer	*Olive*
LCDR Chester Brown	Maint. Material Control Officer	*Chet*
LT Mike Rhodes	Strike Fighter Tactics Instructor	*Dusty*
LT Mark James	Training Officer	*Trench*
LT John Madden	Quality Assurance Officer/LSO	*Coach*
LT Eric Williams	AV/ARM Division Officer	*Killer*
LT Jacob Jensen	Airframe Division Officer	*Big Jake*
LT Ryan Rutledge	Line Division Officer	*Ghost*
LT Conner Davis	Personnel Officer	*Irish*
LTJG Tiffany Rourke	Schedules Officer	*Macho*
LTJG Joe Kessler	NATOPS Officer/LSO	*Jumpin'*
ENS Quan Smith	Material Control Officer	*Quan*
ENS Shane Duncan	Intelligence Officer	*Wonder Woman*
CWO4 Christian Short	Ordnance Officer	*Gunner*

PROLOGUE

(Over the Yucatan Channel)

Doctor Leighton Wheeler suppressed a yawn as he arched his back and stretched his arms. With nearly two hours to go in the cockpit of the Beech *King Air*, he fought the urge to sleep. Mercifully, a half-moon high above kept him company and provided a horizon out in the middle of the Gulf of Mexico, but he lightly slapped his face to stay awake. He knew he was now, at this 1:00 am hour, in the trough of human performance, and he had to concentrate on his gyro horizon and altimeter. Five hundred feet—even with altitude hold engaged, it was unnerving to be so low over the black water underneath. He figured it didn't make much of a difference. One hundred feet or one thousand feet; it looked the same over a dark ocean. He was tired, and the energy drink he had downed before take-off was now wearing off. He considered another one, but the physician in him rejected the idea. He twisted off the top of a plastic water bottle instead and took a long swig. He carefully replaced the top, and as he put the bottle back in the cup holder, he glanced at his fuel...a little over 2,200 pounds with 453 miles to go and fifteen knots of wind in his face. He would make it, but barely.

Wheeler twisted the heading select switch to 324, and the aircraft rolled gently right as it steadied up on course. *Nothing out here,* he thought, unlike the Yucatan Channel some forty minutes earlier. He had not been able to avoid flying right over a half-dozen lights below him. Not knowing what they were had bothered him, but they were most likely fishing boats, Cuban and Mexican. He knew it was too early for the motor and sailing yachts, most of which spent the winters in and around the Virgin Islands, and the Belize yacht traffic was another month away at least.

The moon illuminated the low scattered clouds, so typical above Caribbean waters. They cast splotchy shadows on the surface below. Wheeler knew the next hour would be boring, so to pass the time, he thought of his favorite subject...himself.

A youthful forty-seven years old, Wheeler owned, with three partners, the Women's Cosmetic Center, the top plastic surgery clinic in

Birmingham, Alabama. They offered everything from rhinoplasty to Botox…the whole gamut of services, many on an outpatient basis. The overwhelming majority of the procedures were boob jobs, with augmentation surgeries leading the way. For nearly two decades the Women's Cosmetic Center had offered hope and delivered results, with the ladies (and their men) gladly paying top dollar for their services. It was a gold mine.

Just last month two of Wheeler's clients had brought in their teenage daughters for consults. Cullen, his own teenage daughter, wanted him to perform an augmentation for her 16th birthday—to a tasteful C-cup that would "allow her clothes to fit better," an argument that was part of the tried and true cover story. He certainly wasn't about to let his lecherous partners touch her. Cullen would go to Atlanta with her mother, Tammy, for the procedure, allowing time to recuperate before her birthday party next month.

Tammy. A former homecoming queen at Alabama, Tammy had never allowed anyone to augment *her*—not even her husband, despite how much he had wanted to add some strategic curves to her tall and leggy figure. She was all for her husband performing plastic surgery for *other* women, and Wheeler had done work on several of her girlfriends. He had even had an affair with one of them that Tammy probably knew about but didn't press him on. No, all was perfect with Tammy: hair, makeup, body, clothes, house, kid, husband…in that order. Between the Garden Club, the Tri-Delt national vice-presidency and innumerable shopping trips to Atlanta and Nashville, Tammy had little time for her husband. That was all the excuse he needed.

Ten years ago he had taken up flying and now was the instrument-rated owner of a *King Air* twin. He used the plane for trips to South America to perform *pro bono* reconstructive surgery on cleft palates for Doctors without Borders, giving deformed kids a chance for a normal life. Yes, the guys at the Club admired him for it, *giving back* to underprivileged third-world kids and all that.

He accepted their kind words with aw-shucks modesty, never letting on for a minute about his *other* motive: holding heavenly bodies in Bogotá and Cartagena and watching what the owners of those bodies *could do* with them. The coke, the money, the nightlife, and the girls—always the girls. *I'm an American surgeon, here to help children.* He would say it with a shy smile, looking down at his drink. And the girls crumbled before his eyes; leaning in, grateful, fawning, *buying it*, cooing in English or Spanish. It didn't matter. Within the hour, they would lead him out of the hotel lounge and to their rooms or apartments—rich European girls on holiday, local gold-diggers, sophisticated American businesswomen, Asian flight attendants on layover, ages ranging from 22 to 50. A citizen of the world like Doctor Leighton Wheeler believed in diversity.

The first year he flew to South America twice, and now he was on his fourth trip in the past 12 months. Surely Tammy suspected something, but his altruistic alibi provided cover for both of them. She took advantage of his absences with shopping outings with her girlfriends to Atlanta or New York. Both felt entitled.

Yes, the coke! How it felt when it entered his nostrils, the euphoric explosion of his senses. The girls fed it to him! They carried it in their purses and formed neat lines for him on their creamy thighs. And the guys at the airport loved to look at the plane, crawl around inside, talk flying. *Señor Doctor, want a blow before you take off?* And he would take a hit and fly hundreds of miles to the Caymans in what seemed like minutes, alert like he had never been before, feeling like he could fly on to Alaska if he had the fuel. Cocaine just didn't seem to be a big deal south of the U.S. border.

One day a guy he had befriended during a previous trip was at the airport and asked if he could take a package of "product" with him back to Birmingham. "C'mon, man. No one is going to suspect you, Mister Save-the-Children Surgeon!"

The guy tossed a worn duffel bag in back with his other luggage and handed him a black zipped-up folder. Wheeler glanced inside and quickly closed it, but once he got airborne with the autopilot engaged, he laid the contents out on the seat next to him and counted: *five hundred* Ben Franklins and one typed note.

"Mike" met him at the FBO in Birmingham to park him and to service the aircraft, just like the note said. He smiled as he pulled the bags from the compartment, placed the duffel in his tractor, and helped Wheeler button up the airplane. Chatting away, he was a really friendly guy, one of the nicest guys Wheeler had ever met. When they were finished, Mike offered his hand, just as a golf partner would coming off the 18th green. "Enjoyed it!" he said.

Wheeler had found yet *another* double life to lead, one that paid very, very well, more than enough to cover any of Tammy's activities. *Sure, Honey, go to Lenox Square Mall in Buckhead. Take Cullen. Anything you want. Have fun!*

Tonight Wheeler was on his fourth "mission," and it was a big one. He had told Tammy he was going to spend a couple of nights in the Caymans and rest—and get something nice for Cullen—before he took off for home.

Once he arrived at George Town and parked his plane, "Luis" met him and led him to a different *King Air*, one loaded with product worth over $100 million on the street. With a box lunch and a five-hour energy drink, he set off in the aircraft for a dirt strip along the Mississippi coast called Goombay Smash Field. He would abandon the airplane there—the cost of doing business—and "Rich" would pick him up, drive him to Diamond Head, and put him in a G5 for a sprint back to the Caymans. The morning sun would still be low in the sky by the time they landed back at George Town.

After a day of rest at the hotel, maybe a little *senorita* overnight, he would fly his own plane to Birmingham the next day for another hero's welcome—and a $5 million payday. A yacht. Yes, a yacht would look good parked next to their condo in Orange Beach. He would go to Miami next week and make a down payment on a 53-footer. Once the purchase was sealed, he would make a house call on a former augmentation client—to perform an important post-op examination, of course. That client, and many, many others, inspired the name with which he would christen his new yacht: *Two for the Show.*

A sudden *whoomm* on his right startled him. He studied the eastern horizon but saw nothing but ghostly clouds overhead—no lighting flash. He held his gaze and strained his eyes for several seconds. Nothing. He wished this airplane, expendable or not, had weather radar in it and cursed the cheap screw *narcotrafficales* for not getting him a suitable plane for a long, overwater flight. Instead they had put him in this rattle-trap to save overhead dollars. He checked the INS and noted he was making 265 knots ground. The wind must have shifted to the east. And, for the umpteenth time tonight, he checked the fuel, doing a mental time-distance calculation.

What was that? he thought. *A bird? Did I hit a bird?* The airplane hadn't twitched, so he reasoned it may have been an engine surge…but all seemed normal. There were no indicator lights. He shifted in his seat uncomfortably, wishing he had a blow right now, and turned his thoughts back to Miami.

Suddenly, he flinched as if electrically jolted by loud *pops* coming from the right engine. Wheeler let out an involuntary *Fuck me!* as the airplane rolled hard right and the right engine, mere feet away, exploded into flame. *Oh, God, please!* he cried, instinctively pulling the airplane left and up, away from the water below. Red and yellow lights flared on the instrument panel, and the annunciator bleated shrill warnings of danger. He pushed the throttles forward and felt heavy vibration from the right side, so he retarded the right throttle to idle and fed left rudder to stay balanced. He was already passing 1,000 feet, hyperventilating, and was nearly paralyzed with fear at the persistent flames coming from the right engine nacelle. Whimpering in confusion, he noted airspeed rapidly passing through 120 knots. *Don't stall the damn thing!* He let out another involuntary sound as he pushed the yoke down.

His heart pounded as his hand lifted the right throttle around the detent to shut down the engine. *Mayday!* he cried without thinking, then realized he was truly alone over the invisible sea, the nearest land over 100 miles away. Should he turn right to Cuba? Left to Mexico? He hit the right engine fire light, which mercifully doused the flames, and turned the yoke easy left. *What the fuck?* Still breathing hard through his mouth, his eyes went to the RPM gauge in an attempt to identify why the right engine had burst into flame. He was in a positive climb—even a shallow 100 foot per minute rate of climb was welcome—and he calmed down enough to think about a divert into Cancun. As he rifled through the maps to find the low altitude chart and dial up Cancun's VOR/DME, he made a decision. This was it, no more trips to South America, *ever*.

With a deafening series of staccato hammer blows, the right side of the cockpit erupted into fragments. As the instrument panel exploded in front of him, Wheeler drew his hands and arms in by reflex to defend himself from the flying debris. The windscreen shattered, then caved in from the airspeed. Wheeler was conscious of only three things: the rubbish and forced air swirling about him, the loud roar of the left engine permeating the cockpit, and the fact he was crying out in terrified shock.

Bullets? Is someone shooting at me? Why? Who? Mexicans? Cubans? Out here, at this hour? Then, without warning Wheeler was slammed against the left side of the cockpit with more force than he had ever experienced. A metallic wrenching sound accompanied a violent roll right, and he realized he was upside down and still rolling. *An aileron roll in a King Air!* His control inputs were powerless to stop it, and sensing flames again, he began to scream, *Please, God, no! This can't be happening!* Watching the altimeter unwind, not knowing what caused it, not knowing what to do, Wheeler feared the unspeakable. *Not now! Not here!*

Pinned as he was amid the churning chaos, Wheeler's charmed life flashed before his eyes. Brian, his childhood best friend, smiling at him, hair flowing behind as they rode their sting-ray bikes down a steep hill. Tammy's loving brown eyes looking up as they walked hand-in-hand to her dorm. A group of med school classmates laughing as he told a joke at the pub near the hospital. A beaming five-year-old Cullen running up to him as he got out of his car after a day at the clinic. Sitting in the church pew during Easter Sunday services, looking up at his mother—his beautiful young mother in a smart suit, her smooth skin and dark hair in its sixties flip highlighted under a pillbox hat. Her red lips forming a tender smile as she took his hand. *"God loves you, Leighton."*

The *King Air,* one wing gone, corkscrewed through the darkness in a near vertical dive. Trapped by the force of it, Doctor Leighton Wheeler, tears pushed *back* toward his temples, was filled with regret.

"I'm sorry, God," he shouted with eyes closed. *"I'm sorry."* He cracked open his eyes in time to see the yellow light from his burning plane reflected on the surface of the Caribbean as it rushed up to meet him.

Part I

Just say no.

—Nancy Reagan

CHAPTER 1

(USS *Coral Sea*, anchored, St. Thomas, V.I.)

In his summer white uniform Jim Wilson, Commanding Officer of the VFA-16 *Firebirds,* walked briskly through the hangar bay to the fantail. He carried a small overnight bag and was happy to be getting off the ship.

St. Thomas! How many years had it been? Fourteen, he figured. The view of the island through the El 4 opening brought back the excitement he had experienced as a JO at this, his first "foreign" port. The island jutted out of the blue Caribbean, lush and green. The mountaintops were dotted with homes, and brilliantly lit soft cumulus clouds hovered above them in the late afternoon sky.

Join the Navy and see the world. Exotic and tropical, St. Thomas was one of the nicer ports the Navy visited.

Navy ships, however, rarely called on St. Thomas or any of the Virgin Islands. And since the late 90s, when Wilson was here as a new-guy—a "nugget"—it had become rarer still for a *carrier* to "drop the hook" in the roadstead. During that time, the demise of the Atlantic Fleet Weapons Training Facility had been precipitated by a fatal live-fire training accident—one that involved a civilian target range worker on the nearby island of Vieques. The lives of the naval aviators who crashed in these waters during their training over the years were seldom given a second thought by the press or by the people of the United States, the stories typically buried on page six as events involving a "routine training mission," the aircrew "not identified pending notification of next of kin." Yet, public pressure about this one civilian death had caused the Navy to withdraw, and with the inability to use Vieques for training, the Navy had stopped coming to the region. The result was a second-order effect that dawned on the local populace too late: the Navy also closed the massive training base of Roosevelt Roads, Puerto Rico.

As Wilson made his way around the "yellow gear" tractors and engine storage cans stashed at the far end of the hangar bay, he took care not to smudge his spotless trousers or scuff his shoes on a grimy tie-down chain. A carrier visit was special, and the local Navy League was pulling out all the stops with a big reception at the Frenchman's Reef resort. Ship and air wing senior officers were invited, and as a squadron CO, "Flip" Wilson knew better than to miss this "command performance" with the heavies and local mucky-mucks. He was just glad he would be able to join the rest of his squadron, now partying on the other side of the island in shorts and t-shirts, later in the evening.

"*Dude.*"

Wilson turned to face his fellow squadron CO and longtime friend, Commander William "Billy" Martin of the VFA-62 *Hunters.* He had snuck up on Wilson from the starboard side.

"Hey, Billy. Figured a liberty hound like you would already be ashore."

"You confuse me with the junior officer of my youth. It's gotten to the point where I actually *like* going through my in-box paperwork. Heaven help me!"

"Better not let the JOs get wind of this," Wilson answered.

"They are the ones who save it till the night before we pull in! They know I can't ignore a full in-box."

The officers entered a passageway on the port side that led to the fantail. They passed a long line of sailors in civilian clothes who were braced against the bulkhead waiting for the ferry to take them ashore.

Wilson recognized some of his young petty officers and said, "Have fun, guys."

As he strode past, the sailors smiled. "You too, Skipper."

Wilson and Billy walked onto the fantail and assessed the situation. The admiral's barge was standing off the "camel," a floating dock lashed to the ship's accom ladder platform. A ferry was alongside the camel in the process of boarding hundreds of sailors dressed in civilian clothes.

Several Carrier Air Wing SIX skippers and XOs milled about the fantail. They awaited word from the harried Officer of the Deck they could board the admiral's barge for an evening of forced fun. Wilson's Executive Officer, Commander Jennifer Schofield was among them.

"Hey, Annie, what's the word?" greeted Billy.

Jen Schofield's fiery red hair had earned her the call sign, but her personality was easygoing and reserved. She had come up with the F-14 community, transitioned to the FA-18 after one *Tomcat* tour, and was a former CAG LSO. She had over 800 carrier landings in her logbook, along with a fair amount of combat green ink. On her uniform she wore the Air Medal with a numeral 5 and two Navy Commendation Medals with combat V. Where men with this record would be referred to as Salty Dogs, the refined and capable Commander Schofield exuded professionalism and class.

"Hey, guys! I think they're going to board us as soon as they get this ferry off. Saw lots of smiling *Firebird* and *Hunter* sailors."

"Good," Wilson said. "And our JOs?"

"*Oh, yeah!* Trench is leading the charge to a place called Breezy Cay. Been there before?" Annie asked.

"Yeah, but it's been a few years," Wilson replied. "Nice place on the other side of the island."

"We have an admin at the resort next door," Billy said. "Should be plenty of air wing guys." He motioned to the shore and added, "But, by the looks of it, *that* place is nice."

The officers assessed the resort perched a mile away on the rocky shore of Frenchman's Reef. The barge would soon transport them there for the reception.

Annie then said in jest, "Do you see Mark? He said he'd be waving to us." Annie's husband Mark Schofield was in St. Thomas waiting for the ship—and his wife.

"Nope, can't say I do," Billy said, squinting as if he could. He squinted a little harder and smiled. "But I do see a fruity drink with my name on it."

"With an umbrella in it?" Wilson snickered.

"Maybe. Just don't tell the JOs. I want them to visualize me only with a beer bottle or whisky on the rocks. But when I get among the one percent, I can let my hair down with a rum runner, or even a glass of *white wine.*"

Annie shook her head and smiled, but Wilson continued to needle his friend. "Is that your foo-foo juice I smell?

They both looked at Annie. "Don't look at me!" She raised her hands in protest. "That's not my fragrance!"

The ferry pushed off to deliver a full load of sailors to the fleet landing at Charlotte Amalie. As soon as it pulled away, the barge, a motorized 50-foot covered launch for the admiral's official and personal use, came in behind it with *bosun*'s mates positioned on the bow and stern to throw mooring lines to waiting sailors on the camel. Soon the officers would board in the traditional manner of seafaring professionals around the world: junior officers first; then seniors; with the admiral, the last man aboard...and the first man off when they got ashore.

The Officer of the Deck caught their attention. "Lady and gentlemen, you may board," he said and motioned them toward the ladder.

The officers made their way to the ladder in some semblance of seniority. As they flashed their ID cards, they informed the Petty Officer of the Watch, "I have permission to go ashore." Each one of them carefully descended the ladder to avoid smudging their uniforms, but everyone knew their whites would be trashed by the end of the night, if not on this boat ride.

Once on the gently rolling platform, Wilson and Annie queued up to the barge which was bobbing alongside. In a chivalrous move contrary to naval protocol, Wilson boarded first and took Annie's hand. In her heels, she expertly timed the roll and boarded. They joined other air wing officers in the forward cabin, all chatting amicably and excited at the prospect of going ashore. They then heard the 1MC blare from the ship towering above them.

Ding, ding, ding, ding. "Carrier Air Wing SIX, departing."

Ding, ding, ding, ding. "*Coral Sea*, departing."

Ding, ding, ding, ding. "Staff, departing."

Ding, ding, ding, ding, ding, ding. "Carrier Strike Group Eighteen, departing"…*ding.*

Minutes later, the Air Wing Commander, the carrier Captain, the Chief of Staff, and the admiral—resplendent in their summer whites and each with multiple rows of ribbons—emerged from the ship and onto the camel, boarding in proper order. The captain, an amiable helicopter pilot by trade, poked his head inside the forward cabin. "Hi, guys!" he said in his booming voice, quickly scanning the group in an informal muster. Without waiting for a response, he left to join the admiral in the aft cabin. as the seated officers smiled and waved back.

Captain Rick Sanders was a celebrity aboard *Coral Maru*, a nickname the crew used for the carrier. Each day he walked the ship from stem to stern, shook the hands of his enlisted sailors, asked them about their jobs or how things were going at home, and took time to pass the word over the 1MC on the upcoming schedule and to recognize top performers. *Airman Schmuckatelli in the ship's laundry, you are the winner of today's* Coral Sea *"What-a-Guy of the Day"* award. Female sailors appropriately earned the "What-a-Gal" award. Division officers and chiefs sometimes worried that the Captain handed out so many 96-hour liberty chits there would be nobody left to stand duty. Sanders didn't care, and he smiled and pressed the flesh with the skill of any seasoned politician—which he was.

Rear Admiral Roland Meyerkopf, Commander, Carrier Strike Group Eighteen, was at the other end of the personality spectrum. A career submariner, nuclear-trained as was Sanders, Meyerkopf was tight-lipped and taciturn. His eyes lit up when he discussed issues related to the nuclear plant but became bored—or was more likely out of his depth—concerning issues related to the operational employment of this "bird farm." Tall and almost completely bald, he went to the evening's reception as he would to an inspection. Both events were to be feared lest he or one of his staff make an error, and small talk with strangers did not come easy to him. Once seated in the stern, his aide handed him a folder that included two sets of papers: the dossiers of the local civic leaders he could expect to meet, and his prepared remarks for a speaking responsibility he had not sought, but which he knew would be thrust upon him sometime during the evening.

The Wing Commander, or "CAG," filled out the trio of senior leaders aboard *Coral Sea*. Like Wilson, Captain Tim Matson was a *Hornet* pilot, six years his senior. He was also an easygoing friend since Matson had taught him to fly the *Hornet* long ago when Wilson was new to the airplane. Wilson considered himself fortunate that his boss was also a friend, and Wilson's wife, Mary, was close to Matson's wife, Barbara. Tonight, however, Wilson's friend and boss needed to support *his* boss in this forced-fun function.

The barge cast off from the camel, and at the request of the Captain, traversed the starboard side of the ship before turning to shore. The officers' eyes automatically inspected the hull of the steel mountain floating next to them, some looking at spots of rust, others at refueling stations and others at the tails of aircraft sticking over the flight deck sixty feet above. Wilson thought of the immensity of it. He was continually amazed carriers like this were built by human hands. Holding *Coral Sea* in place were three hundred and twenty-five pound links of anchor chain that stretched tight from the hawse pipe to the sea. The coxswain turned the barge left under the shadow of the bow on their way to shore.

The motor thrummed them forward as the boat rolled and pitched gently in the light swells. As the sun sank lower in the western sky, Wilson and the others inspected the green hills of St. Thomas through the windows and watched the waves crash against the rocky shoreline. The smell of hibiscus and agave filled the air when the barge grew close, and Wilson noted a large white-hulled cruise ship standing out from the Charlotte Amalie terminal. The ship was ready to begin her night's voyage on the smooth sea caressed by the gentle trades. Puffy clouds dotted the horizon, and far to the southeast an impressive line of thunderstorms reflected the light of the setting sun.

Ten minutes after leaving the ship, the pitch of the engine changed as the coxswain maneuvered the barge along the wooden pier. Someone commented on the hundreds of wooden stairs along the cliff leading to the resort above. Annie smiled. Navigating the stairs in a skirt was a small price for her to pay, knowing her husband was waiting for her at the top of them.

As the experienced coxswain manipulated the throttles, a deckhand jumped off the barge and tied the bow line to the cleat, then secured the aft mooring line thrown by his shipmate. Once the barge was tight against the pier, the officers disembarked in order of seniority. A lieutenant greeted the admiral with a salute and led him to the reception. The rest of the white-clad officers trudged up the stairs in order, glad to be ashore after two weeks underway. Many of them commented on the iguana that sunned itself on the rocks in the remaining light, its disinterest in the noisy humans quite evident.

The music of Bob Marley greeted them as they completed the last of the steps, and a low wall invited them to pop their heads over it to take in the spacious resort deck, with its pools, lounge chairs, palm trees, and food laid out on long tables. In addition, servers wearing bow-ties moved among the guests offering fare from their trays. White uniformed officers mingled with the local heavy hitters, who, by the looks of them, were mostly elderly. Sprinkled here and there, however, were what appeared to be a few bored college-age granddaughters in cocktail dresses, disappointed at the lack of *Coral Sea* officers anywhere close to their own age. One loud matron grabbed the captain as soon as he appeared and introduced him to a distinguished looking gentleman in white trousers and blue blazer complete with ascot. The heavies seemed to be enjoying the forced fun with their newfound island friends—smiles all around. However, Wilson and Billy, along with most of the pilots, were thinking the same thing: Find a can of beer, fast.

"There's my girl!"

At the sound of his voice, Jen Schofield walked up to her burly husband. Ten years older than his wife, and with a shock of white hair and goatee to match, Mike Schofield could be characterized as a biker—the big, rotund, loud, and uncouth version. He had served on destroyers as an enlisted man in the early 80s, and when he got out, had gone into the automobile sound business. It came as no surprise that he made a fortune selling the best systems to Norfolk area sailors. Annie smiled shyly and then yelped as he enveloped her, lifting her off the ground.

"Ha, haaa.... Welcome ashore, sweetie!" Mike boomed.

"*Put me down!*" Annie said under her breath, and when he did, she quickly scanned the crowd to see who, if anyone, had noticed the display. As she straightened her blouse, Mike moved in for a kiss.

Mike finished and then offered his meaty hand to his wife's boss. "Hey, Jim! Good to see you!"

"You too, Mike. You know Billy Martin?"

Mike squeezed Billy's hand in his vice-like grip. "Ha! 'Billy' Martin! You guys have the best handles! How you doin', man?" Annie watched the men, no longer as a senior fighter pilot but as a demure wife giving her husband the stage. Not that she had much of a choice when Mike was around. Larger than life and completely comfortable in his skin, he was a good husband and father to their eight-year-old son. Wilson knew Mike was the right guy for Annie. Knowing her when they were both lieutenants, Annie had confided once that her boyfriends could not deal with the fact Annie's job was way cooler than theirs. She could overlook the white hair and beer belly of a man who could accept her for who she was and still treat her like a woman.

The loud matron had the admiral, captain, and CAG cornered as she presented them to more St. Thomas A-listers. In this situation, the squadron COs and XOs were the *de facto* junior officers, and as they had learned over the course of their careers, knew to hit the bar and buffet table early, and in that order. They made small talk with some of the civilians, mostly retired businessmen from the eastern seaboard who made fortunes in clothing, or investment banking, or real estate. All of them peppered Wilson and the others in uniform with questions about the ship, incredulous that they could actually fly high performance airplanes off it. They asked the usual questions about how high and fast the planes could fly and sincerely thanked them for their service. Wilson nodded and smiled. "It's our pleasure," he told them.

Heads turned to the steps leading to the pool deck when a middle-aged man appeared. He was of medium height, with receding hair slicked back into curls, wearing a blue blazer and peach shirt open to reveal layers of gold chains against his brown, leathery skin. Conversation stopped, however, because of the stunning woman who accompanied him. Tall, with flowing brown hair and a brick-house figure spilling out of her too-short dress, she towered over the man in her five-inch spikes.

For a moment, all the assembled men were slack jawed. "*Whoa!*" muttered Billy.

With a satisfied smile, the man led her down the steps while the matron rushed over with the admiral in tow. The man looked important, enjoying the attention from everyone, and the girl was clearly an armpiece, dutifully offering obligatory saccharine smiles at each introduction. Almost a full head length above her companion, she surveyed the crowd, bored and uninterested.

Amused, Annie broke the silence. "You guys never seen a trophy wife before?"

Billy answered, "*That* is an accoutrement, and if she *is* his wife, she's number four or five."

"That's what you red-blooded American men are fighting for!" Mike boomed, too loud as usual. "Me, I've got my honey right here!" He pulled Annie close to him, almost causing her to lose her balance. Wilson watched her give him a look to calm down, which he playfully ignored.

"Think she's a pro?" Wilson offered to anyone.

"If she is, she's not from around these parts," Mike answered. Annie turned to her husband and raised an eyebrow.

"And how would *you*, know?" she asked him with a half playful, half withering look.

"Hey, I was once a sailor on liberty in Saint Thomas, and I don't remember her—or anyone that looked like her. Not that I was looking! And I'm not looking now! Actually, I'm not sure I was ever here! Ah, what were we talking about?" Mike guffawed at his own infectious humor.

Annie, feigning disgust, nodded slowly at her husband as he pulled her to him once again. Mike ignored the Navy's rules about public displays of affection in uniform that pertained to his wife, not to him.

A microphone appeared and the matron took it, gushing over the assembled *Coral Sea* officers, especially the admiral, with whom she appeared to be smitten. At the appropriate time, Admiral Meyerkopf took the microphone and graciously thanked the Navy League and the people of Saint Thomas for their warm hospitality. Professional and confident—and well prepared—he didn't leave anyone out as he thanked the locals by name and impressed upon them the importance of this port visit to the Navy. The civilian guests beamed.

Once the perfunctory remarks concluded, the steel drum resumed the island beat and everyone was ready for another round of drinks. In the dimming twilight, Wilson walked to the railing and viewed the 100,000-ton ship at anchor. Resplendent in "dress ship" lighting that cascaded from the mast to the bow and stern, with row upon row of gray aircraft parked on her deck, she dominated the entry to the harbor. A ferry had just left, chugging across the gentle waves with another load of sailors ready for a night in town. They had five hours until midnight when *Cinderella Liberty* would expire for many of them. Plenty of time, he surmised for them to find fun—or trouble. As Wilson pondered the good ship *Coral Maru* from a mile away, he imagined himself abeam, hook down, through the 90, picking up the ball, easing the power as he slid across the imaginary wake, on centerline, on glideslope…

"Hey."

Wilson turned with a start. The tall brunette stood right next to him waiting for a response.

CHAPTER 2

(Frenchman's Reef Resort)

"Hey," Wilson replied. She looked directly at him. Her soft smile suggested she was his friend and wanted to talk.

"Come here often?" she asked with a coy turn of her head. Wilson tried to place the accent.

"Couple of times a career. How about you?"

"First time. *Love* it," she drawled. *Texas? Mississippi?*

"What brings you here?" Wilson asked and turned to face her. *Billy was right. Whoa!*

She motioned toward her companion who was engaged in conversation with a group of men on the other side of the pool. "*Him.* Sugah Daddy. His name is Marvin, and I met him three days ago."

Wilson was intrigued. "Three days, and here you are on his arm in Saint Thomas?"

"Uh-huh. Anything *wrong* with that?" She was locked on Wilson, playing with him just by *standing* next to him. Having been made the center of attention, Wilson sensed he was at a disadvantage. He wanted to continue the conversation, though, so he played along.

"Where did you meet him?"

"At work – *Ruby Redds*, in North Richland Hills. I dance there."

"*Do* you?"

"*Yes!* Have *you* been there, Mister Hero?"

"Can't say that I have."

"Well, you do look *familiar*. Maybe I've seen you in Austin, or Houston."

"Don't think so, but tell me, why are you here with…?"

"Marvin…he needed a girl on his arm, so I said *fine*. He flew me down on his private plane to stay in a deluxe suite at this here resort and sun myself all day by the pool. And all I have to do is walk in with him and walk out with him. *That's it.*"

17

Wilson gave her a look, skeptical.

"It's *not* what you think. You *spectators* can look all day long, but no *touchin'* and that goes for my rich friend over there. He stays on his side of the room, and he gets nothing, and if he comes over to me, he'll be singing soprano in the shower." She giggled, then added, "He don't care anyway, he just wants you guys to *think* he's gettin' it. Look at him, talking to those *important* men about investment banking...or about *frackin'*." She gave Wilson a devilish smile.

"What's your name?" Wilson asked.

She smiled. "*Mysty*, with two 'Ys.'"

Wilson smiled back. "No, your *real* name."

She looked out to sea and hesitated, but was still very much in charge of the conversation.

"Mary Martha. And you, Officer Wilson?" she answered, after a look at his nametag.

"Jim. Nice to meet you, Mary Martha. Mary is my wife's name."

Mary Martha cocked her head. "I don't see a *ring* on your finger, Mister *Husband*." She turned away in mock disapproval.

Wilson felt his hand. She was right. He had left his ring in the stateroom. He pointed to the carrier across the water. "It's on the ship."

"Um, hummm," she sniffed. "*Just forgot*. I get it. You told me you're married, but I see no ring. Guess you're holding out for somethin' better to come along tonight. *I understand*." Then she changed the subject.

"Where'd you get that Navy Cross?"

Wilson snapped his head and looked at her in amazement. She had correctly identified the Navy Cross ribbon on his chest, something that no civilian had ever done—with any of his ribbons. Maybe Mary Martha wasn't a brainless bimbo after all.

"Iran...a few years ago. But how did you know it was the Navy Cross?"

"My cousin got one. He was a Marine. Long ago, when I was in high school. Two thousand four, I believe. He died."

"Iraq?"

"Yeah, a place called *Fallu'jah*. My aunt got this blue and white medal—and a flag. He's buried at Arlington—Virginia, not Texas." As she gazed out to sea, her voice took on a wistful tone. "I never forgot *that* medal, almost as high as the Medal of Honor, I'm told. The Marine who gave it to her got down on one knee. He was *hot*." She once again locked eyes with Wilson and twisted her hair. "Girls are *suckas* for guys in uniform."

Intrigued by her cousin's story, Wilson ignored her overtures and asked, "What was his name?"

"Rocky. Rocky Roberts. He was a Staff Sergeant." Wilson was impressed Mary Martha knew *that* about her cousin. Most civilians would leave it at *sergeant*.

"How was he lost?" Even as he asked the question, Wilson couldn't help but notice how the trades gently moved wisps of her hair about her face and shoulders.

Her face became pensive as she considered her answer. "He ran into the open to help some of his men and was gunned down in some filthy-ass raghead street. That's all I know. Killed my aunt. Rocky was her pride and joy, and he had a wife and baby boy. Kyle is almost ten now."

They both realized the conversation had taken a turn for the worse. Wilson glanced over her shoulder and saw that Billy and the others were sending amused looks in his direction. *Oh great.* He then locked eyes with Marvin, still in the middle of the group of men, and received a tight-lipped frown in return.

"Mary Martha, it has been a pleasure to meet you."

"Where *you* going? The night is *young*," Mary Martha purred, unloading a full broadside of sexual energy.

"I'm sure there are others you'd like to talk to."

She shifted her body toward him. "I'm not interested in talking to them. I'm interested in talking to *you*."

Wilson now knew he was in trouble. *Get over here, Billy.*

"Are you staying here tonight, or on that *awful* boat?"

"Neither. We're going to the other side of the island."

"You *sure* you don't want to stay here? Daddy Warbucks is going to take me out of here soon so he can go *beddy-by*. Then I can come back out to *play*."

Wilson gave her a slight smile. "My apologies, Mary Martha..."

Now spurned, her eyes flashed as she cut him off. "Okay, *darlin' Jim*. Wifey should be proud of you." She then quickly softened her tone.

"If you change your mind, I'll be here tomorrow morning, sunning myself, wearing three *band-aids* and some fishin' line...You need to get a good look. Everyone else does. *Bye*." She turned and walked slowly across the pool deck to Marvin, who, along with the other men, watched her approach with approval. Billy appeared next to Wilson, and the two of them witnessed the beaming middle-aged men envelop *Mysty* within seconds.

"Wow. *That* is a bundle of fun. And you were talking to her."

"Yep."

"Now that you are returning to earth, care to hobnob with the heavies? But before we do, can I buy you a drink? After that performance you've earned it."

Wilson nodded. "Yep. *The night is young.*"

When the reception began to wind down, and before the heavies left, the aviators jumped in a rental car and headed to the squadron admin at Breezy Cay, a thirty-minute drive through the darkened two-lane roads. Several of the squadrons had admins nearby. They served as bases of operations as the squadron officers explored Saint Thomas. A portion of each squadron also had officers standing duty aboard *Coral Maru.* They would get a chance at liberty tomorrow when the first wave returned back to the ship to relieve them.

Wilson sat in the back seat with Billy and the CO of the *Rustlers*, one of the helicopter squadrons. Looking across the water at the shadowy island of Saint John, Wilson's mind wandered. Once this port visit ended they would get underway for the *western* Caribbean, south of Cuba and east of Belize. *Belize?* A nuclear-powered aircraft carrier was going to conduct exercises with Central American navies from Honduras and Belize, which consisted of little more than harbor patrol boats and *Jet Ranger* helicopters? Carriers hadn't operated in these waters since the mid-80s when Nicaragua was a communist base that fomented revolution throughout the region. Then, later in the decade, Panama under the Noriega regime had drawn U.S. interest for a while. But, when the fleet could no longer train at Vieques, there was no reason to come to the Caribbean at all. Carriers were needed in the Indian Ocean, and Afghanistan combat was where the action was. But that was all changing, and the Navy was signaling that new deployment cycles to "new" locations were in the offing. *Coral Sea* was the first of many more planned carrier deployments here.

As they drove through Red Hook, Wilson's mind continued to wander as he watched the locals gather in restaurants and walk along the road, enjoying the warm evening. To the east a gibbous moon burst out of the Caribbean, illuminating the clouds and lush islands. He thought again of Mary Martha's smoldering sexuality and her lonely existence, then of his own Mary. They passed a lighted billboard for Red Stripe beer. *Yes, a Red Stripe on the balcony overlooking the Caribbean would be good right now.*

Ten minutes later they pulled up to the Breezy Cay resort, where the advance party of *Firebird* JOs had set up "shop" in one of the suites. One of his senior lieutenants, Mike "Dusty" Rhodes, clad in shorts and a tank top, beer in hand, happened to pass by as Wilson got out of the car with his overnight bag.

"Hey, Skipper! Welcome to paradise!" Dusty greeted him.

"Yeah, I'll say. You guys broken in the admin to an acceptable degree?"

"Yes, sir, we are fully qualified—since about noon today! Cold beer, warm water, island tunes. Fully qualled, sir!"

Wilson smiled as Dusty led him up a series of concrete steps. Their suite, located in a complex of buildings, was situated along a hill and surrounded by island flora. The moon had risen higher into the night, above the soft cumulus build-ups that floated over the island. A beautiful scene that Wilson wished "his" Mary could experience.

Thumping club music grew louder and louder as Wilson followed Dusty down a breezeway to a door at the far end. On the door was a VFA-16 sticker, a "zapper" to indicate this room belonged to the *Firebirds* of VFA-16. "Welcome aboard, sir," Dusty said as he opened the door for his CO.

Wilson was met with the blast of an *Outkast* favorite, a gaggle of his pilots in swim trunks and sandals, all with a beer in hand and big smiles on their faces. Teetering on a chair next to the balcony railing was Lieutenant Mark "Trench" James. He wielded a 3-wood and was about to propel a golf ball placed on another chair into the Caribbean night—either that or ricochet it off the railing and back into the living room at high speed.

"Skipper!" a drunken Trench exclaimed as Wilson entered. *"Watch this!"*

"No!" Wilson warned as he raised his hand and shook his head smiling, knowing how this story was going to end.

"Oh, *c'mon*, Skipper! Coach bet I couldn't hit the ocean from here, but I can. I mean, it's *right there!* I don't even need a driver!"

"Now, Trench," Wilson, still dressed in his white uniform, admonished him as he good-naturedly approached him through the laughing JOs. "If you put the club down and get off that chair, we won't have to convene a mishap board tonight."

With mock indignation, the JOs roared their disapproval. They had wanted either to witness the spectacle of Trench lofting one into the sea or lofting himself over the railing and into the bay tree branches that brushed the balcony.

Smiling, a wobbly Trench stepped down from the chair. "Okay, Skipper. *But I could've done it, Coach!*" he bragged, generating derisive hoots from his squadronmates.

"If you hadn't screwed around so much before the CO got here, you could have at least taken one swing!" Lieutenant John "Coach" Madden answered with a broad smile. Like Trench and Dusty, Coach was another senior lieutenant. This trio formed the nucleus of the *Firebird* JO pilots, whom Wilson could depend on tactically and whom he needed to show leadership to the nugget aviators.

As he surveyed the room, Wilson's eyes met those of the only woman there—Lieutenant Commander Kristin "Olive" Teel. Before Wilson entered the room, she had been the senior officer present. Olive looked back at her CO with an awkward smile.

"Well," Wilson said as he approached Olive. "Everything is well in hand...the *Safety Officer* is present!"

Olive knew she should have put a stop to Trench's antics before Wilson arrived. "Sorry, sir. I couldn't resist seeing it for myself!" Wilson nodded with a smile. Then, so only she could hear, he added, "This is not like you, *Safety* Officer."

Olive was now mortified at her lapse in judgment. "Yes, sir, I'm sorry... It's just that they already think I'm a stick-in-the-mud. Bad decision. Won't happen again, sir."

"I know it won't," Wilson said. "It can be lonely at the top, especially in that middle place."

"Sir?" Olive asked.

Wilson smiled at her. "There are old fudds and young studs. *Then* there are lieutenant commanders."

"Yes, sir," Olive answered with a sheepish grin. She didn't know what else to say as she reflected on the meaning of his message. *Olive, you aren't the boss, but you aren't an irresponsible kid anymore either...not that you ever were.*

"Forgotten. Where can I change?"

CHAPTER 3

(Breezy Cay Resort, St. Thomas)

Lieutenant Mark James led the junior officers from the admin and down the hill. At six-foot-three and 225 pounds, "Trench" was the ringleader of the *Firebird* JOs, a role he enjoyed immensely. Nowhere did he shine more than when leading them on liberty. Their destination was the beachside cabana where pilots from Billy's squadron, the *Hunters*, and the lone FA-18F *Super Hornet* squadron, the VFA-23 *Blue Lancers* had already gathered. A bonfire was raging and spirited aviators in aloha shirts were having fun sipping on their beers and telling sea stories.

Trench liked being the center of attention. With good looks chiseled by nature and a body cut by daily workouts in the foc'sle, he was olive skinned and wore his wavy black hair longer than most and unlike most kept it moist with mousse. He could easily pass for a cast member of the reality show *Jersey Shore*, using that to his advantage in a never ending quest to bed as many women as he could. He seldom lacked volunteers.

Trench was obsessed with the score. Having earned his call sign from his large stash of porn magazines, he was not about to squander his current target-rich environment—a tropical beach adjacent to several resort properties. The women of Carrier Air Wing SIX knew to give him a wide berth—some unfortunately learned too late and became figurative kill markings on the fuselage of his *Hornet*. It mattered not to Trench. Once he got to the beach, his eyes were in track-while-scan mode as he searched for the talent he had spied on the sand that afternoon. Fellow lieutenants Coach and "Ghost" Rutledge were "flying wing" on him to pick up any leftovers.

Trench and his wingmen stopped at the bonfire and popped open a Red Stripe. The moon, now halfway up the eastern sky, bathed the point and the cay behind it in a warm glow. Paradise. Nugget pilots Conner "Irish" Davis and Joe "Jumpin" Kessler were already there stoking the flames, beer bottles in hand.

"Bro! Check out the biscuit, nine o'clock long," Ghost volunteered. They all eyed a tall, buxom blonde as she joined what appeared to be a group of giggling college coeds on holiday. Each of them held a jar of Long Island Iced Tea from the cabana bar, and they were well on their way to losing their inhibitions.

Trench snapped his eyes to the left. "*Hoo, baby!*" he said. "Look at the milk jugs on that bitch!"

Just as he uttered those words, the mood of the group took on a noticeable chill. When Trench did not get the reaction he expected from the guys, he turned to see Nugget pilot Lieutenant Junior Grade Tiffany "Macho" Rourke glaring at him.

Macho Rourke was his nemesis. Barely five-foot-three, she had a round face and wore her hair in a Navy-regulation bob. The most junior of the three female *Firebird* pilots, she was outspoken and coarse as she endeavored to rule the nugget pilot roost. Because she always bristled at Trench's sexually suggestive innuendo, he knew to keep his distance from her. As a protected minority, a woman, Macho had demanded respect from day one before she had earned any, and silently chafed under the derisive meaning of her call sign. Sadly for the male *Firebird* pilots and luckily for Macho, *Battle Axe* was already taken.

"Oh, sorry, dudes! Thought it was just us bros here. Where were we? Oh yeah, Irish, you were going to lead us in the next song. *I'm a little teapot...*"

As the men laughed, Trench reveled in the attention. Smiling at Macho, he sipped on his beer, *daring* her.

"Go ahead, *men*, undress those little girls with your eyes," Macho responded. "At least slip them a twenty for bouncing around in their bikinis for you."

"Darn, I left my wallet in the room," Trench shot back. "Besides, they look like *classy* college girls, probably Southeastern Conference types. Maybe I should—dare I say it—walk over there and *introduce myself.*"

Coach jumped in. "Bro, let *me* introduce you. 'Ladies, may I present Lieutenant *Hugh Jardon?*'"

"Thank you, *Lieutenant John Mehoff.* Girls, you can call him '*Jack.*'" Trench said, playing along, with more chuckling from the guys.

"Those *children* aren't going to give you the time of day," Macho interjected, not afraid to be on her own defending the sisterhood, despite the fact the college girls were oblivious to the pilots talking about them from over 50 feet away. Trench picked up the gauntlet.

"Yes, Macho, you are *so* right. We *don't* have a *chance.* We have *zero game* here on this tropical paradise with these girls on the prowl who are what, six, seven years younger than us, and about *twenty* years younger than you."

The guys roared as Trench waited for Macho's comeback. He didn't have to wait long.

"You guys know that hitting on those students is child abuse, if not pedophilia. And...*both* you guys have girlfriends back home." Macho folded her arms in smug superiority.

A hush came over the group, with Trench and Coach giving her a hard look. Trench spoke first.

"*Abuse* is staying here arguing with Little Miss Can't-Be-Wrong on a moonlit beach in St. Thomas. Come on, Coach, you lecherous *cad*, let's go make some new and *attractive* friends."

The two senior pilots trudged over the sand to the coeds, who watched them approach with excited smiles. Ghost joined them, and within minutes the men had their new friends laughing and giggling, the night full of anticipation.

Irish and Jumpin stared into the dying fire as Macho stared out to sea in haughty defiance.

"What a *great* team bonding experience," Jumpin muttered.

Irish pulled on his beer and added, "Yep, our first liberty port and the JOs are divided into the cool kids and the snot-nosed nuggets."

"Go ahead and join them," Macho snorted. "Nobody is stopping you,"

Jumpin replied, "Macho, you are such a frickin' Debbie Downer. *You* are the one who ruined this night for *us*."

Pointing at Trench, she exploded. "*He* shouldn't be talking about girls' body parts in front of me! He's always making snide comments under his breath about the *talent* aboard ship, and that's total bullshit. Damn frickin' right my antenna are up for a hostile work environment, because I hear it. I dealt with it all through flight school, and..."

"*Bullshit,* Macho," Irish snarled. "I was with you in flight school, and all of us had to walk on eggshells around *you*, especially the instructors. We'd be happy with two above averages on a hop, but *you'd* be pissed and mutter under *your* breath about sexism. The airplane doesn't give a fuck if you're a man or a woman. And it will kill us if we let it, so don't fuckin' let it."

Absorbing the blast, Macho turned away and folded her arms again. Jumpin spoke first.

"It's up to you, Macho. You can be a dude with hair and one of us, or you can be Gloria Steinem looking for trouble. You weren't here when

Trench started checking her out, and besides, Trench is probably going to die alone."

Irish added, "Just give him a look next time. Girls—I mean *women*, sorry—know how to do that. And knock off the 24/7 sexual assault crap. If he directs his comments to you or the other squadron women, then I'll back you, but it's not *always* about you." The night ruined, he shook his head. "I'm outta here."

"Me, too," Jumpin agreed. "Let's douse this fire."

Macho took a step to pick up a plastic pail, but Irish snatched it up first. "No, no, I've got it! Not asking you to do anything menial. We can do it." He headed to the gently lapping water to fill the pail.

Before she spun on her heels and headed to the room, Macho's eyes met Jumpin's. Humiliated, she hoped the darkness hid the tears running down her face. *You stupid bitch!* she berated herself as she slogged across the sand with arms folded.

The sound of female laughter wafted over the tropical beach.

Macho woke up early after a fitful night of sleep on the couch, her male counterparts sprawled about in chairs and on the floor. Olive was sacked out in a lounge chair on the balcony. As Macho gazed through the window past the uninhabited green cay to the blue Atlantic, she could tell paradise was going to offer them another gorgeous day.

Today was her turn to be on duty as the *Admin Queen*. One of her most important responsibilities was to make sure the snacks and beer were well stocked. Another duty was to go to the airport and pick up the new guy. Ensign Shane Duncan was reporting to the *Firebirds* as the new squadron Intelligence Officer.

She looked around but didn't see Trench, her archenemy. She figured he spent the night in an orgy with the college girls and shivered at the thought.

To not disturb her squadronmates—and incur even more ill will than she had last night—she carefully stepped around the sleeping pilots and into the kitchen. Just then the front door opened; Skipper Wilson returning from an early morning run.

"Hey, Macho," Wilson whispered.

"Hi, Skipper. How was the run?"

Wilson reached into the refrigerator and pulled out a bottled water. "Good. Going to the café for a cup of coffee. Want to come?"

"No thanks, sir. I need to police this place and then pick up the new guy at the airport."

"Okay. You guys have fun last night?"

"Yes, sir!" Macho lied.

"Great. See you later. Bring the FNG down to the beach when you get here."

"Yes, sir."

After Wilson left, Macho changed her outfit, pinned her hair, and covered it in a ball cap. She then grabbed the keys to the rental car and slipped out of the still quiet admin.

CHAPTER 5

(St. Thomas, V.I.)

Macho set out for the airport on a two-lane road that bisected the island. *Off to get the new guy...he'll no doubt be easy to spot.* Macho knew the type: slight, withdrawn, a pimply faced geek right out of college. First time out of the states, his mouth full of *ma'ams* and *sirs*. She shook her head. She hated the thought of delivering fresh hazing meat to Trench and his fellow frat-boy abusers.

As she climbed the lush mountainside to Skyline Drive, she became lost in her thoughts. She began to enjoy the day and the spectacular view of the Caribbean—until she noticed *Coral Sea* anchored in the roadstead.

Screw them, she thought. Trench and the other cliquish senior lieutenants were dividing the squadron, not her. After all, *she* was in the right; they were not allowed to say things that made her uncomfortable. And, despite the fact that VFA-16 had a female XO and Department Head, Macho was clearly in the minority. And minorities needed to be protected. Hadn't Trench gotten the memo? Women were *commanding* squadrons, air wings, ships, and even strike groups. Treating women like pieces of meat and was going to *stop* in VFA-16. And Lieutenant Junior Grade Tiffany Rourke would lead the way in getting rid of this boy's club unprofessionalism. *The hell with Irish and Jumpin, too,* she thought. *They are just worried about fitting in with those bastards.*

As Macho wended her way through downtown Charlotte Amalie, she spied pockets of *Coral Sea* sailors mixed in with middle-aged tourists on the sidewalks, both carrying packages of cheap jewelry and other souvenirs. She turned west to the airport. She had just parked the car when she heard the roar of an airliner rolling out with engines in reverse thrust. She saw that the 757 was from the correct airline and on time. *Ensign Duncan, arriving.*

She waited in the airy terminal as passengers from the Miami-originated flight filed past. Macho saw families on holiday, sunglassed businessmen in loud shirts, with blazers added to keep it real, Rastafarian locals, college kids, and European twenty and thirty-somethings seeking work at the resorts. She searched for a typical Navy intel weenie, one with a clueless and bewildered look of apprehension, eyes searching for someone, anyone, to help.

Among the crowd of arriving passengers, she spied a tall, female ensign in a summer white uniform. In her left hand she carried a small bag and held her combination cover against her body and under her arm. Macho watched her approach, her big eyeglass-covered eyes searching for a friendly face. With her dark hair pulled back into a regulation bun, her white pumps added three inches to her statuesque height, and she wore a skirt.

I hate skirts, Macho thought, wondering if *this* was Ensign Shane Duncan. As she drew closer, Macho could read, with her 20/17 vision, the black nametag over the right uniform pocket above the ensign's full bosom: DUNCAN.

Oh, no, Macho thought, before she walked up and extended her hand. "Ensign Duncan, hi, I'm Lieutenant Jay Gee Tiffany Roark. Welcome to the *Firebirds* of VFA-16."

Startled by Macho's informal appearance, Duncan stopped and returned her handshake. "Hi! I'm Shane Duncan! Nice to meet you, ma'am!"

Macho cringed, and quickly corrected her. "Look, it's Tiffany—*Macho*—and cut the ma'am thing. Lieutenants and below are all JOs, all first-name basis. Even the hinge-heads go by call signs, but it's smart to throw a sir or a ma'am in there once in a while."

"I'm sorry, please forgive me…and I'm sorry but what is a hinge-head?" Shane asked, looking crushed as if she had blown her only chance for a good first impression.

"*Relax*, for crying out loud. You're the *Fung*, and you have a lot to learn. Six months ago *I* was the Fung, and someone showed me the ropes. *Hinge-heads* are the department head lieutenant commanders who nod up and down enthusiastically at anything the CO says."

"Fung?" Shane asked.

Macho realized this "kid" really was wet behind the ears. However, she looked like an Amazon goddess, and should have *exuded* confidence, but she was more like little Bambi than Wonder Woman. *That's it*, she thought, *we have Wonder Woman!*

"F-N-G. Frickin' New Guy. That's you until we get you a call sign."

"Oh," Shane replied uncomfortably, not sure she liked the *F* in FNG.

They got her luggage off the carousel, and Macho was impressed Shane could lug her sea bag as well as any guy. Hell, she was *bigger* than her fellow pilot, Ghost. Walking to the car, Macho asked, "Where you from?"

"Pocatello, Idaho. Graduated from the University of Idaho last spring with my commission, and I came here straight from Intel School. I'm really excited to be in a strike squadron!"

"Strike *Fighter* squadron, dearie." *Does this chick know anything?* Macho wondered.

Macho pulled onto the main road while Shane sat in the passenger seat. Fascinated by the flora and fauna of St. Thomas, she commented with excitement about everything she saw. As they climbed the narrow switchback roads above the city, Macho stole glances at her new squadronmate. Shane sat demurely with hands folded on her lap, a faint smile on her lips as she marveled at the sights. The understated makeup on her peaches-and-cream complexion highlighted her deep blue eyes, almost hidden by big glasses. Her brunette hair was professionally pinned in place according to uniform regulation. Shane was a big girl, and she was *built*. Simply put, the newest addition to VFA-16 was a *bombshell*, even in her summer white uniform. And Macho didn't see any rings on her fingers.

Macho did not fear female competition from Shane. After six months in the squadron, Trench and his sidekick, Coach, had established themselves as near mortal enemies, but her fellow nuggets were like kid brothers. None of the junior officers in Carrier Air Wing SIX was of interest to her, but she instinctively knew any attention she had hoped to receive from them would now be superseded by the arrival of *Wonder Woman*. Then it dawned on her—the squadron thinks Ensign Shane Duncan is a guy, a geeky intel guy they can abuse. Were they ever in for a surprise.

"Look!" Shane exclaimed as they drove along the summit, which offered a magnificent view of the harbor roadstead. "Is that the carrier?"

Macho glanced at the ship and answered her. "Yep. *Coral Maru*, all 100,000 tons of her. And I *think* she is the only carrier around here."

"Goodness! A real carrier! I've never seen one except in pictures! Oh, Tiffany, this is *so exciting!*" Shane was almost beside herself in excitement, sharing this moment with her new-found sister. Macho, giving in to a dark impulse, decided to have some fun at the FNG's expense.

"Yes! And wait till you meet the guys! You'll *love* them! True officers and gentlemen who open doors for us and pull out chairs for us in the wardroom! Our XO is a woman. And one of the hinge-heads, I mean *department* heads, is a woman, too. She goes by Olive. The guys absolutely *adore* us, and we have so much fun together! And they are all *McDreamy!*"

Shane squealed and hunched her shoulders together. "Ohhh, I can't wait to meet everyone!"

"Yes, and they treat us like the ladies we are. Now, mind you, we are a working squadron. The pilots are going to *depend on you* to teach us about the enemy order of battle and what the bad guys are up to. The *Firebirds* are a team, and we need you to be a contributing part of it."

Shane's big eyes became serious, and she nodded emphatically. "Oh, I will! You can depend on me!"

They pulled into the resort parking lot, and Macho led Shane to the admin as she lugged her sea bag up the steps. Mercifully, her CO was up and dressed in shorts and a polo shirt. Wilson stood as they entered, and Macho introduced him to his newest officer.

"Skipper, allow me to present Ensign Shane Duncan."

"Welcome aboard, Shane. Jim Wilson," Wilson extended his hand.

"Thank you, sir!" Shane gushed. "I'm honored to be here!" Wilson immediately noted her height and the fact that he had to look up to her. Because the others were lounging at the pool or sunning on the beach, they were the only three people in the condo

Wilson led them to the sitting area and motioned both women to have a seat. Macho relaxed and crossed her ankle over her knee like a man. Shane sat up straight with her back off the chair, eyes locked on her new CO.

"Please tell me about yourself," Wilson began.

"Well...I'm from Pocatello, Idaho, and I was in Navy ROTC at the University of Idaho. My grandfather served in Vietnam on a cruiser, and I loved his stories of exotic ports and the romance of the sea. Here in St. Thomas, I now see what he meant!" she giggled. Macho rolled her eyes. Wilson nodded and smiled, waiting for her to continue.

"Soo...I went into ROTC and was drawn to the Intelligence field. I hope to be able to serve you well and to help the pilots learn about ships and aircraft and air defense systems."

"I'm sure you will. Do you have other work experience, or is this your first job?"

"Well, I'm Mormon, so I was on a mission trip a few years ago that split up my college studies."

"Family?" Wilson asked.

"I'm single. My family lives in Pocatello, and we have some relatives in Oregon. I'm the oldest of six: four girls, and the two youngest are twin boys. We dote on those boys!"

Wilson smiled, impressed with Shane's positive energy. He could also see she was stunningly beautiful. The combination of her striking good looks and innocent naiveté could pose a challenge for her—and his command.

"Again, welcome aboard. You are joining a fleet *Hornet* squadron, the *Firebirds* of VFA-16, and we've been a winning team since the Vietnam War. Our job is to be *ready* to deliver *credible* combat power with no-notice as part of the Carrier Air Wing SIX/*Coral Sea* team. We fly the FA-18C *Hornet* strike-fighter, and we employ all manner of weapons against all manner of threats. We deploy anywhere in the world Washington sends us, and we live with strict rules of engagement. And we need *you* to learn how we employ our aircraft and to prepare our pilots with the latest intelligence and capabilities of any potential adversary, and that includes me."

Shane nodded purposefully, riveted on her CO. Wilson then turned to Macho.

"Macho, when we go back aboard, where is Shane going to bunk?"

That morning Macho had expected to pick up a guy at the airport, so, on the way back, she had given this some thought.

"We have an open bunk in my stateroom, sir. Probably there."

"Great. Well, okay. Welcome aboard, Shane. It's good to have you in the squadron." Wilson stood to shake hands.

Beaming, Shane replied, "Thank you, sir!" Welcomed as a full-fledged and vital member of the *Firebirds*, she accepted his outstretched hand.

Macho, who had a plan in mind, then spoke. "C'mon, and I'll introduce you to the rest of the guys. They are probably down at the pool. Do you have a swimsuit?"

Shane appeared uneasy. "Yes, I do, but...."

"Great, let's get changed! Please excuse us, sir."

Wilson nodded. As the women left, he sensed Shane's unease with meeting her squadronmates in a swimsuit and wondered if he should stop them.

CHAPTER 5

At that moment, one thousand miles to the west, Enrique Martinez had to take a leak.

Pounding over the choppy seas at 80 kilometers an hour, the cigarette boat transferred continuous rapid-fire shocks to his spinal cord. They were taking a toll, especially after their mid-point "meal" aboard the trawler some forty minutes earlier. At this rate they were three hours from landfall at Banco Chinchorro, an atoll just north of the Belize coast, and the weather looked to hold. How he wanted a shower. After they'd spent hours loading product into the hold and forward sleeping compartment, the sonofabitch Pablo said the boat was out of balance and had to be reloaded.

All that work for nothing. And Pablo just stands there pointing his finger while we break our freakin' backs.

The men had to take it all out, then load it back in. And as soon as it was secure, Pablo got spooked by headlights on the wharf and frantically motioned for them to shove off. *Now!*

Enrique hated Pablo and all the fancy-suited *narcotraficales* with their gold chains and thick-necked muscle, who pushed him and his partner, Jorge, like dogs. *We are the ones taking the risk out here.* Pablo and his *prositutas* just sat around the pool until the next shipment. Middlemen, that's all they were, and Enrique was filled with contempt for them, all of them. Ashore the *campesinos* grew old before their time with the drudgery of cultivating and harvesting product, and now he and Jorge risked their lives on the open ocean or, if caught, in prison. *And the pigs—like Pablo— take a big cut and do nothing. They are the ones who should be in prison, the bastards.*

Enrique scanned the horizon before his face was lashed with spray. Wiping the water off with his right hand, he held the wheel with his left. Even in the open cockpit of a boat with over 40 knots of wind, he could smell the familiar odor of marijuana wafting up from the cabin door next to him.

"Jorge. *Jorge!*" Enrique yelled to his partner below.

Jorge stumbled to the hatch and looked up at Enrique with squinty eyes, a lighted joint in his hands. "What the fuck do you want?"

"Take the wheel. I need to piss."

Disgusted, Jorge stepped up from the cabin and hung on to the railing as the boat pounded each swell. Once he got on deck, he flicked the half-smoked joint over the side and scanned northwest toward the bouncing bow.

"Just hold this heading. Haven't seen anything since we left the damn *barco.*"

"*Si. Si.* Just go below and take your piss. And hurry the fuck up."

Enrique grunted and got out of the chair as Jorge grabbed the wheel. Though the men had known each other for years and crewed these boats before, they were not friends. Their frayed nerves, due to lack of sleep, coupled with the constant pounding of the choppy sea, did nothing to improve their moods.

Eat shit, Enrique thought as he went below. He'd had enough of Jorge's pissy attitude for today. His partner had been a complete ass to the *mujer* on the "trawler," probably the ugliest woman Enrique had ever seen, but she had made them sandwiches as the boat was fueled. *Cold sandwiches!* Enrique thought. *We are making millions of dollars, and we can't afford at least a hot meal at sea on a decrepit fishing boat?* His thoughts then returned to Pablo. He wished Pablo could at least assign one of his idiot whores to make the sandwiches so they didn't have to look at the stomach-turning *fish-wife* on the trawler. *Cold freakin' sandwiches.* Still, Jorge didn't have to be mean to her. He then put the thought out of his mind,

Three more hours and he would have his wad of hundred dollar bills and a hot shower. Then a hot meal, *Bistec Encebollado* with vino and rum. *Without Jorge, the prick.* And a *chica bonita* for the night. Then sleep. As he swayed in the stuffy compartment to the boat's heaving and rolling, he thought he might make sleep his first choice.

Lieutenant Mark scanned the horizon and picked up the wake. "Got it," he murmured over the ICS, alerting the three other crewmen they had a visual on their quarry.

His co-pilot, Lieutenant Todd, studying the Forward Looking Infrared display, lifted his head. As the Helicopter Aircraft Commander of the MH-60S *Seahawk*, Todd wanted to work them into an optimum firing angle for the *Hellfire* missile hanging from the "wing" off his left shoulder. He saw a faint white smudge, about seven miles distant, that pulsed from left to right as the boat heaved up and down on the waves at high speed.

"Great, let's fall off left and come up his starboard quarter. Take us down to fifty."

"Roger," Mark acknowledged and smoothly rolled the aircraft left. He allowed it to descend to 50 feet above the waves, a dangerous altitude that required his full attention to maintain.

The data link steering from the E-2 overhead was tight, and Todd toggled back to the MIDS display on the tactical page glass cockpit display. The smugglers' support vessel, designated as track number 1182, was approximately forty miles southeast. Knowing such vessels were typically disguised as fishing trawlers, he made a mental note of a rough heading and distance to it after they completed their task here. With the track ball he "hooked" the cigarette boat, track 1147, an action that gave Mark a steering cue on his display. He then went back to the FLIR, placed the cursors on the bouncing white slash, and designated it. Once the FLIR was tracking the infrared image of the boat, he transmitted over the radio, "Tango Lima, track one-one-four-seven is captured."

"Roger, Delta Charlie," the E-2 controller answered. "*Captured.* Do you have VID?"

"Affirm, appears to be *moonshine*," Todd answered, using the code word for smuggler.

Todd zoomed in on the boat and took a photo. Using the keypad, he sent a text message over encrypted data link with the photo attached to the E-2 controller high above and miles away. He then typed the word

DECLARE

"Stand by for combat checks. This will be a LOBL shot, Mark. Set up for a five-mile run in."

"Roger that," Mark replied.

Todd then saw a flashing "M" on the bottom left of his display, an answer from the E-2. *That was fast,* he thought. With the trackball, he clicked on it.

HOSTILE

Todd typed back an acknowledgment, and keyed the ICS. "Okay, guys, we have a declared hostile. Gunners, you are cleared to lock and load."

"Aye, aye, sir." Each door gunner answered, their faces covered with a "windshield" mask under their helmet visors that made them look like aliens from another world. On the left side door was the heavy 50 caliber GAU-21. The right gunner operated the smaller M240 using 7.62 ammunition. Over the constant whine of the jet engines and the thumping of the rotors above them, the pilots could hear the breech mechanisms slamming rounds home as the gunners prepared to engage on their signal. Todd lifted the switch over the MASTER ARM button and pushed it.

Allowing Mark to fly the aircraft, Todd continued with his *Hellfire* checklist: "AVT lock on target, reticle position…let's pop up to one-fifty…mobility kill."

"Roger, climb to one-fifty," Mark replied, then added, "Turning in."

"Roger," Todd acknowledged.

The aircraft banked right, deepening the *whup, whup, whup* sound of the rotor blades as it dug harder into the Caribbean air. Mark placed the boat on his nose and lifted the aircraft to 150 feet. Todd was now head down on the FLIR. As he studied the boat, he was able to pick up contours from the heat contrasts, especially the four white-hot engines on the fantail. With the hand controller, his finger squeezed to the first detent.

"Ranging…six thousand meters."

"Roger," his co-pilot replied.

"Give me three degrees left, please…" Todd requested, lost in his concentration as they crept up on the boat, holding course and speed. *They haven't seen us. Good.*

"Comin' left three," Mark answered. "Slowing to one hundred."

The range steadily decreased, and Todd transmitted their status to the E-2. "Tango Lima, ten seconds." He then said over the ICS, "*Designate*…good heading, good offset…solid constraints box…solid seeker head."

"Roger, Delta Charlie," transmitted the disembodied voice of the E-2 controller.

With the laser designating the boat two miles ahead of them, Todd kept up a running commentary for the benefit of his crew.

"We're armed up, good laser…five seconds." He concentrated on holding the reticle on the middle engines, and when the range was ideal, squeezed the controller trigger to the second detent. After a familiar and unnerving delay, and sounding no different than a bottle rocket, the

Hellfire shot past his shoulder. It left a white plume as it climbed gracefully ahead. He then transmitted;

"*Rifle* away, *now, now, now*…fourteen seconds."

"Roger, Delta Charlie," the E-2 calmly responded.

While Todd concentrated on reticle placement, Mark watched the missile fly away. It became a white point that abruptly stopped in midair halfway to the boat as the rocket motor burned out. The missile immediately became invisible, and his eyes then went to the boat, bounding northwest as before.

Todd watched the seconds-to-go display count down as he kept the reticle on. "Five seconds," he whispered into his lip mike, keeping his eyes on the display. *They still don't see us,* he thought, transfixed by the infrared image casting off spray from the bow. When the missile exploded on the engines, the display went nearly white, and Todd instinctively looked up to see his target.

"Nice shot," offered Mark, as if Todd had driven a ball into the fairway on a relaxing Saturday morning round of golf.

Todd watched the boat suddenly stop in the water as a mixture of white and black smoke rose into the air. "Impact. Cease lase." he transmitted to the E-2.

Enrique, pants down around his ankles and sitting on the toilet, held a lighter flame to the end of his own joint and puffed. A terrific shock, accompanied by an ear-splitting *boom,* jolted him off the seat. His body bounced against the thin fiberglass of the head as toilet water splashed everywhere. Stunned and on all fours, he felt the boat pitch and roll out of control. His first thought was that Jorge had run into a floating log or some other piece of flotsam. Warm blood ran down Enrique's forehead into his right eye socket, and he felt pain in his right knee. A loud *screeeee* emanated from the fantail, and he headed aft as the hull continued to roll. At the hatch opening, he recoiled in horror—the severed leg of Jorge lay on the steps.

Jorge!

Three of the four engines were burning. The one still running on the port side was chugging and bucking hard in its housing as it ate itself trying to provide horsepower to the propeller. Wide-eyed with fear, he stepped over his partner's leg and entered the cockpit. Jorge was slumped motionless over the wheel, and his head and shoulders, peppered with shrapnel, formed a bloody mess that stopped abruptly where his back met the seat. The deck was awash with seawater as the boat turned to the right under the power of its one malfunctioning engine.

The heat from the fires, coupled with the gore of his partner's body, drove Enrique over the side, but not before he grabbed a waterskiing vest for flotation. When he hit the water, he frantically backstroked away from the burning derelict.

The blood!

In his haste to get off the boat, he had forgotten he was bleeding heavily, and that fact filled him with more terror than seeing Jorge's body in pieces. He jerked his head to the left and to the right in search of the shark fins he knew were only minutes away.

Then, he heard a strange noise. From the south and coming out of the sun, he saw a helicopter approaching. *Rescue!* He thanked God for his good fortune, and as the aircraft approached, he got into the vest, clipped it secure, and began to wave and shout.

"Aqui! Aqui!"

He watched the helicopter veer to the right and continue, not slowing down. It was a military helicopter, painted gray, and it appeared to be an American design. Yes, he had seen helicopters of this type flown by the American Coast Guard, but painted in the characteristic white and orange scheme. He splashed water up in the air to catch the pilot's attention. As the helicopter flew past, he saw the pilot looking at him. And behind the pilot was a gunner—also looking at him.

As they approached the boat's burning hulk, Lieutenant Todd keyed the ICS. "Thanks, Mark, I've got the aircraft."

"You've got the aircraft," Mark replied.

Todd now addressed the gunners behind him. "Guys, we are coming inbound for an assessment pass. Be ready to return fire. Bringing him down the right side."

"Roger, sir," Petty Officer Mike answered.

On the FLIR Mark saw movement. After a few seconds, he keyed the ICS. "Looks like we have a survivor."

Todd lifted his visor and spotted splashing in the water near the hulk. "Oh, yeah, visual on the survivor. Don't see any small arms. The boat looks like it's toast."

The aircraft slowed to 80 knots and stood off a few hundred yards from the still burning boat. Todd initiated an easy turn to the left as the crewmen circled their prey, assessing the situation. After verifying only one survivor, still splashing water in the air like a madman, Todd was satisfied.

"OK, guys, we're going to reverse to the right. Petty Officer Jason, get ready."

"Aye, sir."

Rolling out of his right turn, Todd continued, "Target is one o'clock coming to two...Petty Officer Jason, your target is a single individual in the water next to the wreckage."

"Tally, sir."

"You are cleared to open fire. We're gonna stay about 100 meters off."

"Aye, aye, sir."

Enrique was incensed. When are the fucking Yanquis going to rescue me! he thought.

He watched the helicopter circle lazily around him. Surely they had spotted him with all the water he was throwing into the air. He hated the Americans, hated their rich Coast Guard sailors who offered him clean bottled water and good food in their cookie-cutter blue uniforms—after they had boarded his go-fast boat five years ago. Yes, it was jealousy. They had so damn much, stealing resources and money as they did everywhere around the world. And the sailors looked down on him, including the women sailors in their blue coverall uniforms. That was an unbearable insult, and Enrique would one day avenge the dishonor. He could kill the weaklings with his bare hands, and given the opportunity after they rescued him, he would.

In the distance he saw the helicopter turn away from him. Turning away?

He couldn't believe the helicopter was leaving him to die! That feeling quickly subsided when it turned around and flew back toward him. Finally, the cocksuckers! As the aircraft drew near, he scanned nervously for sharks. Hurry up, dammit!

He saw the aircraft approach, but it did not slow down. He could clearly see the pilot, and behind him, the gunner—with his gun pointed. With clarity Enrique saw what was going to happen...

The Yankees are going to shoot me like a dog!

In a frenzied state of terror, his hands worked to open the vest toggles. As he moved to duck underwater, he took a last look at the helicopter and realized it was too late.

Santa Maria! Ayudame!

Enrique Martinez' last image was a flash from the side of the gray aircraft.

The M240 spit a stream of bullets that churned up the water around the man and covered him in spray. After two full seconds of fire the gunner stopped and watched for movement. From his left seat, Todd had to look across the cockpit to see the target.

"See any movement?"

"No, sir."

"Roger, we'll do another circle. Petty Officer Mike, you want some target practice?"

"Yes, sir!" the GAU-21 gunner crowed.

Todd reversed his turn to the left and answered, "OK, your target is the floating boat hulk. Mark, you've got the aircraft. Have a Tally?"

"I've got the aircraft. Tallyho." Mark replied, taking the controls and keeping the turn in.

Todd kept control of the tactical situation. "Your target is nine o'clock coming to ten. Let's stay off about 500 meters, Mark. Petty Officer Mike, call Tally."

"Tally," the gunner answered.

"Roger, open fire."

A tongue of flame leapt from the 50 caliber barrel with a deafening chainsaw sound and cordite smell that filled the cabin. Splashes bloomed next to the hulk as the heavy rounds punched big holes in the fiberglass hull. The gunner fired several bursts, tearing the floating bow to pieces before it slipped below the waves.

Todd was back on the MIDS display as he keyed the mike to transmit to the E-2. "Tango Lima, Delta Charlie is splash-one complete. Standing by for steering to track one-one-eight-two."

The E-2 rogered the transmission and sent Todd steering directions to his next assigned target, the trawler 40 miles south. He would need the three remaining *Hellfires* to sink this larger and heavier vessel, with the GAU and M240 to complete the job.

The *Sierra* accelerated as it turned southeast. It left behind floating pieces of fiberglass—and slicks of blood.

CHAPTER 6

(Breezy Cay Resort)

Stretched out on a lounge chair with his eyes shielded by his Wayfarer shades, Trench surveyed the scene at the resort pool. The college girls he had slept with last night were not out yet, and he wondered what he should do when they showed up. Play it cool and chivalrously buy them a drink at the cabana? Hug them as friends and spend some time before making an excuse to leave? Which one to hug first? Hug, hell, he was *in bed* with them six hours ago! *Two* of them—a first, even for Trench.

Coach, lounging next to him, could have had the redhead, but he had bagged out. *Fine, head on back, loser.* And now Coach wanted the details. As Trench relived the night, many of them were fuzzy—and he couldn't remember much anyway. He remembered the girls were completely blotto and literally bounced off the walls in silly hysterics in the early evening, but were mercifully still passed out when he slipped out in the morning. After the ouzo shots, however, he wasn't sure about all that had happened—*Did I do it with* both *of them?*—and he didn't like it. His head was still throbbing, and lying out in the sun wasn't helping, but in his image-is-everything world he had to show the JOs what a stud he was, 24/7. Even to all-talk-and-no-action Coach.

"What do you want to do today?" Coach asked.

"I dunno... Dry out. Go back to the ship. Get a sunburn. Get laid."

"In that order?"

Trench took a swig of water. "You had your chance, man."

Coach said nothing. The other squadron pilots were playing water volleyball in the pool, which was lined with tourists sunning themselves in lounge chairs.

Trench noticed Macho come into the pool area from the jungle path. "Oh, shit," he groaned. "Here comes *Nurse Ratched.*" Behind her was a girl, tall and trim...and Macho was talking to her! Together they walked up to the group of *Firebird* pilots poolside, and it appeared Macho was introducing the girl to them. She shook hands with each one.

42

Trench propped himself up on his elbows to see better. "You gotta be shittin' me," he muttered.

Coach was watching, too. "You think that's the new guy?" They observed her for a few moments: long legs, flowing dark hair, and then a shot of the goods once she removed her beach cover-up.

"Whoo, baby," Trench answered, a small smile forming on his lips.

Shane was excited to meet her new squadronmates. She just knew Tiffany was going to be her new BFF, and meeting these fleet aviators wasn't as bad as they said it would be at Intel Officer school. They seemed nice, and clearly Commander Wilson was an inspirational leader. And surrounding them was a tropical paradise the like of which she only seen in the movies. She couldn't wait to tell her mother.

"You 'girls' done with volleyball?" Macho asked the men.

"Just waiting to thump you," Irish said in retort. "Let's go!"

Macho whipped off her t-shirt and jumped in the water, while Irish smiled at Shane. "C'mon, *Fung*, you're on our team!"

Shane looked about, nervous. Fearful of showing too much at this first meeting, she should have *insisted* on remaining at the condo. Boys looked at her body differently than they did other girls, had since middle school. She couldn't help her height or what God gave her. *Yes,* her girlfriends always said, *you are* blessed, *but there are worse problems for a girl to have.* Shane Duncan, though, wanted to be known for her professional ability, and this first impression was not the one she had wanted to make.

"New guy, you in the squadron or not?" Irish persisted. From the water Macho looked at her quizzically, as if to say, *What's your problem?*

Now sensing the eyes of everyone at the pool on her, Shane whispered to herself, "Let's get this over with." She quickly unbuttoned her cover-up and removed it. The black one-piece suit was at least sensible, and she kept her arms drawn in as she gingerly slid into the pool. She waded to the net on Irish's team as two more guys joined them in the water.

"Macho, is this the new guy?" Trench asked with a friendly smile, looking eye-to-eye at VFA-16's newest officer.

Macho's plan was working. "Yeah, this is Shane Duncan. Shane, this is Mark 'Trench' Jones and John 'Coach' Madden."

"Hi, sir," Shane replied with a shy smile as she extended her hand awkwardly.

"Welcome aboard, *Fung*, and cut the 'sir' crap. We're all JOs. You know what you're doing, here?"

Shane nodded. He *was* cute, they *all* were. And Mark—*Trench*—was paying attention to her. Maybe this wasn't so bad after all. She could relax with her new squadronmates.

The game commenced, and Shane kept missing the action as Trench took the shots whenever the ball came their way. Soon, though, the ball came to her, and she needed to jump up and hit it.

Trench's body crashed into her hard, knocking her down with a splash. She immediately felt his arm around her waist, pulling her up.

"Whoa, sorry, new guy!" Trench apologized as he released her and backed off.

"C'mon, Fung," Macho chided her. "That was *your* shot!"

Shane smiled and got ready for the next serve. *What fun!* Everyone was so friendly and welcoming, smiling at her, embracing her, right off, as one of the group. Tiffany was right, the guys were so friendly and nice, like big brothers, their hands helping to steady her when she was off balance. Within minutes she felt protected by them. Playing pool volleyball with her new squadron friends in this tropical paradise was like living a dream. She found herself beaming as the water ran down her face and a dozen wet and friendly faces smiled back at her. Her grandfather had told her of the "work hard, play hard" culture of the Navy, and the play hard part was off to a great start. The *Firebirds* seemed to accept her for who she was, their new Intelligence Officer who would make them better aviators.

Next to her, with one eye on the game and one on Shane, Trench got his second wind like no hangover remedy could have done. Fate had delivered this dripping *centerfold model* practically into his lap! He would nail her by the time they returned to Norfolk, and he would make sure he was the first.

Trench then noticed the girls from last night had arranged their towels on the poolside lounge chairs and were taking furtive glances at him. They seemed miffed that he was not coming right over to join them, or at least to acknowledge them. They were no worse for wear he figured, and would probably snag some other guy tonight. He had duty back at the ship anyway, and the two coeds, together, couldn't compete with the smoking hot six-foot *juggernaut* next to him. He'd say goodbye of course, being a gentleman and all. He might even buy them a drink before departing for the sea and disappearing into their clouded memories.

Meagan is the redhead, and... Oh, what's the other girl's name?

CHAPTER 7

(USS *Coral Sea*, underway, St. Thomas roadstead)

The shrill sound of the bo'sun pipe over the 1MC sounded throughout the ship: "Ta-Weeeet...Underway. Shift colors."

From his ready room chair Wilson glanced at the PLAT image of the flight deck and noted the time: 0905. *Coral Sea*'s anchor was up and soon they would be heading southwest into the central Caribbean. On the black-and-white television screen he could see the rugged shore of St. Thomas, and reflected the port visit had been fun and was over too soon, as all port visits were. The JOs had done a good job on the admin and seemed to welcome Ensign Duncan all right. No surprise there; she was friendly, pleasant...and gorgeous. He already had heard some of them refer to her as *Wonder Woman*, and he knew he needed to keep an eye on Trench and Coach.

"When's the meeting again?" Annie asked from her chair.

"Zero nine-thirty," Wilson answered. "All COs and XOs, and COs from the strike group ships. Guess our advanced training cruise just got changed."

"What do you think's going on? Venezuela?"

"Too provocative. Actually heard we might be operating in the vicinity of Panama. Maybe we'll get to fly some close air support with the Army and some dissimilar hops against F-16s.

"Drug ops?"

"Nah, we're too much of a national asset for that small stuff. Besides, they come through here, too. I think Panama, with the Chinese interest in building their own canal through Lake Nicaragua. Send 'em a signal we're watching them."

Annie nodded. "Makes sense. Hey, thanks for the leave."

"You and Mike have a good time?"

"Yeah, we went to St. John and Tortola. Beautiful. Boating, snorkeling...just beautiful. Met some fun Brit ex-pats living on a sailboat. What a life."

45

"You could live like that, too, after you retire."

"Yeah, but our little guy is thriving in Virginia Beach. Can't do it," Annie said.

Wilson smiled and shook his head. "You are such a mom. To *both* of your boys."

"Yes, and Mike would agree with you." Annie chuckled before she changed the subject. "How's Mary?"

Mary. Wilson wondered himself. She was distant when they had talked on the phone and seemed further away than the actual 1,200 miles between them. He knew her seeming preoccupation was more than catching her at a bad time on a bad day. Derrick, now in sixth grade, was becoming moody with his video game obsessions. With that, and eight-year-old Brittany's sexualized cultural desire to be thirteen, she had her hands full. But there was more. For the first time in their married life, he suspected her of having an affair.

Against his desire, Mary had taken a job in Suffolk, and the daily scramble—to get the kids off to school, fight the I-64 traffic, and deal with the guilt of after-school daycare—was taking its toll on her. And where was he? At sea or on a detachment for weeks or months at a time, preoccupied with the squadron and bringing the job home, not engaged with his family. And yesterday he was in "paradise," partying it up—and talking to strippers.

Who is Mary talking to? Probably the guy in her office, Tom, divorced, outgoing, a single parent—*like Mary.* They had lots "in common," lots to share. *What else are they sharing?*

"She's doing great, kids are great. All good," Wilson quickly responded.

Annie smiled and nodded her approval. "She's such a doll. Mike says she's doing a great job taking care of him and all the squadron girls in the spouses' club." Wilson didn't want a reminder of *more* of Mary's responsibilities. He needed to change the subject.

"I hear a bunch of fleet training guys came aboard. Have you seen any of them?"

"Yes," Annie replied. "My red-haired brother Weed is in the group, and some other guys I don't know. TOPGUN types."

Wilson smiled. Mike "Weed" Hopper had been his roommate in the *Ravens*. Promoted to the rank of Commander and serving as a staff member on the Operational Test and Evaluation Force, Weed had hoped to get his own squadron command; however, his career timing had gone against it. This Caribbean at-sea period would be a fun opportunity to fly together again.

Just then the ready room door burst open. *"Kemosabe!"*

Beaming, Wilson rose to greet his friend and grasped his outstretched hand. *"All right, Weed!* Welcome aboard!"

"Hey, Flip! Hey, Annie! Great to be haze gray again! Only been aboard thirty minutes and I'm tired, hungry, and—well—never mind!"

"Glad to see you in a flight suit," Wilson said. "How hard was it to extricate yourself from your desk?"

"I managed. Part of my job description is to bag traps with fleet pilots like you so I don't go insane. And down here, in our sunny warm-water playground, like the old days."

"What are you guys doing aboard this time?" Wilson asked him.

"Well, we're working a project with DARPA on some cool new sensors. We're going to run some profiles with them, maybe drop a few precision weapons to get these boxes a full test. What's coming down the road is incredible."

Annie asked, "Whose jets are you going to fly?"

Weed turned to Flip and suppressed a smile. "Well, ah, *yours*, if you have one to spare. You'll be happy to know, Flip, that I asked for the *Firebirds* by name."

"Just for you?" Wilson deadpanned, suspecting the answer.

"Well, no... A TOPGUN guy they call *Chainsaw* is also flying with you. Doesn't talk much and may have killed a man once. Got off on a technicality. *But hey*, that's all behind us now!"

Wilson smiled. "How is he behind the ship?"

"Oh, just like me! Solid as a rock. Gets aboard two out of five tries and had only one blown tire last time out! You can sleep soundly!"

Wilson smiled again at Weed's banter. *Same old Weed. It will be fun to have him out here*, he thought. And maybe they could find an excuse to fly together. Such opportunities were rare, but as the CO, he was in a position to make it happen.

"We better get going," Annie said.

The three commanders left the ready room and headed forward to the Carrier Intel Center, or CVIC. The other strike group commanding officers were gathered there to hear from the admiral on the upcoming at-sea period.

Once they arrived at the restricted space, they showed their ID cards to the sailor in the window. Satisfied, the sailor hit a switch to unlock the door, which buzzed until Wilson opened it. When they stepped inside and went to the main planning room where the rest of the "heavies" were gathered in light conversation, Weed boomed an exaggerated *Hey!* at seeing former shipmates after many years apart. The trio found seats among the folding chairs and joined in the socializing. A few moments later, the murmur of conversation was broken by a sharply raised voice.

"Ladies and gentlemen, the admiral."

The room snapped to attention, the silence broken by the footsteps of the admiral and his entourage as they walked up to the lectern. CAG Matson and Captain Sanders were right behind the admiral, and all were dressed in khaki, the admiral sporting his characteristic navy blue pullover sweater.

With the officers still at attention, the admiral pulled out a folder and placed it on the lectern. "Pleased be seated," he said.

The group took their seats and waited.

"Ladies and gentlemen, I trust everyone had a nice time in St. Thomas. You are all to be commended on the conduct of the liberty party. Now that everyone's batteries are recharged, we have a full four-week tailored training period ahead of us. While we are in these warm waters, we'll be doing reactor drills in preparation for the upcoming Operational Readiness Inspection, as well as ongoing qualifications of new personnel, some of whom have just joined us. Damage control preparation and material readiness are also areas of concern, so we'll be conducting general quarters drills and take a strain on material conditions and personnel qualifications."

As the admiral talked, Wilson wondered why he had gathered all commanding officers here for this routine stuff. And why the dramatic entrance? Meyerkopf was different from other admirals Wilson had observed. He appeared to be uncomfortable around the aviators. Wilson also noticed the admiral did not discuss air wing training.

The admiral continued.

"While we can conduct this training anywhere, Fleet Forces has sent us here to show the flag in this part of the world. Carriers haven't spent time much time in these waters in years as they've been wed to Central Command needs in the Middle East. SOUTHCOM has been asking for carrier presence for some time, and even this short cruise down here is welcome. We'll be operating in the middle of the Caribbean basin, between Hispaniola and South America, with a swing by Panama and Nicaragua. You aviators will fly and do what you do during this time, but the focus will be on the upkeep of *Coral Sea's* nuclear plant, which is critical to the tasking of this capital warship."

The focus? Wilson thought. He sensed his fellow aviators, sitting silently around him, were also troubled by Meyerkopf's tone-deaf remarks. By gauging their blank stares, Meyerkopf realized he was not connecting and picked up the pace.

"We are also in these waters to help prosecute the War on Drugs, to help the Coast Guard stem the flow of illicit narcotics into the United States. Eighty percent of this traffic is seaborne, and the routes traffickers use are many and varied, from the Pacific coast, through the Yucatan Passage, Windward and Mona Passages, and up the Lesser Antilles and the Bahamas. When you come across cigarette boats, low-slow flyers, submersibles, or anything that looks suspicious, report it, and we'll contact the Coast Guard to prosecute it."

Wilson knew this was something the aviators could get excited about, but he had been there and done that. The vaunted *War on Drugs* that had begun in the late '80s was, by any measure, a failure. While there were individual battles won—most notably the battle for the soul of Colombia, at one time a narco-state—the cartels had just moved over to friendlier Venezuela. It seemed the decades-long efforts by the U.S. to stem the tide of drugs had done little more than put a small dent in the pipe. Handing off air and surface contacts to the overworked and overextended Coast Guard had not stopped the trade, and American kids—and their parents—were puffing and snorting away, while sending a constant demand signal to willing suppliers.

Meyerkopf wrapped up his wooden delivery and seemed thankful he could now escape the skeptical eyes of his aviators. "Well, that's all I've got. Ah, Captain, do you have anything?"

Captain Sanders scanned the room behind him until his eyes settled on his Intelligence Officer, Commander Norb Hofmeister. "Hof" was a favorite among the pilots for his quick wit in daily briefings and for knowing his business. He led a team of squadron intel officers—of whom VFA-16's Ensign Duncan was the newest member—tasked to provide actionable intelligence to the aviators before they had to fly into harm's way.

"Yes, sir," Sanders answered as he stood. "Commander Hofmeister has a run-down on the local situation. Hof…"

In his khaki uniform, Hofmeister bounded to the front of the room as a chart was projected behind him. "Admiral, good morning! We are going to remain in the vicinity of Puerto Rico for the next two days requalifying your aviators in day and night carrier landings before we transit west southwest to this position north of the Panama Canal so we can do our reactor and damage control drills unmolested by ship traffic. This is about 750 miles from our current position, and we'll be flying while en route. With a fifteen-knot speed of advance, we should be there in two days."

Wilson was confused. The position Hofmeister had pointed to was right in the middle of the Caribbean basin, over 200 miles from the nearest land. His pilots could operate "blue water" and depend on tanker aircraft to keep them fueled if they had difficulty getting aboard. But what was there *to do* out there? The drills Meyerkopf wanted to do could be done here, near Puerto Rico, just as easily, and the current location would allow his pilots better training opportunities.

"What are we doing now?" Weed muttered next to him. Wilson nodded slightly, hoping Hofmeister, who was on his best behavior with the admiral and the other heavies sitting in front of him, had *some* good news.

"While the ship is in this vicinity," said Hof as he pointed again to their destination, "we'll be engaged in an exercise called *Assured Promise*, which will involve training with local air forces in Panama and Colombia. Each day and night we'll have KC-135 and KC-10 tankers to fill you guys up before you bump heads with these guys to exercise their air defense systems."

The aviators perked up. *Yes!* Dissimilar Air Combat Training! And "gas" from big wing Air Force tankers. Lots of it, for them to burn! This was turning into a good deal after all, and the cheesy name of this exercise, *Assured Promise*, could be ignored like all the other politically correct names the heavies in Washington or SOUTHCOM gave these things. *Whatever.*

"The Colombians fly refurbished *Kfir's* sold to them by Israel. They are older jets but are capable of Mach 2 and present a forward quarter threat. They also have a modified 767 tanker you guys may be getting gas from. The Panamanians have nothing more than light civil aircraft in their glorified police force, but the Air Guard is sending a *Viper* squadron from South Dakota and an F-15 squadron from New Orleans to give us some good training. They and the big wing tankers will be operating out of the old Howard Air Force Base at the southern end of the canal."

Cool! Wilson thought as he and the other aviators murmured their approval. Hofmeister shifted gears.

"We also have riders here from the Operational Test and Evaluation Force staff who will be flying with you. They will be working with the guided missile destroyer USS *Max Leslie* which has a *Fire Scout* UAV detachment aboard, evaluating it for fleet interoperability. Part of that evaluation is to release inert practice ordnance on floating targets and smokes. They will be operating independently. Welcome aboard, gentlemen."

Weed whispered to his friend, "Damn, was hoping to get a fun fighter weps hop with you instead of the test profile crap we have to fly."

"Maybe we can work you in," Wilson offered.

"Maybe, but the coke-bottle engineers on *Mad Max* have a test program the size of a phone book, testing every little tron in every condition. Hope it works out, but I think our dance card is full."

Wilson nodded. He felt a twinge of sadness for Weed, his roommate when they were in the *Ravens*. Both had air-to-air kills from the action five years ago with Iran, but Wilson had *two*, and he was now a squadron commander. Weed had gone to routine test duty, primarily a desk job at a backwater staff where promotion was not assured. It wasn't fair, and Wilson was grateful Weed didn't resent him for it. Hoped he didn't. At least Weed was flying.

To move on to a new subject, Hofmeister changed the slide behind him.

"While out there you may come across *go-fast* boats, what we know as cigarette boats. These guys are carrying two to three tons of product, anything from cocaine to marijuana, and they are sometimes serviced by trawlers that they rendezvous with mid-ocean. If you see a go-fast, report it back to the ship: time, lat/long, course and speed, yadda yadda yadda. When these things get cranked up on a smooth sea, they can get up to *eighty* knots. *Yes, eighty.* If you come across a trawler with a bunch of 50-gallon drums on the fantail, that boat is operating illegally. In either case, report it and we'll relay the info to the Coast Guard. If they have a cutter nearby with a helo or a rigid hull inflatable, they can deal with it as a law-enforcement issue. You can't—so just report back."

One of the squadron commanding officers asked if they could contact a cutter direct to help coordinate an intercept. Hofmeister looked at the admiral and captain for guidance. Not receiving any, he answered, "Well, you could talk to them on emergency GUARD or find them on an HF frequency, but we don't have any plan to assign discrete frequencies for direct coordination." He looked again to his leadership for help, and CAG Matson stood up to address the group.

"Guys, we are not going to get involved with prosecuting the War on Drugs beyond reporting what you see, just as we would with any surface contact of interest. Maybe the E-2 will vector you to identify something for them, but that's pretty much it. Same with low-slow fliers, and it is unlikely we'll see any of those. This interdiction stuff is in the Coast Guard lane, and to keep all of us busy, we have our exercise and the ship has their engineering drills. If you see something unusual, sing out, and we'll task some of the sorties to do routine surface search around the ship as we always do. Nothing new here."

That was fine with Wilson, but he remained skeptical. Why bring the ship way down here, except to placate the State Department? Or the general in SOUTHCOM who wants some toys to play with so he can pretend to be a big time theater commander? Whatever the real reason, there were worse places to operate. Maybe, on the way home, they would get a port visit to Fort Lauderdale as a reward.

When Admiral Meyerkopf rose to leave, the room popped to attention. With the Captain and CAG in trail, he waited until he was almost outside before he released them with a terse "Seats."

Annie gave Weed a smile. "Well, you gonna fly with us?"

Gesturing to Wilson, Weed answered. "If *Kemosabe* here will have me! Actually, we have about eight of us from OPTEVFOR on this test program. Seriously, can I bring one of my pilots to join the *Firebird* ready room? We'll pay for the gas we use, and you'll get extra sorties to pad your total. What a deal!"

Wilson smiled and nodded. "Sure, but who is the pilot? Not *Chainsaw*?"

Just then an imposing lieutenant commander in a flight suit walked toward the group. Well over six feet tall, he held Wilson's gaze with his unsmiling, cold dark eyes as he approached. Weed introduced them.

"Flip, Annie, this is Keith Meadows, one of our flight test pilots. *Mongo*, this is Skipper Wilson and XO Schofield."

Mongo, tight-lipped and businesslike, threw in a curt *sir* and *ma'am* as he shook hands with the two commanders. Having his hand squeezed like a vise did not leave a favorable impression on Wilson. He'd seen this air of condescending superiority and evil-eye gaze before in the overachieving population of fighter pilots he part of, but it was rare. There were many, many more gregarious *Weeds* than taciturn *Mongos*.

"Mongo comes to us from the West Coast where he just finished his department head tour."

"Oh, yeah?" Annie asked. "What ship?'

"*Nimitz*," he answered. Offering the minimum response possible, the pilot effectively brought to the conversation to a halt, and Mongo excused himself with a pained smile.

"Are all your guys so affable?" Wilson asked Weed.

"Okay, he's no Regis Philbin, but he's a Jedi Knight when it comes to the *Hornet* and sensor fusion. My best tester. And, in his spare time, he paints with watercolors and arranges flowers. Yeah, okay...he's a geek."

Annie smiled. "Does he need to bunk with our JOs?"

"Nah, we're good. The ship found a bunkroom for my guys."

"Can he fly?" Wilson asked.

"Yeah, he can fly. He has that ability—like you guys—to use his head to analyze the airborne situation and transfer that into stick and rudder skills. He's solid around the ship. Seriously, you won't have to worry about him."

Wilson nodded. "Okay, welcome to the *Firebirds*. We'll get Stretch to put you guys on the day/night qual schedule—for *tomorrow*."

"Stretch Armstrong is your Ops Officer? Terrific. And, hey, no rush for the night stuff. In a few weeks, when the moon is fuller, I'll be ready to go!"

Wilson smiled. *Same old happy-go-lucky Weed.* He was pleased to have his old roommate back in the squadron with him. He looked forward to a fun at-sea period.

CHAPTER 8

(USS *Coral Sea*, underway)

Shane Duncan had never been so nervous.

With sweaty palms she sat next to Macho and Jumpin in the last row of high-backed chairs in Ready Room 5. The folder on her lap consisted of "Order of Battle" information on drug cartel go-fast boats and the Colombian Air Force. After Skipper Wilson finished talking she expected to be next, and while she wanted to listen and absorb his every word, her mind wandered. In five minutes, she would be giving her first presentation, ever, in front of *real pilots* in this fleet *Hornet* squadron on an aircraft carrier at sea. This was the big leagues, for sure.

Mercifully, she wasn't seasick; she detected no motion at all even though she could see by the closed circuit TV image of the flight deck that they surely were moving across the water.

How beautiful St. Thomas was! And by the looks of it, the day outside was gorgeous. She couldn't wait to go outside to smell the salt air from the flight deck, to see the blue Caribbean. And later in the day, the pilots were going to fly! *So exciting! I can't wait to watch* that*!*

Everyone in the ready room—except for Shane—wore green flight suit. Like a real sailor, she wore a wash khaki shirt and slacks, another first. She admonished herself for not concentrating on the CO, and once again gave him her attention.

Wilson wrapped up his comments about the upcoming exercise and how he wanted his squadron pilots to behave.

"Remember, our job is to support both the ship's drills and tasking from SOUTHCOM. We've got a nice exercise for us to get some training and have fun, and we'll hear more about that in a minute. If you are called off an exercise intercept, do it without backtalk and investigate what they want you to look at. If the ship can't schedule our hops when we want them, too bad, we'll fly when available. Also during this time we'll have testers from OPTEVFOR flying with us, like Commander Hopper and Lieutenant Commander Meadows here. They'll be helping test some *Fire*

54

Scout UAVs from the small boy *Max Leslie*, and that ship could be anywhere. So, it's going to be a fun and diverse three or four weeks in this new and beautiful part of the world for many of you: both exercise and real-world operations, lots of gas from big wing tankers, and *flying*, which is always a good deal.

"So, we've got day and night ops today after a nice week off in port. Now we need to refocus on routine carrier operations. Flight leaders, we need solid preflight briefings, and because the jets have sat for a week, they'll have some bugs to work out. So don't press it. Fly smart and fly the brief. Okay, enough motherhood. Stretch, what's next?"

"Sir, we have the *spy* next," answered "Stretch" Armstrong

Wilson gestured to the back of the room. "Okay, new guy, Ensign Duncan, come on up here."

With heart pounding, Shane gathered her folder and slid out to the aisle and strode forward. Wilson motioned her to stand next to him.

"All right, we've got our new guy spy, Shane Duncan, who comes to us from the University of Idaho via a little stop at intel school. Shane, it's good to have you in the squadron as we've been without an intel officer for some time. We need your analysis and knowledge of the local situation, and we look forward to your brief. *Firebirds*, let's welcome Ensign Duncan."

"HELLO, FUNG!" the pilots boomed.

Shane flinched from the blast. "Thank you, sir!" She said smiling, feeling the blush of embarrassment that covered her face. For a moment after Wilson took his seat and the floor was hers, she froze. Knowing that all eyes were on her, she took a deep breath, picked up the projector remote, and brought up her first slide.

Three rows back, Trench and his sidekick Coach indeed had their eyes on Ensign Duncan, now known throughout the wing as *Wonder Woman*.

As Shane delivered her briefing and pointed to various positions on the chart of the western Caribbean, her figure a distraction even in her regulation khaki uniform. The two pilots were watching, but weren't listening, to her presentation.

"*Mmm-mmm*" Trench sighed as Shane pointed high to show a divert field in Jamaica.

"Roger that," Coach responded in a tone only Trench could hear. As she continued with the exercise slides, Shane briefed the ready room with increased confidence.

"The Colombians will be flying C-10 and C-12 *Kfirs* from Barranquilla here on the coast. These are rebuilt Israeli aircraft obtained in 2009, and they are Mach 2 capable, used mostly for strike missions, have an internal gun and the forward-quarter *Python* missile. Good thrust-to-weight, not much of a turn rate, but they do have canards for enhanced slow-speed handling, and a glass cockpit. The pilots are fairly well trained in air-to-air and fly their aircraft to the limit. Typically, they fly in pairs, and we can expect them to operate under strict ground control."

As they feigned attention, Trench and Coach were not thinking about strict ground control.

"You'll be conducting mock attacks against the mainland, and *Kfirs* of the *Fuerza Aérea Colombiana,* or *FAC,* will be intercepting you off the coast."

As Shane spoke, Macho surveyed the pilots as they watched her. The heavies up front, adults like Skipper Wilson, gave her the professional attention she deserved. It was plain to see, however, that back in the cheap seats Trench and Coach and probably the others were undressing her with their eyes. She had set Shane up in St. Thomas: *Sure, meet the guys by the pool in a swimsuit. We do it all the time. Play grab-ass volleyball with them in the water.* And *Wonder Woman* had played it perfectly, enthralled by the pilots' attention, gushing like a schoolgirl, the naïve and delicate princess whispering to Macho at night in their bunks about how *cute* Trench was. Yes, Shane was the perfect bait to catch Trench and his bastard side-kick, Coach. They were *going* to slip up: a stray public comment, causing Shane grief and creating a hostile workplace, and Macho would be there to "protect" her frail roommate—and the sisterhood, in general—from these lecherous assholes. She envisioned Trench standing tall in front of the XO having to explain himself, and a smile formed on her lips. *Just a matter of time…*

On the other hand, Macho was impressed. *Thrust to weight? Turn rate? Slow-speed handling?* Wonder Woman had done her homework, and here, on day one, was talking to her aviator squadronmates on their level.

"Are there any questions?" Shane asked the group with a pert smile.

There were none, and Wilson looked over his shoulder to see for himself. "Nice job, Shane. Thanks," he told her. Flushed with pride, she returned to her seat next to Macho.

"*Well done!*" Macho whispered and patted Shane's knee.

"Thanks!" Shane replied. She radiated satisfaction with her performance, which she hoped made a difference to the fleet strike-fighter squadron. She felt she was off to a good start with a great group of people, like her cool roommate, Tiffany, er, *Macho*.

CHAPTER 9

As he sat at the head of the table in his flag meeting room surrounded by *Coral Sea's* brain trust, Admiral Roland Meyerkopf was perplexed.

To him, with his submarine pedigree, a nuclear-powered ship was a nuclear-powered ship, and if it floated on the surface or submerged under, it mattered little. No, it was all about the *plant*, and in the case of *Coral Sea*, the *plants*. The carrier he was on had two Westinghouse AW4 nuclear reactors that drove four massive shafts that delivered a mind-boggling *260,000 shaft horsepower* that pushed the 100,000-ton steel mass of *Coral Sea* over 30 knots and could do it non-stop for *twenty years* if the machinist mates could keep the shafts and reduction gears lubed. Indeed, this *national asset* would serve the Navy and the nation for *half a century* before it wore out and needed to be decommissioned. During those decades, it would serve many roles: deter aggression and occasionally respond to it; deliver relief supplies; project national power, or the threat of it, well inland. And *Coral Sea* could do this from anywhere on earth.

A capital warship of this stature was vital to the nation's military policy of forward deployment, the 800-pound gorilla that could be moved to trouble spots quickly and remain on station for weeks or *months* to maintain—or restore—stability ashore. In that sense, to Meyerkopf, the tactical war fighting capability of these ships was a sideshow. To him, the nuclear carrier fleet—like his submarine navy—was in greater danger from neglect and accidents, the insidious march of corrosion and mismanagement of planned maintenance shipyard availabilities that put unnecessary wear and tear on the plant and associated equipment. Vigilance through exhaustive and repetitive training, strict adherence to preventive maintenance schedules, and thorough inspections could mitigate this danger. Therefore, Meyerkopf was the right man at the right place at the right time.

He wasn't the captain of the ship, but it was the flagship and the center of gravity of his strike group. As the senior officer aboard, he certainly shared some responsibility for her upkeep. After giving Sanders a fair shake, Meyerkopf's measure of him was that he was shockingly detached from the engineering spaces, delegating them to his Executive and Reactor Officers in a way that appalled Meyerkopf. Sanders seemed to spend an inordinate amount of time pressing the flesh like a politician as he strolled through the passageways and mess decks, handing out his silly and monotonous daily "awards" to junior sailors only a year or two removed from their everybody-gets-a-trophy civilian upbringing. When Sanders wasn't "campaigning for office," he was on the bridge when the Airedales flew, day and night, another disturbing waste of time. Surely the aviators were professionals, and appeared to depart and return to the ship without trouble. No need for coddling by the captain for hours on end. The wing commander, Matson, seemed to be doing his job with the flight suit crowd, but running a ship was something Meyerkopf knew how to do, and Sanders clearly needed help.

With this focus, Meyerkopf asked probing questions about the plant each day in his morning staff meetings. The operational employment of the ship, even deployed far from home waters, would take care of itself. His flagship wasn't going to deteriorate on *his* watch.

"Captain, these elevated dosimeter readings in Main Machinery Room One concern me."

Sanders, ready for the daily quiz, answered with confidence.

"They concern me, too, Admiral, and while radiation levels *are* within limits, the Reactor and Medical departments are working side-by-side to find causal factors while closely monitoring our personnel. The XO reports to me each day. This has our full attention."

Meyerkopf frowned as he shifted uncomfortably in his chair, mindful of the dozen senior officers present. He did not want to humiliate Sanders but needed to make a point—for the benefit of all. "Captain, the data indicate *Coral Sea* has elevated readings compared to other carriers, and they seem to elevate once underway. I mean, does it have your *full* attention? Do we need to ask for an assist team to fly down and help? Is it a training issue, or is it a sign of impending mechanical failure? What is it?"

"Sir, while the readings are elevated, they've remained steady. They are within limits, and we are watching them like a hawk." Sanders regretted his last point, mentally scolding himself for not saying *I* am watching them.

Meyerkopf exhaled as he reviewed the report in front of him. "Rick, we can't live this way. What if the readings get out of limits?"

"Sir, if they do, we can shut down Number One and operate on Number Two to complete the mission down here. Meanwhile, yes sir, if an assist team from Norfolk can visit us and give it a look, we'd love that. We're always open to help and to increasing the knowledge of the crew. While we wait for their arrival, we are still operating the plant within limits."

Shooting Sanders a sharp look, Meyerkopf pursed his lips. *Enough for today,* he thought. *Point made.* Operated by aviators the whole time, *Coral Sea* was less than ten years old and, in his view, showed signs of premature aging. It was good, he reflected, that the Navy occasionally assigned a submariner who "grew up" around nuclear power to oversee a carrier strike group and ensure the sound material condition of its vital flagship for future operations.

After Sanders' come-around was complete, the meeting adjourned with no discussion of the air wing flying operations other than the previous days' sortie count and expected weather for today. Meyerkopf seemed uncomfortable—or disinterested—in what the aviators were doing, even in support of the significant muscle movements involved in *Assured Promise,* drug interdiction ops, or unmanned helicopter test operations. As they left the room and entered the passageway, Sanders' eyes met those of CAG Matson, and they both grinned knowingly.

"I guess bad press is better than no press, huh?" Sanders said under his breath.

"Yep, are there airplanes on this ship? Wish I could take some of the heat off," the Air Wing Commander answered his friend.

"Thanks," Sanders chuckled. "I'm off to go help my engineering department find a within-limits-and-holding-for-years radiation leak. You have a great day."

"You, too." Matson clapped Sanders' back in encouragement.

As the little political drama played out in the flag spaces of *Coral Sea,* Wilson had just completed his flight briefing with Macho in Ready Room 5. Test pilot Lieutenant Commander Meadows was also scheduled to fly during this event, and Wilson wanted to know what he was up to with one of his jets.

"Mongo, what kind of testing are you doing today?" he asked.

"Interoperability tests with a *Fire Scout,* sir. We want to see how this unmanned aerial vehicle performs data-link transfer with a fleet aircraft."

"Great, why don't we rendezvous overhead the ship at recovery time?"

Without taking his eyes off Wilson, Mongo refused. "No can do, Commander. I may need to stay out if the tests go long or if the bird can't get airborne in time."

Wilson was taken aback. *Nobody* called him Commander, especially in his own ready room. It was either *Skipper* or *sir*. While Mongo wasn't officially a *Firebird* pilot, even the "guest" aviators, as a sign of respect, referred to Wilson as Skipper. Mongo's stiff demeanor was different from the other pilots of his rank, most of whom were easygoing and completely respectful. Mongo gave Wilson the impression that he was holding Mongo up from something more important. He took another approach.

"Fine, if you get back to the ship when we do, then join up and you'll be Number Three as we enter the landing pattern. Where are you operating?"

"In the vicinity of the ship, sir."

Puzzled by this answer, Wilson was beginning to lose his patience. "We are operating *in the vicinity*, too, and so that we can deconflict our airspace, I want to know what sector you plan to be in. We are going to operate south if we can find a clear area."

"That will be fine, sir."

Mongo's robotic answer irritated Wilson. He was "giving the keys" to one of his jets to this guy and he was...*weird*, weird compared to anyone he had ever met wearing a flight suit. Mongo was Weed's guy, though, a *Jedi Knight* Weed had called him. And if the test community sent a detachment down here and needed one of Wilson's jets each day to test a new unmanned helicopter, he had to defer. He was thankful that chasing a drone and collecting data-link numbers was Mongo's job instead of his on this glorious day.

CHAPTER 10

Peering over her oxygen mask at the yellow shirted flight deck director, Macho released the brakes and added power as she pulled out of her parking spot on Elevator 2. She tapped the brakes once to check them and continued forward, goosing the throttles to advance no faster than a man could walk. Macho kept her eyes locked on the director, using the rudder pedals and nose-wheel steering, she made slight turns under his direction. He taxied her past other parked aircraft, all "turning" with jet engines at idle and awaiting yellow shirt directions to taxi. Outside the cocoon of Macho's cockpit, the flight deck was a high-pitched whine of screaming machinery. Hundreds of sailors in multicolored jerseys and "float-coat" life vests wore dark visors on their cranial helmets to shield eyes from the brilliant sun overhead. Puffy white build-ups, radiant in the dazzling midday light, towered above the ship as it slowly turned to a launch heading.

Coral Sea was preparing to launch fifteen aircraft on the first scheduled event of the day, a short 45-minute "cycle" that the *Hornet* squadrons used for their fuel-consuming air combat training. Though fuel management was always foremost in their thoughts, the pilots could breathe a little easier on a shortened cycle than they could on their typical hour and thirty minute cycle. Operating 200 miles southeast of Jamaica, with the South American landmass over 200 miles further southeast, *Coral Sea* was right in the middle of the Caribbean and working "Blue Water." This meant that low-fuel aircraft would have to "plug" from an orbiting *Super Hornet* tanker to take on fuel in order to remain airborne and attempt a carrier landing. Varsity for sure, but even nuggets like Macho, with only 70 carrier landings under her belt, were confident and excited to get airborne in this tropical playground.

The director turned Macho left, and she crept past the parked *Seahawk* helicopters next to the island. She could see she was in line for one of the waist catapults as the yellow shirt stopped her. With a delay until launch time—the ship was still in a turn—she set the parking brake and waited.

Macho used the time to enter some navigational waypoints in her computer and fiddled with the brightness of her multifunction display. On the horizon, she saw a nondescript merchant ship heading north, and, in the distance, the familiar lines of a white-hulled cruise ship. She smiled when she thought that she was getting paid to be here, and that nothing on the "fun-ship" was as much fun as she was going to experience in ten minutes.

She lifted her head to the island and blinked in surprise. From the "Vultures' Row" catwalk, Wonder Woman waved at her wildly. Next to her, on either side, were two air wing pilots from the *Raiders*, smiling down at Macho with smug grins. *Well, it didn't take the air wing studs long to roll in on Wonder Woman.* Oblivious to their motives, Shane was waving and beaming like a schoolgirl, even more ridiculous in her "Mickey Mouse" sound attenuators. She was causing a scene.

In an effort to get her to stop, Macho lifted her hand in response. Shane blew her a kiss and shouted something to one of the men next to her and pointed at Macho. Macho gratefully found a reason to look away to the catapults on her right. *How can a chick be so smokin' hot and so uncool at the same time?* she thought. Macho knew the air wings guys thought she was a girl just this side of "Peppermint Patti," and *she* had no desire to date one of them. Still, she was becoming slightly jealous of the attention Shane, the friggin' *intel weenie*, was receiving from her peer group. Macho made a mental note to have a talk with Shane after she got back and explain how to act on the ship.

The launch was about to begin and the yellow shirt motioned Macho ahead. She released the parking brake and, against her better judgment, looked up. Shane smiled proudly down upon her and clapped her open palms together as if she were watching a small child in a school play. One of the smug *Raiders* also waved with his fingers, as if to say "Bye-bye!" *Compartmentalize! Compartmentalize!* Macho scolded herself. She kept her eyes locked on the director, refusing to look at Vultures' Row.

The E-2 and tanker aircraft ahead of Macho were shot into the moist tropical air to take their places overhead, and a director led her to the catapult. On signal, she spread her wings and locked them in place. Once over the shuttle, she lifted her hands above the canopy rail while the ordnancemen "armed" the captive *Sidewinder* practice missile on Station 9. Unable to resist, she slowly turned her visor-covered eyes to the right, moving her head as little as possible, and caught a glimpse of Shane. With the two *Raiders* still by her side, Shane's attention appeared to be elsewhere on the flight deck. She nodded as one of the men pointed at something on the bow. *Just my luck,* Macho thought, *to get "Miss Idaho" as a roommate.*

Macho was led forward and the catapult petty officer directed her to "take tension." Shoving both throttles to military power, she felt the airplane tense up underneath her. She then "wiped out the cockpit" by moving the stick to the four corners of travel and pushed the rudder pedals to their full extent. Ready, she popped a sharp salute to the catapult officer. When he returned it, she placed her head back in the headrest and grabbed the canopy bow "towel rack" and locked both arms in place.

From the island catwalk, a thrilled Shane watched the scene. *That's my roommate in that big and powerful airplane!* She squealed with delight as Macho suddenly roared down the track and went airborne with a *boom* as the catapult shuttle slammed into the water brake. Shane watched Macho fly away until she could follow her no longer. She was thrilled.

I am so proud, so amazed, and so fortunate to be here!

CHAPTER 11

Mongo was shot off the bow a moment later and sucked the gear and flaps up. Leveling at 500 feet, he then energized his radar and Forward Looking Infrared sensor, or FLIR.

Like the other aircraft, he began to climb at seven miles ahead of the ship. Unlike the others, he set out to the west, on his own.

Mongo climbed at a shallow angle, the blue surface slowly falling away as he concentrated on setting up his cockpit up for the mission. He soon passed 20,000 feet—and had almost another 20,000 feet to go.

Passing 30,000 feet, he was well above the white buildup columns that cast shadows on the surface below. To his right, and about 50 miles north, a storm with an anvil-topped cloud sat over an open patch of ocean. Far to the south, at a distance he guessed was over the South American landmass, he saw other towering cumulus thunderstorms with more anvil-tops. His radar detected contacts on the surface, four total, and he commanded his FLIR sensor to lock on them one at a time. The binocular power of the sensor helped him identify them as merchants: two containerships, a tanker, and one car carrier that resembled a floating rectangular box. Mongo guessed the car carrier to be coming up from the Panama Canal.

He still had over 100 miles to go.

At 36,000 feet, Mongo leveled off but stayed underneath the contrail altitude of an airliner about 15 miles ahead of his nose. He glanced over his shoulder to see if he was "marking" himself and, as he had planned, saw no contrail behind him. *Good*, he thought and watched the airliner on his FLIR. The silhouette looked like a Boeing widebody, and the closest he got to the aircraft was three miles as it crossed right-to-left in front of him.

Mongo wasn't worried about being detected by the airliner, and out here in international airspace, it was unlikely anyone was watching either one of them. *Big sky, little airplane.* The white contrails the aircraft engines generated were long, and with nothing better to do, Mongo wondered where the flight had originated. He guessed Dallas, as good a

65

guess as any. As the airliner gradually receded to the south, Mongo figured it to be a 767, and, by the paint job, he could identify the U.S. flag airline.

While Commander Wilson and his wingman Macho were returning home to *Mother* after their training flight, Mongo was just beginning his. After 30 minutes airborne and over 200 miles from the carrier, Mongo retarded the throttles and entered into a shallow descent. Fuel management around the ship—and especially in an FA-18—was critical, and Mongo would need to refuel in-flight before he recovered in two hours. But this was risky. He had to complete his mission with just enough reserve fuel to find the big wing Air Force tanker near *Mother,* someplace 200 miles behind him. He could then get a drink before the engines flamed out.

Risky. Mongo was not given to worry. He was doing his job, and, if the ship weenies did theirs, this mission would be successful. If he ran out of gas and had to punch out, fine. If he died on this flight, fine. He had no one waiting for him in the states, and while he was in the service of something bigger than himself, the *United States Government*, he was drawn to the challenge: to manage every aspect of this mission, *perfectly*, and only *he* would know exactly how perfectly, leaving nothing to chance. And if the weak links in the chain broke, *he* would save their bacon. He even hoped they would drop the ball so he could pick it up.

Enjoying an unobstructed 360-degree view, he basked in his solitude as he descended in a lazy turn to the right. He knew he wasn't, and at five minutes past the hour, the MIDS display showed a message:

READY FOR MISSION 45B AS FRAGGED?

Mongo selected his response:

WILCO

He wasn't sure of the location of the controller he was communicating with. On the "small boy" guided missile destroyer? In an AWACS or E-2? Nevada? It didn't matter, and Mongo wasn't going to waste brain power speculating. This controller had come up on the right frequency at the right time with the right mission number. The controller answered him:

ROGER TAKE STATION AS BRIEFED PACKAGE ON SCHEDULE

COI BULLSEYE 315/35 TRACKING NW 330 40 KTS

REPORT PLAYTIME

Mongo called up his bullseye waypoint and calculated a course to the contact of interest about 30 miles away. Cruising at 20,000 feet, Mongo scanned the surface of the ocean. On the other side of a column of puffy cumulous, he saw it: a go-fast with a big wake. Taking care not to lock on the boat with his radar—for fear of setting off any RF detection equipment it may have—he overbanked the jet to put his nose on the smuggler. Viewing it through the FLIR, he bumped the castle switch to "grab" the IR contrast. Picking his nose back up, he leveled off, sauntering toward the boat from a position behind it. He maneuvered to conceal himself in the sun. In no hurry, he energized the video recorder.

CAPTURED he signaled to the nameless, faceless controller. He then used his data link to send a picture of the contact. The reply was swift:

VERIFIED HOSTILE

COMMENCE LIMA IN 1 MIKE

Mongo punched his timer and scanned the surface as he performed lazy S-turns to stay behind the go-fast and to stay in the sun. He saw the gray *Fire Scout* UAV, the *package*, three miles below him, heading for the same "skunk." He scanned the water out to 20 miles around them—nothing—and felt satisfied. No witnesses...and no rescue.

When the timer passed 60, he engaged the laser and kept it on the go-fast, now only five miles ahead. Mongo's geometry was perfect. He estimated the *Fire Scout* to be less than two miles from the boat. A MIDS display message warned him a shot was imminent. Seconds later, a fiery flash sprinted forward from the unmanned helicopter to the boat, a guided 2.75- inch rocket trailing a brilliant white plume against the blue textured sea below. Mongo returned his attention to the FLIR display, holding the laser on target, and waited for the rocket to enter the picture.

When it did, the display was washed out by the explosion, and Mongo could tell the boat was knocked off its keel by the force of impact. As the flash subsided, the boat careened wildly and rolled upside down with a huge splash. He saw debris splashes around the smoking hull, but no flame. The white fiberglass hull floated as the concentric impact rings and smoke subsided. On the FLIR he observed no movement around it.

Mongo circled like a vulture, keeping his FLIR—and eyes—locked on for signs of survivors. There were none, and Mongo wondered what the controller had in mind. He sent another photo of the hulk as a prompt. Within a minute, he received his tasking:

STAND BY FOR SHOT

LIMA IN 1 MIKE

Mongo acknowledged and set himself up for another south to north run. As he descended to below 10,000 feet, he worked to keep his aiming diamond low on the hull. He saw the *Fire Scout* launch another guided rocket from inside a mile. The rocket motor was still burning when it exploded into the upturned hull, cutting it in half and sending a spray of debris that churned up the water on the far side. Within seconds, both pieces of the hull slipped below the waves. Now down on the water, he saw no signs of life, not even a floating body. The controller messaged him again:

GOOD WORK

CLEARED RTB

Mongo rogered the message, and, climbing through the buildup columns, set a course back to the ship. It was now time to pay more attention to his low-fuel state. Soon he was back at 35,000 feet, heading east with the sun high above.

Cruising at a transonic airspeed, he felt he was floating above the earth, in total dominion of it, *looking down* on the hapless merchant ships and dirty little fishing boats. They were *clueless*, like dumb sheep grazing in a meadow, protected by him who keeps watch, killing the wolf without remorse. He killed *perfectly*, as they had briefed it...and would not say a word about it, ever.

At 100 miles out, he keyed the mike and checked in with *Strike* control for vectors to the KC-10, the first words he had spoken in the two hours since he had manned the jet on the flight deck. The tanker was orbiting southeast of him at sixty miles, and he pulled power to enter a fuel-conserving descent as his radar locked it. He was low on fuel but would make it before the FUEL LO caution appeared on his display. After all, he was a professional, handpicked for this mission.

And ready for more.

CHAPTER 12

Several days later, after another long day at sea, Macho sat at her stateroom desk emailing her sister back home in Virginia. Today's dissimilar air combat training hop against the Colombian *Kfirs* had been exhilarating, and as the XO's trusted wingman, Macho had felt a kindred bond of sisterhood. Annie had led them out of the sun, gaining two early tallies. She had directed Macho to take the far *bandit.*

Macho came in high-to-low taking a big bite— the guy didn't see her until she was almost saddled in for guns—and when he did, he took it up...a mistake.

Macho followed his predictable flight path with ease. Unable to maneuver hard, the gray delta-winged jet hung against the brilliant blue sky as it bled airspeed. It fell off right, and Macho followed it with her gun sight pipper on. *Ho hum. Another day at the office.* Staying behind her *Kfir,* with its nose buried, she noted Annie pushing her bandit around a mile away. White condensation poured off the *Kfir's* wings as the pilot struggled to get his nose up and get the *Hornet* off him. Macho imagined "writing her name" on the fuselage of the aircraft in front of her with the imaginary bullets she was pumping into it. Satisfied, she called "Terminate," and Annie soon followed. They joined up and returned home, logging some "practice plugs" on the *Super Hornet* tanker that orbited overhead the ship, and in sharp formation came into the break, both of them logging OK-3 wire passes. A great hop all around, Annie was a big sister she could look up to and a leader she could emulate.

Shane entered the stateroom after her day in CVIC, the carrier intel center. Her duty included debriefing pilots and updating launch and recovery information for their event briefings.

"*Hiii!*"

"Hi. How was CVIC?"

"Omigosh! It was so cool today! Commander Hofmeister assigned me to get the weather information for the flight briefings. The sailors in the meteorology office took me up to the tower and showed me how they launch weather balloons and take wind readings. It's incredible up there! And they told me how the Captain turns the ship any way he wants in order to get the winds down the runway for you *exactly* the way you need them. Really cool! And everyone is so nice!"

I'll bet, Macho thought.

"What did you do today?" Shane asked.

"Two-v-two with the XO against some Colombian *Kfirs*. We bumped heads about a hun'erd miles south of here."

"How were they?"

Macho wasn't expecting this question, but answered as if she were a pilot.

"They came at us in an echelon, not much in the way of pre-merge maneuvering. XO led us out of the sun, and we each glommed on to our own guy and pushed him around a bit. I think I had the new guy in their formation, and we were pretty far out to sea; they were probably worried about losing sight of land!"

"What kind of radar indications did you get?"

Impressed by the technical question, Macho remembered that the "Sweet Polly Purebred" who stood in front of her did have an understanding of threat radars.

"*I was clean.* Maybe that was their plan—so you *spies* couldn't glean any intel. But they didn't seem to lock us, and that makes sense because we were already rolling in on them when they began to turn."

Shane nodded her understanding. "Yeah, they may have gone in silent." After a moment, she changed the subject. "Are you writing your boyfriend?"

"No. Don't have one. How about you?"

"I had one, but it didn't work out." Shane's answer left a question hanging.

"What happened?" Macho asked her.

Shane formulated her answer and took a breath. "We met in college. He was a year older, good-looking, brother of my roommate. We dated, while in school, for three years. After he graduated, he asked me to marry him, and I said yes. He took a job in Alaska, and before he left, he wanted pictures of me "to keep him warm" at night and all that. You know...*those* kinds of pictures. Now, we had never done it, we were saving ourselves, but he begged and pleaded and we *were* engaged, so I took my top off. *That's it!* And I covered myself with my hands and my hair. He took pictures with his smartphone, and...*I was such an idiot.* Months later, he called one night crying. He had shown the photos to some guys. No, he had *sent* the photos to some guys! I couldn't believe how he had betrayed me! And, sure enough, it got out there, and people started whispering at school. *Praise the Lord!* I kept my commission, but I called off the engagement. It just *killed* his parents and his baby sister. We had gotten close. I was upset that *I* let them down."

"Wow," Macho said.

"You can't tell *anyone!*" Shane flared. "I had to go away on a *ship* to leave Idaho behind, and here there are lots of cute guys, and they aren't going to want a *slut* like me."

"Oh, stop! *He* betrayed *you!* You're not a slut. You're the victim. And I wouldn't give these guys here a free pass. There are plenty of pigs to go around."

"I know, I know. And I wouldn't date a squadron guy, but it is a big ship. Maybe one exception," Shane offered with a smile.

"Who?"

"Trench is cute." *Wonder Woman* shrugged and smiled as she said it.

"Oh, no! You need to give him a wide berth, girlie. He's interested in only one thing."

"Don't worry. I wouldn't start an office romance...*but those muscles!* Are *you* interested in him?"

"No way! He's the lead pig! He doesn't respect you, and you are just a notch in his belt. Besides, the *Firebird* guys are like brothers, and they call me a dude with hair. But Trench—and Coach, too—are two guys I avoid."

"Why don't you like him?" Shane asked.

"Because he thinks he's God's gift and that all women are his playthings—to be abused, verbally and otherwise."

"Did he...?"

"Omigosh, *no!* Look, he's nice to you *now*. Hell, every swingin' dick on the *ship* is nice to you, but you are a piece of meat to him. He's a *Neanderthal* and doesn't think any of us chicks should be here, even the XO."

Troubled, Shane looked away. "I just want to do my job and be respected for it."

Macho rolled her eyes. "Do you think those guys in the metro office give the snot-nosed *male* intel officers personal tours of the tower? Or horse-faces like me? *Fuck no.* Your face looks like Miss America, and your body looks like Miss July. They are *guys*, young virile guys, and they're *after you.* And if you don't watch yourself, you're going to get hurt."

Stung, Shane said nothing, and an uneasy silence filled the stateroom. Shane checked for something on her desk, and Macho went back to her email, both still conscious of the exchange.

"I'm sorry," Shane said.

"Hey, *I'm* sorry. It's just that I want to protect you. Girls come aboard and are the flavor-of-the-month until the next one shows up. You're showing your chops as an intel officer and gaining credibility around here, and that's hard to do with these a-holes. The non-pilot males have it much harder. If they shrink away from the needling, they're treated like shit. At least you have their attention. I'm not sure how much *listening* they're doing, but you have their attention. Keep giving good briefings and it will sink in."

Shane smiled in appreciation. "I think your face is pretty."

Macho exhaled and smiled back. "Thanks," she replied, grateful—as any woman living on the gray warship would be—for a rare personal compliment.

CHAPTER 13

(USS *Coral Sea*, underway, Central Caribbean)

Wilson climbed up the ladder steps in his flight gear, carrying his helmet bag in one hand and steadying himself on the rail with the other. At the top, he reached the O-4 level and undogged the hatch that led to the flight deck and stepped outside.

A week had passed since they had begun *Assured Promise,* and the ship and airwing were in a routine. First launch at noon. Last recovery at midnight. Lots of routine surface search around the ship interspersed with fun intercept hops against the Colombians who, like the Americans, were honing their air-combat maneuvering skills against a dissimilar adversary. The *Kfirs* were hard to see until the merge, and the Colombian he had fought yesterday had a good understanding of his jet to fight it slow. However, the *Kfirs* were no match for the *Hornets.* When not "fighting" the Colombians, the airwing pilots had scoured the surface around *Coral Maru.* The ship knew what every passing vessel was and where it was going, and the airwing pilots were competing against each other for the best still pictures of the same ships. As the merchants plodded through the Caribbean in the vicinity of the carrier, the American jets buzzed around them like troublesome insects. The "kids" in those cockpits found ways to compete in everything.

According to the schedule, *Coral Sea* was to remain *here* in this same piece of water for the next two weeks, with Wilson and the other airwing pilots doing routine searches and bumping heads with the Colombians while the nukes below carried out their arcane engineering drills. The daily repetition was like *Groundhog Day,* and, as Wilson walked to his jet parked on the fantail, he wondered once again why they were doing this basic meat-and-potatoes training *here* and not closer to home. Air Force and Marine fighters based in the Southeast could give them better flight profiles and provide several overland targets for training. In fact, the carrier could be in port for much of the training and drills. *And why do the reactor guys care where the ship is anyway?*

Weed and the test guys seemed to be busy, and that was the biggest mystery of all. *Why test this stuff here when the test infrastructure was back in home waters?* Sending *Coral Sea* here, and keeping it in one area for weeks at a time, was strange. He could only surmise it was to placate the ego of the four-star Combatant Commander in Miami who wanted some Navy assets to control. Or some regional State Department initiative: *Sure, send 10,000 sailors to sea to show Colombia we care.*

Oh, well, he thought, as he neared his jet, *Firebird* 301. *It's a beautiful day, and my job is to fly.*

"Good morning, Dubose," Wilson said as he returned the salute of his plane captain.

"Good morning, sir!" the young man replied, standing at attention in front of *his* jet. Although Wilson's name was stenciled under the canopy, Dubose's name and hometown were stenciled in black letters on the nose wheel door. Dubose felt as if he actually owned the multimillion-dollar jet and *let* the pilots fly it.

Wilson stowed his gear in the cockpit and began his preflight routine as Airman Dubose followed. On one wing station was a rack of six Mk-76 practice bombs. He and new guy LTJG *Jumpin Joe* Kessler were going to drop them on a towed target in *Coral Sea's* wake before they set out to update the surface picture around the ship. All was in order, as usual, and Wilson chatted with some of the flight deck troubleshooters before he climbed into the cockpit.

He saw Weed preflighting a jet next to him, a single-seat *Rhino* from the *Hunters* of VFA-62, and noted his jet was carrying *two* racks of five practice bombs. Wilson shrugged off the double load of ordnance to the test program. He called to Weed and pointed at the weapons.

"Where you going with those?"

Weed smiled as he walked over to Wilson. "More *Fire Scout* testing. I'm gonna drop these things on smokes, and the *Fire Scout* will record the hits."

"What fun," Wilson said. "Where you going?"

Weed hesitated just long enough for Wilson to notice. "Depends where the *Fire Scout* is. I'll find out airborne. What are you guys doing?"

Wilson gestured aft. "Dropping these on the sled, then searching around the ship. Showing the nugget the ropes."

"As you have done so well for so *many* years, old man," Weed joked.

Wilson smiled at the barb. "You were right alongside me most of those years."

"But you are senior, and you're a *skipper* now, the *old man*. Sorry to have to point all this out."

"See you out there," Wilson chuckled. *Same old Weed.*

With nimble steps Wilson climbed the boarding ladder and plopped himself in the ejection seat. Dubose followed. After connecting Wilson's oxygen and g-suit hoses, he slammed home the upper Koch fittings that attached Wilson's harness to the parachute embedded in the seat mechanism.

"Where are you going, sir?" the plane captain asked his CO.

"We're gonna stay here and bomb the spar, that sled they're towing behind us."

Dubose looked over the fantail and saw a white spray being kicked up by the target sled in the wake behind the ship.

"Cool, sir."

"You gonna watch us?" Wilson asked with a smile.

"If I can, sir," the teenager replied. Both knew that the flight deck was not open to a lot of sightseeing.

Dubose descended the ladder and then stowed it in the LEX. Standing next to 301 at parade rest, he waited for engine starts.

Across the deck Wilson saw Jumpin in 307 and noted several troubleshooters around the aircraft. *Oh, oh.*

Like clockwork, at thirty minutes before launch time, the Air Boss came up on the 5MC flight deck loudspeaker to set the familiar ballet in motion with his singsong cadence:

"On the flight deck, aircrews have manned for the fourteen-thirty launch. Time for all personnel to get into the proper flight deck uniform. Helmets on and buckled, goggles down, sleeves rolled down, life vests on and securely fastened. Check your pockets for loose gear and FOD. Check chocks, chains, and loose gear about the deck. Stand clear of intakes, exhausts, prop arcs, rotor blades and tail rotors. Let's start the go aircraft! Start 'em up!"

Dubose lifted his arms to signal ready, and Wilson gave him a thumbs-up to proceed. Dubose, like the other dozen *Hornet* plane captains on deck, signaled for Auxiliary Power Unit start, and Wilson lifted the switch to energize the APU that would soon provide starting air to the jet engines.

The jets scattered about the flight deck cranked to life, a whirring growl of machinery, and with the APU's online, the plane captains led their pilots through engine starts in practiced order. A *whoosh* of air entered the engine bays to start the turbines as the pilots ignited fuel in what soon became a screaming, high-pitched whine of jets. The *hummmm* from the E-2 turboprops and the *whirrr* of the MH-60 *Sierra* plane guard filled in the background. Sailors in multicolored jerseys scurried about with varied tasks, flight deck tractors weaved among the aircraft, chiefs identified by their khaki trousers walked about supervising the young sailors like Dubose. Arguably the most dangerous work environment on earth was aroused to conduct another "routine" launch and recovery.

A warm breeze circulated among the aircraft as the ship moved through the gentle swells, the sun high overhead and the afternoon buildups gaining strength. To the west were two small rainclouds dumping gray sheets of water on the sea, and high on the tower mast the Stars and Stripes flew above the white and red signal flag for flight ops, FOXTROT.

With his canopy down to drown out the din, Wilson flicked on avionics and radios and punched in the frequencies and waypoint coordinates he would need for this flight. He did love it down here and, by the look of the flight deck, the crew did, too. As they went about their tasks in the warm sunshine, they knew that, if the ship went into the squall, many could find a reason to go below.

Wilson and Dubose went through the post-start checks in familiar sequence, and when complete, a nearby yellow shirt hurried over to take control of 301. Dubose and two blue shirts scurried underneath the jet to remove the chocks and tie-down chains, and when Dubose reappeared, the chains were draped around his neck, adding another layer of flight deck grime to his already filthy brown float coat. He pointed to the yellow shirt and saluted Wilson, control of 301 now in the able hands of the young flight deck controller.

Obeying the yellow shirt's hand signals, Wilson eased out of his spot, passing dozens of sailors tending other jets waiting their turn. He was passed off to another yellow shirt who took him along the foul line past the island. It seemed Wilson was being taken to the bow behind Weed, who had taxied ahead of him.

Weed was positioned on Cat 1, and, as the Jet Blast Deflector slowly rose out of the flight deck, Wilson stopped behind it, mere feet from the steel shield. Troubleshooters ducked under the jets and walked along the fuselages, making last-minute checks of their charges with practiced eye and loving hands.

The *Hawkeye* was shot early off Cat 2 with a resonating *whooommm*. After a short lull, and with the other aircraft positioned behind them, the catapult crews began hooking up the jets to the shuttles. Red-shirted ordnancemen pulled pins to "arm" the practice ordnance and the 20mm cannons of the fighters. Off the waist, a tanker-configured *Super Hornet* roared into the air to take position overhead *Coral Sea* to transfer fuel to thirsty jets.

The crew waited through a five-minute break for the Air Boss to give a green deck. The goal was to shoot the first airplane at *exactly* 1430, to the second. Circling overhead, small formations of aircraft from the previous event waited for their turn to land and watched the progress of the launch so they could enter the break as soon as the angled deck became clear.

The ship steadied on launch heading—with the squall now right in front of it. Concentrating on the dangerous task set before them, the sailors didn't seem to notice the foul weather ahead—which would soon drench them.

On the other side of the JBD, Weed added some power, and Wilson knew that soon his friend would be placed in tension. Seconds later the twin F414 engines of the *Rhino* thundered to full strength. The waves of kerosene exhaust pounding on the JBD caused everything in the vicinity to vibrate. Wilson was buffeted in place and would have been blown over the side were it not for the JBD.

Wilson saw Weed's rudders and stabilators move and watched the edge of his friend's helmet in the canopy. Wilson saw Weed salute to signify ready, and seconds later Weed roared down the track and into the gray gloom of the squall. The JBD lowered, and the catapult crew turned their attention to 301.

Big raindrops began to pelt Wilson's canopy, and then sheets of rain beat down on the flight deck, giving a welcome fresh water wash down to everything on it. In his dry cocoon, Wilson taxied as his yellow shirt directed him, lining up on the cat.

"Flip, Jumpin," Kessler called to him on the tactical frequency.

"Go."

"I'm down, sir."

As he lowered his launch bar, Wilson absorbed this information. Jumpin's jet was down for some maintenance malfunction and would not be launching. Wilson was now "alone" for this flight.

"Roger, see you later," he transmitted.

Wilson came up on the power to tension the holdback and seat the launch bar in the shuttle. The rain obscured visibility ahead of the ship, and near the shot line he saw some teenaged sailors laughing at the absurdity of their drenching shower. Then, through the squall, he saw sunlight on the water.

Dripping wet, the yellow shirt gave Wilson the take-tension signal. The rain subsided as quickly as it had started, and Wilson shoved the throttles to military power and cycled the controls. With all well, he popped a sharp salute to the catapult officer and held on, waiting to be shot. Seconds later, he blazed down the track kicking up billowing clouds of spray. The warm Caribbean air would soon act as a 25-knot blow dryer for the sopping sailors remaining on the flight deck.

Wilson cleaned up, energized the radar, and accelerated ahead of *Coral Sea*. He couldn't begin to drop bombs on the wake until the airplanes on the previous event were recovered so he had 30 minutes of time to kill. To the west, he saw the dot of a climbing jet silhouetted against a white cloud and figured it was his friend, Weed. *What the hell*, Wilson thought. He had some time and decided it would be interesting to follow his former roommate and watch an operational test live.

CHAPTER 14

(*Firebird* 301, airborne, Central Caribbean)

With his radar in Range-While-Search mode, Wilson elevated the antenna and soon found Weed, about seven miles distant. Above his canopy bow about 30 degrees left of his nose, Wilson could see the speck that signified Weed's aircraft. He climbed to place himself about 5,000 feet below Weed who appeared to be level around 15,000 feet. Wilson did not "lock" his friend on radar; he did not want to distract him with a radar warning receiver indication. Weed continued west at a moderate 300 knots—no hurry—and Wilson matched him, having fun with his impromptu "tail" as he weaved among the afternoon buildups that drifted like hot-air balloons over the sea.

After 10 minutes of cruising, which took him over 50 miles from *Mother*, Wilson commanded his radar to scan the surface. He saw nothing. Back in RWS mode, he still couldn't pick up anything. This surprised him because he figured the *Fire Scout* UAV Weed was working with on this test must be nearby. Bored, Wilson was about to turn around when he noticed Weed turn right to the northwest and begin a shallow descent. Wilson stayed to investigate.

Taking care to remain hidden behind Weed and among the low clouds, Wilson watched Weed descend toward the surface. Staying under the ragged bottoms, Wilson now picked up a lone *Fire Scout*. Weed turned west, and Wilson gave both aircraft a wide berth. Struggling to keep sight of them, he held at a max-endurance fuel setting to watch the test from about five miles south.

For a moment, Weed disappeared from view. Using raw radar return, Wilson reacquired him and saw Weed in a dive. A puff on the surface revealed one of Weed's Mk-76 practice bombs hitting the water, accompanied by its white-smoke spotting charge. Intrigued, Wilson flew closer.

Minutes later, two puffs appeared on the surface. Wilson wondered what Weed was bombing. The *Fire Scout* orbited nearby. Wilson had no idea what was going on, but could not pull himself away.

Another puff of white smoke shot from the surface. Then, Wilson was surprised to see froth develop as an object appeared on the disturbed water. Commanding his radar to air-to-ground, Wilson locked this new surface contact and bumped his FLIR to it. On his display, it appeared to be a boat, a long raft, very low in the water. The next image astounded him. He detected movement on it.

Lifting his head up from the display, Wilson saw a fiery streak extend from the *Fire Scout* toward the object. His eyes darted back to the FLIR in time to see the missile hit, followed by a bright explosion. With his naked eyes, Wilson saw the black and gray cloud of the live-weapon explosion hover over the unidentified surface contact. Back on the FLIR display—which Wilson was recording—he saw that the object seemed to have pivoted up in the water.

It now dawned on Wilson. *They just hit a drug smuggler submersible or submarine!*

Alarmed that he was intruding, Wilson shoved the throttles into burner and departed the scene. Horrified by what he had just witnessed, he looked over his shoulder and saw Weed in a strafing run. White geysers lifted around the area of the missile detonation. *He's finishing them off!* Wilson thought. Shocked and sickened that smugglers, albeit criminals but human beings nonetheless, were trying to escape the vessel's final plunge only to be torn to pieces by Weed's 20mm cannon rounds. *Holy shit!* Wilson's his heart beat faster as he tried to comprehend what he had just witnessed.

He got into the clouds and headed south, darting from cloud to cloud. After twenty miles, he turned east toward the ship and climbed to 10,000 feet. Selecting a max-endurance fuel setting, he undid his mask. He let it hang as he took in lungfuls of air, still shaken by the incident and Weed's role in it.

Weed. What is he involved with? Murder? Summary execution?

Wilson's mind raced. The *Fire Scout*, a new and valuable asset, had a weapons capability he had not known it possessed. What he had seen, and Weed's involvement in it, was an ominous revelation that signified close coordination with higher authority.

What is this? National Command Authority and an undeclared war? CIA? Who is Weed working with?

The recovery was long complete, and he could now go and drop his bombs on the towed spar in the wake. Still disturbed by the experience and troubled by what it foreshadowed, he decided to make one run on a low-stress delivery. *The United States had just crossed a line.* And Wilson trembled to know he was witness to it.

He switched up tower frequency and listened while he found the ship on radar. He locked it and saw on the FLIR there were no airplanes buzzing overhead as the carrier turned back to the east. *Good*, Wilson thought, and set up his switches for his weapons delivery. Willing himself to compartmentalize, he began an easy turn to the northeast.

Rolling out of the turn, Wilson scanned ahead of his flight path and confirmed no aircraft near the ship, which was now less than 15 miles off his nose. Ingrained habit caused him to swivel his head to search for aircraft at his altitude—especially important around the ship. With his head craned to the right, he flinched in surprise and caused the jet to twitch as he tightened his grip on the stick. Next to him, on his right, was a *Super Hornet* in welded-wing parade formation. Inside the jet, eyes covered by his dark visor and his oxygen mask dangling, was Weed. He was not smiling.

CHAPTER 15

Shock, as strong as an electric charge, coursed through Wilson's body at the sight of Weed's jet next to him. Separated by only thirty feet as they cruised at 250 knots, Weed offered no hand signals. Wilson lifted his hands above the canopy rail and shrugged his shoulders to convey *What gives?* Weed had no reaction at all and continued to fly perfect form on Wilson's wing. Weed then lifted his arm in salute and pulled up and away. Wilson watched him turn southwest.

As an incredulous Wilson closed the ship and took extra glances behind him to see if Weed reappeared, his mind replayed the scene. *What did I just see? What did Weed just do?*

It made sense. *That's why we're down here,* he thought. *Weed and his "Jedi Knights," like the weird Mongo, are working with the new* Fire Scout *drones to attack drug smuggling submersibles.* Wilson had heard of such drug-smuggling vessels. He wondered how many the drug runners had, and how did Weed know where to find it? *He must have had tipper information but from where, from whom? Is this the kind of "testing" they are doing every day?*

Wilson continued to replay the event in his mind. It was as if Weed had kicked over an anthill, seen the agitated ants swarm to the surface, and then blown them away. Wilson had seen Weed drop the Mk-76's on the water—on the submersible—and if 25 supersonic pounds of kinetic energy hadn't punched a hole in the vessel, it had scared them enough to "blow tanks" and surface. Or to open the hatch and abandon ship. It must have been enough of a signature for the *Fire Scout* to launch a missile, which Wilson figured was something like a *Hellfire*.

Then, Weed had finished them off.

The submersible had lifted one end out of the water and had sunk like the *Titanic* in her death plunge. Then Weed had strafed the spot it went down. Had Weed seen people struggling in the water? *My gosh! We're the Americans and, we* pick up *survivors.* Wilson followed that thought with another that was just as disturbing. In an action of this type, witnesses—like Wilson had become—could pose problems.

Wilson remained troubled as he went through the motions of his practice bomb delivery on the wake. In a gentle dive he placed his string of Mk-76's "behind" the spar as it dragged through the water 1,000 feet behind the ship. As he then went off to hold for the recovery, his mind unable to concentrate on anything except what he had seen.

As the recovery neared, he dropped his tailhook and joined the aircraft holding above *Coral Maru* in lazy circles. All were waiting for the aircraft on deck to launch and be clear of it for their recovery. Fuel was on everyone's mind, and the aircraft maneuvered to fly over the ship in practiced sequence.

Wilson entered the circle at angels three, 3,000 feet. Below were two flights of *Rhinos* from the *Raiders* and *Hobos*, and across the circle was a section of two *Hunter* FA-18Es. Weed was also flying a *Hunter* aircraft, and Wilson searched for him. Wilson would have joined up on him and come into the break together, like the old days, when they were friends—like they were a few hours ago. But what had transpired *one* hour ago, and without one word being spoken between them, seemed to change that. Wilson feared the harm to their friendship was irreparable.

Wilson saw Weed's jet enter the circle from the opposite side. After 180 degrees of turn, it was apparent he was not going to join on the other *Hunters* or on Wilson. Wilson knew Weed knew Wilson was in the only FA-18C overhead the ship, and he wasn't joining up. The two pilots were ignoring each other from a distance of three miles, like friends with a strained relationship at a party, knowing full well the presence of the other.

Coral Sea began to launch aircraft, and soon each of the waist cats had only one more jet to shoot. The game now began, with the *Hobos* first to enter the break, followed by the *Raiders*. Wilson followed and entered the pattern. As he bumped up his airspeed and came into the break from a position three miles aft, mind and habit shed thoughts of the incident with Weed. He took a distance interval behind the second *Raider* jet and whipped the stick left. He then pulled into a knife-edge turn as he brought the throttles to idle.

With the stick in his lap, he bled airspeed, slapped down the gear and flaps, and worked himself on speed, on altitude, and abeam with a good interval. As he turned off the abeam position, the *Rhino* ahead of him rolled into the groove. *Perfect!*

Wilson concentrated on flying a good pass, working hard, checking rate of descent, angle of bank, and holding proper airspeed. He was *locked-in,* in control of his jet, placing it *exactly* where it needed to be. For a short moment, green lights appeared above the lens, his indication that the LSOs had cleared him to land. For the next 25 seconds, he was absorbed in the task of putting his 16-ton airplane on a targeted 40-foot patch of moving flight deck. He was in a sense relaxed as he concentrated on his approach—not having to dwell on either his command responsibilities nor on the new and troubling relationship with his friend.

As Wilson slid across the wake, making minute corrections with the stick and throttles, he took some power off and nudged the stick. He held a constant rate of descent, and the amber "donut" of his indexer lights showed him "on speed." He ignored "the ship" that loomed larger with each second and concentrated on the lights of the meatball, centering it between the rows of green datum lights which showed him to be on glideslope. He picked up slight movement in the ball and *felt* the jet alternately settle or balloon as he worked the controls to keep himself in parameters. The stick and throttles now acted as extensions of his brain as he flew the jet.

Wilson held 135 knots of airspeed, his entire being locked in on the approach. As he approached the ramp, Wilson felt he was hovering over it, able to move the jet inches up and down the imaginary chute that led to an arrestment.

As he slammed into the deck, his hook picked up the three wire and threw him forward against the straps. His left arm pushed the throttles to full power, and the force of the arrestment caused him to bounce in his seat as the deck edge rushed up. *Home.* But within seconds Weed and the image of him strafing helpless survivors returned to mind.

As he retracted the flaps and folded the wings, Wilson raised the hook on signal from the yellow shirt and followed his directions to the right. He gave a thumbs-up to Chief Sutherland in a gaggle of green-shirted maintenance sailors. Dubose, burdened by his tie-down chains, followed Wilson's jet to its parking spot.

Wilson could see they were taking him to Elevator 2, and he crept forward until his nose was out over the edge of the deck. The yellow shirt turned him right, and, for a moment, Wilson saw the frothy white waves from *Coral Sea's* wake, sixty feet below him, radiating into the blue Caribbean. He inched forward, and after another quarter turn, Wilson's left main mount skirted the deck-edge coaming. As he moved ahead, his nose came within feet of the *Growler* next to him. The yellow shirt had him lock his right brake, and Wilson came up on the power to pivot his nose right. Sailors helped by pushing on 301's nose in the delicate maneuver. Once lined up, sailors swarmed over the jet, taking care to remain clear of the dangerous jet intakes. On the yellow shirt's signal, they pushed Wilson *back* into place with the tail of *Firebird* 301 out over the water.

The yellow shirt gave the signal to wrap it up, and Dubose began to place tie-down chains on the landing gear to secure the still running *Hornet* in place. Wilson pulled the parking brake and began to relax.

Mongo then appeared next to Wilson's jet. He stood watching Wilson, his face expressionless.

What does that sonofabitch want? Wilson thought.

CAG, wearing his float-coat and cranial over his khaki uniform, then walked up next to Mongo. *Highly unusual.* CAG, too, was looking at Wilson, and both of them were waiting for him to shut down and deplane.

What the hell is this? Wilson thought. *What is happening out here?*

CHAPTER 16

(Flight Deck, USS *Coral Sea*, Central Caribbean)

After securing the avionics, Wilson shut down the jet. He popped the canopy open as he brought the throttles to off. Surrounded by the deafening noise and the not insignificant danger of the everyday flight deck, CAG and Mongo still watched him with cool detachment as they waited for him to climb down.

Wilson stepped onto the LEX, removed his videotapes from the machines behind the ejection seat, put them in his helmet bag, and descended the ladder. Mongo brushed past Airman Dubose and reached toward Wilson's bag. "I'll need those tapes, sir."

Bristling, Wilson clutched his bag, and bared his teeth under his helmet visor. "Excuse me, *Lieutenant Commander*, I am post-flighting my aircraft!" CAG stepped in to defuse the situation.

"Guys...guys.... Let's go below. Nice job, Jim," he shouted as he put his hand on Wilson's back, pulling him toward the island. CAG turned to Dubose, who was as puzzled by this reception as was Wilson, and pointed to 301. "Nice looking jet, airman! Keep it up!" Dubose nodded as the three pilots walked away toward the island, shrugging his shoulders at more strange officer behavior he couldn't begin to figure out.

Wilson fumed as Mongo led them to a catwalk abeam the island and descended to the O-3 level where he undogged the hatch so CAG and Wilson could enter the ship. Once inside and away from the flight deck chaos, they removed their helmets. CAG spoke over his shoulder as he led them down the passageway.

"Jim, we need to go to CVIC. No worries, but we need to talk there."

The carrier intel center was where Wilson was going anyway to debrief, as would any aviator after a hop. He could see that he was going to be debriefed by CAG himself on what he had seen out there. But one thing was sure: From this point on, he would not allow Mongo to step into his ready room, much less fly one of his jets.

Once at CVIC, the sentry buzzed them in, and CAG led them past the tables of intel officers taking aircrew debriefs. Among them was Shane who smiled at her CO. Wilson nodded back, mindful of the need to look as normal as possible, despite his high-ranking escort.

A conference table sat in the middle of the small room they entered, and workstations with computer monitors ringed the perimeter. Charts of the area were displayed on the bulkheads, and in one upper corner the ubiquitous PLAT monitor showed the recovery that continued on the flight deck. They heard the roar of a *Growler* trapping aboard one deck above them.

Mongo closed the door behind them and went to a file cabinet to retrieve a folder. CAG motioned for Wilson to take a seat.

"Jim, what did you see out there?"

Feeling Mongo's hostile stare on him, Wilson began. "I saw a *Rhino*, flown by my friend, drop 76's in a patch of ocean. Suddenly, an object, which I assumed to be a submarine, surfaced where he was bombing, and a *Fire Scout* shot it with a missile. On my FLIR display I saw the object as it began to sink, and after it did, Weed—that is, Commander Hopper— strafed the water where it went down. Then I left."

"How do you know it was Weed?"

"He was ahead of me on the cat. And, when my wingman went down, I had time on my hands and decided to follow him. We've been friends for years, and I wanted to see what kind of tests he was doing with the *Fire Scout*." Wilson paused as he looked at CAG. "I now think I know."

CAG took a few steps and sat down in a chair on the other side of the table. "Do you know we are at war?"

Wilson let the words sink in. "Yes, sir, several of them ongoing. If we'd just *win* one, we could lower that number." CAG Matson let Wilson's sarcasm pass.

"We are at war down here. Remember the war on drugs?"

"Yes, sir, been going on 20-25 years, I think."

"Are we winning?" CAG asked.

"Not from what I can see."

"Well, we're trying to. Mongo, go ahead."

Mongo, still standing, placed an open folder on the table in front of Wilson. Inside was a nondisclosure agreement.

"Commander Wilson, you are being read-in to a special access program that involves restricted information. You are being read-in as a 'need-to-know' as a result of a breach of operational security during the normal course of your duties. The information you are about to receive is classified TOP SECRET NOFORN, SCI, and will remain so until rescinded by controlling authority. Do you understand, sir?"

"Yes," Wilson answered Mongo with a frown.

"This classification level has no expiration date and will remain in effect after you leave the service and until your death. Do you understand this, sir?"

"Yes."

"Please sign and date."

As CAG watched, Wilson took his pen, scanned the agreement, and signed his name at the bottom. They heard a knock on the door, and Mongo cracked it open to see who it was. He then opened it to allow Weed to step inside. Wilson's eyes remained on Weed as he walked around the table and pulled out a chair next to CAG. When Weed sat down, he made eye contact with Wilson.

"Kemosabe."

Wilson glared at him.

"Sorry to give you a start as you were coming back home. How was your pass?"

Wilson's eyes narrowed. "If Paddles can find me, I'll get a debrief—if I ever get out of here," he said, trying to mask his disgust. CAG took over.

"Jim, here's the deal. The United States is engaged in a covert program to stem the flow of illegal narcotics from South and Central America. Smugglers are using air, surface, and, as you saw today, *subsurface* means to traffic product. Navy is the lead agency, and we have assets here in the Atlantic, and in the Pacific, to interdict the flow."

"How long has this been going on, sir?"

"That's need-to-know, but we've been involved since we arrived here. Weed and Mongo and the other operational testers *are* involved with testing of the *Fire Scout* based on *Max Leslie*. That much is true. But they are also involved with kinetic operations like you saw today. This operation hides in plain sight, and you stumbled across it. So now you're read-in. The name of the program is called CENTURY RATCHET."

Wilson took it in, his mind full of questions. "Who else aboard is read-in, sir?"

Matson glanced at Weed, then back at Wilson. "Several. Without naming them, I'll allow you to ask, and I'll answer with a nod."

Taken aback, Wilson formed a mental list of likely confidants for CENTURY RATCHET. "The captain?"

Matson nodded.

"Ship's Operations Officer?"

Another nod.

"The admiral?"

CAG shook his head no. Wilson was stunned. The strike group *admiral* was not read-in? He continued.

"Other aircrew like me?"

"Yes, two JOs from another squadron, in a similar scenario."

Wilson absorbed this information before he asked the question he knew he must: "So, no one in my squadron?"

Matson pursed his lips and shook his head. "There is one."

"Who, sir?'

The airwing commander pointed toward the other room. Wilson reacted with wide-eyed shock when he realized CAG's gesture meant his new intel officer. *Shane Duncan.*

"My wet-behind-the-ears ensign! *She's* read-in?" he asked, astonished.

"Intel needs to be collected and recorded, and cleared people need to do that."

When Wilson slumped back in his chair, Weed piped up. "Sir, may I take over now and spend some time alone with Skipper Wilson?"

"Yep," CAG agreed. "You've got it." As he stood, he said, "Flip, you know the gravity of this. CENTURY RATCHET is a classified term, and we are not going to discuss it further. As far as you are concerned, our activity down here is ops normal. Make it fast, Weed, so he can get back to his squadron."

"Thanks, CAG," Weed replied. He then turned to Mongo and said, "Mongo, why don't you take a walk?"

"I need his tapes, sir."

Weed raised his hand. "I've got it, Mongo. You can go now." With a scowl, Mongo followed CAG out the door and closed it.

Wilson spoke first. "Is he really a naval officer?"

"Yep."

"Could've fooled me. I don't want him flying my jets. I don't want him to even set foot in my ready room."

"Fine. Anything else?"

Wilson looked at Weed as if to say *Really?* Considering what he had seen, Wilson was still skeptical—and worried about the implications for his friend and his country.

"Where do I start?" Wilson asked him.

"Why don't you let me begin? Do you know how much the cartels make each year on the cocaine trade? Total?"

"A gazillion dollars."

Chuckling, Weed said, "You know, that's about right. It's eighty-six billion a year. Do you know how much of that is overhead?"

"No."

"*One billion*. The cartels are making 98.8% profit, numbers that would make Amazon and Apple blush. And they are using old, beat-up, twin turboprops; cigarette boats; nondescript fishing boats; and, yes, as you saw today, submarines. They have fucking *submarines*, Flip, not low radar cross-section submersibles. Submersibles are *so* last century. Their subs can carry 10 tons of product that they take to Mexico where it walks across the border, or they can take it to the Bahamas, Puerto Rico, or even right up to our gulf coast and transfer it to a waiting cabin cruiser offshore. And they ditch the vessels or aircraft, no need to reuse them, and if two out of four shipments are intercepted by law enforcement, they are *still* making a mint. And that's *just* cocaine, not pot, not meth, not heroin. The stuff then gets into the distribution network in the states or Europe, wherever, and it's no longer the cartels' problem. They've long been paid. That's all this is, Flip, one big and very well oiled production and distribution machine. You gotta hand it to these guys."

"They can abandon all that?"

"Hell, Flip, they've flown damn *airliner* packed to the gills into a dirt strip, unloaded it within minutes, and abandoned it to the desert. They don't need it again. They've made their billion off it."

"So what is this? You guys are going out there, with tipper info from someplace, to find a go-fast and blow it away just like that? And it's all covert, even as you hide with your bogus cover story in plain sight aboard the ship. Do I have it right?"

Weed's eyes held no expression as he mulled his answer. "In so many words, yes."

"Lying to me and everyone else?"

"*A bodyguard of lies*, Flip. We need to keep this black to deny the enemy any intel for as long as possible as we attrit as many of their on hand transportation assets as possible."

"Come upon them with no warning? Shoot with live ammo? Shoot survivors? Is this what we've come to, Weed? Is this how far we've devolved?"

Weed's face turned dark as he leaned forward in his seat and growled. *"Don't give me your Marquess of Queensberry bullshit!* These guys are sending poison into our society each month. It is a fucking *deluge* and law enforcement can't handle it. Decades of interdiction have barely made a dent in the trade, and the cartels' networks are stronger than ever. Dollars are washed with increasing sophistication. Look at Panama! It's the financial capital of Central and South America, and it ain't from collecting fees from banana boats going through the canal. If we don't stop these guys, or at least slow them down, they are going to become a major power right on our front porch. Are we supposed to just watch that happen? Do we have to just sit back and go through the farce of this endless 'drug war' while our inner city kids kill each other, generation after generation of them unemployable. The suburban kids grow up wasted and useless, and even the country kids have figured they can make meth themselves and eliminate the middle man. Everyone acts rationally except us, and you want to see no evil?"

"I just saw you commit murder, and you are telling me it is officially sanctioned? Fine, let's march the cons on death row to the firing squad tomorrow. Let's send the damn lawyers home if we have no more rules of engagement. I mean...I can't believe we're having this conversation, Weed. What have you gotten involved in?"

"What did you see out there? A U.S. Navy warplane catching a smuggler in international waters and taking it out. What is the difference between that and a UAV blowing away a terrorist in any number of sovereign nations? Happens all the time, doesn't it? How about a sniper defending a company of soldiers. No warning, bang, here comes a *Hellfire* or a high caliber bullet. Precise and quick. Would you rather we waste the coastal village from where they started? The poor farmers who are growing this stuff and still live in squalor? The bottom line is everyone gets screwed but the kingpins down here and the dealers back home."

"No survivors! Why? Just tell me why?"

"The gloves are off. It sends a message when Juan and the boys go over the horizon and are never heard from again. Before, the Coast Guard would capture some guys after they tossed everything overboard. They would then do some amount of time, then it's 'Back, Jack, do it again.' I'm thinking, after this month, the recruiting offices will have a tougher time making their quota of mules if the mules know there's a pretty good chance they'll disappear forever. That fear is another weapon, asymmetric at that. If those guys want to play without rules, we can do that."

Wilson was still struggling to understand. "How did you get involved in this?"

Weed's familiar smile returned.

"After I left the *Ravens,* I was 'approached.'"

"Approached? I wasn't '*approached.*'" Wilson regretted his words, and Weed didn't disappoint.

"Yes, you, the hero of Yaz Kernoum! Navy Cross, two air-to-air kills— never mind that one of them was *mine,* you dick. Then, boy-skipper. I guess the CNO aide job took you out of the pool, and they had to approach little-old-me with my measly Silver Star."

Wilson knew he deserved it and knew Weed had to get this off his chest.

"You know, that Silver Star...people notice it. You are King Kong, instant credibility, but when your freakin' *roommate* has a Navy Cross...." Smiling at the incredulity of it, Weed shook his head and exhaled. "I mean, you're the guy the CNO wants. *Everybody* wants you on their team. You get command of the *Firebirds* early; you're on your way. Me? I'm the perennial second-banana to Flip Wilson, Tonto to Kemosabe. I'm out of the limelight—and that's why I was approached."

"Are you still in the Navy?" Wilson asked.

Weed chuckled. "Yes, currently hanging out with Mongo and other fun personalities in a dark cyber-locked dungeon on the Fleet Forces staff. We're the Atlantic Fleet operational test guys. *The land of the misfit toys,* I like to call us. We are everyday fleet knuckleheads involved in some programs—so we have cover stories—and we just read you in to one of them."

"One of them?"

"One of them."

Wilson pressed him. "You've done this before?"

"Yes, several times. Mostly go-fasts and submersibles like today. Months ago I bagged a *King Air* near the Yucatan Peninsula; low-slow flyer on the deck, non-squawking, lights out, heading north...that guy isn't a tourist. I flew close aboard to ID him, then chipped away at his right engine with guns before finishing him off. The guy was a fucking plastic surgeon from Alabama carrying a load of poison for *our* kids. Yeah, I sleep soundly."

Wilson sat absorbing it, stunned.

Weed broke the tension that followed with his familiar grin. "Skipper, you better get back to the squadron. We've been alone here for some time, and people are going to talk."

Wilson, still in his flight gear, gathered his helmet bag and stood. "We will talk again?"

"Sure, Kemosabe! But not about CENTURY RATCHET. That is discussed here *only*, and I cannot emphasize enough, my friend, the importance of operational security. You have some experience in this area, and, if I were you, I wouldn't sneak up on me and hide behind clouds again." Weed's face went from jovial to serious as he spoke the words.

In the past, Wilson would have made a crack about Weed's poor lookout doctrine or his poor eyesight. Not today—and maybe never again.

CHAPTER 17

(Garcia Estate, Peninsula de Paria, Venezuela)

With a cup of coffee, Daniel Garcia enjoyed the sunrise over the *Golfo de Paria* from his mountaintop estate above Puerto Hierro, the dark landmass of Trinidad barely visible from thirty miles away. As the red warmth began to break through the clouds that hung over the mountainous island, Venus showed itself in the royal blue sky. To the south a large ferry plied the gulf. *En route to* Port a Spain, he surmised. *Unusual for this hour.*

To his left and north the Caribbean met the Atlantic, the limitless ocean, now dark and serene as the glow from the east began to illuminate the cottony clouds that floated above the peaceful waters. From his picture-window observatory, he had a near 360-degree view of the sea and sky around the Peninsula de Paria. Here, as the day began, long before Annibel and the girls awoke, he could think.

Medellin. A continent away and a lifetime ago.... In reality, it had been only ten years since he left the city where he had made his fortune. Not that he missed it. The *Pacific* was what he missed, his boyhood home of Buenaventura along the coast. A boy as restless as the Pacific surf, he had left paradise for Cali and the coke, the girls, the money—and the *power* a tough, smart kid like Daniel could wield at a young age. He regretted the murders, and was glad he no longer had to burden himself with the violent end of the business. He didn't regret leaving bitchy Marta, who had refused to leave Cali and her super-bitchy mother. Marta did not know how close she came to death when she lit into Carlos that night in Medellin. *She has her money now,* he thought, *and her annulment.* If she remarried, however, he would have her new husband killed. Daniel would ensure she spent the rest of her days alone.

Yes, this mountaintop estate, far from Medellin, far from Caracas, was where Daniel and his cartel had moved in order to stay in business. Why had Colombia turned on him? He and the others had paid off all the senators, the generals, the police. The *campesinos* loved him. Why did they do it? Colombia was the perfect base to ship product up the isthmus, along the vast Pacific or through the Caribbean islands and wash bushels of money in Panama. Yet, almost overnight, the *Ejército Nacional* had pushed out the FARC. How? With help from the hated Americans, of course.

Reports from the field were troubling. Not only were shipments not getting through—although a fraction still meant a handsome profit—but the mules operating the vessels and airplanes were missing. *None* of the seaborne shipments were showing up in the Yucatan distribution centers and just a trickle in the Bahamas through Puerto Rico, overall a net loss. Baja distribution networks using the Pacific routes were down but acceptable, but his main territory was the Caribbean through Yucatan. While mules could be replaced with eager recruits, they were still an asset, and losing *all* of them was bad for business and recruit training. He knew of the whispers on the waterfront: You move product these days and chances are good you won't come back. His intel was drying up, as was his reserve cash.

And it wasn't just Daniel; all the cartels were feeling the pinch.

Who could it be but the Americans? he thought as he sipped his coffee. Learning their tactics, and how to counter them, was his immediate challenge. The sun was up now, bright orange rays signaling that the day was here, *reality* was here. Sadly, the magical twilight period of tranquil magnificence in this lush tropical paradise had transitioned all too quickly to harsh responsibility.

Soft footsteps from the stairwell indicated he was about to have company. A moment later, Annibel appeared in her nightshirt with fresh cups of coffee for each of them. She placed a cup next to Daniel, kissed his head, and curled up on the sofa next to him. Lost in her own thoughts, she, too, gazed out at the sunrise as she sipped her coffee.

"Where are the girls?" Daniel asked.

"Emma is still asleep, but Juliana is up. She was up most of the night. Maria has her."

Daniel admired his wife, the former *Miss Aragua State*, as she gazed at the dawn in silence. Hair tousled, no makeup, she still looked incredible. Her beautiful smile, however, was missing.

"What are you doing today?" she asked.

"Meeting with Marco and Paul at ten, then fishing this afternoon. Why don't you join us?"

She took another sip and said nothing. She then answered. "No. I won't have them leer at me, and who's going to watch the kids?"

"Bring Maria and the kids."

"No, Maria gets seasick, and I won't subject the children to your crude language when you men are together. I'll just stay here in this palatial estate—my prison."

Here it comes, Daniel thought. He turned away as he shook his head. "Then go to Caracas. See your friends and go shopping. You can be there by lunch."

Annibel shook her head. "No, I've been away from the girls too long, and I think Emma is coming down with something."

"Fine, then, Maria can watch her, and I'll send the plane, and your friends will be *here* after lunch. You'll have the afternoon to sun yourselves and my 'leering friends' will be far away from you. Why do you do this to me?"

Annibel said nothing as she took another sip. Though fifteen years younger than her husband, she was his intellectual equal and took no crap from him. She was careful, though, not to humiliate him in front of the men, a behavior that kept her alive. If she feared his wrath, she didn't show it, and Daniel respected her ability to spar with him. He liked having at least one member of his train that kept him honest. She then spoke.

"You've become distant. You all but ignore the girls, and you do ignore me—unless I come up to your lair before Pepé and the others get to you. You haven't touched me in days, and you are snapping at everyone."

"Didn't I just invite you to go fishing?"

"*Daniel, not with them!*" Annibel shot back, pointing downstairs. "And even if you took me out on the boat alone, they would be following us in the other, keeping 'security watch' over the most powerful man in Venezuela. I can't be myself with you out there, but at least I can understand why. Up here, in our *home*, I cannot understand why. You tell me I have everything. *You* have everything, including me and the girls, and yet *you* are unhappy. Why? Just talk to me!"

The most powerful man in Venezuela assessed her in silence. Her eyes not blinking, Annibel waited for his answer. He put down his cup and opened up to her.

"Shipments are way down. In one area, they are down to zero, completely cut off. People have gone missing on the high seas without a trace. *Not one trace*, and we don't know why. We suspect the Americans, but maybe it's another cartel."

"Sinking your boats? Who would be so stupid?"

"You never know."

"Then *ask*. Ask if they are experiencing losses, too."

"You know it's not that easy, and I don't want them to see me sweat."

"Fine then," Annibel shrugged, exasperated. "You are concerned about business, yet plan to go fishing this afternoon."

"*Something is happening out there!*" Daniel growled, careful to keep his voice down and temper in check. "And, if we don't figure it out soon, the money is going to dry up *fast*. When it does, not only are your shopping trips to Caracas over, but *we* are over. The jackals will be on our doorstep. If I don't keep the money flowing to the army and the politicians and my network, or if I show weakness for even a moment, then we'll be surrounded. *Fast*. So, yes, I'm going fishing, as much to relax as to *show* that I'm not too concerned. Those jackals *are* watching."

Annibel now showed concern. "How do you intend to find out?" she asked him.

"I think it's the Americans. Pepé thinks it's a rival cartel, that the *yanquis* are too inept at keeping secrets and that the American media will expose it for us anyway. But who else has the intelligence and sensors to find a damn *skiff* on the open and know what it is, destroying it without a trace before anyone can even radio for help."

"Do your skiffs have radios?"

Daniel said nothing, not knowing the answer to her question. Such details were left to others. Even if they did have radios, the mules were conditioned not to highlight themselves in any way. They would die before they radioed for help.

"Better yet, just send girls to their bars. Men like to talk and boast, don't they?" Annibel asked.

"*American* men. Down here, talking can kill you."

"Yes, of course, *American* men," Annibel snickered as she looked out to sea. "Well, then, you have a strategy."

"Maybe, but I need more than that," Daniel responded, lost in his thoughts.

Annibel got up from the sofa and moved toward him. "Then I won't disturb you as you think about your multinational business." She stopped in front of him and bent over to whisper in his ear, the lace neckline of her nightshirt hanging low.

"Think about business today, and think about *me* tonight."

She walked away carefree and in charge. "I'll take you up on your offer of Caracas," she said over her shoulder. "If you call for the plane, I'll be ready in an hour. Maybe I'll pick up something for you." She turned her head to leave him a coy smile as she descended the stairs.

Daniel smiled back, thankful for a moment of peace to dream about his firecracker wife before he turned his eyes out to sea—toward the Americans. He had some ideas.

CHAPTER 18

(USS *Coral Sea*, underway, Central Carribean)

Macho entered the "dirty shirt" Wardroom with her tray of food and set it down at the unofficial *Firebird* table. Situated up forward under the bow catapults, the dirty shirt allowed flight deck clothing, and the olive drab flight suits of the aviators mixed with the multicolored flight deck jerseys of various maintenance and flight deck officers. The initial crush of hungry officers had, for the most part, melted away, and Macho, taking a late lunch, found herself alone at the squadron table.

Her roommate, Shane, was the talk of the ship. Stunning *and* knowledgeable about enemy threat systems, she was friendly, *nice* to everyone. Macho found this unusual in a young woman of such head-turning beauty, expecting bored-with-it-all aloofness rather than sincere interest and a willingness to pitch in. In the weeks since Shane's arrival, Macho had watched as several airwing players rolled in on her, and Shane spurned their advances with her sweet smile and, in several cases, even gained their respect and friendship. Though no beauty queen, Macho wasn't ugly, and was one of the few "available" female aviators aboard who were surrounded by dozens of available male aviators. The young officers—male and female—were all attractive to one another, more so as the days at sea built up one by one. If anyone tried to roll in on Macho— and some had—they were dispatched by her biting rejoinders, and the guys kept their distance.

After she took her first bite, Macho saw Trench, followed by sidekick Coach, pop through the knee-knocker opening and into the wardroom. *Oh, great,* she thought. Avoiding eye contact, she hoped they would sit with some of their airwing friends at other squadron tables. When they stopped beside her, thoughts of enjoying her own company at lunch were dashed.

"I see you sitting with all your friends. May we join you?" Trench said.

"*Screw you*," Macho muttered into her plate.

"Why thank you, even though that's against squadron rules. And, despite my endowment, I doubt I could accomplish that even by myself, but thanks for thinking I could. Lieutenant Madden, please be seated."

Coach placed his tray next to Trench as they faced Macho, two poisonous snakes facing a mongoose. Trench continued to taunt his prey.

"And what do we have on the schedule today? Beat up on the Colombians? Find a fishing boat around the ship? Write a whiny letter to *Navy Times* crying about the mistreatment of women who call themselves warriors?"

Macho raised her chin, shot him a look, and answered his question with a question. "And what do *you* guys have on the schedule? Circle jerk in the bunkroom?"

Feigning indignation, Trench grinned. "Well, I believe there are certain rules, command directed and moral, against that sort of thing. So, no, that's not on my schedule. How about you Coach? Circle jerk in the bunkroom for you?"

"No, thanks, and actually I have no experience with this. Macho, please explain," Coach said.

"You guys wrote the instruction manual," she replied as she wolfed down another forkful of rice.

"Oh, you got us on that one, Macho. Coach, we don't stand a *chance* against her wit, and her brawn, and her big rippling eyebrows. And our enemies don't either. Macho, you are a one-woman strike force, our secret weapon, the face that sunk a thousand ships. Glad we're on the same team!"

Macho's eyes narrowed on Trench as he smiled back at her, satisfied his blow had landed hard on her ego. *I'm going to enjoy bringing your career to an end*, she thought. Trench changed the subject.

"Where's your roommate? She's made a splash…professional, pleasant, helpful. Quite an addition to the junior league here aboard *Coral Maru. You* must be learning a lot."

Macho smiled as she ignored the barb and, now that the opportunity had presented itself, was ready to spring her trap. Trench continued their sarcastic banter.

"Yes, Wonder Woman, the perfect helpmate. Probably down in the photo lab going over the latest recon images."

"Yes. I imagine she has some experience with cameras," Coach added.

Macho lifted her eyebrows in response as she poked at her food, a gesture not unnoticed by the men. Trench smelled blood.

"I'm sure she did some modeling in her day. I'm thinking a hand model," Trench volunteered. "What do you think, Coach? Hand model? She *does* have beautiful hands, not that I've noticed them, or any of the physical attributes on her or *any* of the women aboard. Especially *you*, Macho."

"Haven't noticed either, dude," Coach confessed. "She's just the squadron intel officer to me. Besides, she's much too straight-laced to be a model."

Macho, building energy, answered in exasperation. "Just because a girl wants to be feminine you think she's a slut. Who hasn't taken some images she regrets? Everyone does it these days."

"Yes, *everyone*, before you get to be twenty-three and it's too late. If you've got it, *get* in front of the camera. Guess you were best *behind* the camera. Right, Macho?"

"You *dickheads* better leave her alone!" Macho lashed out in a tone low enough not to attract attention. "She's a girl, and she's not perfect, and you guys don't have girlfriends who pressure *you!* Not that any girl would ever be your girlfriend! I'm outta here."

Macho got up and stalked out, biting her cheeks to keep from smiling. Her trap was sprung, and they were caught in it. *Yes! I've got 'em!*

As they watched Macho storm off, Coach turned to Trench and shook his head. "Guess we're going to die alone, bro."

"*Yes*," Trench agreed, "we're pigs. But, first, we have some research to do."

Later that day, Olive placed her wardroom food tray across from Annie. "XO, may I join you?"

"Please do," Annie replied, taking a bite of salad.

Olive removed her food from the tray and arranged it on the table. A sailor took away her tray. Having arrived late in the lunch period, the two *Firebird* pilots were alone at the squadron table.

"What do you have today?" Annie asked.

"Night intercept hop with Macho. How about you, ma'am?"

"Bombing the wake with Killer this afternoon, then a night surface search with Jumpin."

Both pilots took a bite of their food. Olive continued, "XO, when do you think we're going to leave here?"

Annie shrugged. "I don't know. Haven't heard anything from above, and the skipper doesn't know either. Getting to be like *Groundhog Day*, isn't it?"

"Yeah, I mean, bumping heads with the Colombians is cool and all, but we're searching the same patches of water day after day."

"The test guys need to finish up, too, and they are taking forever. But it's beautiful down here. Guess only us aviators can complain about lots of flying in clear skies."

"*Touché*, ma'am," Olive responded with a smile.

Annie changed the subject. "How's our Ensign doing these days?"

"She seems to be okay, liked by all, has a smile on her face."

"She's okay with being *Wonder Woman*?"

"Doesn't seem to faze her. Macho has her under her wing and is only too happy to blast anyone who shows disrespect."

"Like Trench and Coach?"

"Yes, ma'am. I keep watch from afar, and they seem to be behaving."

"How about the rest of the air wing guys?"

"So far, so good. She knows her job and she's *nice.... And* looks like Miss America. Don't you hate her?" Olive said as she smiled.

Annie smiled back, and then added, "I just don't want to see her get hurt. She's pleasant, but she also seems naïve. And her flight deck jersey and khaki uniform show too much of her figure. Let's get her a flight suit."

"Yes, ma'am, but she's still six-feet tall and built. Hard to hide that— even in a flight suit."

"Yes, but I think she also needs a motherly talk from me. I'm not sure things are as rosy as they seem for Ensign Duncan, and she needs her shields up. You, too, need to watch out for her."

"Always."

"And Macho and Trench...are they still at each others' throats?"

"Probably, but, from what I can see, it hasn't spilled over into their jobs."

"Good," Annie said as she nodded. Good order and discipline for all hands was a key part of her job as squadron XO. As the senior woman in VFA-16, an unwritten part of her job was to look out for the fifteen percent of the squadron who were female, most of whom were young sailors, many of them right out of high school. While the junior officers had a few more years of maturity under their belts, it wasn't *that* many more, and she was glad to have Olive as a wingman to help keep everyone focused on their jobs. Shane Duncan, in particular, had a bright future as an intel officer, and while it wasn't her fault, she could also be a distraction.

Fifty frames aft, Coach couldn't believe his luck.

Yes!

Before him on his computer screen was an email with a special attachment sent to him by a stateside buddy. Coach opened it, and before him were three photos of the squadron Intelligence Officer wearing blue jeans—and nothing else.

At that moment Trench walked in. "Dude," he said as he flicked on the light to his desk.

"Just in time," Coach replied. "Lookie here. We got skin. We got ink."

Trench walked over to Coach and checked the screen. "*Yes!* I *knew* it!" he said as he peered in close. In the photos Shane wasn't wearing her glasses, but her arms covered her breasts. She appeared withdrawn if not perturbed, and one photo displayed her bare back with a tattoo design over her waistline. While the images were not R-rated, the pilots knew they weren't anything Shane would want shared.

"Is that really her?" Trench asked. "Zoom in on her face."

Coach complied, and they studied the high-definition image. "Look," Coach said. "See that thing above the corner of her right eye? What is that? A mole, a freckle?"

"I think it's a freckle."

"Does she have a freckle there?"

"Dude, I haven't noticed!"

"Yeah, I know what *you've* been noticing!" Coach shot back. He got up from his chair and grabbed his cell phone from the charger.

"Where you going?" Trench asked.

"Going to find out for sure. I'll leave you two alone while I head down to the ready room. Be right back."

Coach closed the door behind him, and Trench stared at the computer screen. *Yes!*

A booming roar from a jet recovering on the angled deck above vibrated the passageway as Coach headed aft. Bounding over knee-knockers with purpose, he turned amidships and then aft on the starboard main passageway to Ready 5. He found Shane sitting in the back alone.

Perfect!

"Hey, Shane, how's it going?" he asked her. *There it is,* he thought as he spied the small brown mark above her right eye.

"Great! How about you?" she beamed back at him.

"Great. Hey, we're sending the spouses photos of us at work, and as the new guy, they will want to see you. Let me get a photo of you here on duty."

"Okay," she answered, brushing back a wisp of her hair as Coach framed the shot.

"Glasses or no? How about one with each and you pick?"

"Okay," Shane said and posed for each with her dazzling smile.

Coach showed her the photos. "Here, you go. This one…or this one?"

Replacing her glasses, Shane compared both. "I think the one with glasses."

"Glasses? You sure?"

"Yeah, that's kind of who I am. Glasses!" she said, blushing.

"Okay, you got it. Thanks, Spy."

"You're welcome. Thanks!" Shane called as Coach spun for his stateroom to compare the evidence.

Once there, Coach opened the door and closed it behind him. "I think we have a winner," Coach said to Trench. He placed his phone next to the computer screen, and they compared the images of Shane. Coach pumped the air. "That's her, man! Same spot right there."

"Are you sure?"

"What? You need a fuckin' *micrometer* here? It's her. See, it's right above the right corner, same ratio from her eyebrow. We have an intel officer *and* a centerfold model in the squadron."

Trench smiled. Maybe Shane wasn't such a little *ingénue* after all. And, with the right amount of charm, maybe *he* could photograph her and…. He was now as determined to bed her as he was to earn his wings. He *had* to have her, and it made no difference whether it was aboard ship or ashore.

Coach, on the other hand, was thirsty. He knew of a JO in the *Hunters* who had the hots for Wonder Woman, and these photos should be good for a bottle of whiskey.

CHAPTER 19

(Garcia Estate, Peninsula de Paria, Venezuela)

Daniel got up and walked over to the wall-sized map of the Caribbean basin. Seated at the table were José Ramos and Eduardo Ramirez, kingpins of the Lara and Sabana cartels. Colombian expats like Daniel, they, too, were feeling the pinch of an unknown chokehold on their supply lines. Agreeing to meet at Daniel's mountaintop lair was a rare occurrence for the cartel executives, who eyed each other with wary suspicion. Sharing the common hardship of severe losses and the disappearance of skilled *mules*— plus the harm that brought to their recruiting efforts—the trio had to pool resources and cooperate to restart the profitable flow of product north. Also seated at the table were their number twos who listened and spoke little. Standing around the perimeter was the muscle, in dark suits and glasses, showing no emotion and taking in everything. Daniel pointed to the map.

"I am effectively shut down in the Yucatan. We haven't seen a shipment come ashore in two weeks, and have had two get through in the past month. *Seven* of our nine aircraft are missing, and we have only a *Mayday* call from one in the Windward Passage that had left Haiti thirty minutes earlier, reporting a fire before the radio went dead. Three of my lily pad trawlers are missing—*without a trace*—and with all this, over forty *mules* have disappeared with the vessels. At some point, even the mules have value when they make multiple trips and splash cash around their towns to gain new recruits."

"I'm moving product along the Pacific, but only half of what I send out." Ramos growled. At 300 pounds with slicked-back hair and dark glasses, he was a repulsive and feared thug.

Ramirez looked like a movie star. His tan set off the little bit of gray at his temples, and gold chains were visible under his open shirt and blue blazer. Like Ramos, his dark side was to be respected, and he spoke next.

"Had you not fought me, Daniel, we would have shared these losses in 'Your Yucatan.' Like Ramos to the west, I am having success up the

105

Leeward chain, but, once in the open, my shipments are lost. Last month one vessel and three aircraft got through to the Bahamas."

"How are you doing with containers?"

"Acceptable, but they are difficult to load and not as precise and responsive to demand as go-fasts and planes."

"I had a *submarine*," Daniel told them, "that went missing off Nicaragua two weeks ago. Twelve tons of blow. Three mules." The hundreds of millions in lost product was a huge hit, but a show of emotion at the loss was blood in the water to the others, especially Ramos.

"It is dangerous under the sea," Ramirez shrugged. "How do you know it was not a mechanical failure or human error?"

"I don't know, and *you* don't know either. *None of us do,* but we have to find out."

"What's in it for me?" Ramos asked. "I'm still making a profit. Why should the fact that you are having trouble with your supply chain concern me?"

"We are not talking about a little disturbance to be addressed. We are talking a near shutdown of our operations, including yours. And when they finish in the Caribbean, they'll be coming to you in the Pacific."

Ramirez made a pyramid with his fingers and took Daniel's measure. "You are convinced it is the Americans?" he asked.

"Yes. And probably the British, Dutch, and Canadians. All have warships and helicopters, patrol planes, surveillance aircraft."

"The Americans are clumsy, and they telegraph their every move. They *talk*—they can't help themselves!"

Daniel took a drag on his cigarette. "The fact remains, gentlemen—and it affects you, too, my dear Ramos—that the majority of all our Caribbean open-water shipments are missing. They are *shutting us down*. You want a telegraph, Eduardo? They have a damn *aircraft carrier* out there working with our former Colombian countrymen, and they base airplanes in Puerto Rico, Guantanamo, the Keys. They can take advantage of the natural chokepoints throughout the islands, and they can see us before we can see them."

"Yes, an aircraft carrier that can destroy the world!" Ramirez answered. "What good is such a ship without the will to use it? They have fought the sticks-and-stones Arabs with these ships for *decades* and still can't defeat them. For all its muscle, Washington doesn't have the stomach to fight us, and addicts are found in all parts of their society, even at the top. *They want what we are selling*, so whatever this is will pass. We should be more concerned with their legalization efforts. Do you know of the state they call Colorado?"

Exasperated, Daniel threw up his hands. "Eduardo, send your boats and planes if you wish, but I propose we stop our shipments and wait them out. The three of us can continue our activities in the Pacific...."

"Both of you are wrong."

Daniel and Ramirez turned to look at Ramos, who sat there expressionless. Showing fear to each other could be fatal, and Ramos was the master at keeping his emotions in check. Daniel berated himself for showing a flash of frustration.

Ramos repeated himself. "Both of you are wrong. If, as you say, the Americans are destroying our boats and planes one by one, they are doing it because we allow them. We send the mules out alone, at night, so not to attract attention, but the very fact that they are alone in the open attracts the attention of their satellites and radars. We should husband our resources and send them in a wave, a convoy as they call it."

"Yes, hiding in plain sight," Ramirez added. "They cannot attack all our vessels at once, and there will be witnesses if they try."

"Yes. Obtain lookouts with radios and cameras to report and record any activity, a minor overhead expense," Ramos answered.

"A diversion...." Daniel said, thinking out loud.

Ramirez looked at him. "What are you talking about?"

Daniel walked to the window, the blue Caribbean radiant before him.

"A *diversion*, a military term. Ramos is right; if it is the Americans who are behind this, what do they fear the most? Instability. Their stock market gyrates at the slightest bit of bad news. We know they and NATO are here, and we need them to show their hand. Let's give them instability."

"What is your proposal?" Ramos asked.

"Let's start a war with them."

Ramirez studied Daniel, trying to read him. "How?"

"I do not propose full-scale *war* with the United States, which the Bolivarian Republic would lose, but we can tie them down with diversions, *feints*. Raul receives millions from us; he can mass forces near Guantanamo. The Russians will do anything we ask for cash; they can fly warplanes here tomorrow to collect it, and the Americans are powerless to stop them. And since we've lined the pockets of the generals here for years, they can rattle their sabers for us. The politicians can concoct some foolish slight to cause a diplomatic crisis. The Americans would then move their forces to *send their signal.*" Pointing to the sea, Daniel continued. "I want to see an American aircraft carrier *right there.*"

"And this saves our boats and planes?"

"Yes. The Americans will overreact as they always do. Their media will become breathless reporting on war clouds in South America, *¡ay, caramba!* Their focus will be defending Guantanamo, Roosevelt Roads, and the canal. Go-fast boats with product will be small potatoes. They can't be everywhere."

Ramos was unconvinced.

"If the Americans want, they can shut us down, and we still don't *know* what is happening out there. Yet you seek *more* attention, *more* forces from the Americans?"

"Yes, Ramos. Call their bluff."

"And how do you propose we do this?" Ramirez asked him.

Daniel now motioned to the "seconds" at the table who were taking it all in. "That's in the details. Details to be left to others." The men shifted in their chairs, knowing they would have to deliver a plan of action to their kingpins, and soon.

CHAPTER 20

(USS *Coral Sea*, underway, Central Caribbean)

The duty officer in the ready room called Trench to the phone. "XO's on the line."

When Trench answered, Annie ordered him to report to her stateroom—with Macho. An uneasy Trench replied, "Yes, ma'am," and motioned to Macho in the back of the ready room. *This could not be good.*

"What?" Macho asked in a condescending manner as she walked up to him between the rows of high-backed chairs.

"XO wants to see us in her stateroom. Together. Now," Trench said under his breath.

Macho felt a surge of adrenalin. *This could not be good.*

Trench and Macho walked from the ready room through the O-3 level passageways together. With Trench in the lead, the two pilots walked single file to squeeze past sailors transiting in the opposite direction. Both of them were troubled by the unexpected summons to their XO's stateroom.

"What do you think this is about?" Trench asked.

"I don't know," Macho answered. They continued in silence. Although their "hate-hate" relationship was common knowledge among the air wing JOs, the two of them kept it professional and cordial in front of the heavies. When they arrived at Annie's stateroom door, painted with a large *Firebird* emblem and the words EXECUTIVE OFFICER, Trench rapped twice.

"Come in," Annie said. The pilots found her wearing her flight suit. Olive, one of their department heads, stood in the corner.

Oh, shit! Trench thought.

"Please, have a seat," Annie said, motioning them to her couch. Trench and Macho sat down and faced their XO, waiting for her to speak first.

"I'm sure you are wondering why I've called you here together. It's no secret there is no love lost between you two. As your XO, I see things, and

I hear things. I want to offer my help before things get out of hand. What is going on between you two?"

The tight-lipped lieutenants avoided eye contact, each waiting for the other to speak first.

"Trench, as the senior, why don't you start?"

Trench opened his mouth and tried to find the words. "Ma'am…we do our jobs, but…I mean…. We're not friends, but we can get along."

"And you?" Annie asked Macho.

"Ma'am, I have no problem with Trench," she lied, wondering if she could fool her XO. She didn't have to wonder long.

"Macho, you are full of baloney. I would use a stronger word, but, in the presence of ladies, I defer. Frankly, I don't believe you're telling me the truth. So, with that little *lie* out of the way, let's continue. We're going to resolve this *right now*. Do you read me?"

"Yes, ma'am."

Annie cast a cool gaze at Macho. "Are you going to lie to me again?"

"*No, ma'am!*" a shaken Macho answered.

Annie waited a few seconds before she responded, an eternity to Macho. "Good." When she continued, she set her sights on Trench, which allowed Macho to catch her breath.

"Trench, you are the quintessential air wing *playa*, think you are God's gift, have a disgusting porn habit, and snicker too much in the back of the ready room. Are you seeing someone on this ship?"

"No, ma'am!"

"Good. Are you making women on this ship uncomfortable?"

"Ma'am?"

"Flirting with some but not others in the wardroom? Being overly solicitous of Airman Jackson on the flight deck? Snickering when our intel officer is briefing the squadron? Any of that ring a bell?"

Trench looked down, not knowing how to respond.

"We XOs have eyes in the back of our heads. Being a mom helps, too."

"Yes, ma'am," he stammered, blood flushing his face, but Annie wasn't finished with him.

"Are you attracted to *some* women on this ship?"

Trench glanced at her, then Olive. His worst nightmare was coming true. *Where is the XO going with all this?* he thought.

"No names, but tell me the truth."

"Yes, ma'am, as much as the next guy."

"Are you attracted to me?"

Trench moved back in his seat, not knowing what to say. He sensed, though, he had better figure it out fast. He again opened his mouth, but no words formed.

"How about Lieutenant Commander Teel? She's a woman, and, unlike me, she's single."

Trench took a quick look at Olive whose face remained expressionless.

"Ma'am, no..."

"Oh, are we too old for you? I'm a *hag,* of course, at 38, but Olive is much closer to your own age. And, as I said, she's available."

Trench's forehead was moist.

"Ma'am, I haven't.... It would be wrong to pursue...."

"Because we're senior officers, right? In your chain of command? Wouldn't be proper, would it?"

"No, ma'am."

"But Ensign Duncan and Airman Jackson are in *your* chain of command. You are their senior officer. Perhaps they are flattered by your attention. Perhaps it makes them nervous. Whatever it does, we call undue familiarity *fraternization,* and it's really, really bad for good order and discipline. It doesn't have to be sexual either. If Olive and I go shoe shopping together, or go in and buy a Cessna to fly on weekends, it's still undue familiarity. She is at an advantage over her fellow department heads as they compete for promotion. And that generates mistrust, which is *bad* for good order and discipline, which, in turn, degrades combat effectiveness. And *my* job is to help the CO ensure that the *Firebirds* are combat effective."

Trench remained still, his humiliation almost complete.

"I see things, Mark, and so do others. You are a superb aviator and can go far. You are a warrior I want leading a group of JOs down the road. I suggest you take these words to heart, and stay away from women in this squadron and, I would say, the entire ship. It can only lead to ruin."

"Yes, ma'am."

"One more thing, and this is for both of you. Your job is to fly *Hornets* off this ship in support of national tasking. You must work together and fly together in formation. You must not undercut each other in front of the others, especially the sailors. You must do the job together, *but you do not have to like each other.*"

The chastened junior officers nodded. Annie then changed course.

"Very well. Trench, you are now dismissed. Lieutenant Commander Teel, you may leave as well. I have something I want to say to Macho, alone. Please excuse us."

"Yes, ma'am," Trench said, still troubled by the experience. Olive followed him out, closing the door behind her.

With the others gone, Annie studied Macho for a moment before speaking.

"Why did you join the Navy?"

Unsure of the reason for the question, Macho answered. "I wanted to prove something to myself, do something exciting."

"Not many women fly jets. There's only five of us on the whole ship. You are in rare air."

"Yes, ma'am," Macho agreed, grinning with pride.

"So, have you proved anything to yourself?"

"Well, yes, ma'am. Here we are in a man's world, you know, *succeeding*. I mean, we know that women can fly and do anything the guys can. I appreciate that you were one of the women who paved the way for us in the '90s. And I want to build on that."

Annie nodded with a smile. "We can do anything the guys can."

"Yes, ma'am," Macho gushed, lowering her defenses further.

"Then what is your goal this tour?"

"Well, I want to help you and Olive lead the women here. To ensure that guys like him are not harassing or assaulting them—"

"Assaulting?" Annie asked, concerned.

"Well, you know, ma'am, the whispered comments, the frat boy antics on liberty…like in St. Thomas. Girls have to stick together against those guys."

"Yes, *assault*. Those stray comments, men being men…. Why, a girl could go to pieces under the pressure."

Macho realized that the conversation was taking a troubling turn.

"*Pressure* is a low-fuel jet trying to recover on a pitching deck on a black night, or Marines screaming for help in an Afghan valley while you try to find them. You've been here a while, and you are doing well enough, but you've not experienced pressure like *that* yet."

"Yes, ma'am, I'll be…."

"You know, Tiffany, this is a tough business. You are expected to *kill*, and you can be killed out here. You want a challenge? You've come to the right place. But it's not about *proving* something to yourself or others. The bottom line of our business is combat effectiveness, not agendas and not revenge. Certainly not the PC crap Washington cares about. We are warriors, you and I. We are also adults, old enough to know the ways of the world. If you want to be offended you can be, but if you want to make a difference and contribute to the unit cohesion and *combat effectiveness* of this squadron, we need you to do that. Frankly, we demand it. If you cannot give us that, you need to do something else. If I catch him behaving untoward to *anyone* in this squadron or aboard this ship, I'm going to rip his lips off. He can see he's been warned and you saw it. But if I catch *you* sowing discord and forming your own little clique that can tear this squadron apart, I'm going to *hammer your tits*. Do you understand?"

Taken aback, Macho answered her. "Yes, ma'am."

"If, in the future, any of your fellow officers act in an immature way that doesn't cross the line, then shoot them a condescending look. I believe you have some experience in this area. Then *drop it*." Macho nodded her understanding, her eyes locked on Annie.

"I've lied before in my life. We're only human, and we must be forgiven. But if you ever lie to me again, it will be bad for you. *Very* bad."

"I'm sorry, XO. Won't happen again."

"I know it won't. That's now behind us. You have a problem, come to me first."

"Yes, ma'am."

Can you fly on his wing?"

"Yes, ma'am."

"He's a solid pilot, and you can learn from him."

"Yes, ma'am."

Annie smiled a warm smile at her nugget pilot. "Great. Have a nice day. Dismissed."

CHAPTER 21

(Safe house, Maracay, Venezuela)

Daniel drew on his cigarette as he observed *Mayor* General Edgar Rodolfo Hernandez through the smoke. The two of them were at a safe house near the *Aviación Militar Nacional Bolivariana de Venezuela* base at El Libertador in the coastal city of Maracay. Previously known as the *Fuerza Aérea Venezolana* or FAV, the Air Force brought to the Bolivarian Republic a modern fourth-generation threat that included a squadron of older model F-16s and 24 more modern Suhkoi Su-30 multi-role fighters, and a few squadrons of light attack aircraft. The force was well suited for internal security and air sovereignty alert missions, possessing a 707 in-flight refueling tanker and a handful of electronic warfare aircraft.

While no match for a concerted American effort, the AMV was a capable South American air force that could pose problems for the Americans should they decide to test Venezuela, the topic the two men were discussing in the dimly lit room in a non-descript neighborhood. Hernandez, who wore civilian clothes for the meeting, had only his aide and a bodyguard outside. He knew they were no match for Daniel's team. Hernandez hoped the meeting would be over soon. He couldn't wait for his reward and found it difficult to concentrate on Daniel's words.

"Edgar, my supply lines are almost completely cut. I haven't had a single shipment of any kind make it to the Yucatan in almost two months, and my operations in the islands are severely curtailed. Unlike normal interdiction efforts, my mules are disappearing. They go over the horizon in a plane or boat and are never heard from again. They disappear, as if in the Bermuda Triangle. Even my lily pad trawlers. Some of my best men, men who know how to outfox the *Yanquis*, are gone without a trace. And it's becoming a challenge to replace them. Not only for me, but my colleagues are also feeling this new phenomenon, and we do not know what it is. I suspect the Americans. Who else has the intelligence to locate my shipments and the firepower to destroy them without warning? Their elite soldiers know their business. *Without a trace*, Edgar. We have a problem, mí General."

Hernandez was a fighter pilot by trade, one of the youngest FAV pilots to fly the F-16 when it was purchased by Venezuela in 1983. He survived the 1992 coup by being on the loyalist side, and, because there were so many openings in the officer corps, he moved up fast. He was the Commanding General of the Venezuelan Air Force, now known as the *Aviación Militar Nacional Bolivariana de Venezuela,* or AMV in the Bolivarian Republic. While he had never flown in combat, Hernandez knew how to survive—not only in the air force bureaucracy, but while currying favor with the politicians in Caracas. Having a friend in Daniel—who saw to it that one million dollars a year appeared in his offshore accounts and that some of the finest mistresses in Aragua State appeared at his plush safe houses—made life worth living.

Hernandez, in Daniel's debt, knew the account had come due.

"Señor, we have a small number of open-ocean patrol planes. We will find the Americans and report on their movements...."

"Edgar, I do not want to know where the American are. I want my supply routes open. It's the Americans that are stopping my shipments, I'm sure of it. They've changed their tactics, and I want to take their minds off me and focus them on *you.*"

"Señor?" Despite being ten years older, Hernandez deferred to Daniel, but the bill—*starting a war with the United States*—was more than he had ever thought he'd be asked to pay. He was now focused, but soon his mind wandered back to his conditioned obsession. He couldn't help himself. Daniel continued.

"I want you to start a war, or make the Americans think you are. Rattle your sabers, move provocatively. I want to see an American aircraft carrier outside my window dealing with *you* and the threat posed by *your* expensive warplanes. I want them to ignore my little boats and bug-smashers. I want to hear—on the BBC and CNN—about war clouds, the threat of Russian overflights, partnering with Cuba, whatever. Invite the Russians to your bases and have a party when they arrive. The Americans will go *loco* with fear and will take their hands off *me.* All this is to *your* benefit, Edgar."

"Señor, I do not see how increasing the American presence in the Caribbean can open the sea lanes and air corridors?"

"Edgar, in my experience the Americans, as they say, cannot walk and chew gum at the same time. They can focus on one thing only, and the AMV in the defense of the Bolivarian Republic is a worthy opponent."

"While I work for you in private, señor, I work for the President in public. I must have orders." Hernandez was too savvy in the ways of politics to proceed without all the bases covered.

"Yes, of course, orders from above. We have several friends in Caracas, men you are familiar with, who will assist you. Surely the Americans have committed some diplomatic slight or have designs on our nation's oil wealth that our intelligence operators have uncovered. Perhaps we can accuse a diplomat or businessman of a trumped-up charge. Events will occur—within days—that will assist you in your efforts so you can send your men into battle with a clear conscience. *All of us* want a clear conscience, Edgar."

Daniel's words reminded Hernandez of another military commander who had served masters who did not appreciate what they asked of him. After masterminding the attack on Pearl Harbor, Admiral Isoruku Yamamoto was said to have lamented his orders. At least Yamamoto had been able to "run wild" for six months, which he did. Hernandez knew that against a determined United States, he didn't even have six days.

But what choice did he have? Daniel was gracious and attentive, refined in speech and dress. However, Hernandez harbored no illusions that his friendship with Daniel would "save" him. He knew Daniel was ruthless, capable of killing him while smiling into his eyes. And, if that failed, the muscle who waited outside the door would do so the moment Daniel snapped his fingers. A quick bullet to the head or a slow squeeze with their bare hands. Hernandez had seen it with others over the years; Daniel had seen to it that he *had* seen it. Hernandez thought of some of his F-16 pilots—Falcon and Rico, Gunnar. In just a few days, he would be sending them to their deaths. At the memorial services, he would console their grieving widows and pat their small children on their heads in sympathy as his own wife stood next to him. The money, the girls....

Hernandez stiffened his back. He had known this day would come. *Maybe I can lead a formation of fighters into battle. I've lived fifty-five years, many more than I deserve.*

"Señor, the AMV and all the forces of the Bolivarian Republic will fight to the death to uphold our sovereignty and freedoms. I will set about these tasks as you request." He was trembling and wanted to get on with it.

"Excellent, General!" Daniel beamed as he poured them another glass of wine. "And when the Russians visit us, please throw them a large party. I'll cover the costs, of course, and send you a list of *entertainers* all of you will enjoy. And I'll have a handsome gift for our friends to take with them when they return to Moscow—or wherever they live! Come!"

With Hernandez' heart pounding in anticipation, Daniel led him to a modest patio and small pool surrounded by high hedges to discourage prying eyes. The invitation to the patio was his reward for the Pavlovian stimulus/response to his master's request. Under the shade, a folding table of warmed food and chilled wines awaited them, and plush couches, stacked with luxurious towels, lined the walls. In the pool, three showgirls in bikinis, new to him, smiled at the men, beckoning them to remove their clothes and join them. For a brief moment, Hernandez realized his own daughter was older than any of these girls. Aware of the cameras mounted on the eaves and trees to record the event, Hernandez wondered if Daniel would view these tapes himself. Who would he show them to? Would he share them after Hernandez was dead?

One of the girls stepped out of the pool and, dripping wet, picked up a silver tray. She smiled up at Hernandez as she offered it to him, the dog-treat reward for his faithful military service to the Bolivarian Republic. General Edgar Hernandez knew the drill and forced a smile as he picked up a straw and took a blow, shedding his inhibitions. He had shed his honor and dignity many years ago.

CHAPTER 22

(USS *Coral Sea*, underway, Central Caribbean)

Since his encounter with Weed, Jim Wilson had gone about his day-to-day existence and command duties aboard *Coral Sea* in surreal disbelief. Read-in to a Top Secret program, he was now complicit in an undeclared and "black" war involving *his* airplanes and maintenance crews, although it was unknown to them. He couldn't believe it. *Unknown to the damn admiral!* Each day Weed would fly a *Firebird* jet in an effort to seek drug runners and execute them on the spot. It rubbed him the wrong way, as *unrestricted submarine warfare* and *destroy the village to save it* had in earlier times. Weed was right, though; the United States was using drones overseas to good effect, and sniper operations had valid military legitimacy. If in combat he snuck up on an enemy aircraft, he would shoot it down and be proud of it. The difference between the circumstances was whether or not there was a declared war, or at least the legitimacy of clear orders passed down from National Command Authority, open and known to the public.

He was not so naïve as to think that classified or clandestine operations were in some way morally wrong. Wilson was a realist. *Why* should *we telegraph our every move?* He didn't lament the lack of media involvement—they always got it wrong anyway—but the cover story troubled him. He wished the United States would just say the Caribbean drug trade is going to be shut down, effective immediately, in order to give the enemy in this phony war fair warning. Then, Wilson himself would blow any blockade runners out of the water without a second thought, and shoot down, without remorse, any non-squawking, low/slow flyers. Just say it and then do it. *If you are going to take Vienna, take Vienna.*

It had to be the media, he surmised. For all the platitudes to the military, they did not tell America the truth about much of anything. They seemed to just fill their programming with fluff. *Contempt.* That's what Wilson and many of his shipmates had for the media, and maybe that contempt was shared by National Command Authority or the combatant commander to send them 2,000 miles to do "operational testing" and to "train" with the Colombian Air Force. At some point, that story would begin to crumble, and Wilson wondered what the next training evolution would involve.

He was at his stateroom desk going over work-center audit paperwork when there was a knock at his door. "*Come in*," he called.

Weed opened the door and poked his head in. "Can we talk?"

Wilson motioned to his couch. "Yeah, c'mon in."

Weed closed the door behind him and took a seat on the couch. At night, Wilson folded it out to make a bed.

"You fly today?" Wilson asked, knowing the answer.

"Yep, just got back."

"Successful test?" Wilson asked.

Holding eye contact, Weed nodded. "Successful test."

Wilson nodded back. "Good. What can I do for you?"

Weed gathered his thoughts. "Our friendship is important to me."

"Me, too."

"I have a job to do."

"Doing it well from what I can see."

As Weed hesitated, Wilson eyed him with disdain.

"I'm not sure why I came here, or what I was going to say, because.... Well, I'm here. And I want to.... How's the squadron?"

"Fine," Wilson answered. "Our new intel officer is the talk of the ship, and I can see the sharks circling. Stretch, Blade, and Olive are doing well. I'm concerned about one of my chiefs. The usual stuff."

"I miss it," Weed said.

"*Then why did you leave it?*" Wilson raged, surprising both of them with his intensity. "You were on track for command! You'd be here now with your own squadron, and *don't* give me that bullshit guilt trip that it's my fault!"

Weed shot back. "You tell me, *Skipper*. I wasn't privy to the screen board results that selected *you* and not me. I went to operational test because I couldn't get out of the damn Pentagon fast enough! Maybe that's it. I got off the fucking career track because I couldn't put up with the *bullshit* in the five-sided wind tunnel. Glad *you* could."

"You think you're making a difference?"

"I know I am."

"At what cost? You've become an *executioner*."

Weed shook his head. "Ha, and you aren't? How about that truck you turned into Swiss cheese in Iraq? You didn't give *them* a chance."

Knowing Weed was right, Wilson didn't have an answer.

"I thought so, Mister Holier-Than-Thou. You don't want a fair fight. *None* of us do. The *cartels* don't fight fair with uniforms and set-piece movements, but they're fighting us and *winning!* How old is Derrick now? Ten? Eleven? Given the chance, they are going to *poison* him. And you are going to let them do that to your son because you follow fucked-up rules generated by lawyers. They don't."

"Are we a country of laws or not?" Wilson asked.

"Yes, and I am following them! Just because the news networks aren't here doesn't change that. *You* live by need-to-know, and they don't need to fucking know! Hell yeah I'm following orders, valid orders delivered by National Command Authority, reviewed and blessed by the damn lawyers. You're pissed because you're missing out on the fun. Well, you're the CO with a formal photo, twelve-piece band at your change of command, following your orders and tasking, a bright future in uniform ahead of you...you earned it so be happy with that. I'm happy with my lot...making a difference and protecting our kids."

"You could have been a CO," said Wilson.

Weed looked at him with a blank expression. "What makes you think that I'm not?"

Part II

Beloved: Where do the wars and where do the conflicts among you come from? Is it not from your passions that make war within your members? You covet but do not possess. You kill and envy but you cannot obtain; you fight and wage war.

The Letter of St. James 4:1-4

CHAPTER 23

From 10,000 feet, Trench checked the time. He had almost 40 minutes to screw around.

His *Hornet*, 302, had needed a routine post-maintenance check flight for a new right trailing edge flap actuator. After Trench had "wrung it out," he was satisfied the sailors in the airframe and aviation electronics shops had done their jobs well, as usual. He was now alone, 50 miles south of the ship, on yet another gorgeous blue day in the Caribbean. Chances were he could find a sailboat down there hoping for an impromptu air show. Trench was the perfect guy to deliver.

His radar was showing several blips to the southwest, and he reduced power to near idle to conserve his fuel so he could show off later. In an easy turn, the midafternoon sun moved left to right across the top of his canopy bow, and he opened the distance between him and *Mother*.

Alone—and *free!* Only the single-seat *Hornet* pilots could really be away from others at moments like this, free to roam over the open ocean in silence, alone with their thoughts. Away, even, from wingmen in formation, away from the ship controllers, airspace controllers, the CO and XO. Away from ball-busting Macho and all the *crap* back there aboard *Coral Maru*.

Yes, Macho, *Little-Miss-Can't-Be-Wrong*...ugly freakin' bitch. *She* was the reason for the come-around with the XO. *Screw them*, he thought. For an hour or so, away from the ship and the regimented military *control* of it, he could be *free* in his single-seat rocket ship. Want to whip the stick hard left and do an aileron roll? Go ahead. Want to cloud surf, rolling and pulling the jet along the nooks and fissures of the brilliant cumulus buildups that dotted the sea all around? Why not? The weather was perfect and such opportunities didn't happen every day.

In another ingrained habit, he kept his head moving to search for other airwing jets around him. They were also free to roam and goof off in this beautiful tropical playground before the ship summoned them home. Running into each other would ruin everyone's day.

He rolled out due south in a shallow dive, headed for a small canyon of cloud, an opening like that between the thumb and hand of a mitten. The cloud formation reminded him of Michigan and his home, Bay City, at the base of Saginaw Bay. Nothing for him there anymore, not that there ever was. His jag-off high school friends were going to drink 12-packs of Pabst from the back of their pickup trucks until the day they died. They were already dead with their bitchy, ball-and-chain wives and rat-tailed kids who spilled cereal everywhere. He was flying through, and past, Saginaw Bay, the scuffed rust-belt patina of his youth, which in his mind was washed away in the radiant whiteness of the clouds here, or the Med, or the Indian Ocean. *Lieutenant* James was free—and *powerful*—flying a high-performance jet with *firepower* at his fingertips they could only imagine. He had used it, too, in Afghanistan last cruise, strafing a mortar position to the cheers of the Marines on the radio. Angel of death. Agent of deliverance. An officer and a gentleman when it suited him. And God's gift when....

Trench spotted a squall up ahead and continued down to 500 feet as he put it on his nose. He knew the maintenance chiefs would appreciate a freshwater wash for 302, so he decided to bring them an "up" jet with the sea-salt and shipboard grime cleaned off by a natural, 300-knot spray hose. He leveled off under the bottom of the gray cloud...no lightning observed...and, as he entered the veil, the rain beat down hard on the canopy, drops rapidly moving aft from the slipstream. In less than a minute he was out of it, sunlight and air friction drying the water on the jet's skin, entering an open area, his personal playground, and on the blue surface he saw what he'd been looking for...some toys to play with.

The big blip on his radar was not a gleaming cruise ship but a drab merchant heading northwest trailing a white wake, and far to the south was a white object he would check out later. Disappointed, he banked left to approach the ship from the starboard quarter. It appeared to be 500-feet long with a black hull, superstructure aft, cranes amidships. Old bulk cargo carrier. Slewing the radar cursor over the return on his digital data display, he bumped the castle switch with his right thumb to lock it. When the computer settled down, it showed the ship on a heading of 315 and making 10 knots. He scribbled the latitude/longitude numbers on his kneeboard card and noted the time: 1054.

He slowed as he crossed the wake to fly up the port side. On the stern he read the name and noted the country of registry: *Panama,* like most merchants in these waters. Light gray smoke trailed from a single stack, and four sets of large horizontal doors lay on the deck. As he flew past the lonely ship, Trench figured it to be a grain carrier of some sort. He looked for signs of life on the bridge or weather decks and found none. *Damn thing must be on autopilot,* he thought, and figured the sudden roar of a *Hornet* whizzing past the bridge would be the only excitement these guys would get all day.

Reversing his turn to the left, he doubled back to the surface contact to the south, and spotted the white object at 20 miles. He locked it with his radar and tracked it heading west at five knots with no other contacts around it. This one could be interesting. Remaining low on the water, Trench picked a heading to let it slide down his right canopy so he could sneak up behind it like the merchant. He commanded the radar to air-to-air and scanned the sky around him. *Nobody else out here.*

A wall of white buildups hovered over the eastern boundary of his playground, but he saw the silhouette of another merchant to the southeast. Checking his fuel—7,000 pounds—he had more than enough fuel and time to check out his personal contact of interest to the south.

As he expected, he soon identified a motor yacht with a pointed bow and sleek, raked lines. A smile formed under Trench's mask. Yachts meant money, and money meant girls…and girls in the tropics are outside.

The yacht was cruising west, the dazzling sun still climbing toward its noon apex. Trench rolled easy right and peered left over his leading edge extension to check for any other airwing knuckleheads who had the same idea he did. Doing his duty, he wrote down the course, speed, lat/long and time.

Like he had with the merchant ship, he approached the yacht from the aft to surprise it, and got down to 300 feet as he came up along the boats' starboard side. The noise from his engines would alert the people on the yacht to his presence only seconds before he roared over unless somebody happened to be scanning the horizon. Inside a mile, he didn't see anyone on the fantail. He surmised it was about 100 feet, with a rigid hull inflatable boat hanging from davits on the top deck aft of the flying bridge. Atop the mast was a SATCOM dome and marine radar spinning around looking for surface returns.

Approaching the bow, his suspicions turned out to be true. There, Trench's trained eye saw two bikini-clad girls lying on their backs, and one was waving at him.

Jackpot!

With heart pounding, Trench shoved the throttles to afterburner and pulled hard across the bow. He craned his head to keep sight of the yacht while he formed a plan. He would turn hard, extend for a few seconds, then pull hard again back to the yacht. He would then slow himself down to 200 knots and descend to 100 feet for another pass.

While turning back, he set the radar altimeter bug to 80 feet—if he broke 80 feet it would warn him—and paid close attention as he pulled back to the yacht. Keeping the engines spooled up, he extended the speed brake to remain slow and got as low as he dared as he crossed the yacht's wake. The small craft continued on course, as if to beckon him to come back for a closer look. He scanned the skies again for air traffic.

He was alone.

Stabilized, he slid up next to the yacht, his hand shielding his eyes from the sun glinting off the deck. *There they were!* Still on the bow waiting for him, jumping up and down and pointing with excitement. Trench banked left and waved as he passed only 100 feet over the girls, getting a good look all right. Despite the glinting sun off the flying bridge, he was ready to set up for another pass when...

He blinked his eyes. And blinked again. He lifted his visor and rubbed his eyes, opening them wide. *I can't see!* In horror and unbelief, he shouted into his mask, "I CAN'T SEE!"

CHAPTER 24

Terrified, Trench half-rolled right by feel and shoved the throttles into burner while he pulled back on the stick. Breathing heavily into his mask, he realized he had some peripheral vision, but when he tried to focus his eyes ahead, he saw only black. With the marginal vision he had, he sensed he was in a climb. *Yes, get away from the water!* He forced his eyes open, causing them to bulge in an effort to regain sight and focus. *I can't see! God help me! Please God help me!*

Trench couldn't believe what was happening and didn't know his altitude. *Didn't know the aircraft attitude!* Too steep and he could run out of airspeed and stall it, even in burner. He looked up and right, hoping what little he could see on the periphery would guide him. It was no use. He could see the green pitch lines generated in the Head-Up-Display, but he couldn't decipher them. He sensed he was flying west and by instinct rolled to the right, easy, and still in burner. Talking to himself, he counted the seconds of his turn, as if he were back in flight school, to determine a rough heading to north—and home.

This must be a nightmare, he thought and whimpered as he breathed through his mouth, not knowing his altitude, airspeed. *I don't know where the motherfucking ship is! Dammit!*

"Please help me!" he screamed in the cockpit, frantic with nerves and moaning, crying in mortal dread. *This is really happening!*

Fuel. *What's my freakin' fuel?!* He then realized with more shock and horror that the burners were still plugged in! With a frustrated cry, he pulled the throttles to a midrange setting.

The clouds! He was heading toward the clouds. If he went into one, what little peripheral vision he had would be gone. He would be in complete blindness!

I need help! his mind screamed as he rolled left to stay clear of the cloud. Without depth perception, he was unable to determine how far away it was.

Knowing the XO and Big Jake were airborne on this event, he keyed the mike on the Comm. 2 squadron tactical frequency.

"Any *Ridgelines* up? This is Trench in three-oh-two! *I can't see! I can't see!*"

Silence.

He then keyed the Comm. 1 radio to call the ship. "*Strike*, three-zero-two!"

After a short delay, the *Strike* controller answered. "Go ahead, three-zero-two."

"*Strike*, three-zero-two is south of *Mother*. I can't see! I'm blind! I need someone to join up on me and guide me!"

After an eternity of silence, the controller answered. "Roger, three-zero-two, mark your posit." The routine request for position sent an already stressed Trench over the edge.

"Strike, *dammit*, I CAN'T SEE to tell you my position! I'm south about eighty miles. I think I'm heading north." Even in his panicked state, Trench could sense the controller on the other end of the radio transmission had never heard a call from a pilot with this problem. Willing himself to calm down, Trench fought to remain patient with the only lifeline he had.

"*Ridgeline* three-zero-two, *Strike*, looking…can you squawk seventy-seven hundred?"

In front of Trench at the top of the instrument panel was the Up Front Control, a keypad for all his avionics. This included his IFF transponder that broadcast a code that controllers could use to identify specific aircraft with course, speed, and altitude. Without it, Trench's *Hornet* was just a mark on a scope. His left hand moved to the UFC to change the code as he had done hundreds of times before—and he froze. The IFF pushtile under the UFC was marked, but he couldn't focus on it!

Which one is it?

Once again, Trench felt the frustrating dread of not being able to do the simplest of tasks. In the back of his mind, he considered ejecting.

"*Strike*, three-zero-two, stand by."

Annie in 305 and Big Jake in 307 were forty miles west of *Coral Sea*, low on the water and playing with the bathtub toys they had found in *their* personal playground.

In combat spread formation at 360 knots, they were approaching a fleet of about ten fishing trawlers spread over a few miles of ocean. They were small craft, no more than forty feet long, all painted white, some with outriggers deployed. On the northern horizon she picked up the silhouette of an unusual looking vessel, a large ship with a huge crane-like object aft. Once they finished with these little fishermen, Annie would lead Big Jake north to check it out.

As they came upon the fishing fleet wallowing in the swells and appearing dead in the water, she concentrated on one of the boats as she thundered over it. She and Big Jake were freelancing after dropping their practice bombs on smokes they had laid down, killing time as much as honing their skills before the scheduled recovery in thirty minutes.

"Three-zero-five, Alpha Sierra." Annie was surprised to get a call from the ship surface search controller.

"Alpha Sierra, three-zero-five, go ahead."

"Are you in touch with three-zero-two?"

This was an unusual question. *Trench is in 302. Is he okay?* she thought as she keyed the mike. "Negative, but I can be. What's the difficulty?"

"Three-zero-five, Alpha Sierra. Three-zero-two is reporting he's blind."

Annie let the fishing fleet pass underneath as she let the message sink in. *Blind?*

"Alpha Sierra, is he lost-plane?" Trench had a combat cruise under his belt, and Annie was incredulous that Trench could be *lost* and unable to find his way back to the ship, especially on this gorgeous day.

"Negative, three-zero-two reports that the *pilot* is blind, cannot see, and needs assistance. He's talking to *Strike*."

Stunned, Annie began a climb, and on the tactical frequency transmitted, "Annie's, go squadron tac." On Comm 1 she told Alpha Sierra they were on the way. "Alpha Sierra, *Firebird* three-zero-five flight switching *Strike*." For Big Jake's benefit, she added, "Annie's, go button three."

"Two," her wingman responded.

As if pushing preset buttons on an automobile radio, nimble fingers flew over the UFCs in both cockpits, punching in the new frequencies. After a few seconds on *Strike* frequency, Annie keyed the mike. "Annie check?"

"Two," Jake replied. Satisfied her wingman was up the proper frequency, Annie keyed the mike again.

"*Strike, Ridgeline* three-zero-five flight with you on *Mother's* two-six-zero for thirty-five, passing angels five. We understand three-zero-two needs help."

Miles away, Trench heard the exchange. Overjoyed when he recognized the calm and welcome voice of XO Schofield coming to his rescue, he keyed the Comm. 2 mike.

"Annie, Trench. You up tac?"

"Yes, got you loud and clear, Trench. We're comin' to ya."

The three *Firebird* pilots were all up the same two frequencies, and the chances of "stepping on" each other when transmitting were reduced. However, the ship was not monitoring the squadron tactical frequency, and before Annie could respond to Trench, they called.

"Three-zero-five, *Strike*, radar contact. *Ridgeline* three-zero-two reports he's blind approximately eighty miles south of *Mother*. We are looking and have several aircraft in that vicinity."

Big Jake was now close enough to Annie to use hand signals as she led them up. Using triangulation geometry—thirty miles west to eighty miles south—she figured a heading of 150 would put them on a vector to intercept Trench and banked the formation right. Both she and Jake had their radars searching in the 80-mile scale to find their stricken squadronmate.

Blind? She wondered how this could have happened to Trench. *A popped blood vessel under g-force? Unseen chemical in the cockpit?*

Like all carrier pilots, she was mindful of fuel, and through hand signals with Big Jake learned they had about 6,500 pounds each, some 45 minutes with a bare minimum cushion for the recovery. How much did Trench have? And where was he going to land, even if he could see to do it? The nearest land was Kingston, Jamaica, over 200 miles northeast...from the ship! For Trench, the nearest land at the moment was Colombia, which was some 250 miles south of *Mother*. Both options were bad: it was going to be the ship for Trench or nothing. All they could do was hope some semblance of sight returned to him, but before they could do anything, she needed more info.

"Trench, what's your angels?" she asked him.

After a moment he answered. "I can't tell...think between five and ten."

Leveling at 15,000 feet, she accelerated to the southeast. Big Jake held his position on her in a loose cruise formation so he could also work his radar. She heard *Strike* ask Trench to squawk emergency in an effort to find him *now*.

"Trench, can you squawk emergency?" she asked him.

"Trying –fumbling with the switches because I can't see them."

"What's your state?"

"Don't know. Was in burner a long time to get away from the water. I think it's around four-K."

Annie thought, *Four thousand pounds*, with over 30 minutes till the ship was in a position to recover aircraft. Trench would be on fumes by the time he even had an opportunity to trap, and Annie needed to know if the ship was working on a plan to do that.

"*Strike*, three-zero-five. Is a *Firebird* rep working this problem in air ops? Once we find three-zero-two, we can guide him back for a Mode I approach. Recommend emergency pull-forward."

Yes, Trench thought. A Mode I "hands off" approach was the only way he was going to get aboard—unless his sight reappeared in the next thirty minutes. He hoped his auto-throttles, flight control computers and data link were all up to the task. But first, the XO and Jake needed to find him. His mouth was bone dry from fear, and he reached down into his g-suit pocket to grab his water flask. He didn't know how high he was and, for a moment, was afraid to unhook his oxygen mask. *Screw it,* he thought and removed his oxygen mask, allowing him to take a long drink from his canteen.

"Three-zero-five, *Strike*. We've passed your recommendation."

"Three-zero-five, roger," Annie answered. She needed to get Trench to squawk emergency to help everyone find him.

"Trench, Annie. Can you select IFF? Under the UFC, second pushtile from your left."

With his XO's helpful reminder, his thumb found the IFF pushtile—*of course!*—and Trench pushed it. With his peripheral vision his saw the display illuminate, and then punched in 7700 on the keypad by feel: left row, bottom, seven, twice; center row, bottom, zero, twice. Out of habit, and by feel, his mind guided his thumb to hit ENTER.

"*Ridgeline* three-zero-two, *Strike*. Radar contact on *Mother's* one-six-five for seventy two."

Roger, *Strike.* Say my angels!" *Thank goodness,* a relieved Trench thought. *They've got me!*

"Three-zero-two, you are at seven thousand, three hundred feet."

"My heading?"

"Three-zero-two, you are heading zero-five-zero."

Annie realized that Trench was moving away from them. "*Strike*, three-zero-five. Can you get him to turn north toward *Mother*?"

Trench could turn the aircraft left, and maybe use the sun overhead to gauge a general heading, but he needed help until Annie showed up. He still didn't know his airspeed—he *felt* like he was fast—so he pulled the stick into him a little. When he felt a few g's on his body, he figured he had at least 300 knots. Annie called to *Strike* again.

"*Strike*, three-zero-five. Bogey dope to three-zero-two."

Strike responded that *Ridgeline* 302 bore 160 degrees at 65 miles, and gave them a heading of 140 to intercept. They still needed to get 302 heading north.

"Three-zero-two, *Strike*. I'm going to call your turn. At a standard rate turn, turn left."

Rolling left, Trench did his best, by feel and what sense of the horizon he had, to hold 30-degrees angle of bank. He waited for *Strike* to tell him to roll out, using a procedure he had learned in flight school and had never used since. He was beginning to gain confidence despite blinking his eyes hard to snap out of the loss of sight. *Nothing.*

"Stop turn."

Trench did as he was told. "What's my altitude now?" he asked.

"Angels six-point-eight," replied the controller. Trench added power and eased back on the stick to stop his shallow descent.

C'mon, XO! Get down here! he cried to himself as his panic returned.

CHAPTER 25

Wilson sat in the back of the ready room with the briefing guide open on his lap as he led Ghost through the conduct of their upcoming flight. Killer, the duty officer, walked up to them with a grave look on his face.

"Sir, Air Ops says Trench in three-zero-two is reporting he's blind and trying to find his way back."

Wilson was incredulous. "*Blind?* He can't find the ship?"

"No, sir. They say he *can't see.*"

Jolted again, Wilson absorbed the news in shock. After a moment, he stood and headed for the door.

"I'm going to Air Ops," he told them both.

Looking at Killer, he added. "Find Olive and get her up there, too. Call CAG Office and inform them to get the word to CAG if they haven't already."

Glancing at the status board, he saw Annie and Big Jake were also airborne. With thirty minutes to recovery, Wilson knew they were low on fuel.

He flung open the ready room door, startling a passing sailor, and bolted for Air Ops some 20 yards forward. *Air Operations* was the nerve center of the air traffic control functions involving *Coral Sea's* aircraft, of which fifteen were airborne at the moment.

As he strode past sailors and over the knee-knockers, his mind raced. *Blind? How? Where? How do we get him back? Can Annie find him? Can we bring him aboard hands-off?*

Wilson opened the hatch to Air Ops and stepped inside the darkened space, relieved to find CAG and Lieutenant Commander Mike "Rat" Fink, the air wing Landing Signal Officer, conversing with Commander Chris Maher, the Air Ops Officer. CAG saw Wilson approach.

"Flip, what's the story?"

Unsure himself, Wilson responded. "Sir, I've just learned one of my guys is blind. What's going on down here?" Maher answered for CAG.

"*Strike* is in contact with James about 60 miles south and vectoring Schofield in three-zero-five to intercept him. How much gas do you think he has left?" All of them knew the answer to this question would narrow the options available.

Wilson glanced at the digital clock mounted on the bulkhead "Little over an hour. Maybe. Has he reported a fuel state?"

"*Strike* says he can't read it to tell them," CAG replied, then turned resolute.

"Okay, I'm going to call the Captain and recommend we scrub this launch and pull all the jets forward. We need to get three-zero-two aboard ASAP. Chris, suggest you get the alert tanker airborne as a backup and recommend you get with *Strike* to bring everyone airborne back *now*. I think we have less than an hour for Annie to find him, guide him back if she can, and set him up for a hands-off approach. Do you have your best approach controller ready to go?"

"Yes, sir," Maher replied.

CAG then turned to Wilson. "Flip, what was he doing?"

"Sir, he was on a post-maintenance check flight—flight control actuator. Routine, and Trench is experienced." CAG nodded his acknowledgement.

"Sir," Wilson said. "I want to talk with him, or at least listen to what's going on over Strike frequency."

"Yeah, let's go over to CDC," agreed CAG. When Olive entered the room, Wilson motioned her over.

"Olive, we're going over to Combat. Hang out here, and help Commander Maher with his questions. We should be back shortly."

"Aye, aye, sir," she replied.

Combat Decision Center was another cool and dark room located in an adjacent space forward. The ship's command center, it was filled with digital displays of the air and water space around *Coral Sea*. Shadowy figures wearing jackets and sweaters sat in cushioned chairs bolted to the deck in front of a maze of tactical displays.

"Where's three-zero-two?" CAG asked as he rounded a console to meet the Watch Officer. CAG and Wilson sought to find Trench themselves on the big display.

Pointing at the display, the Watch Officer responded. "He's here sir, and three-zero-five is *here*, about twenty miles away on the join-up." The two pilots watched the blips slowly converge, one of them flashing an emergency code. *About fifty miles out,* Wilson surmised. Just then he recognized Annie on the radio speaker.

"*Strike,* Ridgeline *three-zero-five. Contact one-four-five, eighteen miles, angels eight.*"

Wilson heard the sailor on the console speak into his lip mike. "*Ridgeline,* that contact is three-zero-two."

Wilson stood over the controller's shoulder and watched his scope. The radar blips signified that Annie and Big Jake were tracking east-southeast in an effort to rendezvous on Trench who was heading north.

All knew that a "Mode One" hands-off approach was the only way to get 302 aboard. The aircraft had an automatic throttle control (ATC) that kept the jet at the proper landing airspeed once the gear and flaps were down. It also had a fly-by-wire flight control system that could be "coupled" to respond to commands sent via data link from the ship. For things to work properly, 302 needed the ATC, flight control computers, and data link to be operational; any single malfunction was a showstopper.

The ship's final control radar needed to work, too. At least the weather conditions were not a factor. CAG put in a call to the Captain.

"Rick, Tim down in CDC. We've got Annie Schofield joining on three-oh-two. They are about fifty miles south. What are you thinking?"

Wilson watched CAG nod and tried to decipher the conversation. CAG Matson continued.

"Okay, great, if Annie can get him back here in a position to couple-up, we'll have a chance. I've got Flip Wilson standing next to me, and he'll check with his people on the aircraft status. Rat is here, too, and I'm sending him up to the platform now. Roger, thanks."

CAG turned to Wilson and filled him in on the plan. "Okay, once Annie can talk him into a position behind the ship, we're going to bring him aboard. Right now the airborne aircraft are being recalled, and they are going to do an emergency pull-forward on the roof to make a ready deck. We'll recover what we can until three-zero-two is ready to come aboard. After we trap him, we'll get the rest of the airwing. Call down to your maintenance and see if three-zero-two's systems are up for a Mode One."

"*Yessir,*" Wilson answered.

From the flight deck above them, they heard the voice of the Air Boss over the 5MC loudspeaker as he commanded his sailors to carry out the orders passed down from *Coral Sea*'s brain trust.

"On the flight deck, emergency pull-forward! Emergency pull-forward! We've got an incapacitated pilot in Firebird *three-zero-two! Chop chop!"*

CHAPTER 26

Against a backdrop of white cumulus clouds, Annie saw the "dot" in the middle of the green target designation box on her Heads Up Display. Inside that dot was Trench.

Moving from right to left off her nose, he was heading north, about 300 knots of airspeed, at 8,000 feet. She keyed the mike. "Trench, we've got a visual on you. Maintain your heading and airspeed. You are about angels eight."

"Roger," he replied.

She turned a few degrees left to sweeten the intercept as the familiar outline of Trench's *Hornet* began to take shape. She checked her fuel and her clock—20 minutes to recovery time. But the recovery for Trench would not begin until after the airplanes on deck were launched. It could be 40 minutes before Trench got an attempt to land, *if* they could coax him into a position behind the ship *and* if all the black boxes worked properly.

Inside two miles she allowed Trench to drift left on her canopy, and, after checking to see that Big Jake was clear, she pulled hard into him to intercept the bearing line of his wing. As Annie slid up this imaginary line formed by Trench's wing, it occurred to her that she needed to start a running commentary, one that wouldn't end until Trench was aboard the ship.

"OK, Trench, we are on your left bearing line. Hold what you've got. *Mother* is about forty miles off your left nose."

Annie then switched to the Comm 2 auxiliary frequency.

"Trench, Annie on Comm 2. Can you see anything?"

"Peripheral vision only. It's like a black ball is right in my face, and I can only see around the edges."

"What's your state?"

"Don't know. When I focus on the fuel indication—or anything—the black ball jumps in the way. I have to look away to even get a sense of anything."

"What do you think happened?" Annie continued.

"I was rigging a boat. On the second pass I lost sight.... May have been a blinding laser."

Annie felt a chill as she let this sink in. *Lasers...out here.*

Word of the recall to *Coral Sea* was out, and as other air wing aircraft returned to her, they clobbered *Strike* frequency with their voice calls. If Annie was going to "fly" two airplanes, she had to have a clear radio frequency. She called to *Strike*.

"*Strike*, four-zero-five is joined on four-zero-two. We need to get off this freq and over to approach so we can minimize frequency changes."

Strike approved the plan. "Roger, three-zero-five, go button one."

"Three-zero-five. *Ridgelines* go button one."

Now Annie had to get Trench to change his radio, and if she lost him, it could spell trouble. She called to him on aux. "Trench, on Comm 1...turn the knob two clicks counter-clockwise." After waiting a few seconds, she called.

"*Ridgeline,* check Comm 1..."

"Trench is up!" In their cockpits the *Firebird* pilots let loose a collective sigh of relief that they were still communicating on both radios, their only lifeline.

"Roger," Annie answered, then called to approach. "Approach, *Ridgeline* three-zero-five with you on *Mother's* one-three-five for thirty, angels eight, low state five-point-oh. We are holding hands with three-zero-two who is incapacitated due to blindness. Need to set up for a Mode One." The approach controller answered with the plan.

"Roger, *Ridgelines*, Mother is conducting an emergency pull forward. Expected BRC one-four-zero. You are cleared aft at ten miles. Take angels one-point-two."

After Annie acknowledged the instructions, she visualized the ship heading southeast. She had to set up behind it, or to the northwest, and to do that Trench had to turn—and descend. *Here goes,* she thought as she keyed the mike.

"Okay, Trench, we're gonna turn. Easy turn left."

After a moment, Trench moved his stick left with Annie's coaching.

"A little more angle of bank.... Good...hold that.... *Mother* is twenty-five miles off the nose.... Okay, roll out. Back to the right. Good. Let's pull some power now, and bunt the nose down.... Too much. Pull it back up a little.... Twenty-four miles."

And so it went. Big Jake, in loose formation behind them, watched for traffic while Annie flew next to Trench and guided him down. Her calm voice carried over the radio to his brain where the message was transferred by his hands to the flight controls. This came with an inherent lag, but Annie still had to anticipate one step ahead.

"Drop your hook," Annie directed. By feel Trench found the hook handle and lowered it. "Good," she said when she saw it extend into the slipstream.

In his cockpit, Trench found reason to chuckle. It was as if he were Stevie Wonder or Ray Charles at the piano, looking up and away as he flew his multi-million dollar warplane. He sensed the blue Caribbean below and saw they were surrounded by cottony clouds as his XO led them down and behind the ship. She sounded confident, and it looked as if they could get set up with plenty of "straight in" to get the system to lock-on and allow the ship to fly him down to the deck. He had a few Mode One approaches under his belt, but the air wing pilots seldom used it. He hoped 302 and the ship's system were up and up.

"Fuel low. Fuel low."

Instant fear and dread shot through his body as he absorbed the meaning of the message his plane had relayed to him. Trench had at most 20 minutes before his aircraft ran out of fuel.

"Sonofabitch!"

Now back in Air Ops, Wilson heard Annie's alarmed voice deliver the dire news of 302's low fuel state. *Dammit, only twenty minutes!* he thought. On the PLAT he assessed the deck, jammed with airplanes being towed forward by tractors with yellow shirt directors extorting the deck crew to move faster. He figured they had 15 minutes to get Trench aboard.

South of *Coral Sea*, Annie knew she would have to guide Trench into a "basket" behind the ship at the proper bearing, altitude, and airspeed to allow the ship to lock him and guide him down to the deck automatically as he selected the automatic carrier landing switches in order, precision flying for any pilot. Annie had to fly Trench's airplane by voice, and Trench had to respond exactly. So far he was doing a good job following her directions, but once they were behind the ship, things were going to happen fast.

She led them through an opening in the scattered clouds that hovered 2,000 feet above the sea. When Trench had informed her he had a low fuel light, she hit the countdown timer of her clock. She figured they had 15 to 20 minutes left before his engines flamed out, and she settled on 17 minutes as a baseline. Annie was going to stay with him until he was aboard, acting as his eyes and hands in their one shot to get this right. First, she had to level him off at 1,200 feet…. Then both the aircraft auto-throttle and Automatic Flight Control Systems had to work. "How you doing, Trench?" she asked him on Comm 2.

"OK. Seems like we're getting close to the water."

"Affirm, passing angels two. *Mother* is about two o'clock for fifteen miles heading southeast. We're gonna do a right one-fifty-degree turn to hook in on final."

"Roger."

"We're a little fast here. Tweak the throttle back a little and pick up the nose—just a little. *Good.* We're gonna level off now. Engage ATC. We're at two-fifty knots…. Good. Can you engage radar altitude hold?"

"Think so," Trench replied.

Annie helped guide his fingers over the radio. "OK, select, AFCS…far left pushtile under the UFC. Now, the fourth option, switch down. Got it?"

Trench pushed the switches in sequence and lifted his arms above the canopy rail to show Annie before keying the mike. "How's that?" Trent asked. The flight control computers were now flying the aircraft "hands off."

"Good, we're stabilized at angels one-point-three. Close enough. How you doing back there, Jake?"

"Good, fuel state four-point three," Jake answered from his position behind and to their right, riding shotgun for the formation and scanning for traffic ahead of their flight path. With Trench stable for the moment, Annie needed to coordinate with the ship.

"Approach, three-zero-two with you on *Mother*'s one-eight-zero for ten, estimating low state one-point-five, requesting Mode One on arrival. The pilot is blind and wingmen are guiding him to final. Say expected final bearing."

"Roger, three-zero-two, radar contact. Expected final bearing one-four-zero."

"Roger, approach, and we're gonna need a ten-mile hook, plenty of straight away. Can we expect a ready deck?"

"Expect that, three-zero-two."

In their respective cockpits, Annie and Trench let go a sigh of relief. The ship was going to be ready.

Trench prepared himself for the approach, which he sensed would be his last—ever. *Blind! Blind in the cockpit of a* Hornet *behind the ship with fifteen minutes of fuel!* His best window to the outside world was his peripheral vision, low and to his left. He moved his head in deliberate motions to take in anything he could. Outside he sensed two shades of blue, light blue sky over deep blue sea, and he could make out the outline of the cockpit. He could even see his hand move over the switches, but he couldn't focus on anything.

Trench had gotten better control of his panic, and he trusted Annie would set him up in the proper window for lock-on. Even if he survived, though, he figured this was the end, with a changed and uncertain future awaiting him. In fifteen minutes, he might be dead; if alive, he would *still* be dead. Either way, his life was over, and he felt the panic return. Annie brought him back.

"Looking good, Trench. We're downwind now, and *Mother's* over your right shoulder inside ten. Let's get your data link up...fourth pushtile from the left."

Trench engaged the data link that would receive autopilot commands from the ship. He sensed the frequency come up in the window and lifted his visor. As he leaned in close, placing his eyes mere inches from the display numerals, he determined the frequency was correct. *I can read!* he thought with jubilation.

Aboard *Coral Sea*, the last aircraft was being towed forward and the recovery stations reported manned and ready. Air Ops had rousted Petty Officer Conley, their best final controller, from his rack, and he hooked his headset microphone up to the console so he could guide 302 on the most unusual approach of his career. The mood was tense, and all eyes were focused on the PLAT screen.

On the LSO platform, "Rat" Fink scanned aft as the phone talker plugged in his sound-powered phone. Lost in his thoughts, he knew the last twenty seconds of this approach would be up to him. *A blind pilot!* Trench James was a solid pilot, but could he—could anyone—get aboard while blind? Even on a hands-off Mode One, this was a tall order. Commander Schofield was going to guide him in position, but Rat would be responsible here. The phone rang, and he reached down to answer it.

"Lieutenant Commander Fink, sir." Rat pressed the receiver close to his ear as the 25-knot wind whipped around him.

"Paddles, this is the captain."

"Yes, sir!" It was the first time Captain Sanders had dialed the platform.

"Three-zero-two is about ten miles aft with his XO guiding him, and we're hooking him in now. He has some limited vision that we think allows him to determine up from down, but that's about it. Now, I'm conveying this to you direct. If you need to jump in there and talk to him, do it. And if he is not in a position to land, wave him off. We get one chance. If he doesn't get aboard, his XO is going to coax him back in the air, and he can eject. We'll rescue him. So, do what needs to be done, and I'll back you up. You ready?"

"Yes, sir. We'll get him."

"Roger that, Paddles. We'll have about twenty-five knots down the angle for you, and Petty Officer Conley controlling him. I'm confident in all of you. Good luck!"

"Thanks, sir. Appreciate it," Rat answered, grateful for the vote of confidence.

"Roger. Out here," the captain said as he hung up.

Firebird LSO "Coach" Madden joined him on the platform. "Can I back you up, Rat?"

"Yeah, please. Captain just called. Trench is ten miles aft, and they are hooking him in for a coupled approach. Hopefully, we just watch him, but if he drops radar lock, you've got line up. Captain said if he's out of position, wave him off."

Coach nodded, tight lipped and uneasy. Seeing Coach's reaction, Rat added.

"Let *me* make that call. You help with line up and talk to me over my shoulder, but I'll be responsible for taking him—or not. Got it?"

"Got it," Coach replied, relieved that Rat was removing accountability or blame from his shoulders.

"He's your roommate, isn't he?"

Coach nodded.

"If you pray, I'd say one. Want to pray?"

Coach wasn't the praying type, even as he realized his head was nodding yes.

"Okay," Rat replied as he turned to the young sailor on the sound-powered phone and shouted over the din of the flight deck. "Airman Friddle, you want to join us in a prayer?"

The enlisted sailor looked at him for a moment in confusion, then answered, "Yes, sir."

"Okay, let's bow our heads." With the high winds whipping at their clothes and sun shining on them, Rat led them in prayer on the exposed Landing Signal Officer platform of the great carrier. "Lord, help us guide our friend down. He needs you, and *we* need you. Please give us the strength and grace to make the right calls and the right decisions. *Your will be done always*. Amen."

"Amen," Coach muttered as the sailor blessed himself. Soon other LSOs arrived on the platform, all scanning the distant horizon for signs of Trench. "Visual," Coach said, and pointed at a series of three dots low to the west.

Hornets. Each with a squadronmate inside.

CHAPTER 27

(USS *Coral Sea*, underway, 225 miles northwest of Barranquilla, Colombia)

Olive joined Wilson in Air Ops as he stood with CAG Matson. The three of them contemplated the status board and listened to the controllers talk to Annie as she guided 302 in an easy, right-hand turn. Wilson leaned toward his Safety Officer.

"Any gripes on three-zero-two?"

"No, sir. I just reviewed the book in Maintenance Control. There's no throttle or flight control gripes, and the data link is good. We should be okay."

Relieved, Wilson nodded and then turned to CAG. "Sir, we believe three-zero-two has a good system for a Mode One."

"Great. Now it's up to Annie to get him in the window."

Helpless, they listened to the controller guide 302 toward the ship.

"Three-zero-two, *Mother*'s steady now. Turn right. Intercept final bearing one-three-one."

Annie responded, "Roger, approach, final bearing one-three-one. Trench, turn right...a little more angle of bank. Good. Twenty degrees to go...eleven miles.... Okay, roll back to the left a little.... Good."

Annie knew that once Trench lowered his gear and flaps, he would need to hand-fly 302 before re-engaging the autopilot. She watched Trench in the cockpit and saw him lean close to the instrument panel to read what he could from it. "Can you see your fuel?" she asked.

"Negative," he replied, "not enough contrast."

Both knew he had less than fifteen minutes of fuel, probably closer to ten minutes.

"Okay. You ready to dirty up?" she asked.

"Affirm," Trench replied. Things were going to happen fast now, and the last chance for the ship to lock a "stabilized" and linked-up 302 was coming up in five miles.

"Okay, let's roll out left. Good. You are level and just right of course, ten miles. Now disengage the ATC and autopilot. Drop your gear and flaps."

With some trepidation, Trench did as he was told, finding and lowering the gear and flaps controls by feel. He felt the aircraft "balloon" with the increased lift provided by the flaps. Annie and Jake lowered their flaps to match their stricken mate. To be at the same configuration as the aircraft she was guiding, Annie also lowered her landing gear, while also "flying" the aircraft next to her.

"Okay, a little nose down....Gear coming down, drifting right. Back to the left. Slowing below two hundred.... Come up a little on the power, a little nose up. Trim it. One-seventy...nine and a half miles...one-fifty. A little nose up. Trim out the stick forces.... Now engage ATC."

Trench nodded as he did so, and felt relief as the throttles moved to keep him at the proper airspeed, which at this light fuel weight he figured would be less than 130 knots. One variable—airspeed control—was out of the way. Annie continued.

"Nine miles, and we're high, so a little nose down.... And we're still right, so a little left bank.... Good. Keep it in. Now roll out right. *Hold it*.... Good. *Approach,* three-zero-two has three down and locked at eight miles."

"Roger, *Mother*'s steady. Final bearing one-three-one," Petty Officer Conley answered her.

Trench flinched when he heard a MASTER CAUTION audio tone in his headset. He placed his head next to the left digital display to try and discern what the caution was, and a chill came over him.

"Think I've got an AMAD caution here!"

"Roger that, continue," Annie reassured him. "We're four minutes from touchdown." The Airframe Mounted Accessory Drive powered the generators on each engine. Fuel cooled the AMADs, and 302's low-fuel state at low altitude on a hot tropical day was causing one of them to overheat. If the situation continued, the associated generator could fall off line, and a hiccup in AC power delivery could affect the flight controls and the data link systems, spitting 302 out of a coupled approach. In Air Ops, Olive was on it.

"Skipper, the book says to leave the generator and engine alone if you can land within fifteen minutes. Recommend we ignore the AMAD."

Feeling CAG's look of apprehension, Wilson nodded. "Concur, and Annie is on it. Rick, can I talk to him?"

The Air Operations Officer handed him the radio handset.

Wilson took it and transmitted. "Three-zero-two, *Firebird* rep."

Recognizing his skipper's voice, Trench answered, "Go ahead, sir."

"Just leave everything alone, you are inside fifteen minutes to landing. You're doin' great. Out here."

"Roger, sir."

Annie jumped back in. "You're settling...you're low. Pick the nose up. Okay, bunt nose down and hit altitude hold. Airspeed good, just under one-thirty. Just slightly right of course, six-point-five miles."

What everyone involved knew, and what Trench sensed, was that the invisible last-chance "window" for the ship to lock him was looming just ahead. Actually, they were inside it, and Trench wanted them to lock him up now so he and Annie could stop struggling with calls over the radio.

"Three-zero-two, approach. Are you receiving landing check discrete?"

"Affirm!" Trench lied, hoping but not knowing if he had a good landing check. It was now or never. Annie kept the calls coming.

"Okay, stabilize. Trim the stick forces out. Doin' good...roll a little left.... Approach, lock him now."

"Four-zero-two, report coupled."

"Trench, push the bottom push button," Annie guided.

With his fingers, Trench felt for the push button that would link 302 to approach control, and pushed it.

"Coupled!"

"Sending commands..." the approach controller continued.

Trench felt the aircraft twitch and throttles move under his left hand. *Yes!* he thought as a wave of relief swept over him. The ship had him now.

"Command Control!" he transmitted.

"Roger three-zero-two, slightly right of course and correcting at five miles. Nice job."

On the bridge, in Primary Flight Control, in Air Ops, and in Annie Schofield's cockpit, all those monitoring the situation breathed a sigh of relief. While continuing to fly escort on Trench, Annie kept her jet at a safe distance from him so the ship's final control radar would not jump over and lock *her*.

Wilson and the others in Air Ops watched the "dot" of 302 loom larger as it gravitated closer to the glide slope "crosshairs" on the PLAT camera mounted in the flight deck. All of them knew what could happen. The ATC or flight controls could "kick off," and it would be too late to lock Trench inside the window. When the controller said, "Three-zero-two, you're on course at four miles," they knew they were committed. Above them on the flight deck, Wilson heard the Air Boss on the 5MC loudspeaker; "*Make a ready deck.* Firebird *three-zero-two is at four miles. Stand clear of the foul line!*"

Trench let his hands rest on the stick and throttle, feeling them move under the data-linked commands sent from the ship. With his limited peripheral vision, all he could discern was water and sky. In two minutes, he was going to be aboard—hanging from a parachute—or dead. He sensed this was it, the end of his flying days, the end of his military career, not that he had ever wanted one. But now he did, and would stay for thirty years if he could just see. *Please God!* he cried in his mind, begging to wake up from his nightmare, begging for a second chance. *Damn yacht!* He had to warn the others. Approach kept the calls coming.

"Three-zero-two, approaching tip-over. Up and on glide slope at three miles."

"Roger," he acknowledged. He felt the airplane lunge as the throttles moved back, then forward to keep 302 on speed. He was now on glide slope, an imaginary 3.5-degree ramp that would take him all the way into the wires, and he couldn't even see the ship's wake. Annie reassured him on Comm 2.

"Looking good, Trench. Deck's clear. You've got a centered ball. Gear down, hook down. You're all set." Trench nodded, then keyed the mike to warn everyone.

"It was a yacht, about a hun'erd miles south. I was rigging it, and it blinded me. White yacht, heading west."

"Three-zero-two, approach. Say again?"

"I'm telling you, *it was a yacht!*" an exasperated Trench boomed. "With a blinding laser. Now you know, so get me aboard!"

In Air Ops, Wilson and Matson exchanged glances. CAG stepped over to the console and picked up a phone. Wilson went back to the PLAT display, helpless to do anything more.

"Three-zero-two, roger. On glideslope, on course.... Two miles."

To Trench, the controls seemed to be working hard to keep him on glide slope, and he was fearful they would "kick him out" of the ship's data link control. He had no choice but to ride and wait.

All eyes looked aft at the formation of *Hornets*, knowing that a blind pilot was in the lead aircraft. They also knew this approach could end in a fiery crash, and the Air Boss had instructed nonessential personnel to go below. Descending from her cockpit on the bow, Macho asked Chief Hauber, the squadron flight deck chief, what was going on.

"Three-zero-two is coming back. He's blind."

Stunned, Macho asked, "Who's in three-oh-two?"

"Lieutenant James," he answered.

With her mouth hanging slack from disbelief, Macho saw the formation of *Hornets* on final. *Blind? Trench? How? What was he doing?* These questions cycled through her head as the aircraft grew closer.

"We better get below, ma'am," the chief said to her.

"Yes," Macho replied, trying to process the news that Trench was in extremis. Despite the fact she considered him her mortal enemy, she wanted to stay and watch—not to watch the train wreck, but to provide support, to *see him make it* for herself. She didn't want this, but stepped to the deck edge and down a ladder, taking another look at Trench as the formation drew closer. Unable to force herself to go below, she disobeyed and stayed in the starboard bow catwalk forward of the foul line—and waited.

Through habit, the controller called to Trench one last time; "Three-zero-two, on and on, three-quarter mile…"

"You're *on and on,* Trench! Workin' twenty-six knots, clear deck!" From the LSO platform, Rat jumped on the radio to reassure the pilot that he "had" him now, even though the ship's equipment was still flying Trench down to the deck.

In the cockpit, Trench could sense the ship's wake below and a mass of gray ahead of him. The ride was smooth despite the jerky movement of the throttles. Next to him, Annie slid further away and leveled off at 200 feet. Rat was in control now.

"About a half-mile, Trench. You're on and on."

"Roger," Trench answered. Knowing he was seconds from touchdown—or ejection—his breathing had become rapid and clipped.

"On glideslope…*onnn* glideslope," Rat continued with his comforting calls.

Trench then felt the throttles under his hand stop moving. Panicked, he keyed the mike for help. "Manual throttles!"

This call electrified the LSOs and, behind him, Rat heard Coach call to him. "He's settling!" Rat was on top of it and transmitted.

"Roger, manual. You are in-close, a *little* power."

Nobody involved with the evolution had experienced this before. With five seconds to touchdown, Trench now had to manually manipulate his throttles, requiring a delicate touch even with pilots who could see. The ship had his flight controls, but now Trench had to add and retract power through the throttles from calls Rat gave him. Trench responded to Rat by adding a shot of power. Rat fought to remain calm as Trench was now getting too fast.

"*Easy* with it, you're fast.... On glideslope, fast, approaching the ramp."

Approaching the ship's flight deck ramp, the flight controls could not keep up with the erratic throttle movements. With a routine advisory cockpit tone and the stick seeming dead in his hand, Trench knew he had both controls, elevating his fear.

"*Manual! I'm manual!*"

Rat jumped in as he saw 302 balloon too high for landing. "You're going high. Drop your nose! *Drop your nose!*" Trench did so, but overcorrected and was now at risk of crunching his jet on deck. Behind him Coach cried, "He's drifting left!" *Screw it*, Rat thought, knowing this was it.

"*Attitude, idle!*" Rat shouted into the handset as Trench roared past him and came down hard. He slammed onto the deck, the jet bouncing back into the air but not before his tailhook snagged one of the arresting wires to keep it on deck. By reflex, Trench went to full power as he felt himself decelerate on the violent roll out and sensed nothing but water on his left side.

"We got'cha. *Stay with it. Stay with it.* Keep a little power on," the Air Boss radioed. Crash and salvage crews ran out to his jet, and a flight deck tractor trailing an aircraft towbar chugged over to his nose. In his cockpit, Trench slumped in his seat, but he unhooked his mask and gulped in one lungful of air after another. Alive—but, at the same time, dead.

"Safe your seat and open the canopy, three-zero-two. Nice job, we've got you. You can shut down the engines," the Air Boss transmitted.

From her vantage point in the catwalk Macho climbed the ladder to the flight deck and moved toward 302. The jet was now surrounded by personnel, the Boss barking orders on the 5MC. Overhead, she saw aircraft circling, waiting for their turn to land. Confusion reigned. Nobody knew if they were going to recover the aircraft overhead or launch the ones on deck first. She moved down the bow toward the angle, toward 302 as activity swirled about her. She saw Trench stand up in the cockpit, assisted by crash and salvage sailors and corpsmen from Medical. The approach had not been smooth, and the jet had hit the deck hard.

Was he coupled all the way to touchdown, or did he fly that blind? Macho wondered. She was shocked to see 302 so close to the deck edge and realized that another ten feet left would have put him into the catwalk, and probably over the side. *How did this happen?* she thought, even while knowing that things can happen in this business with no warning. Trench was her enemy, and she hated the Neanderthal misogyny he represented— but he was also her squadronmate. The XO's words rang true. *You don't have to like each other.*

Trench was out of the jet now. A throng of sailors guided him toward the island, putting their arms around him as they led him off the deck— maybe his last time on it. Macho watched from a distance, confused, trying to comprehend what had happened and what it meant.

"Ma'am."

Macho flinched in surprise as Chief Hauber approached from the left.

"Ma'am, they're gonna recover the birds overhead then launch you. They want you pilots in the jet and ready."

She looked at him, uncomprehending, dumbfounded that the chief was talking to *her.* She looked toward the gaggle with Trench and the gaggle as they disappeared into the island, then back at the jet parked on the bow. The open canopy and the empty ejection seat waited for *her* to get in and to *fly* 22-ton machine off the ship and into the air, over the ocean. On a mission, a *routine training mission* like Trench was on. She tried to form words but could not, and without looking at the chief, she walked toward her assigned jet as if to the gallows.

What's out there? she thought. *What's out there?*

Chief Hauber watched with concern as she walked away, knowing enough about pilot mindsets to know that Lieutenant Rourke was not in the proper frame to get in the jet, *his* jet. Should he stop her? Find a reason to "down" her jet before she launched? He would watch her during the start sequence, and wondered if she, too, was thinking about not flying.

A call from the Air Boss over the 5MC made the decision for them, a decision that everyone on the roof welcomed. "On the flight deck, we're gonna catch the recovery aircraft and secure from flight ops. Make a ready deck. Land aircraft."

CHAPTER 28

(Sick Bay, USS *Coral Sea*, central Caribbean)

After they watched Trench trap and watched the corpsmen lead him to the island, Wilson and CAG left Air Ops. They headed to sick bay to see their stricken pilot and find out what happened. Matson summoned his Wing Intel Officer, Commander Hofmeister, to join them.

They descended four decks below where sick bay was located on the "mess decks," the large open dining facilities where the crew took their meals. Sick bay was a small hospital that provided for the 5,000 men and women of *Coral Sea*. There they found the emergency medical response team leading their young pilot into an examination room. Still in his flight gear, Trench seemed confused, fearful, and relieved, all at the same time. Wilson called to him.

"Trench, Skipper. Welcome home."

"*Skipper!* It was a yacht! I was rigging it, and on the second pass I lost my sight. About eighty miles south of *Mother* when I found it. Heading west."

"Describe it." Wilson asked him. The medical personnel were in the process of removing Trench's torso harness.

"White hull, sleek—about 100 feet long. Tinted cockpit glass. Boat davits aft."

"Trench, this is CAG Matson. How close did you get to it?"

Trench hesitated, then answered. "Right on top of it, sir, about 200 feet down its starboard side. I made two passes."

"Did you get a photo?" Wilson asked.

"Not a hand-held, sir, but I believe it's on my FLIR tape."

"Okay, we'll take a look."

Just then the flight surgeon interrupted. "Gentlemen, we need to get vitals and examine his eyes. Can you give us 20 minutes?"

"Yeah, Doc, go ahead," answered Matson. "Trench, *nice* job. We are going to take care of you now. We'll finish the debrief later."

151

"Thanks, sir," Trench responded, still shaken and unsure.

Wilson grabbed Trench's arm. "We'll be back to check on you soon. Relax now."

"Sir?" Trench whispered.

"Yeah, go."

"Sir, there was some...scenery on the bow."

"Got it. We'll come back later."

"Thanks, sir."

Matson and Hofmeister waited for Wilson in the passageway. "What was that?" he asked.

"There was a girl or girls on the bow as he rigged the yacht. I think it had a blinding laser, just waiting for one of us to fly by."

"Yeah, we're all lucky he lived to tell the tale. Let's get his tapes reviewed, and I'm going to see the admiral. I want us to stay on top of this yacht. Come with me."

They returned to Combat Decision Center located between Air Ops and the flag spaces. Scattered about were large radar repeater consoles with track-balls, communications handsets and controls, and manuals of standing orders and directives the size of phone books. Bulkhead displays showed the sea and air contacts located about *Coral Sea*, contacts called *tracks* in the vernacular of the watchstanders, and Matson asked the Battle Watch Captain, one of the admiral's staff officers a question.

"What tracks do you have south of us?"

The Watch Captain studied the screen. "Sir, we have well over two dozen *south* of us. Can you narrow the bearing and range?"

Matson frowned, and gave it a shot. "Look from one-five-zero to two-three-zero, eighty to one hundred fifty miles.

The Watch Captain narrowed the search by "grabbing" that patch of waterspace and hit ENTER. The display expanded the tracks in the selected "pie" and Matson inspected them.

"Do you know what they all are?"

"Most of them, sir. These two guys are containerships. This is a fishing boat. This one is a DDG, USS *Norman Kleiss*. And this track—what is this guy?"

The officer moved the tracking ball, "hooking" it to read the heading and speed plus the identification assigned to the contact. Wilson watched with interest. Seeing his CAG take action was not only heartening but exhilarating, and he sensed, by the end of the day, *Coral Sea* could have a chance to enact some payback.

"Not sure of this one, sir. It's moving southwest at 20 knots. Track 1724."

"When will 1724 be in Colombian waters?" Matson asked.

Using his fingers, the Watch Captain measured the distance between the contact and the 12- mile territorial limit of Colombia. Outside 12 the vessel was in international waters.

"Four hours, sir. Maybe three, if he kicks it up."

"I want you to find out what 1724 is," Matson ordered. Turning to one of his staff officers, he added, "Rich, when you find out what 1724 is, come tell me, I'll be in CVIC."

"Yes, sir."

Matson spun for Flag plot with Wilson in tow. When clear of CDC, he turned to Wilson. "Find Weed ASAP, and let's meet in CVIC in five minutes."

"Aye, aye, sir." Wilson answered. He was certain that *Coral Sea* would resume flight quarters very soon.

Once in CVIC, Wilson called Ready Room 5 and the duty officer, Killer, answered the phone.

"Ready Five, Lieutenant Williams, sir or ma'am."

"Killer, Skipper. Find Commander Hopper ASAP and have him meet me in CVIC. Do you have Trench's tapes from 302?"

"Yes, sir."

"Good, have a pilot bring them to me in CVIC *on the double.*"

"Yes, sir!"

"Get the Ops Officer to find four pilots to brief with me in an hour, three primaries and a spare. And get maintenance to prep five birds, four and a spare. We launch in two-point-five hours."

"Aye, aye, sir!"

"Out here—but *find Hopper.* Get the ready room to help, and get him up here now."

"Yes, sir!" Killer answered.

Wilson hung up. He knew he could not schedule a launch for his squadron, but, after watching CAG Matson and sensing his thoughts, the *Firebirds* would be ready.

Matson entered CVIC with the Chief Staff Officer Captain Ed Browne and motioned for Wilson to follow him into a debriefing room. Billy Martin and Commander Hofmeister joined them and, moments later, a breathless Irish handed Wilson two 8mm tapes, the tapes Trench was flying with.

"Pop them in, Flip," Matson ordered. "Let's see what he was looking at."

Wilson did so and rewound the tapes to the time Trench estimated he had rigged the yacht. The men watched in silence as the yacht came into view. Matson led the commentary.

"That's it, our track 1724. Look at the time...almost two hours ago. And there's his Nav readout. He was on *Mother*'s one-seven-zero at eighty miles. Okay, Norb, check with the bridge. Find out where we were at 1102, and work backwards to plot where *Ridgeline* 302 was. The contact next to it is our contact of interest, and it may be track 1724. Ed, we need you guys to find where this guy is now, and I'm requesting a SEAL mission to take it down. We need to capture these guys and see what they are carrying—and who is ordering them."

Just then Weed entered the room.

"Weed," Matson asked. "What assets do you have south of here?"

Unsure of what was going on, Weed took a moment before he answered to do a mental roll call that all present were read-in to CENTURY RATCHET.

"*Norman Kleiss* has a *Fire Scout* detachment and one *Sierra* with two crews. Not sure where they are now, but they've been working south."

"They are still down there," Captain Browne nodded.

Matson nodded. "Great. Okay, Weed, contact them and get the *Fire Scout* airborne. Need to find these fuckers *now*."

Captain Sanders joined them, and the officers plotted their next moves. With time short—the yacht moved one mile closer to the safety of Colombian territorial waters every three minutes—they had to act. There was no time to "ask" Washington for orders, no time to ask SOUTHCOM in Miami for guidance. A clear act of war had been committed, and the brain trust of *Coral Sea* was in no mood to let the perpetrators squirm free without any effort to stop them. Forgiveness could be sought later. Sanders called the bridge and spoke with the Navigator. Within minutes, they felt the ship heel to port and accelerate.

The chase was on.

But one other person aboard *Coral Sea* needed to be part of the decision-making process.

CHAPTER 29

Meyerkopf was incredulous. In his thirty years in uniform he had never heard of such a thing. He was the *Strike Group Commander*, the *Senior Officer Present Afloat*, and he was *in the dark* about what his strike group was involved in! *Subordinates* on his own flagship were fighting a quasi-war under his nose! Why hadn't he been briefed on CENTURY RATCHET?

He glared at Sanders and Matson—and at his own Chief of Staff, Ed Browne, aviators all. Betrayal. Confusion. They seemed to be running the show. *And who is this commander they called Weed? NSA? CIA? What the hell is going on?* After Weed finished reading him in, Matson spoke first.

"Admiral, I'm sorry you weren't on the cleared list for CENTURY RATCHET, but our orders were clear."

"You've been sinking and shooting down drug runners for the past three weeks?"

"In a manner of speaking, sir. Commander Hopper's personnel are using your ships and aircraft."

"*Behind my back?*" Meyerkopf shot back. Matson didn't have an answer.

"Sir," Captain Sanders jumped in, "we didn't ask for this arrangement. This came from Fleet Forces with elaborate cover stories and a small need-to-know contingent for this strike group. All of us are in the middle here, but after what happened this morning, and the fact that time is of the essence, we needed to act first and bring you in second. *Right now,* admiral, my people are building up weapons to load on Tim's aircraft. We are moving south at best speed, and Tim's pilots need to launch in about an hour to find this contact, this yacht. We need to disable it so we can capture it and the crew."

"From a standing start you can capture a civilian vessel and potentially start a war?"

"Sir, one of your pilots is in sick bay—*blind.* Something happened to him out there, and this contact is suspect number one. We are tracking it and working backwards to see if it's the same contact Lieutenant James

155

flew past. If yes, we're going to stop it and capture what crew we can and interrogate them."

"*Why not just blow it out of the water like everything else?*" Meyerkopf asked, perturbed.

"So we can *exploit* it, sir," Weed volunteered, ignoring the brusque jab. "We need to see what we're up against and forward that to Washington for them to make a decision."

"Who *are* you?" Meyerkopf asked Weed with disdain.

"Commander Mike Hopper, sir, a naval officer like you, subject to orders, including yours, sir."

"Who do you work for?"

"Fleet Forces Command—like you, sir."

At that, Meyerkopf made a face and brushed Weed away with his hand. Seething, he turned to address his trio of captains. "So we take orders from Commanders, now?"

"Sir, *all* of us are following orders," Matson answered. "We've been read-in to CENTURY RATCHET on a need-to-know basis. Events have transpired to read you in, sir. Now, Admiral, our people are preparing for a mission to find, disable, and exploit this yacht—"

"On whose orders?"

"*Mine*, sir, but only with your concurrence now. Rick and I are still in command of our forces, and we were attacked. We have a plan to stop further attacks, and we are keeping you, our senior, informed. You can stand us down, if you wish, and all will file incident reports to Norfolk. Now sir, while you decide on how you'd like to proceed, we must to oversee the efforts of our people while there's still time."

Ed Browne spoke up.

"Guys, let me talk to the Admiral. Please excuse us."

"Yes, sir," Matson said and led the group out of CVIC.

Once alone, Meyerkopf frowned at his Chief of Staff, fuming. "I'm all ears."

"Sir, your pride is wounded. Fleet Forces tagged us to come down here and show the flag and exercise with the Colombians. While we are here we can train on the damn reactors, fly the kids in the air wing, and get some good port visits for the crew. All of that was a cover story for this, and Hopper and his guys are doing good work out here. They are practically shutting down the seaborne drug trade."

"I'm certainly capable of safeguarding classified information!"

"I'm sure there were times in your career you were privy to classified info your superiors didn't have access to. And now you are on the other end, and it is not *wrong*. Sir, I recommend you call Miami and tell them what happened and how *you* are dealing with it."

Just then a staff officer entered. "Excuse me sir, but we've done the radar and data link forensics. Track 1724 is a yacht."

"Very well," Meyerkopf responded. "What do we have tracking it and how far away?"

"An E-2 sir, and a *Fire Scout* from *Norman Kleiss*. It's 110 miles south of us, and we are closing it at 15 knots. We expect it to be in Colombian territorial waters in two hours."

"Very well, please keep us updated."

"Yes, sir!"

Once the officer left, Meyerkopf turned to Browne. "We are steaming at flank speed to catch this guy? Isn't Sanders paying attention to his reactors?"

Exasperated, Browne answered him. "Sir, the reactors are fine. The shafts are fine, and the dosimeter readings are *fine*. We are in *combat mode* now, sir, and your people are briefing to deal with a proven blinding laser threat they will face in an hour. My recommendation, sir, is that you call the Combatant Commander and tell him *Coral Sea* has a plan and is ready for any and all tasking."

Still sulking, Meyerkopf shot Browne a look before he turned on his heels for CDC. Browne wasn't sure how his admiral was going to handle the next two hours, but *Coral Sea's* aviators had work to do, and minutes counted.

CHAPTER 31

With only thirty minutes to start engines, Wilson had no time for an elaborate strike brief. His *Firebird* division would consist of Dusty, Ripper, and Olive, with Coach as spare. Billy Martin was there with four of his *Hunter* pilots flying the FA-18E *Super Hornet*, and two crews from the *Rustlers*, the MH-60S squadron, were also present. A lieutenant from the SEAL detachment aboard stood next to him with a small notebook.

In minutes, Wilson and Billy had devised a plan: All the aircraft would launch and *buster* south as fast as they could, wasting no time for a rendezvous or a launch sequence plan; if the carrier aircraft could join up en route, that was good, but it was not required.

The *Fire Scout* drone aboard the destroyer *Norman Kleiss* would put a *Hellfire* missile into the fantail of the yacht—at the waterline if possible. The plan was to disable the yacht's screws and/or rudder. With the vessel drifting, SEALS from the two *Sierras* would board the yacht, capture the crew, and gather what intelligence they could. With the vessel secure, *Norman Kleiss* would take it under tow.

All this would happen in broad daylight, and they could expect the yacht crew to be alerted for trouble. Chances were they were armed with automatic weapons, RPG's and hand-held SAMs—plus the laser that had already blinded one pilot.

Wilson's eight jets carried two 500-pound, laser-guided bombs each and full loads of 20mm High Explosive Incendiary bullets. With little time, the ordnancemen assembled the weapons in the magazine and were now in the process of transferring them via the weapons elevators to the flight deck where they would be loaded as the pilots were preflighting their aircraft. Wilson imagined the aircrew listening to him as he if were drawing up a sandlot football play in the dirt. *You do a buttonhook. You go long. You hike it and go down-and-out...*

Checking his watch, Wilson gathered them around him in the front of the ready room with a navigational chart of the Caribbean. "OK guys, the yacht is here tracking south at twenty knots. Looks like it is heading for

Barranquilla. Let's everyone start up on *Firebird* tactical freq to check in, and I'll pass any updates. Once you are ready, the yellow shirts will break you down and shoot you ASAP. No waiting. If you are ready and a catapult is ready, go. Turn south immediately off the cat, and we'll get together en route.

"By the time we get down there an hour from now," said Wilson, pointing to a spot on the chart, "the yacht should be *here*, about 25 miles from the coast and only thirty minutes from the 'safety' of Colombian waters. Let's haul ass supersonic in the low 20's. Once I'm on station, I've got the mission lead with Skipper Martin as back-up. Let's all check in with *Condor*, and we can expect data link from them to the contact. We're going to call the yacht *Lauderdale*, and, when we refer to the laser, it is *Lightshow*."

The aviators nodded and scribbled Wilson's instructions onto their kneeboard cards. All of them were experienced, no nuggets on this impromptu combat sortie. Wilson continued.

"Once we are on top of this bitch, we'll look for the *Fire Scout* to disable it. It has boat davits and a rigid hull inflatable. If they try to escape in the RHIB, strafe ahead of them to stop them until the *Rustlers* show up. *Rustlers*, pour fire into the yacht as required to neutralize it, and fast-rope the SEALS when you and the SEAL lead determine it is safe to do so.

"If they light us up with the laser, we back off. To mitigate that risk, let's stay high and get on top of the yacht and stay tight on it. Try not to look at it with your naked eyes, Use your sensors to the max extent. "

"Sir, why do we have the weapons?" one of the *Rhino* pilots asked.

"If the *Fire Scout* can't disable the yacht, we have to. Let's use the FLIR and aim for a spot just off the fantail. Delay fuses. We want a water burst close aboard that disables the screws or rudder, maybe pops some engine room piping, or even holes the hull."

"What do we think the effective range of the laser is, sir?"

Wilson opened his mouth—and realized he didn't know.

"One mile, sir," Shane answered, and the group waited for her to continue.

"One mile *effectively*, and we believe it needs 15-50 kilowatts to build a charge. Not sure how long a yacht would take to build up a charge, or if it's capable of more than blinding a pilot. We suspect a Russian design— there is evidence they are working with the cartels on a variety of high-tech projects—but that distance is an estimate. We've tested a laser weapon with a range of ten miles."

Wilson pursed his lips and nodded. "Thanks, Shane. If you and the other *spies* can relay the likelihood of a burn-through capability, and any sanctuaries we can exploit, then get that relayed to us through CDC."

"Yes, sir."

"Thanks. Okay, gas. The ship is going to add on a tanker after we leave, but don't bet on it. Manage your fuel, and, if you have to come back, do it. If they send us a tanker or two, we'll play it by ear about who gets what. We need to keep at least two of us overhead. We can also expect the *Raiders* and *Hobos* to send some jets down to relieve us after about 30-45 minutes."

The pilots nodded.

"All right. Anything else?"

The pilots shook their heads. All were ready to get airborne and on top of the yacht.

"OK, pass your aircraft lineups to your ready rooms. We need to get airborne in less than 30 minutes. If you only get one bomb or half a load of bullets, take the jet anyway. If you don't get any chaff or flares, take it."

The pilots wished each other well. "Nice job, Flip, Semper Gumby!" Billy told him with a smile.

"You got that right. Good hunting down there. We gotta move," Wilson answered.

Good hunting!" Billy said as he led his squadron out of the *Firebird* ready room.

Wilson noted the time: 1345. He grabbed his helmet bag and went next door to maintenance control to check out his jet, 301. Olive followed him.

"Good brief, Skipper. We'll catch these guys. Do you think they're Colombian?"

"Maybe. Maybe Venezuelan, or maybe not even from the western hemisphere."

Olive nodded as she reviewed her discrepancy book and then noticed that the Maintenance Control Chief and two sailors were listening to their conversation. The Chief spoke.

"Skipper, are you going to find the guys that blinded Lieutenant James? Is there a fleet we are fighting out here?"

Wilson shook his head. "There's a contact of interest south of us that we need to check out, and it's not a combatant. We have a small boy with a drone nearby, and we're going to support them. As soon as we can get up there and started, we are going. So tell the guys on the roof, chop, chop."

"Yes, sir, they're ready for you! You're on the bow."

"Thanks, Chief," Wilson said and smiled as he signed the book. He then grabbed his helmet bag and hurried for the paraloft. They had little more than an hour to go.

CHAPTER 32

A determined Wilson moved up the flight deck in long strides, leaning into the 30-knot wind. He saw Billy get into his assigned jet, 404, next to the Cat 1 jet blast deflector. Wilson's jet was three up from him, with Olive next to Wilson in 303. Dusty and Ripper were starting someplace aft, with Coach as the spare. The red-shirted ordnancemen continued to wheel 500-pounders into place under the wing racks of the jets and to crank 20mm rounds through the feeder mechanisms. Wilson knew he did not have time to wait on them to finish. Whatever was hanging from his jet was what he was going to have to take.

The ordies were manually lifting the bombs into place on the weapon pylons of 301 when Wilson arrived. He caught the attention of Gunner Short, the Ordnance Officer.

"Gunner, we have no time. After I preflight this jet, I'm starting it up."

Worried, Gunner responded. "OK, Skipper, we're going to connect this one on station two and load up eight as fast as we can."

"Do it!"

Wilson preflighted the aircraft in practiced sequence, thinking about the yacht, the SEALS in the helos, CAG's intensity. He had not awakened this morning expecting to expend weapons in anger on a vessel underway, much less a pleasure craft. With Trench blind, the combat capability of the *Firebirds* was degraded, but Weed could fill a flight schedule slot. Wilson would let a jet go empty before placing that sonofabitch Mongo in it.

Weed. CENTURY RATCHET. *This* was the reason they were down here, the reason Trench was blind, not knowing of the quasi-war Weed and the "testers" were fighting in secret. *Secret?* To keep it from the press or from operational security? Wilson suspected the former. *If our country knows Venezuela or Colombia or Panama—any of them—is growing and shipping poison to ruin our kids, then blow 'em out of the water.* Wilson would gladly participate. *Just declare it, and don't screw around! Win it! Take Vienna.*

Wilson finished his preflight and bounded up the ladder. As he dropped himself into the ejection seat, the plane captain began hooking up his mask and g-suit connections, and the Air Boss yelled something over the 5MC flight deck loudspeaker. As Wilson was hooking up his leg restraints, his eyes met those of Chief Royal, the Ordnance Chief. Royal's crew was finishing up on station 2, and the laser-guided bomb for station 8 was still in its dolly cradle. They weren't going to load it in time, and Wilson sensed Royal's concern.

"Chief, I'm taking it as is. Work on the next jet!" Wilson shouted to him from the cockpit.

Royal nodded. "We did our best, sir."

Wilson pointed to the nose. "How many rounds have I got?"

Royal lifted him a thumbs-up. "Full up, sir!"

"Great. Thanks, Chief!"

Wilson's 19-year-old plane captain, Airman Hodges, helped attach the upper Koch fittings to Wilson's harness as Wilson finished strapping himself into the ejection seat. Conditioned not to ask questions of officers, especially of the Skipper, Hodges couldn't help himself.

"Sir, are we at war?"

"Maybe. We have reason to believe a vessel south of here attacked Lieutenant James in international waters. We aim to stop it and find out. Hodges, let's start this thing up *now*. We've gotta move."

"Yes, sir! Have a good flight, sir!"

Hodges descended the ladder and folded it into the LEX. Wilson caught the attention of a flight deck yellow shirt controller and shook two fingers, the hand signal to start. The yellow shirt nodded, and when Hodges reappeared, Wilson began the start sequence, the first jet on the bow to do so. The flight deck was a scene of confusion as sailors and aircrew darted among the bombs, fuel hoses, and electrical cables in an effort to get the jets started and airborne. *Now.*

With both engines online, Wilson lowered his canopy and continued turning on radios and navigation systems. On the angled deck and saw the SEALS loading in the two *Sierras*. Machine guns bristled from the sides of both aircraft, and one *Sierra* had a *Hellfire* missile attached. The ship was pounding south through the gentle swells at thirty knots to close the distance to the yacht. Wilson guessed, at launch, his quarry would be about 100 miles south. He could make that in roughly ten minutes.

The flight deck, under time pressure to get the aircraft airborne, was a scene of controlled confusion as the red-shirted ordnancemen and white-shirted troubleshooters jockeyed for position on their jets. Wilson smiled at the thought that the sandlot "football payers" he'd talked to a moment ago now sat in their jets with technicians around them as if involved in a NASCAR pit stop. The yellow shirts and blue shirts, impatient to get the jets off the bow, milled about near the aircraft as they were being prepared. The green-shirted cat crews were also impatient to move the jets off their catapults.

Wilson checked the winds. At high speed, the ship was generating its own wind right down the deck, and Wilson didn't think the ship would have to slow and turn to a launch heading. The weather was beautiful, as always, and offered ten miles visibility, gentle clouds floating about, scattered-variable-broken.

Once ready, Wilson signaled to Hodges, and the yellow shirt stepped up, signaling his blue-shirted apprentices to remove the wheel chocks and tie-down chains from 301. The yellow shirt now motioned 301 forward, inches from Olive's folded wing. Hodges saluted at attention with a dozen grimy tie-down chains over his shoulders, a salute Wilson returned with a smile. He tapped the brakes to check them, and continued forward, eyes locked on his young director.

On signal, Wilson turned to head aft between the two rows of screaming jets. On Cat 3, an E-2 was hooked up with launch bar down, waiting for the two *Sierras* to get airborne with their SEALS. A *Rhino* tanker was on Cat 4.

Wilson taxied past Billy and gave him a wave as he was handed off to another director. This one took him aft along the spinning rotor blades of the helos on the angle as sailors warily watched the clearance. Wilson glanced up at the island. Hundreds of sailors in the galleries were observing, and on the signal bridge he saw the signalmen break the FOXTROT flag from the yardarm. The Stars and Stripes snapped in the stiff wind above the 4.5 acres of sovereign U.S. territory.

The helos lifted one after the other and flew straight ahead on their long journey south. Wilson now passed mere feet from the spread wings of the E-2, still watching his assigned yellow shirt and monitoring all the activity around him. He noted Ripper in 310 waiting his turn on top of the one-wire. *Good.*

At full power, the *Hawkeye's* prop tips generated white condensation from the moist air before it lumbered down the angle and jumped into the air, cleaning up as it, too, headed south. The *Rhino* on Cat 4 then went into tension. As the pilot cycled the controls, the surfaces moved at full deflection, as if a bird were ruffling her feathers. Wilson saw the pilot salute as the catapult officer looked up and down the track, touched the deck, and pointed forward in a crouch. Seconds later, the thundering *Super Hornet* bolted forward as it accelerated down the track, attaining airspeed of 200 miles per hour in the length of a football field.

Wilson saw he would be the first "attack" bird to be shot on this event. As he was led to the catapult by a yellow shirt straddling the track, he noted Billy, Olive behind him, taxiing aft to the waist. Dozens of sailors in multicolored float coats moved about with their important tasks—or watched from the sidelines until they were needed. On signal, Wilson reached down and cranked the wingfold handle to the right to spread the wings for launch. As the wings spread, he was directed to lower the launch bar. Troubleshooters each took a side of the aircraft as they checked for loose panel fasteners and leaks. Wilson inched forward under the guidance of the yellow shirt and locked the wings in place.

"Three-zero-one, you are cleared for an immediate turn and climb," the Air Boss radioed from the tower above. Wilson rogered him and nodded, appreciating that someone had cued the Air Boss in on the plan. The ship was pretty much heading in the proper direction, and Wilson calculated a 10-degree right turn off the cat.

Wilson raised his hands above the canopy rail as Gunner Short's red shirts armed his gun and his one laser-guided bomb. Once arming was complete, he was directed forward until he felt tension on the holdback fitting that prevented him from moving forward. With no delay, the director extended his arms, and Wilson shoved the throttles to military power. With habits formed from hundreds of catapult shots, Wilson cycled the controls to full extension and checked the engine instruments and flight control computers. He then waited for the catapult officer to look at him. Once their eyes met, Wilson touched his helmet visor in salute and braced himself by grabbing the "towel rack" on the canopy bow. In anticipation of the shot, he locked his arms in place and waited.

His 44,000-pound airplane leapt forward and pinned him back in the seat under its sudden g. The *Hornet* whizzed by the blur of airplanes and sailors to his right as the deck edge rushed up. At the same time, he extended his left arm to full extension, shoving the throttles into burner to use every available second. Once airborne, the g subsided, and he was "thrown" forward in the straps as the jet rotated to a climb attitude.

Wilson grabbed the stick and glanced at the bow of the carrier as he roared past—nothing ready to launch—and followed the Air Boss' orders with a gentle roll to the right on course. Keeping the burner plugged in, he raised the gear and flaps in almost one motion. He got the radar going and energized the targeting FLIR, setting a shallow climb angle that would allow him to best accelerate and climb to his planned 25,000 feet. The others would follow him as fast as they could in a single-file chase.

In no time, Wilson was passing 300 knots, then 400, as he began to weave between the cumulus buildups. To his left, a few miles ahead, he saw the E-2 in its slow climb to altitude, Then, on the surface, he saw the two helos heading for the contact yacht, a flight that would take them about 45 minutes. He checked his computed navigation to the expected latitude/longitude of the yacht. He had eight minutes to go and was accelerating past 500 knots.

With Colombian territorial waters on the horizon, the margin to intercept the yacht was small.

CHAPTER 33

Wilson's radar cursor bounced back and forth across his right Digital Data Indicator screen. He saw over a dozen surface "blips" he had to inspect, one by one.

He began his inspection with the radar returns at the bottom of his display and slewed the Throttle Designator Controller over each. With his thumb, he bumped the "castle switch" to the right to lock the raw return, and, within seconds, his FLIR seeker head slewed to align with the radar target. The IR images on his left screen allowed him to reject a LNG merchant tanker or a fat fishing boat and move on to the next unknown contact. With his altitude in the high teens now, he held a near supersonic airspeed in his shallow climb as he continued to inspect each synthetic blip on his screen.

Wilson was impatient. Holding too much airspeed, he was in danger of running past a contact before he could identify it or of stumbling across the yacht—with its suspected blinding laser—before he was ready. This close to the continent there was a lot of surface traffic for the yacht to "hide" among as it fled to the "safety" of territorial waters. The E-2 could help, and Wilson energized his data link and called the *Hummer* on the briefed frequency.

"*Condor, Ridgeline* three-zero-one's up for tasking. Any luck with *Lauderdale?*"

"Negative, *Ridgeline,* still trying to sort all the traffic. We have *Mike One Juliet,*" the E-2 controller said, referring to the guided missile destroyer *Norman Kleiss,* "about fifty miles east of you with a *Fire Scout* airborne."

Ripper then checked in with *Condor,* followed a minute later by Billy Martin. Now, the E-2 had some assets to work with as it built the surface picture south of *Coral Sea.* Wilson feared the yacht could have doubled back or changed course toward the west and Panama; therefore, each contact would have to be identified.

But in Wilson's gut the yacht was still heading south and closing Colombian territorial waters. He and the others had to get down there to shut the door, leaving the jets behind them to sweep up unknowns from the north in order to positively identify all the traffic.

"*Condor*, three-zero-one is going to buster down close to Waterloo. Will ID what I can en route."

"Roger, three-zero-one. Fly your pointer to first skunk."

The E-2 sent data-link commands to Wilson's navigation computer that provided him steering cues to an unknown surface contact. Wilson saw a contact close to the steering cue and locked it with the TDC. The FLIR image revealed the heat signature of a coastal merchant ship heading east at ten knots.

"*Condor*, your contact is a merchant. We think our guy is booking it south at twenty-five for the coast."

"Roger, *Ridgeline. We*'ve got lots of traffic in your vicinity, but we'll concentrate on the skunks heading south."

While Ripper and Billy received instructions from *Condor*, Wilson continued south just under the supersonic "number." His radar now showed him fewer than 60 miles from the coast, with the buildups increasing in size and number as he neared the South American landmass. Thirty miles to the west was a lone thunderstorm topping around 40,000 feet, and to the southwest a line of cells was approaching Barranquilla. Believing, through experience, that "a peek is worth 1,000 scans," Wilson peered over his left LEX at the water four miles below. In the shadow of a little squall cloud, he saw something light on the water. He pulled power and slewed his radar way down to the surface and locked the object. Once the FLIR matched his radar, he studied the image. Sleek, with raked lines, the vessel was motoring south. Wilson determined this could be the yacht, but it appeared to be in no hurry.

A few miles to the east, he spied another coastal merchant, and to the south and west he observed other small boats. No matter what happened now, the Americans would have company.

"*Condor*, three-zero-one is marking on top of what could be *Lauderdale*. I'm going to stay high above. Can you send the UAV to look?"

"Roger, *Ridgeline*. Will be a few minutes."

Wilson acknowledged the transmission and scanned the surface for the *Fire Scout*. He took care to remain high above the contact, which, by the wake, seemed to have picked up speed. The clouds concealed the vessel, at times but Wilson knew it couldn't get away from him. The UAV would fly close aboard to do what Wilson and the other pilots wanted to avoid—risking their eyes to identify it.

When Olive showed up, Wilson directed her to take an altitude above him and help keep eyes on the contact. Now transiting south at fifteen knots, the contact was headed for another squall. Olive's *Hornet* was loaded with two bombs and, like Wilson, had a full load of bullets. They were inside fifty miles from the coast—an unexpected cushion from Colombian territorial waters, even if the suspected yacht kicked it up to full speed. They had breathing room for the moment, but Wilson knew he would have to return to the ship for fuel within an hour.

He saw the *Fire Scout* approach from the east and reported he had a visual on it. Three miles from the contact, the little unmanned helicopter bore down on it unafraid, taking pictures and gaining what intel it could. Wilson didn't know if the UAV was armed or not, and thought of the *Sierras* and the SEALS who were about thirty minutes behind.

The contact slowed as it entered the squall—an innocent enough maneuver for any pleasure craft entering bad weather—but Wilson sensed they knew they were being watched and knew the rain squall could offer some concealment from the American aircraft. *That sure looks like the yacht from Trench's FLIR tape*, thought Wilson. He was reminded of a small rodent hiding in a crevice from birds of prey overhead.

With the *skunk* on the outskirts of the rain band, the *Fire Scout* continued toward it at high speed. From overhead, Wilson watched the aircraft veer left to circle the vessel, but the movement seemed strange. The *Fire Scout* then appeared to tumble, and with a big splash it fell into the sea.

"*Condor*, the *Fire Scout* just crashed about a mile abeam the skunk!" Wilson transmitted. He then called to his wingman on his Comm 2 radio. "Olive, you see that?"

"Affirm, and I may have it on my FLIR tape," she answered.

"Roger."

After a few minutes, the E-2 came up with a dire message to the Air Wing SIX aircraft circling above. "Ninety-nine *Broadsword*, we believe the UAV was downed by a *lightshow*."

The contact, the last indication of innocence now gone, was not moving. It was in the middle of the rain squall that was drifting southeast, and the thunderstorm was nearing: two weather developments that would help the vessel hide from American eyes and weapon sensors. Because Wilson and the others didn't have unlimited fuel, time seemed to be on the side of the contact.

Wilson *knew* this contact was the yacht that had blinded Trench. It had also just shot down the UAV before his own eyes. Sure, the lawyers could point to circumstantial evidence, but with the *Sierras* inbound and as the senior on scene, he needed to make a call.

"*Condor*, this is *Broadsword* lead in three-oh-one. Declare the *Lauderdale* I'm marking on top of."

Wilson and the other air wing aircraft waited for a reply. The tactical coordinators in the E-2 had access to secure communications with several tactical intelligence and signals reconnaissance sources in the region. Wilson knew it could be a while before they came back with an answer. Now joined by Ripper and Billy Martin's *Rhinos,* he and Olive circled overhead, and Wilson directed traffic by assigning deconfliction altitudes.

The yacht remained in the relative safety of the squall, rain still beating on it, as the carrier aircraft remained overhead. As they waited for an answer from E-2, the pilots watched both their fuel and the thunderstorm bearing down on all of them.

The storm was now five miles away and pushing the squall ahead of it to the safety of territorial waters, but before that happened it would envelop the squall and yacht, escorting it in a cloak of rain and lightning. The *Sierras* were five minutes out. Wilson needed an answer, now.

"*Condor, Broadsword* lead. What's the story?"

"*Broadsword, Condor.* Stand by."

"No time, *Condor*. You've got sixty seconds to give me an answer. *Lauderdale* is going to escape."

Wilson was now at 16,000 feet, with the other jets stacked above him, and, through the buildups, noted the *Sierras* coming from the north. He called to them.

"*Rustlers, Ridgeline* three-zero-one is on-scene commander. Hold your position there until we straighten things out here. We've got the contact of interest in a squall, and we're getting direction from above."

"Roger, sir. We've been monitoring. Standing off."

With the helos holding away from danger, Wilson knew the yacht now had plenty of time to recharge their laser to blind or to shoot down any aircraft that approached. Fuel was dwindling, and the thunderstorm bore down on them with no let up, blocking out the sun. As Wilson circled in its midafternoon shadows, he formed a plan.

"*Broadsword* lead, *Condor*."

"Go," Wilson replied.

"Your contact is declared *hostile*."

Wilson rogered and put his plan into action.

"Olive, take trail on me. Ripper, Billy, you guys hold high. You have me, Olive?"

"*Affirm!*"

"Follow me down."

Wilson overbanked and traded his thousands of feet in altitude for airspeed as he accelerated toward the water and *away* from the yacht. With the yacht still under the squall, Wilson's line of sight was obscured by the clouds, but he planned to disable the yacht so the SEALs could take it down. He would come in low and fast and "throw" his bomb into the crevice between the sea and cloud bottom, aiming for a position just aft of the fantail—a mobility kill. He radioed his wingman.

"Olive, take some offset, and, after my run, spray them with bullets. Don't press it, and keep your knots up."

"Roger," Olive answered.

"Billy, lead your guys behind us and set up a strafe wagon wheel to keep their heads down while we escort the *Rustlers*. Ripper, remain high cover."

You go down and out. You go long. All rogered the impromptu plan as they armed up and took position. *Showtime.*

Now near the water and five miles from the yacht, Wilson reversed his turn and descended down to the surface at military power. As he held the tight turn, straining under the five g pressure, he struggled to crane his head out of the top of the canopy to keep sight. He saw the silhouette of the yacht in the gloom as he brought it to his nose and leveled off just above the waves. Station selected. Fusing set. FLIR – ON. LASER – ARMED. MASTER ARM – ARM.

Wilson sweetened the radar cursors and locked his target as he approached from the northeast. Again entering the shadow of the storm, he thought about how tracking an unmanned helicopter was one thing, but how doing the same with a transonic fighter moving in three dimensions was something else. So far, his ability to maneuver hard had posed a problem for the yacht, but the yacht had advantages. Wilson needed to lob the weapon in there, hold his FLIR on the aiming point, and fly his jet close to the water. If he pressed it too close…well, who knew what the laser was capable of?

Wilson took a glance behind at Olive about a mile on his four o'clock. *Good.* At his planned distance, he yanked the jet up and right. Fearful of looking at the business end of a laser, he watched the picture build on his FLIR and flew the jet "on instruments." He pulled back into the yacht as he leveled off his climb, needing to stay underneath the cloud ceiling. He then watched the computer symbology give him steering indications and weapons release parameters on a delivery he had just dreamed up. He had never practiced anything close to it.

With the yacht obscured by his nose, Wilson held his heading for a bit. He wanted to take a look at the vessel, but at the same time appreciated the momentary "cover" the fuselage gave him. However, the *Fire Scout* was shot down by what the research guys called a laser cannon, and Wilson knew he could be in their sights right now.

He mashed the pickle down as he lofted the weapon toward the computed solution on his Head Up Display. Once he felt it come off, Wilson overbanked left and pulled across the horizon, watching the time to impact and keeping the aiming diamond on the fantail of the yacht. The twelve seconds after he pulled power to stay in position were an eternity. Fighting every urge to *get the hell out of there,* he held the aiming diamond and monitored his altitude over the water, making sure he didn't get too low to spoil the computed weapons solution. He seemed to be flying in front of the yacht as the laser weapon guided, by spastic movements of the attached wing control surfaces, to its aim point. With three seconds to go, Wilson noted on his FLIR display a sudden light from amidships the yacht. Even "protected," with his belly up to the threat, Wilson couldn't tell if his jet was being burned right now.

Two seconds....

C'mon, dammit!

One second....

Once the weapon flew into the FLIR field of view and exploded near the yacht, Wilson overbanked again and pulled hard away from it. "Olive, they may have a *lightpost.* Just spray them and get out!"

"Two's popping," Olive called as she pulled her jet up and away from the water. Wilson watched her over his left shoulder as he leveled off and sped to rendezvous with the *Rustler* MH-60s. He watched Olive spray the vessel with a long burst from her 20mm cannon before she jinked away, safe.

Billy then called. "*Ridgeline* lead, nice hit! Looked like twenty feet off the fantail. He appears to be circling. Not sure he's in control. And nice strafing, wingman. *Arrows* take interval. Lead's turning in."

Wilson watched Billy lead his jets into a makeshift strafing "pattern" as he, with Olive following, made for the two *Sierras* holding north of them. Fuel, always an issue, was becoming a real factor. They had to get the SEALs aboard—and off—ASAP.

After Billy and his wingmen made one strafing run each, the vessel was dead in the water. Wilson and Olive escorted the helos in, directing the *Arrows* to hold clear. The yacht wallowed in the seas as Wilson called to the lead helicopter.

"*Rustler* from *Ridgeline*, looks like it's neutralized. I think they tried to laze me from amidships."

"Roger, *Ridgeline*, we're locked and loaded. Going to put a *rifle* into them before we insert. Stand by."

"Roger that," Wilson replied. Circling a few thousand feet overhead, he watched the helos approach the yacht, which was now smoking from the fantail. Without warning, a missile shot forward from the lead *Sierra*, and Wilson watched a yellow flame trailing white smoke streak to the yacht. Seconds later, a small explosion occurred on the yacht's amidships superstructure.

The helos bored in, and Wilson thought they would overshoot the yacht before the lead pilot stood his aircraft on its tail as the wingman circled the damaged vessel. Wilson then observed the number two helo pump some machine gun rounds into it before the lead aircraft hovered over the bow to fast rope SEALs onto the smoking hull. The yacht didn't appear to be fighting back.

The operation was now to capture survivors, collect intelligence, and put the derelict on the bottom. Wilson was surprised how fast things had moved since he had first learned of Trench's blindness. While he was certain this had to be the vessel that had lased Trench and shot down the *Fire Scout*, unease gnawed at him.

The first helo flew away and assumed cover as the second one approached the bow with its load of SEALs. Wilson could see sporadic fire from the door gunners of both aircraft. The yacht picked up a list to port as white smoke continued to pour from the fantail. The white hull, as pockmarked with gunfire as it was, gleamed in the sunshine as the squall moved off. The thunderstorm was close at hand—they had to move fast.

The first helicopter returned and hovered over the bow. Wilson watched as it hoisted objects—probably people—inside. It took several minutes to complete, and the radio was full of pilot chatter about the approaching thunderstorm. On the southern horizon Wilson saw a ship, a merchant. He directed Ripper to stay high and check it out.

Wilson watched in fascination as the yacht rolled on its side. The helo crews screamed directions to one another on the radio as the thunderstorm moved over them. The aircraft cleared, and Wilson—suspecting there were SEALs still aboard—was horrified as the yacht's fantail sank lower and lower into the turbulent water kicked up by the storm. Helpless, he saw figures on the upturned hull as the rain beat down on them and lightning flashed here and there. All the aircraft had to move away, and Wilson's *Hornets*, lowest on fuel, had to return to the ship. Billy assumed on-scene commander as the helos waited for the storm to pass.

As Wilson and his wingmen climbed back through the buildups toward home, Wilson reflected on what had just happened. Unsure about whether or not the SEALs had suffered losses, or if they'd had time to collect evidence, he knew the United States had crossed a line. The yacht matched Trench's FLIR tape, Wilson had seen it shoot down the UAV, and *Condor* had declared it hostile. Still, it bothered him...and the same two questions ran over and over through his head. *What just happened? What is my role in it?*

Witnesses. With all the vessels around, he knew this could be world news by the time he returned to the ready room. He snapped out of it and concentrated on the return home, only sixty miles away, and obtained fuel states from his wingmen via hand signals.

Wilson called the ship with a mission report.... He figured the admiral and CAG were listening real time to their operations. He then checked in with Marshal for landing instructions.

The controller acknowledged radar contact as Wilson and his low-fuel wingmen maneuvered to enter the low holding pattern overhead the carrier. With a free moment, he couldn't bear to wait for the end of the story and called Billy on his tactical frequency.

"Billy, Flip. What's the latest?'

"The yacht just went to Davey Jones' locker. *Rustlers* are still here picking up survivors. Hope our buddies made it. They got two captives— male and female."

Sunk. Wilson thought about the implications. The potential loss of the SEALs aboard was primary, followed by the loss of actionable intel and exploitation of the laser. He wondered if the bad guys scuttled it on purpose or if the hull took too many holes from a combination of bombs, missiles, rockets and .50 cal fire. And two captives.... Wilson wondered if the woman was one Trench saw, but she was there with bad guys who had gone down with the ship. *They are probably already dead.*

Wilson lowered his tailhook. The others followed suit and prepared their cockpits for the recovery. Hidden by the buildups, he locked *Coral Sea* on radar and noted her still heading south toward them. He took an offset heading to avoid launch traffic and continued his easy descent to

3,000 feet. He, like CAG and the admiral, would have to wait for the repercussions—and the cost—of this quick-reaction strike.

CHAPTER 34

(USS *Coral Sea*, Central Caribbean)

Rear Admiral Roland Meyerkopf had never seen anything like this in his career.

Submariners lived in a world of rigid procedure and strict accountability, and he did not know how to react to the aviators aboard *Coral Sea*. They were *making weapon release decisions* on the spot and then justifying their actions. CENTURY RATCHET be damned! *He* was the strike group admiral and had not been consulted before *his jets* attacked the helpless yacht. That his staff and the frickin' CENTURY RATCHET assholes devised rules of engagement with positive identification conditions that were met didn't mean that the flyboys could just go ahead without him. Or did it? This was a new Navy, one he little understood. As Ed Browne tried to calm him down for the second time in one day, Meyerkopf wished for the "comfort zone" of a submarine control room.

"Admiral, when the ROE were met and the yacht positively identified through several network inputs, *your* strike lead, Commander Wilson, acted on *your* behalf to disable the vessel and effect conditions for our SEALs to board it. The druggies scuttled it, but we got some intel and two captives."

"We are damn lucky the SEALs survived," Meyerkopf shot back.

"We are, sir. They chalk it up to another day at the office, but they got photos of the laser and the laptop and other stuff. We are putting them in for medals. Commander Hofmeister and his team will interrogate the captives, and we'll send all we collected off ship for analysis."

"Get me on the phone with General McGovern at JIATF South."

"Yes, sir."

"Head us north toward GITMO at a 20-knot speed of advance. I want to get out of these waters and get the captives off the ship by tomorrow."

"Aye, aye, sir."

"Then get Matson and Sanders in here. When I finish with Jimmy McGovern, I want them waiting for me."

"Yes, sir."

"Then I want to have a one-on-one with you." Meyerkopf held Browne's gaze to convey that it was not going to be a friendly chat.

"Aye, aye, sir."

Commander Hofmeister led Shane down four ladders to the mess decks where they proceeded forward to medical. The ship's Master at Arms had secured the portside passageway so foot traffic could not pass by the entrance to sick bay. When Hofmeister identified himself and his business, the petty officer nodded to allow them to pass, after giving Hofmeister and Shane a skeptical if not contemptuous look. Ignoring the disrespect for the time being, Hofmeister brushed past, and the Ensign followed. They entered sick bay and were met by a chief who led them to the secured area where the male captive was being held. In critical but stable condition, the man's right arm was missing below the elbow.

Hofmeister and Shane entered with an armed escort. The captive, about thirty, was strapped down on his back on the hospital bed, his dark hair matted with dried perspiration. His dark, hostile eyes followed the officers as they stepped to the foot of his bed. Hofmeister pulled a cigarette from his pocket and motioned toward the captive. The man looked back at him, confused, then understood and nodded. The chief objected, "Sir, we don't allow smoking—"

Cutting her off, Hofmeister answered, "I have a waiver from Captain Sanders. Will that suffice?"

"Yes, sir," the chagrined chief replied.

Hofmeister handed the cigarette to the captive. He took it without a word, staring him down with contempt, his hate-filled eyes conveying more ill will than his broken body. Shane thought she was looking at the face of evil. Hofmeister then produced a lighter and held the flame so the captive could light the cigarette. The MAA moved closer, ready in case the captive were to grab Hofmeister's arm.

The man took a puff and seemed to relax. Hofmeister began.

"*Como esta usted, señor. Que es su nombre?*"

The captive stared back with cold eyes.

"Please forgive my grade-school Spanish," Hofmeister continued. "And how presumptuous of me... Please, what is your name?"

The captive took a puff and said nothing.

"You are not in uniform. You refuse to give your name. And you make war against the United States. Would you care to visit Guantanamo Bay? Because that is where you are going, *mi amigo*. Or, you can answer my questions, and we can turn you over to the Coast Guard who is equipped to deal with law enforcement problems like you. A little criminal smuggling? Or illegal combatant status? It's up to you, señor. A short jail stay in Miami, or years and *years* at GITMO with the jihadists. You decide. Now, what is your name?"

The captive looked at Hofmeister, and then turned away, mumbling.

"*Que?*" Hofmeister prodded.

The captive mumbled something again, and Hofmeister leaned in.

With no warning, the captive lunged and spit at Hofmeister who, without hesitation, slugged him across the jaw and swatted the cigarette from his hand. The guard punched the captive's rib cage, and he screamed in pain, cursing them in Spanish.

Wiping his face, Hofmeister nodded. "Very well. GITMO it is. Chief, until further notice, bread and water for this one."

With her aircraft aboard, *Coral Sea* sped north toward GITMO some 500 miles away and to distance itself from the South American landmass. While surface traffic was prevalent in all parts of the Caribbean, it tended to cling to coastal waters and funneled into and out of the approach to the canal. Meyerkopf wanted to get away from the scene of his greatest humiliation. *In the dark!* He still couldn't believe it, and, after speaking with higher authority, he would have a one-way conversation with his warfare commanders.

Meanwhile, thousands of miles to the northeast, a single Russian Tu-95 *Bear* bomber transited high along the eastern seaboard of the United States under the watchful eyes of the North American Air Defense Command. First tracked by the Canadians, the aircraft was handed off to the Northeast Air Defense sector who decided to scramble two Air National Guard F-15C's standing Air Sovereignty Alert at Otis, Air Force Base in Massachusetts.

The *Eagles* intercepted the ancient propeller-driven bomber at 150 miles east of Cape Cod and escorted it as it passed down the coast, the Russian maintaining 20 miles offshore as it cruised at 27,000 feet. *Bears* were known intelligence collectors, and, while not a direct threat, transits like these were not routine and had NORAD's full attention. Despite the high alert level at headquarters, threat levels were low—this was Russia reminding the Americans not to ignore them. Alert fighters were scrambled from Atlantic City, Langley, and Jacksonville as the *Bear* lumbered down the continental shelf on a crystal blue day.

Further north, Canadian controllers were shocked when they picked up two contacts that seemed to pop out of the North Atlantic hundreds of miles northeast of Newfoundland. With flight profiles much faster than the slow *Bear*, these returns were not squawking an International Friend or Foe code, an action which went against accepted aeronautical convention. Nervous about the identity and purpose of these raw radar contacts, Canada scrambled two CF-18 *Hornet* fighters to rendezvous on the bogeys that were closing North America at a transonic rate of speed. When the excited Canadian fighter pilots intercepted the contacts and identified them as *four* Tu-22M *Backfire* bombers in two flights of two separated by fifty miles, the NORTHCOM Commander informed the Secretary of Defense who at once called the President. In like manner, his Canadian counterpart contacted the Prime Minister of Canada. The fact that these supersonic bombers had "popped out" of the ocean indicated they had flown hundreds of miles from of their Murmansk base and around the North Cape and into the Atlantic at low altitude. This had necessitated a rendezvous with in-flight refueling aircraft south of Iceland, topping off down low, and then climbing to cruise altitude, a varsity military demonstration of capability not seen in years. No one on watch up to four stars had memories of anything like it, and, with the groups separated as they were, every alert fighter on the eastern seaboard was pressed into service. AWACS scrambled to help meet the command and control challenge.

It was into this national security emergency that Roland Meyerkopf placed his call to the Commander, Joint Inter-Agency Task Force SOUTH.

Ed Browne dialed the headquarters of JIATF SOUTH in Key West, and, once placed on hold and according to protocol, handed the receiver to Meyerkopf. "We're on hold, sir."

Meyerkopf took the receiver and held it to his ear as Browne picked up the extension and covered the phone with his hand. After two minutes, Marine General Jim McGovern picked up.

"Roland, Jim McGovern."

"Good afternoon, General, Com Strike Group Eighteen checking in. We've had some activity down here."

"Same here. What are you doing?"

"Sir, earlier today one of my pilots was identifying a surface contact south of us, a pleasure yacht as it turns out, and just as he flew past it, he was blinded. I'm still amazed the aviators got him aboard, but somehow they did. Our docs are checking him out, but it looks serious."

"Go on."

"On the advice of my air wing commander and chief of staff, we threw on a quick reaction strike and identified the vessel as hostile. When intel sensors said it met the ROE, we disabled it for boarding."

"Disabled it?"

"Yes, sir, one of my *Hornets* bombed it, and SEALs boarded it via fast rope. They had to shoot it up pretty bad to make it safe, and we believe the crew of the yacht scuttled it and went down with it."

"Holy shit. *You bombed a fucking yacht?* How big was it?"

"About 100 feet, sir. I've seen video of it."

"Get that to me ASAP." Meyerkopf glanced at Browne, who nodded back at him.

"When did this happen?" McGovern's irritation and impatience were evident in his voice.

"About two hours ago, sir…"

"*Two hours!* When was your pilot blinded?"

Meyerkopf was back on his heels. "Late this morning, sir."

McGovern let out an audible sigh for effect. "Could you not have picked up the phone? Roland, I need to know shit like this when it happens."

"My apologies, General. Things moved fast, and—"

"Fine. Where are you now?"

"We're in the central Caribbean, sir, about 150 miles north of Colombia and 300 southwest of Jamaica."

"What are you doing down there?"

"We're heading to GITMO to MEDEVAC my pilot and deliver the captives."

"*You have captives?* Who are these guys? Druggies? Please tell me they are druggies."

"We think they are, sir, and we have some evidence that should reap an intel bonanza. My people are on it now."

"Okay. Now from the top, I forget.... What are you doing down there?"

"We are doing air wing training with the Colombians, showing the flag, identifying surface contacts and doing lots of damage control drills to identify problems. The ship needs some work." Meyerkopf was unsure if McGovern was familiar with CENTURY RATCHET and, even on a secure line, was afraid to broach the subject. He kept his eyes on Browne as he spoke.

"Okay, and your pilot was out minding his own business and was blinded when he flew by a yacht. A laser?"

"We think so, sir, and one of the pilots reported what could have been a laser during the strike."

"Okay. Captives... Tell me about them."

"One bad guy, critically injured. Lost his arm in the firefight. And a girl. We think she's a prostitute."

"Are you interrogating them?"

"Yes, sir, and tomorrow we plan to fly them off to GITMO. We're running hard and should be there by sunup."

"Okay, speaking of GITMO, the Cubans are mobilizing forces on the western and northern fence lines. At the same time, the fucking Russians are flying *Bears* and *Backfires* down the east coast, and we don't know if they're heading for Havana or Caracas. We're spinning up the Marines to defend GITMO. NORTHCOM and SOUTHCOM are going ape shit, and the Dutch are reporting a hostile gang threatening their frigate tied to the pier in Aruba. The bubble may be going up down here."

"Yes, sir, we'll be on station off GITMO in twelve hours. I need to refuel though—"

McGovern cut him off. "Roland, these *Backfires* took off from Murmansk. They are ship killers with frickin' Kh-22 missiles. They are a threat to *you,* and I want you in the open until we figure this shit out. Stay put for now. Do you have a submarine?"

"Yes, sir. Actually, he's under the direct control of SOUTHCOM at the moment, intel collection."

Meyerkopf heard another sigh as McGovern answered. "So you *don't* have a submarine. I'm going to contact SOUTHCOM and place him in a window to launch TLAMs into Venezuela if we need it. We think they're involved in this, and we're watching to see where the Russians land."

"My staff can help with that, sir."

"Good, we may need you."

Meyerkopf changed the subject. "General, I do need to refuel if we are spinning up, and my oiler is over 200 miles away. I won't be ready to go until morning unless we can close GITMO and rendezvous earlier with him." Meyerkopf waited several seconds for an answer.

"Yes, by all means, *refuel your ships*, Admiral. *Make it happen*, but stay out of sight and out of range. Fly the damn captives to GITMO. We have our *best people* there. And make sure *your* people are connected at the hip with mine. SOUTHCOM is going to grab hold of you real soon, so stand the fuck by and monitor what NORTHCOM is doing with these bombers. Report to me when you are ready for tasking. Out here."

Meyerkopf cradled the receiver, unable to look at Browne. Both men were embarrassed, conscious of the fact the curt and sarcastic responses from McGovern had been just this side of a dressing down. Meyerkopf had absorbed worse in his career and reflected that he, himself, had delivered worse over the years. He would hold back on the salvo he was preparing for his people.

"Okay… First, find a spot for us to refuel that meets JIATF SOUTH's requirements, and get the oiler down here at flank speed. Get that to Ops and the bridge ASAP. Job One."

"Yes, sir."

"Matson and Sanders, and you, in the war room. Twenty minutes."

"Aye, aye, sir."

CHAPTER 34

(USS *Coral Sea*, Central Caribbean)

Coral Sea rose and fell in the gentle swells of the dark Caribbean. Ninety feet to her right, the oiler USNS *Patuxent* maintained steady course and a speed of 15 knots as she refueled *Coral Sea's* aviation fuel bunkers from two large, black hoses. Alongside since midnight, the ships had been linked together for over two hours, and had at least two more to go. On the other side of *Patuxent,* the guided missile cruiser *Gettysburg* also took on fuel for her marine gas turbine engines. The bridge teams made one-half degree course corrections and added and reduced revolutions of their screws to maintain position on the oiler, over 150,000 tons of ship "flying formation" on each other on an easterly heading.

While Captain Sanders monitored his conning officers from the carrier's auxiliary conning station on the starboard side of the bridge, watch team members in NORTHCOM and SOUTHCOM, due to the previous day's activities, were watching the Atlantic Ocean with heightened interest. The *Bear* was a pathfinder and signals intelligence collector for the four *Backfires* that flew close along the U.S. coast before they split up near the Bahamas. Washington was stunned by the complexity of the operation and admired its execution. That the Russians had avoided detection through the Greenland-Iceland-UK gap was impressive, but refueling the big bombers down low in the North Atlantic clag, using the probe and drogue method, was even more so. In a coordinated manner, they had climbed to 38,000 feet, blasting right through the middle of the trans-Atlantic air corridor as they transited southwest along North America. Canadian and American interceptors, having to maintain escort on two groups, had had their hands full all day rendezvousing with the intruders and handing them off from sector to sector.

Near Andros Island, the trailing bombers had diverted to Havana, and the Florida Air Guard F-15's had stayed with them almost to the 12-mile limit of Cuba. The lead *Backfires* were met by another tanker. This one launched out of Havana but cancelled in air, despite its filed flight plan to

Moscow, to rendezvous with the thirsty Tu-22M's. The tanker dragged them along the Bahamas chain before ducking through the Mona Passage and into the Caribbean. All three aircraft then landed in Caracas. The whole operation was an impressive display of planning and execution. It seemed as if the Russians had kicked over an ant hill, and the Americans were left to scurry about in their attempts to figure out how to react.

Not long after Meyerkopf and McGovern ended their conversation, Venezuelan secret police ambushed the American *Chargé d'Affaires* on his way home from the embassy. They held him and his personal security force overnight and charged him with espionage. For the benefit of the cameras, the secret police dressed all of them in striped prison jumpsuits, and the humiliating affront to American sovereignty and honor made world news. If Daniel Garcia and the cartels had wanted to draw American forces off the sea and air drug trade, and to call attention, instead, to American movements in the region, they had succeeded.

Unrelated to the Russian bomber flights and the diplomatic kerfuffle, the assembly of two Cuban Army brigades on the perimeter of Guantanamo drew SOUTHCOM's full attention. This barren and arid outpost, only 32 square miles on Cuba's southeastern coast, was home to the infamous illegal combatant detention facility. The outpost was a valuable logistics hub with its deep-water harbor and airstrip. Compared to Cuban troops massing along GITMO, the State Department's concern in Venezuela was a sideshow. A battalion of Marines, who were outnumbered in this situation, defended GITMO, and SOUTHCOM asked for a Special Marine Air Ground Task Force to help. The Fleet Marine Force Atlantic and the Navy began, in haste, to assemble the task force.

A night owl by nature, Meyerkopf was too keyed up to sleep and stood in the dark on his flag bridge as he observed the replenishment ships. He knew he hadn't been at his best with McGovern that afternoon, but reading the message traffic about the Russian and Cuban activities filled him with excitement. Washington had to be asking where the nearest carrier was, and he knew the answer: *Coral Sea,* with *Roland Meyerkopf* commanding the strike group.

America's backyard, the Caribbean, was heating up, and SOUTHCOM, that sleepy backwater in Miami where guys went to retire, was running the show. He wondered if General Freeman's staff could handle this. It had been *years* since SOUTHCOM had had a carrier to play with down here. Would they know what they were doing?

In contrast, Meyerkopf's strike group was a frontline force, combat experienced from months in the Middle East. No doubt, they would receive rudder orders from Washington and Admiral Peterson at Fleet

Forces. Except for the GITMO operations, this theater was an air/sea theater, and right now Meyerkopf was the only game in town.

The sodium vapor lights on the island bathed the flight deck in an eerie yellow glow, and red lights on *Patuxent* and *Gettysburg* next to her provided her night-adapted crews with enough illumination to work. On the horizon he saw the white lights of some shipping vessels, and starlight revealed cumulus clouds floating above them. All of this was new to Meyerkopf, and he admitted to himself that, because it wasn't second nature, McGovern had him at a disadvantage—and McGovern was a Marine infantryman by trade!

Meyerkopf saw the jumble of aircraft scattered about the deck and wished he had taken Tim Matson up on an opportunity to fly in a *Super Hornet*, just to gain some semblance of credibility. Deep down he knew why he had declined the offer—he would get airsick and make a fool of himself. Here he was, an *admiral*, the *commander* of an eight-ship strike group of 10,000 men. *And aboard this carrier the pilots—junior officers!—could get away with making fun of you—in public!*

Despite the close-knit nature of life on an attack boat under the waves, this just didn't happen in the submarine community, and it did not sit well with Meyerkopf. Alone on the bridge, he watched the ships transfer fuel, as if tied at the hip, while helicopters transferred pallets of dry goods, food and all manner of other consumable supplies. While he could understand and appreciate it, he had no career background in maneuvering such large vessels in close proximity. The nuclear plant—he could be at home *there*, but all of this topside activity was new and unfamiliar. And on his dim flag bridge—which served more as an ego-building penthouse view for embarked admirals than as a war-fighting vantage point—he didn't have so much as a radar repeater to gain any tactical situational awareness.

He regretted he'd been so hard on Ed Browne, Sanders and Matson after he'd finished with McGovern. *But, dammit, they were holding out on me.* They could have petitioned to bring him, their boss, in on CENTURY RATCHET. *Another aviator thing. The frickin' boss is kept in the dark?* As a submariner he'd been read-in on dozens of classified programs. *But on this one, I was excluded?* By McGovern? Peterson? It was all upside down. Regardless, his subordinates had gotten the message.

Aviators. He still didn't know what made them tick. The unprofessional familiarity up and down the chain, the routine mocking of seniors, the silly nicknames they had for each other, the questionable been-there-done-that patches on their flight jackets that served as extensions of their titanic egos. Meyerkopf had been-there-done-that, too—hiding under the polar icecap, reconnoitering a hostile patch of water, prosecuting a contact in a deadly game of cat and mouse hundreds of feet below the surface—and not an individual medal to show for it. His was The Silent Service; theirs the pop culture of movies, fraternal newsletter magazines, and *look-at-meee* You Tube videos of themselves. *For crying out loud, Sanders has elevated dosimeter readings in his reactor compartment!* While within limits, the readings did not seem to alarm him in the least. And now Washington was going to push *Coral Sea* to the limit, and Meyerkopf had to depend on *these guys* to get the job done. Shoot first then ask for forgiveness? He wasn't going to stand for it.

He resumed watching the ships alongside as they rose and fell in formation, transferring gallon after thousands of gallons of fuel through the big hoses. The helicopter continued its graceful hummingbird back and forth between the ships, picking up and dropping off pallets in practiced routine, all of it unfamiliar to him. He realized at zero-three-hundred he needed to be asleep. Sanders could handle this.

Meyerkopf stepped inside his sea cabin and closed the door, lying down on his rack with his uniform on to catch a few hours sleep. As the CO of an attack boat, he had done the same for many years, sleeping mere feet from the control room, ready to spring into action.

CHAPTER 35

The following morning, a Saturday, Chief of Naval Operations Mike Dwyer was at his standup desk wearing shorts and a golf shirt. Up since before 5am, he had worked out at his Navy Yard home before driving himself to the office where his Executive Assistant and aide—a Navy Captain and lieutenant respectively—were ready with a folder of paperwork for him to review and sign off.

It never ended. They could be on overseas travel in an airplane in the middle of the night, and the flag lieutenant would have a folder of paperwork for him. Not that Dwyer minded. He *demanded* it, and tried—in vain, most of the time—to keep up with it. The wrap-up last night had gone late, to almost 7:30, but he and his wife had arrived in time for the Fleet Reserve Association dinner at the Army Navy Country Club which he had graced as guest speaker.

Today, after the Navy League charity golf tournament, he had the forced-fun reception at SECDEF's house. He would be stag because his wife couldn't stand to be around the host couple. He cursed the fact he had promised his retired friend at the Navy League he would be there to support the tourney. All the defense prime contractor reps would be there, pawing at him for "just a few minutes" to tout their latest widget for only one billion dollars, tops, total lifecycle costs, no hidden "tail," you can trust me on this one, and *I love you no shit.*

Mike Dwyer didn't have a spare *million* to rub together, and *all* his weapons acquisition programs were over budget and on sustainment rations. And, now, with SOUTHCOM heating up, he needed to answer *that* demand signal—which would only chew up *more* service life from his tired airplanes and ships. Not to mention his overworked fleet sailors. Pete Peterson was recalling them to ships up and down the east coast. And, worst of all, he didn't control how they were employed. Combatant Commanders, like Walt Freeman in Miami, did that and just sent the checks to him, demanding what they wanted, when and where they wanted it, and caring little how they got it.

Dwyer dove into the folder and groaned at what greeted him first: the latest admiral succession plan from "Flag Matters." *They* always *have a new plan needing approval*, he thought.

Dwyer's aide stepped over and interrupted his review of the folder. "Sir, General Freeman from SOUTHCOM is on the phone for you."

Surprised, but welcoming a call from an active "warfighter," Dwyer motioned toward the phone on his sitting desk and asked his aide to put it through. Dwyer picked up the receiver and sat back as he listened to his aide coordinate with the SOUTHCOM exec to get Freeman, the senior, on the line. He crossed his bare calves over the desk corner just as he heard the general pick up.

"Mike, Walt Freeman."

"Good morning ,General, how are you doing down there?"

"Oh, busy, monitoring the situation, assessing it. Also spending lots of time on the phone with State and, of course, the Secretary."

"Is Pete Peterson at Fleet Forces giving you what you need? If you need another carrier, just let me know." Dwyer then covered the phone with his hand and mouthed a question to his listening EA. *What's the ready ship?*

"Oh, I've been on the phone with Pete, and he's cleaning out half of Norfolk to come down here and help. He said he needs a few days and I appreciate that. Glad we already have one of your flattops in theater."

"Yes, sir, *Coral Sea* is a good ship, the best we have. And the fact she's already there and operating is a huge plus," Dwyer said.

"Yes, it is, and that's one of the things I was talking to Pete about. He asked me to bring it up with you."

"Sure, what's the issue?"

"Your guy on *Coral Sea*.... My task force commander and naval component commander are uneasy about him."

With the conversation taking a more sensitive turn, the CNO sat up. His eyes met those of his aide and EA who were listening and taking notes. Dwyer's instinct was to defend his fellow naval officer.

"Roland Meyerkopf is a capable guy, General. He follows orders. I find him fast on his feet. Is there a problem? Because I hear he's doing good work."

"My Navy and Marine component guys don't think he's the right fit for what we're spinning up to do. Can you send me someone else?"

Dwyer was silent for a moment to consider what had just been requested. Before he could respond, Freeman continued.

"Pete says he can—and will—but he did ask me to inform you."

Dwyer absorbed this blow to his ego. He was the Chief of Naval Operations and had "control" of who was selected for admiral and where they were assigned. But he knew, if Freeman and that bastard Pete Peterson made a "drug deal" to move a task force commander, they could. As Dwyer tried to reason with Freeman, his EA placed a sticky note in front of him: THEODORE ROOSEVELT – RDML Bill Rogers.

"Walt," Dwyer began, dropping the formal "General" in order to talk four-star to four-star. "This is…a surprise. Roland is a fine officer who is going places, and before he even gets a shot, we pull him from command? Just yank him out? How does that look? I mean, no amount of whitewashing is going to remove the stigma of being *relieved* of command. How does a guy recover from that?"

"Mike, *it is hard*, I know, but my people are telling me this guy is out of his depth—if you'll pardon the pun. They ran a little operation yesterday, and one of his pilots was blinded by a laser from a druggie yacht. Meyerkopf's guys found it and sank the sumbitch, but they got some intel. Seems the druggies are raising the stakes."

"I heard. So, that's a good thing, right? When faced with a threat, he acted. And his people did an outstanding job getting the pilot back. He—"

"Mike…Mike, we're gearing up for a fight with Venezuela that is going to be primarily an air/sea fight, and my people are telling me the guy on my carrier is wrong for it. That he's a submarine guy and doesn't have the background."

"General, Admiral Buck Rogers is getting *Theodore Roosevelt* underway in three days. He's an aviator, and senior to Roland, and when he gets down there and working for you, he can be the task force commander doing your will and fighting your naval component. And Roland will do what he says. I have every confidence."

Exasperated, Freeman got to the bottom line.

"Mike, why do I have to live this way? My people— and I—*do not have confidence* in him right now. I'm sure he's a water-walking superstar, but right now I want Pete Peterson to send me a guy who is proven and has the right background. *I'm not asking*, Admiral, and if you elevate this to the Chairman, I assure you I'm going to win it. We're talking about a one-star brigade-level commander who is going to be replaced on the eve of battle. It happens, and I'm not going to give it a second thought. I need support *now*, and it's Pete's job to provide it. He asked me to inform you as a courtesy, and I did."

Dwyer avoided eye contact with his staff as he took another humiliating body blow from a combatant commander, one who knew little about naval warfare. He would get even with Pete Peterson for not pushing back and defending a fellow naval officer—and with the junior admirals on Freeman's staff who put him up to this.

"Thank you for the call, General. How else may the Navy help?"

"Pete's been great, and our staffs are working well together. We are probably a week away from initiating action, but with the hostage situation, State is now pushing for an immediate response. I may not have time to flow forces according to plan. You know what Castro is doing around GITMO?"

"Yes, sir, and we're loading an Amphibious Ready Group of Marines in North Carolina as we speak. You'll have it the middle of next week."

"Yeah, but I'm not sure an ARG is going to answer the mail. We may need to airlift some Marines to GITMO now, so I plan to call Dave Keller over at Air Force after we finish. Mike, I appreciate your position, and I know this is not an easy conversation to have. Pete will handle it, and I thank the Navy for your support. We can't do it without you guys."

"Absolutely, General, all of us service chiefs are here this morning and wish we could be down there in the fight. Please don't hesitate to call anytime you need me."

"Will do, Mike. I'm sure we'll be in touch soon. Bye now."

Dwyer put the receiver down and exhaled. His EA walked over.

"Sir, Admiral Davies just gave up strike group command last week and is still in the Norfolk area."

"Yeah, Devil Davies lives for this shit. He's a warrior...and he's probably who Peterson will send. Draft a P4 message for Admiral Peterson: 'Discussed *Coral Sea* leadership situation with SOUTHCOM. Proceed. Dwyer sends.' That's it. No *warm regards* or any of that happy horseshit. I'm pissed."

"Aye, aye, sir."

Dwyer looked at the plaques and career mementos on the wall of his office, an office occupied by men like Nimitz, Burke, and Holloway. Warfighters who sent forces *and* orders to combatant commanders. Now the COCOMs called the shots and Mike Dwyer was all but irrelevant. He served as the Chairman's butt boy who testified on the Hill and talked to frickin' reporters...and played charity golf with glad-handing beltway bandits.

Damn, he thought, wishing he could be a one-star again on a flagship like *Coral Sea*, gearing for battle.

CHAPTER 36

Seated in his ready room chair, Wilson sipped coffee from his mug as he reviewed the message board. Russian bombers flying down the east coast. Forces massing near GITMO. The American diplomat arrested at gunpoint in Caracas. *Ho-ly shit*. He felt *Coral Sea* vibrate underneath him as it continued east along the southern coast of Hispaniola. They were going somewhere fast, and when they reached "somewhere," the ship would orbit and await tasking in the Navy's familiar hurry-up-and-wait *modus operandi*.

Wilson had visited Trench in sick bay earlier that morning, a difficult visit. The doctors hoped an eye surgeon could save his sight, or somehow improve it, but they weren't too optimistic. Trench was resigned now, but depressed that he had to leave that day on the COD. It was bad enough that he had to leave on the cusp of potential combat, but having to contemplate an unknown future made it even worse. Wilson saw the worry and fear in Trench's face, a fear he could not relate to. *Blind* at 28 years old.

The duty desk phone rang, and Macho, the duty officer, answered it. "Skipper, XO is on the phone for you."

Wilson stepped over and took the receiver. "Skipper."

"Flip, Annie. We have a situation here. May we meet in your stateroom to discuss? Now, if we can."

"Roger, see you there in five minutes." Wilson handed the phone back to Macho. He picked up his mug and washed it out in the sink before leaving the ready room.

He wondered what this was about and hoped it was a material vice a personnel problem. With Trench out of action, VFA-16 had a hole to fill. Air Wing staff officers and Weed could step in to fill the flight schedule requirements, but it wasn't the same as having your own guy. And, if this spin-up involving action all about the Caribbean basin turned into actual combat, any hole in the roster make scheduling more difficult.

He reached his stateroom a minute before Annie arrived. Wilson shared a head with fellow CO Billy Martin, and, instinctively, he and Annie spoke in low tones as they sat facing each other. Annie began.

"One of our junior officers is being bullied by JOs throughout the ship."

Wilson nodded, absorbing the information. "Let me guess. Macho."

Annie shook her head. "Look at this."

Opening a folder, she pulled out a photo and handed it to Wilson. It was a computer printout of his intelligence officer, a photo of Shane taken from behind. She wore blue jeans, but her back was bare. Her face was identifiable in profile as she looked over her shoulder in a pensive pose. A design was tattooed on her lower back.

"Okay, what are your thoughts?" he asked.

"The photo is relatively tame, but I don't think intel officers welcome this in their backgrounds. But it's worse. The airwing guys found this, and the smoking gun points at Coach."

"Others have seen this?"

"Oh, yeah. It's all over the ship, *all* over it."

"Does Shane know?"

"I don't think so."

Wilson exhaled. "I mean—how do they surf the Web from the ship? Don't we have filters for this stuff?"

"Yes, but Coach was tipped off about the photo and had a friend on the beach do the research. The friend then sent Coach the photo in an email— and it has now been distributed locally."

Wilson shook his head in disgust. "What a great squadronmate! So who tipped him off?"

"Macho."

"You gotta be shittin' me! *Macho?* NOW's future president?"

"Looks like. I got this from the *Rustler* XO who leaned on his JO who fingered Coach. I just met with Coach and put the fear of God in him. Seems Macho led him and Trench both to believe Shane had some photos out there."

"Macho told them?"

"Not in so many words, but just put it out there for the guys to research. And, guys being guys—"

"So what do we have here?"

"A compromising situation: Shane opens herself up for blackmail, the officer corps gets a black eye. But it also appears a personal confidence may have been betrayed."

"How?"

"My theory. Roommates. Girl talk. Oversharing."

"I've heard."

"And you *guys* don't? Coach couldn't keep his mouth shut."

"Touché. Does Hof know?"

"Don't think so. Otherwise they'd be coming to us top-down. He can't have one of his intel officers read-in to classified programs with this hanging over her head."

"Yeah, this is JOs spreading this."

"And enlisted," she added.

Wonder Woman was still the talk of the airwing, and Wilson knew that when she briefed the aircrew in the ready rooms or on closed circuit TV the guys were looking at her more than listening to her. He also had heard the snickers in the wardroom and passageways when she passed through. This photo—and there could be more—added fuel to the fire, and it seemed, to Wilson, he was the last to know. One of his pilots, Coach, was the lead distributor, and another pilot, Macho, the catalyst.

Why? Why would she tip them off? he wondered.

Wilson imagined Shane would be devastated. He figured the photo was out of character, but she *was* a young woman. Half the women aboard probably had some Facebook image they regretted. As did the men, he surmised. Shane was such an asset to the squadron and ship.... How would she handle this? How would *he* handle this?

"I think we need to bring Shane in and tell her, if she doesn't know already," Annie said.

"Yeah. How shall we proceed?"

Annie smiled. "You mean how shall *I* proceed?"

"Look, this is sensitive, and she may not want a man, especially her CO, around when she learns about it."

"*Because* you are her CO you need to be here, and you need to do the talking. Your intel officer is in a difficult position, somewhat self-inflicted, yes, but she needs help to get out of it. *We* need to lead the effort."

"Yeah...okay...and with us spinning up for combat.... These things never happen at a good time."

"No," Annie agreed.

"Okay. I'm going to hang out here. You find Shane and bring her here in thirty minutes."

"Roger. Shall we bring in Stretch?"

Wilson thought for a moment. "No, we'll inform her department head after we tell her. Olive, too. And Norb Hofmeister. I'll contact him, and you can brief Stretch and Olive."

"Wilco," Annie replied and stood up.

"Then there's Coach and Macho," Wilson added before she reached the door.

Annie nodded. "How do you want to handle that?"

"After we inform Shane's superiors, you and I together can hear their versions."

Annie opened the door to leave. "Roger that," she said as she closed it behind her.

Alone in his stateroom, Wilson thought about his squadron. Situations like this could tear it apart. His fear, at the moment, was that it may have already broken into armed camps. If Macho was the catalyst, as Annie thought, would she turn into a complete pariah? Was Coach guilty of misconduct? If so, did it rate a formal hearing and punishment? Wilson's quiet posture was in sharp contrast to the thoughts that ran through his head about what was going to happen next.

"Enter, please," said Wilson when he heard the knock on his door.

Annie stepped in with Shane in tow. The Intel Officer's eyes betrayed her nervousness, even fear, at this unexpected meeting in her CO's stateroom. Wilson sat at his desk and motioned for the ladies to take seats on the couch opposite him. When he noted Shane's rapid breathing, Wilson felt compassion for her but knew he had to begin.

"Shane, XO and I have learned of something that you need to know but may not be aware of yet."

"*My grandmother!*" Shane blurted out, her eyes wide with panic. "Is she—?"

"No. This isn't about your grandmother," Wilson answered.

"Oh, good!" Shane exhaled with relief, but, seconds later, her face again registered concern about why she was there.

Wilson paused to gather his thoughts. "Shane, there is an image of you being circulated about the ship."

Ensign Shane Duncan shrank inward, as if her trembling body were being squeezed. Her head drooped, eyes closed, and she tightened her hands into a white-knuckled clasp in her lap. Shane began to breathe through her mouth as she processed the information.

"What image, sir?" she whispered. Wilson sensed she knew the answer.

Annie reached into a folder and retrieved a sheet of paper. When she handed it to Shane, the young ensign only needed to take a glance.

From a place deep inside, Shane sounded a mournful groan. Her body heaved, and she fought sobs at the dreaded realization that her secret was out—and the whole ship knew!

Shane struggled to stay in control as her world collapsed around her. Tears ran past her trembling chin, and Annie handed her a box of tissues from Wilson's fold-down desk.

No one spoke. Wilson and Annie watched with compassion as Shane began to process her situation. She replayed in her mind her former boyfriend's pleading and betrayal. She had hoped here at sea—far from home, far from her mother's condemnation—to escape her shame.

Shane removed her glasses to dab at her eyes. Wilson noted she looked different, the sunny disposition gone from her face. She was more composed now, no, determined. Her jaw was set full of resentment – and anger. Wilson broke the silence.

"We believe Lieutenant Madden obtained the photo, and the XO has talked with him. I intend to speak with the other squadron COs to squash its distribution and to speak with Commander Hofmeister. Shane, you've made a huge contribution to the *Firebirds*, and to the ship. I'm glad you're here. I'm sorry this has happened, but we are going to fix it."

With her glasses back on, Shan studied his face. "Sir, how can you unring a bell? You say everyone on the ship has seen this? No wonder I've been getting more looks than usual."

She looked away, her body trembling again, but only took a moment before she continued.

"*I can't help what the Good Lord gave me.* All I wanted was to be on the team and contribute, to be more than *this body*." She interrupted herself with a soft sob. "I'm minding my own business and working hard, and I'm *still* made to feel like a *slutty tramp*. I *hate* their leering eyes and their snickering when I stand up in front of the squadron—"

"When? I've not seen that!" Wilson protested, unaware of the antics in the back of the ready room when Shane was presenting.

"*I* see it, sir. And, if I say something, I'm a troublemaking *bitch* and get the silent treatment. But, if I remain silent, I get more of it. I really thought I could start fresh here. I was so-o-o stupid."

"Shane, you've done nothing wrong. It's not your fault. This happened because your boyfriend betrayed you," Annie said.

"He's not the only one who betrayed me," Shane answered, her eyes fierce and accusing.

"Who?" Annie probed.

"Tiffany. I told her about the photos. No one else."

Annie nodded. She had called it.

"How would you like us to proceed?" Wilson asked. "What can we do to make this right for you?"

Shane thought for a while. "There's a carrier in Japan. May I go there? I tried to escape from North America to the Atlantic Ocean, but now I'd like to go to the Pacific Ocean—the *western* Pacific Ocean—to start anew."

Wilson remained silent while he considered the request. Losing a good officer was always difficult, and, after only three weeks aboard, Shane had established herself as a hard-working and dependable intelligence officer. She would be missed, but Wilson found her request reasonable.

"We'll see what we can do," he promised.

Shane then straightened her back and spoke with clear resolve. "And I don't want to be in the same room with Tiffany. I mean *Lieutenant Junior Grade* Rourke."

"I can take care of a room reassignment," Annie said, nodding reassurance.

"Thank you, ma'am," Shane replied. Wilson then changed course.

"Shane, I'm going to contact Commander Hofmeister now. He holds you in very high regard, and, while he'll regret losing you, I believe he'll help you with new orders. But we've got a situation brewing here involving two hostile countries, and we need an intel officer—you—to help prepare us."

"Yes, sir," Shane whispered. "I'll help."

Annie spoke up. "Shane, you know this will follow you. People here are friends with people in Japan."

"Yes, ma'am, but no one there has betrayed me like my squadronmates here have."

Shane's words cut Wilson and Annie to the bone. Coach and Macho would be standing tall in front of both of them for what they had done to this promising young officer, but Wilson still didn't know why Macho would assist Coach in this way. That Trench was blind seemed punishment enough for his part. Some would even call it karma. But Wilson could ill afford to lose two more of his aviators on the eve of potential combat with the Venezuelans *and* Cubans. Wilson wrapped it up.

"Okay, Shane, we're going to move you out of your stateroom as soon as the XO can find you a new one. Before tonight. I suggest you go back to CVIC for now and let us work this for you. Meanwhile, make me smart on the Cuban and Venezuelan air forces."

"Yes, sir," she answered and got up to leave. Her forlorn whisper told them, more than anything else could have, that she did not want to go out in the passageway and face any of the Air Wing SIX aircrew. Annie followed her outside.

"Are you really okay?" Annie asked as they walked toward CVIC.

"Yes, ma'am."

"Do you want to talk more, woman to woman?"

"No, ma'am, I'll be fine. Guys are fighting and dying overseas. Humiliation doesn't compare to that."

Annie could see Shane was deflated, *devastated*, at what she had just learned. Annie walked ahead of her young ensign, as if protecting her from anyone coming in the opposite direction, ready to silence them with a look. She left Shane at CVIC with a grim smile. "Remember, let us take care of this."

"Thanks, ma'am," Shane said as the sentry buzzed to let her inside the classified space.

Annie watched Shane disappear into the main planning room. Worried about her, Annie was also worried about how to deal with the lieutenants who had betrayed a fellow junior officer.

CHAPTER 37

(Caribbean Sea, approaching the Mona Passage)

Meyerkopf presided in flag plot while he and his staff officers hovered around a chart of the Caribbean and tried to decide where to best place USS *Coral Sea*. Minutes earlier, as they plotted reported positions of Cuban troops massing near Guantanamo, they had received a message that the Russians were flying two *Blackjack* nuclear bombers down the east coast, again causing NORAD to scramble air sovereignty alert fighters to keep an eye of them. Currently transiting past Prince Edward Island, the bombers were expected to land in either Cuba or Caracas in six to seven hours.

The Venezuelan Navy, while no match for the Americans, was still a threat. It possessed two German Type 209 diesel submarines, and intel reports outlined deliveries of China's Harbin Z-9 ASW helicopter. Because of the potential threat of torpedo attack, Meyerkopf and his staff could be forgiven for their near-catatonic focus on the submarines, despite the fact only one could probably get underway. The Venezuelans possessed six frigates, not all operational, and over a dozen coastal patrol boats.

The Air Force was another concern. Their one squadron of F-16s, while an older model of the aircraft, had to be honored as a point-defense threat if land-based targets had to be struck. The two squadrons of Russian-built Su-30MKV *Flanker* Gs, however, had the range and weapons capability to threaten *Coral Sea* anywhere in the Caribbean basin. While the *Flankers* would have to get past Aegis missile shooters like *Gettysburg* and *Norman Kleiss*, the officers had to honor this threat to *Coral Sea*, which at the moment possessed the only American tactical airpower in the region. From the northwest, the Cuban threat to the ship was minimal. If the Americans had to provide air superiority over their installation at Guantanamo Bay, the ancient MiG series fighters and poor pilot training of the Cubans posed an easy tactical problem.

The media had also become a factor. Fed by the Venezuelans, the "diplomatic crisis" in Caracas was front-page news. Washington's State

Department flacks were back on their heels denying accusations of spying and espionage. Unconvinced, and with the usual suspects led by Venezuela's fanning the flames, the American media were reporting on the heavy U.S. military posture in the region. The presence of an American carrier strike group in the Caribbean *was* unusual, and well-placed whispers told of Americans wantonly attacking innocent fishing boats and pleasure craft that the ham-fisted Yankees wrongly suspected of smuggling.

Just killing them outright with their high-tech savagery!

With no prior warning!

Just to, maybe, stop the shipping of a "few bags" of marijuana, which was now grown and sold legally in the American interior.

Reporters were en route to the Pentagon to query the public affairs officers, opening a new front in the conflict, the battle for public opinion.

Ed Browne studied at the chart and stroked his chin. "Sir, it may be prudent to move into the Atlantic until forces flow into the region. Right now, we are five hours away from the Mona Passage at flank speed, and that's right when the *Blackjacks* are expected to fly by us. Recommend we stay here in open waters, south of the Dominican Republic, until the bombers pass and we can recover the combat air patrol, then get into the Atlantic tonight in a position to support Gitmo." Meyerkopf shook his head.

"Ed, this Venezuelan 209 boat could be anywhere, and we need to run hard out of here and get into the open. *Then* we can bottle up these island chokepoints and find the damn thing."

"Sir, we don't know that it will follow us into the Atlantic...."

"He could be watching us right now, Ed!" Meyerkopf was losing his temper.

"Yes, sir, and we have a heightened anti-submarine alert posture. But, we *know* the bombers are coming down here, and, if we are in the restricted waters of the passage, flight operations are going to be difficult. We have been *tasked* to intercept and escort."

As the junior staff officers watched the admiral and his chief of staff argue, they realized there was no "right" answer. If a signal of resolve needed to be sent to Venezuela, leaving the Caribbean was not the best course. But, if there was concern about the location and intentions of the Venezuelan military and the threat from their capable German-built diesel, then retreating to the open Atlantic and waiting for the submarine to transit through the islands where they had a better chance to catch it was a smart option.

Complicating things was the fact that, in a matter of hours, the *Blackjacks* would be in the area on their probable transit to Caracas. When that happened, *Coral Sea* needed to send fighters to intercept and needed sea room to conduct flight operations. Sprinting to the Atlantic would put them in the Mona Passage at the same time the *Blackjacks* were expected. And GITMO was approximately the same distance as the Venezuelan coast, some 400-plus miles, a considerable distance for their carrier aircraft. SOUTHCOM needed two carriers, but had tasked their one available to do the job of two. However, *Coral Sea* had to be somewhere, and the staff officers knew which of their seniors would get their way.

"Admiral, my best military advice is to stay here, south of the Dominican Republic, close to the Mona Passage. We can launch in three-four hours to intercept the Russians, recover and then transit the passage tonight to take station 100 miles north of Puerto Rico."

"Ed, if the Venezuelans hit us, it's game over. Can't you fly in the passage? I mean, seriously, you are worried about *winds*?"

"Sir, there are islands to consider and shipping everywhere. And, yes sir, the surface winds need to cooperate. Admiral, if you direct it, we'll run up there at flank speed and fly in restricted waters. If we need them, we'll have Puerto Rican divert fields available."

"Yeah, can't you get some Air Force tankers to keep the CAP airborne?"

"No, sir, they aren't down here yet. We'll have in-house *Super Hornet* tankers, and, of course, the shore diverts."

While the staff agonized over the logistical and tactical problems before them, the admiral's aide walked over to him and whispered close to his ear. Meyerkopf excused himself to take a call from Fleet Forces commander, Admiral Pete Peterson.

Stepping into his office, he picked up the receiver as his aide listened on the other line.

"Admiral Meyerkopf, sir."

A disembodied voice on the other end said, "Yes, sir, please stand by for Admiral Peterson."

As he waited, Meyerkopf formulated a 20-second report about his strike group activities. The line clicked.

"Roland, Pete Peterson."

"Hello, Admiral," Meyerkopf answered.

"Where are you guys?"

"One hundred and ten miles south of Hispaniola, steaming at a flank bell to the east. I'm going to launch a CAP in roughly three hours to intercept the Russian bombers. We are also watching to the south as I'm concerned about the Venezuelan 209 boats."

Peterson was silent on the other end. Meyerkopf was ready to ask if he was still there when Peterson responded.

"Roland, it looks like this is getting big pretty fast. We've got *TR* coming down, flying a Marine Air-Ground Task Force to Gitmo, and a five-ship ARG from Morehead City gets underway tomorrow. The Air Force is also sending all kinds of stuff to Roosy Roads and Borinquen. We're deploying a missile boat and two attack boats, and a dozen small boys out of Mayport and Norfolk. JCS is pulling their hair out, and State is deer-in-the-headlights, adding no value. SOUTHCOM is spinning up an op-plan to hit Venezuela and hit Castro if he so much as sneezes. Roland, they want a trigger-pulling aviator to run the task force once it is formed. Don Davies just left strike group command...."

Meyerkopf's blood ran cold. Seniority was a hallmark of the military, the aristocratic Navy in particular. Whoever was senior by even one lineal number—and everyone knew where they stood—had overall command. Was he going to have to work for Don Davies, another glad-handing, pretty-boy aviator?

"Roland, SOUTHCOM has made a request. I need to pull you out of there."

Meyerkopf fell back into his chair as if he'd had the wind knocked out of him. Unable to form words, his mind raced. *Relieved of command? Why? With no chance to defend myself? But what "crime" have I committed to defend—except for being a submariner! Damn Peterson and the aviators!*

"Admiral, you are *relieving me*? Sir, I'm stunned and at a loss. Why sir? What have I done wrong?"

"Roland, it is not anything you've done in command of the *Coral Sea* strike group. It's just that we need the A-team now, and this is going to be an air-sea show. Tomorrow afternoon a COD is going to show up with Devil Davies, and after you shake hands, I want you to get on the aircraft. Leave your staff there. The COD will take you to Roosy or GITMO. Get yourself back up here, and we'll reassign you." Meyerkopf couldn't believe his ears.

"Admiral Peterson! I'm here, and we have the Russians flying by in hours. I've been operating down here for a month. *I've got this*, and my staff and the ship is chock-a-block with aviators that are advising me well."

"Roland, what kind of aircraft are the Russians flying along our coast right now?"

Meyerkopf hesitated, unsure. He knew they were bombers. Hell, Russian bombers! *What frickin' difference does it make?* He had all the subject matter expertise he needed at his fingertips.

"*What kind*, Roland?"

"*Bear*, sir," Meyerkopf replied, before looking at his aide who mouthed the word *Black-jack*.

"They're *Blackjacks*, Roland. What are you doing to counter their anti-ship threat?"

"We are staying outside their envelope, and I have missile shooters all around me. And the entire strike group is on heightened alert. We—"

"Roland, *Blackjacks* don't have ASMs. All they carry are *buckets of sunshine*. Now we are going to stop this little game because you've proved my point for me. Roland, this air stuff is not *instinctive* to you like it is for Don Davies, and Don can add value and not be a damn speed bump when SOUTHCOM is talking to him about employing the strike group."

"Sir, I'll work for Admiral Davies—" Meyerkopf said, listening to his own flat voice in disbelief.

Raising his voice, Peterson exploded. "Admiral Meyerkopf, I'm *not* going to be second-guessed by an officer three pay grades junior to me! You don't know the damn difference between a Mark-76 practice bomb and a *Sidewinder*, and SOUTHCOM needs an aviation warrior down there on the tip of the spear. You are relieved of command of the *Coral Sea* strike group as soon as Devil's tires hit your deck, and I want you to stay in the Caribbean for now and in a position to support GITMO and hit Venezuela with eight hours notice. Am I understood, Admiral?"

"Yes, sir." A chastened Meyerkopf could answer nothing else as his 29-year career disintegrated in front of him. No amount of lipstick was going to change the end effect. Relieved of command! *Sonofabitch McGovern!*

"Now, I'm sorry, Roland, but this is from above. I'm going to need you here to advise me on where to best place the missile and attack boats, and I have every confidence you'll move on up the ladder to four stars. *This is not for cause!* Now, get back with your people and intercept these damn bombers, and keep your heads on a swivel. Out here."

"Yes, sir," Meyerkopf said as he heard the line go dead. He locked eyes with his aide, whose face revealed a mixture of heartfelt sorrow and boiling anger that his boss was leaving the ship tomorrow. *Summarily relieved* of command.

Meyerkopf frowned then said, "Send Captain Browne to my stateroom right away."

CHAPTER 38

Olive sat in the cockpit of *Firebird* 300, and, from 35,000 feet, looked over her right shoulder at the northwest coast of Puerto Rico, some thirty miles away. Below, splotchy white clouds dotted the surface of the Atlantic, with larger concentrations over the island. San Juan was visible eighty miles distant with a towering cumulus cell over the mountains south of the city. On the other side of the cell was the former Naval Air Station at Roosevelt Roads, now known as *Aeropuerto Jose Aponte de la Torre*. Whoever owned it, the 11,000 feet of concrete was still there and could serve as a landing strip. With the ship 200 miles behind, a veteran carrier pilot like Olive was always considering options in case she needed to land her *Hornet* in a hurry.

To her left, flying tac wing formation in 303, was Lieutenant "Dusty" Rhodes, the squadron's senior lieutenant. The JOs regarded Dusty as a steady leader. Olive could depend on him to hang on in what would be a varsity intercept.

Ahead and to the left approximately fifty miles were the *Blackjacks*, cruising at a transonic airspeed in the high 30s. They had been unescorted since they had passed east of the Bahamas. Forty minutes earlier the two *Firebird* pilots had been strapped into their jets on *Coral Sea's* waist catapults waiting for the word to launch. Once the *Blackjacks* indicated they were travelling down the Bahamas chain for a probable landing in Venezuela, the ship had launched the alert. With the *Condor* E-2 already airborne over the Mona Passage to vector them to the bogeys, a *Super Hornet* tanker was launched to refuel the *Firebirds* once relieved on station.

Olive noted the radar symbology on her display as she worked the intercept geometry in her head. She turned east northeast to affect the rendezvous with the *Blackjacks* who were cruising on a southeast heading: 39,000 feet at .95 mach. Olive could not allow herself to get slow or to come in from behind in a tail chase that would chew up gas and time. She had to bring her formation in *acute*, as if she were sidling up to the

Russians from a position in front of them and "stop" while also travelling at .95 on their wing line. She would get one chance, and on her scope had just seen another tactical challenge; the jets appeared to be separated by 1-2 miles.

"*Firebird* 300, your contact is now zero-zero-five for forty miles. Fly heading zero-eight-three to intercept."

"Three-zero-zero," Olive replied in acknowledgment. Using her targeting FLIR she saw the bogeys were indeed in a lead-trail formation with the trailer lower than the lead. On the FLIR, the bombers appeared as white slashes with the outline of a vertical tail at the ends. Although clear of clouds and with visibility unlimited, the drawback of being so high was poor maneuverability in the thin air. Almost at military power to stay fast, Olive checked her fuel flow—one hundred pounds per minute—and did mental calculations as to when they would have to leave for the tanker. Or divert into *Jose Aponte* if the situation required. *Options.*

Referencing her data link, she held course and watched the range count down. She wondered if the *Blackjacks* had any indications she and Dusty were nearby. She figured they didn't since she had not locked her radar on them, but she did not want to surprise or alarm the Russians with a covert intercept. She eased her formation up to 38,000 in a shallow climb, taking care not to lose precious airspeed.

At thirty miles the Russians turned forty degrees toward Puerto Rico. The change in course put Olive and Dusty right on their nose.

Shit! Olive thought as she watched the linked aspect vector turn toward her. She rolled her jet easy left and watched Dusty stay in position on the inside of the turn. Once she rolled out, the Russians would be coming at them—fast—from 180 degrees out, further complicating her intercept geometry. She took a cut to the left to build some offset maneuvering room, but she had to figure a new plan. She keyed the mike.

"*Condor, Firebird.* They've turned into us, on the nose three-six-zero for thirty, thirty-nine thousand. Dusty, go single target."

"Roger, *Firebird* three-zero-zero, that's your bogey. *Mother* directs intercept and escort."

"Three-zero-zero," Olive replied.

While the bombers remained in trail, they presented a slight left-right separation, and the trailer was on the left. Perfect.

"We're gonna go for the guy on the left," she transmitted to Dusty on tac freq.

"Roger, sorted," he replied, indicating he had the Russians broken out on his radar display.

Olive could see them now at twenty miles, dark dots against the white horizon. With both formations almost supersonic, and coming at each other with over 1,000 knots of closure, *she* was the one who had to affect the join up by *turning in front* of the bogeys. Unknown was whether the Blackjacks would turn again into them—or away from them, a move that would require a long tail chase.

The two contacts moved fast down her radar display, and, with the bombers on collision course, she turned into them. Looking over her leading edge extension, Olive continued to monitor the radar. She knew that if she seemed comfortable with the closure rate at this high altitude and airspeed, she was likely slow and behind.

At ninety degrees, Olive had her left shoulder on their noses. Resisting the urge to back off, she kept the easy turn in as the Russians seemed to stop moving on her canopy, uncomfortable the whole time. She was thankful they were bombers and not fighters with forward quarter weapons she would be flying in front of right now. Holding at .98 mach, she saw they were tight on the trailer as Dusty slid under to her right side in order to keep sight on all the aircraft. Olive overbanked away for a count, then eased out. It worked, and the trailer moved forward with a small advantage in relative airspeed. Now Olive could make out a red number on the nose of the light gray aircraft, as well as the Russian red star on the tail. The bomber's wings were swept back as it held a transonic airspeed.

Without having to be told, Dusty eased back for more separation as Olive crept closer. She stepped up on the trailer and peered into the cockpit of the big bomber. She could see the helmeted Russian co-pilot looking back at her—and at the AMRAAM missile under her left wing.

"*Condor, Firebirds* are joined and escorting. Low state seven point four," Olive transmitted.

While Olive flew formation on the trailer, the lead bomber turned easy left, building separation from his wingman who maintained heading. Seconds later, the trailer rolled into her, and Olive pulled hard away to maintain clearance. The bomber rolled out on a southwest heading as the lead continued east. At first puzzled about why they would break formation in such a way, Olive realized it was evident "her" *Blackjack* was going through the Mona Passage, heading right at the ship. *Condor* and *Coral Sea* needed to know this ASAP.

"*Condor*, the bogeys have broken formation. Lead aircraft continuing east. Trailer now heading two-two-zero."

"Roger, *Firebird*. Maintain contact," the E-2 mission commander replied.

"*Condor*, unable on both aircraft. We're staying with the trailer heading southwest."

"*Condor* copies."

Although it was risky to leave the lead bomber alone as it transited north of Puerto Rico, Olive wanted to keep Dusty with her as they escorted the trailing aircraft. She took out her camera and snapped photos of the big Russian as she struggled, even at military power, to stay on its wing. Soon that was not enough, and she had to enter min-range afterburner to stay with it.

"He's speeding up," she called to Dusty. About a mile behind, he could observe the yellow glow from the bomber's four giant engine exhausts.

"Yeah, looks like he's in blower," Dusty replied as all three aircraft became supersonic.

Now inside 200 miles from the ship, the bomber began to descend and headed toward a large cloud buildup on their nose. With the increased drag of the drop tanks, racks, and pods she was carrying, Olive had difficulty staying in full burner. She bunted the nose to gain a few knots as the ambient noise of increased airflow built outside her canopy.

"*Condor*, three-zero-zero. He's descending and accelerating," she transmitted to the E-2. Her running commentary was also monitored by the ship.

The bomber was leading them into a towering column of cloud as it passed 30,000 feet in a shallow descent. Olive was now locked on its right wingtip in full burner, with no excess power if it pulled away. The wall of white loomed closer, and Olive had to decide to stay with it or turn away. In an instant she decided to stay with the *Blackjack*. Its co-pilot continued to stare back at her.

"Can you still see the lead?" she asked Dusty.

"Just a dot now, still heading east. I'm locked on you a mile aft."

"Roger."

With airspeed building to 1.1 times the speed of sound, the bomber entered the cloud with Olive in welded wing. Both aircraft then began to shake in the turbulence, and Olive fought hard to keep sight. They broke free and then plunged into more clouds, the bomber extinguishing the navigation lights as they did so. Olive's initial thought was that the jet was experiencing an electrical failure, but she soon realized they had secured the lights on purpose.

Olive slid behind, and despite pushing the throttles to the stops, she could not slow the rate of drift. The bomber's wingtip was fading from view, and she couldn't stay with it. Before losing sight, she turned away to the right and transitioned to an instrument scan.

"Lost sight. Coming right," she informed Dusty.

"Roger, radar contact."

Olive broke clear and paralleled the bomber's last heading. It soon broke free of the clouds about a half mile ahead, still descending, the yellow glow from the burner cans clearly visible. *Impressive,* Olive thought as the bomber accelerated away from her, wings swept all the way back.

She heard the E-2 coordinate with an incoming section of fighters launched from the ship. At this lower altitude, her *Hornet* devouring fuel in afterburner, she needed them here soon. The good news was they were closing the ship fast. Good news for her, but bad news for the ship and the threat the *Blackjack* represented.

Inside 100 miles from *Coral Sea,* the bomber slowed as it passed 20,000 feet in its steady descent. Olive again joined up on its right side and again saw the co-pilot observing her. She then moved forward in the straps as her *Hornet* shuddered from the invisible transition from supersonic to transonic airspeed. As Olive reported these changes to *Condor,* her eyes widened in shock. With no warning, the large bomb-bay doors opened, and the bomber turned into her in an effort to shield whatever it was carrying inside. Alarmed, Olive keyed the mike.

"*Condor, Firebird.* The bogey just opened its bomb-bay doors!"

This news focused everyone on the frequency, and, in *Coral Sea's* Combat Decision Center, the Tactical Action Officer barked, "Sound General Quarters!"

Within seconds, the 1MC sounded the GQ alarm throughout the ship, and 5,000 sailors reacted with a combination of confusion and apprehension as they scrambled to their stations.

BONG, BONG, BONG, BONG...

"General Quarters! General Quarters! All hands man your battle stations! Up and forward on the starboard side, down and aft on the port side! Set material condition Zebra throughout the ship!"

BONG, BONG, BONG, BONG...

In his ready room chair, Commander Jim Wilson noted this was no drill and felt the eyes of his subordinates on him. He didn't know what was going on but knew Olive and Dusty were out there.

"*What the hell?*"

CHAPTER 39

(Mona Passage)

Olive overbanked down to get away from and to get under the *Blackjack*. She also wanted to see what was in the open bomb bay. The bomber kept the turn in, and when Olive slid underneath, the big jet reversed left, almost like a fighter, so she couldn't get a look inside. The sudden and provocative moves signaled hostility, and Olive, having had enough bobbing and weaving with the 500,000-pound monster, fell back behind the *Blackjack*.

Now at seventy miles, the bomber turned back to *Coral Sea* and headed right at it. Olive wondered what type of targeting information it was receiving. Stabilized, she eased underneath and crept up its left side while Dusty provided "cover." The bomb bay doors were now closed as they approached the ship at nine miles per minute.

At 55 miles from *Mother*, the bomber rolled hard left and pulled, steadying on an easterly heading that would take them south of Puerto Rico. Olive reported the development just as a section of *Blue Lancer* FA-18Fs showed up to relieve the two thirsty *Firebird* jets. Olive set a course for the tanker as Dusty joined on her right wing. The *Blackjack* transited without incident along the southern coast of Puerto Rico, staying twenty miles off the coast, before it veered right and headed south to Venezuela, some 400 miles away.

The *Blackjack* landed in Caracas an hour later. It was soon joined by the other bomber that had transited down the Lesser Antilles chain.

As the ship secured from General Quarters, the confrontation was reported within minutes up the chain of command in Key West, Miami, Norfolk and Washington. While the world's media attention was on the diplomatic crisis in Caracas, SOUTHCOM was trying to make sense of the Cuban and especially the Russian military behavior. Flying a *Bear* down the American seaboard at high altitude, with a wingtip just outside the 12-mile territorial limit, was a routine Russian tactic. However, *a formation* of modern and capable ship-killing *Backfires* just did not "pop up" out of the mid-Atlantic ocean from low altitude, considering the fact they required

209

extensive in-flight refueling coordination. Neither was it normal for nuclear-capable *Blackjacks* to make aggressive movements and open bomb-bay doors minutes from an American carrier. Air Force fighters and early-warning assets were sent to Iceland, and military professionals everywhere concluded the diplomatic "crisis" in Venezuela was a manufactured sideshow.

While the National Security Council at the White House directed military movements and assessed courses of action, USS *Coral Sea* was at the end of the whip. And, at the very tip, the business end, were the *Firebirds* of VFA-16 led by Commander Jim Wilson.

Wilson watched the PLAT in the ready room as Olive and Dusty recovered from their eventful intercept. Around him, the other *Firebird* pilots were busy: preparing to stand alerts in the cockpits, waiting, dressed and ready, for their call, studying charts of Venezuela and Cuba. The word was out—things were heating up all right—and Wilson knew CAG would be calling the COs together soon to fill them in on the course of action Washington was devising for them.

Coral Sea transited south of Puerto Rico, and Wilson could feel the vibration of the deck plates as the carrier's four giant screws, positioned almost 100 feet below him, propelled it through the water at thirty knots. Would they go into the Atlantic? Stay in the Caribbean? Who would they fight first? Cubans? Venezuelans? Wilson knew they had to be ready for any tasking with a few hours notice. And the fact *Theodore Roosevelt* was departing Norfolk to join them meant something could happen, soon.

And the Russians? Would they send more aircraft down the coast of North America and into the Caribbean, to see how high and how often the United States would jump? Wilson knew *Coral Sea* could now expect around-the-clock alerts. With live weapons. How far out would they have to intercept them? How would they intersperse themselves with "white" airline traffic? With tensions high in the region, would someone make a mistake? One of his young pilots? Would he?

Wilson's mind drifted to thoughts of Mary and the kids. He realized he had not emailed Mary, or even *thought* of her, in days. Or the kids. Brittany was still playing with dolls, but Derrick's sullenness and obsession with violent video games troubled him. *Like father, like son.* How Wilson wished he and Mary could raise them safely into adulthood, away from the poison of drugs and digital images offered to them on a daily basis, away from the pressures of hyper-sexualized music and dress that would have his daughter pining for heels and makeup before she turned ten. That would expect Derrick to have a "notch-in-his-belt" before he could drive. At least Weed and Mongo *had done something* about it.

They *had killed* to keep drugs away from his kids. So what if it was a finger-in-the-dike effort. It was something, more than Wilson was doing for his family. He thought again about his children, wishing they could stay kids in a happy childhood as long as possible.

BONG, BONG, BONG, BONG...

Wilson jerked his head up and again sensed the others looking at him as the GQ alarm sounded over the 1MC. *Now what?*

"General Quarters, General Quarters! All hands man your battle stations! Up and forward on the starboard side! Down and aft on the port side!"

With the alarm blaring and the sounds of hundreds of sailors stamping forward and aft past the *Firebird* ready room to their stations, Wilson felt the ship heel to port. On the PLAT he noted the canopy close on a *Super Hornet* positioned on Cat 3. He could see flight deck personnel moving around it as if they planned to launch it on alert.

"This is the TAO. Now launch the alert fighters, initial vector zero-four-zero."

Pilots came into the ready room—their battle station—and Wilson watched the duty officer mark them off as accounted for.

"*Vampire* inbound! Fifty miles!"

Holy shit! Wilson thought. A cruise missile coming at us? Fifty miles? *It will be here in minutes,* he thought. *Coral Sea* was defended by the missile-shooting cruiser and destroyers on the horizon and by the carrier's own defensive missiles and close-in weapons system Gatling guns. *Who is shooting at us—from Puerto Rico?*

As the crew dogged down watertight doors and hatches, they all listened to the Tactical Action Officer call down the range. The first *Rhino* went into tension and launched, followed by another on Cat 4. Both jets whipped it over to the left as soon as they cleared the deck and pulled to the northeast 200 feet above the waves in full afterburner

Aboard *Coral Sea*, in the Combat Decision Centers of the strike group ships, and in the cockpits of the two *Super Hornets*, watchstanders moved switches to arm missiles that would fire when commanded. With trepidation, they watched as the range to the contact decreased. At first, the watch officers on the carrier had thought the contact was a cruise missile inbound, put the Aegis ships identified it as an aircraft. Those in the CDCs breathed a sigh of relief at the momentary reprieve, while thousands of sailors at the battle stations listened to the 1MC speakers and prayed this was all a bad dream.

The two *Rhinos* were ordered to identify the bogey and escort. While he set up for an expeditious rendezvous, the flight lead, a lieutenant, had his fellow lieutenant go straight at the bogey to identify it. The bogey was right on the deck and moving at a high rate of knots. The wingman bore down on the contact and surprised everyone when he identified it while thundering past at 500 knots.

"*Alpha Whiskey*, the bogey is identified as a business jet, heading two-two-zero approximately 300 knots at 200 feet! Looks like a *Citation!*"

Captain Browne stood behind the TAO who looked over his shoulder for guidance. How were they to handle this contact coming at them at only 200 feet, well below a safe altitude for innocent passage and, in the current situation, a hostile flight profile?

Browne studied the screen. He had seconds to make a decision. *Shoot down this bogey? Or risk the ship?*

"Thump them," he said.

"Sir?" the watch officer asked, puzzled.

"Have the damn *Rhino's* thump them, weapons safe, but scare them off. Tell them to thump him. They'll know what you mean. *Now*. Keep warning the unidentified aircraft that they are standing into danger."

"Aye, aye, sir," the watch officer responded and relayed the message to both aircraft, using a tactical frequency for the *Hobos* and the emergency GUARD frequency for the Cessna.

In the cockpit of the lead *Super Hornet, Hobo* 203, the pilot was as low as he dared in a tight turn to affect the rendezvous. When he got the word to *thump* the contact, he pulled hard to an intercept heading and lit the cans. He then leveled at fifty feet over the waves which whizzed underneath him like white lines on an interstate highway. His wingman swung around hard to line up at the *Citation's* six o'clock and make his own run. Recording his HUD and FLIR video the entire time, the lead bore in from the right side of the business jet, looking *up* at the white-painted Cessna to assess closure and range. The intruder continued straight ahead as the lead *Rhino* flew his aircraft to a position in front of its nose and pulled straight up in front of it, overbanking left to watch the result. The *Citation* seemed to veer left, then continue straight.

Hobo 207 was now a mile behind the bogey, unseen, and coming at it supersonic. The lead *Hobo* watched his wingman's shock wave bounce off the surface of the water as it sprinted to catch its prey. Once it got to the

Citation, the *Rhino* pulled hard up and to the left, within a wingspan of the unknown jet. Jolted by another unexpected fighter, the message sunk in. The Cessna now turned away from the ship, which it could see on the horizon, and headed back toward Puerto Rico.

With the speed brake extended, the lead *Hobo* joined on the Cessna's right wing and his wingman soon joined on the left as the *Citation* headed away from *Mother.* The *Hobo* pilots watched the pilots of the jet and could sense that they were nervous. Behind the pilots, through the passenger windows, they saw people with big TV cameras. Soon, one person held up a flag against a window. The lead eased closer, accepting wingtip overlap, to get a better look. Within seconds, the lead identified the flag as a logo of a U.S. network news outlet.

Once this was transmitted to the ship, the lead *Hobo* received instructions. At one hundred miles from *Mother,* with the Puerto Rican coast in sight, the *Super Hornet* pilot pointed his finger at the *Citation* co-pilot, then pointed to Puerto Rico, and brushed his hand as if to sweep them away. In unison, both *Rhinos* pulled up and away from the media snoopers, watching the white jet over their shoulders as they climbed behind it. They orbited high off the coast for a time, keeping watch through the clouds below until summoned home by a relieved Tactical Action Officer.

CHAPTER 40

Macho entered her stateroom and noticed right away that Shane's rack was stripped of linen. Her fold-down desk was up, and Macho lowered it. Empty. She opened one of Shane's metal drawers. Empty. A ship-supplied bath towel was left hanging on a hook, but Shane's robe was gone, her closet empty. Macho opened the medicine cabinet over the sink. All of her roommate's items were gone.

Macho wondered what had happened. Why was Shane gone? Was she still on the ship? Sudden illness or loss of a loved one? She hoped Shane was okay and called the ready room.

"Ready Five, Lieutenant Rutledge, sir or ma'am."

"Ghost, Macho. Is Shane down there?"

"Nope, haven't seen Wonder Woman in a while. What's up?"

"Is she still on the ship?"

"Should be. Let me ask the OPSO."

Macho heard him ask the Operations Officer, Lieutenant Commander "Stretch" Armstrong, if Shane was still aboard.

"Yeah, OPSO says, as far as he knows, she's still aboard. Do you think she's not?"

"She's my roommate, but all her stuff is gone."

When Ghost didn't respond, Macho added, "I'm going to CVIC to check."

"Okay, let me know," Ghost replied and hung up.

Macho closed the stateroom door behind her and headed to CVIC. *Could she have fallen overboard? No, why clean out everything in the room? Suicide? No, she is the happiest person I know.* It puzzled Macho that all Shane's stuff was missing and she had moved out with no warning. She hoped Shane was in CVIC.

Macho arrived and was buzzed in. She stepped into the main planning room and saw Shane seated at a table studying a chart. A wave of relief flooded over her.

"Shane, are you okay?"

Shane didn't lift her head. "Yes, fine."

Macho noted the cold shoulder. "Your stuff is gone. Did you move out?"

"Yes," Shane answered as she stood and walked toward the chart locker.

Macho followed, her face contorted in confusion.

"Why?"

Shane kept her head down and didn't answer. They were now alone, out of earshot.

"Shane...*why?*"

Shane snapped her head to make eye contact. "Because, I don't want to live with someone I can't trust."

Stunned, Macho reeled from the verbal blow.

"*What?* What do you mean?"

"I told you about my boyfriend's pictures. You told Trench and Coach, and now those pictures are all over the ship. Every guy on board has seen me naked *and* my tattoo. I've asked for a transfer, but until I leave, I still have to work here—with everyone looking at me and judging me."

"*I did not*—"

"*Yes, you did.* I told you only, and I *begged* you not to tell. I thought I could trust a girl."

"Shane, I did *not* tell anyone!"

"Then how are the photos all over the ship? Skipper and XO called me in to tell me. *That's* how I found out!"

"These perverts are capable of finding things on their own..."

"We don't have Web access out here. They had help, and they were tipped off. This didn't happen until I opened up to you, my roommate, my squadronmate, my "fellow officer" of honor and integrity."

"It's not a *bad* picture. You can't *see* anything..."

Shane exploded in fury. "I don't care if it's a portrait picture of me with my hair colored blonde! I came here—to a ship!—to escape my shame, to be an Intelligence Officer with a professional image. Free of blackmail! And now that's gone, so I'm leaving."

"When?"

"As soon as the XO lets me."

"I'm going to find out who did this and kill them!"

"Tiffany, it's *you!* Yes, guys are guys, but I opened up to *you*, shared with *you*, my new soul-sister. And *you* spread it. And I'm the one who has to leave."

"I *didn't spread it!*"

Just then Commander Hofmeister appeared. "Shane, when you have a second, I need some help, please."

Shane spun to follow him, but not before she addressed Macho with contempt. "Excuse me, *Lieutenant.*"

Macho watched her walk away and noticed some guys from the E-2 squadron working on something in the corner. Did they know? Have they seen Shane's photos? They didn't seem to notice her as she walked past them to join Commander Hofmeister.

Things aren't so bad. Shane is overreacting.

But Macho had Coach dead to rights! He was with Trench in the wardroom. Trench is off the ship—blinded in combat—but his sidekick is still here. Coach would have to pay for what he did. She would go to the XO and finger him for ruining Shane and causing a hostile workplace for her, and for Macho, and for all the women on *Coral Sea.* He would get his, and the *Firebirds* would be rid of those two pains in her ass.

Her little plan had worked. But would it cost a budding friendship? Until now, Shane had been nice to her, had admired her. She was sure this would blow over, and Shane would come back. XO would talk her into staying after she keel-hauled Coach, and maybe some other worms in the airwing. Once again the boy's club was at fault.

Besides, it's just a bare back! Good grief, Malibu Barbie! You need to lighten up.

CHAPTER 41

Wilson met Billy Martin in the passageway as they both headed to CAG's stateroom for the CO's meeting.

"Did ya hear?" Billy asked him. "Admiral Meyerkopf is leaving the ship."

"Yes. Quite a move on what may be the eve of battle. Have you heard of a relief?"

"Yes, Admiral Davies."

"Devil Davies, a real warrior."

"What do you think's going to happen?" Billy asked.

"I don't know if we are at war with Cuba or Venezuela...or Russia. Guess we're going to find out when Devil gets here—or, maybe, right now."

They arrived at CAG's stateroom and knocked. When he told them to enter, they stepped inside and saw the Deputy CAG Captain, Bob "Not-o" Kay, and a few other air wing COs arrayed on the couch. Once the others arrived, CAG began.

"Okay, guys. First, Admiral Davies is coming aboard on the COD. Word has it we are spinning up, and Fleet Forces wanted a carrier guy here. Admiral Meyerkopf is leaving. I haven't seen him, and he refused my request to meet." CAG raised his eyebrows, as if to say *C'est la vie.*

Wilson reflected on this confirmation of the rumor mill. A new admiral on the eve of battle, and not just any admiral. *Devil* Davies was the closest thing naval aviation had to the Red Baron, a blood-and-guts warrior who, no doubt, was spoiling for a fight. Meyerkopf was a bespectacled nuclear engineer at heart, with little understanding of the combat power he wielded. Now they would be led by old *Devil Dog* himself, who had begun his career as a Marine F-4 pilot and had a full understanding of what the *Coral Sea* strike group could do to an enemy. Just point him in the right direction and give him a green light.

217

CAG had an easel with an aeronautical chart of the Caribbean and Venezuela. He referred to it as he spoke.

"In CVIC there are target folders for you *Hornet* guys. Looks like we need to be ready to hit Venezuela in three nights. *TR* is getting underway and will run down here at flank speed. Once she's in the region, she's going to take a position north of the Turks and Caicos to influence GITMO. We are staying here for a few days, then moving into the Atlantic to take a position south of Barbados. SOUTHCOM is giving us the area here around the Gulf of Paria and Delta Amacuro. The port at Río Salta and their air force base at San Ramón will be our main areas of focus. The USAF is taking the area around Caracas. The F-22 guys are coming down from Langley to stage at Homestead, and they are moving a wing of *Eagles, Vipers,* and *Strike Eagles* to Roosy Roads. The big wing tankers will be bedded down here in Borinquen, and we may get our "own" set of tankers in Barbados once we get there. That will be nice."

The COs studied the charts as CAG spoke, imagining the targets, the weapons required, the readiness of their pilots and aircrew, the state of their aircraft. They were preparing for *combat* with a regional power flying fourth-gen fighters as part of an extensive integrated air defense system. And Wilson was CO of a squadron that would challenge them in mere days. He thought of Trench as CAG continued.

"We're getting a platoon of SEALs. These guys are available to you if you need them in your strike planning. I know you haven't seen your folders yet, but I want you to know that you have the SEALS, and we expect them aboard today, or maybe tomorrow."

CAG Matson looked at the *Sierra* squadron CO.

"Ed, I want you to be responsible for getting them a space to work out of and to stow their gear. And coordinate with the ship for berthing. You can expect one officer and one chief, the rest enlisted, for a total of 16. If you have the space, I'd have them hang out in your ready room and get to know your aircrews and vice versa. You *Rustlers* are going to be the delivery and extraction mechanism for these guys in the short term, so you need to be tied at the hip."

"Yes, sir," the *Rustler* skipper answered. CAG then turned to Wilson.

"Flip, the first strike package is going to San Ramón. You're leading it. And, Not-o, I want you in that package, too. You're going to have *fifty-five* aimpoints, ranging from knocking out EW and SAM radars to cutting the runway and destroying fighters in revetments and hardened shelters. This strike is designed to knock out their IADS in the eastern part of the country, and you're going to have B-2s from Missouri and B-1s from

South Dakota helping you. You're going to need most everything on the flight deck, and, after you're airborne, we're gonna bring up birds from the hangar bay for a follow on raid at Río Salta. Billy, you've got that one, and you're going to have to stay closely aligned to Flip's plan."

"Yes, sir," Wilson and Billy both nodded. *Holy shit!* Wilson thought. *Fifty-five aimpoints!*

"After those two roundhouse punches to bring down their IADS, we're going to chip away at their infrastructure to prevent them from gaining cash and to keep their merchant fleet bottled up. Most of their Navy is homeported in the Caracas region, and we can expect them to remain pier side. That doesn't mean we can discount the potential for combatants underway in the Río Salta area and throughout the gulf."

Wilson raised his hand, already knowing the answer. "Sir, are we in a declared war?"

Matson frowned. "No…and this may be throttled back, but we have tasking to be ready to go with these packages in 72 hours. The Venezuelans still have our diplomat, and they are now threatening Aruba and Curacao which makes the Dutch wig out, the frickin' Cubans are along the fence at GITMO, and who knows what the Russians are going to do tomorrow. These guys are all coordinated and screwing with us, so we are lifting the hammer in the air and waiting for the word to strike—or to set it down gently." The officers in the room nodded their understanding.

"I think we're going to do this," CAG added, "and we need to be in that mindset. Now, go to CVIC and take a look at the folders. Then get your strike planning teams together. Admiral Davies is coming aboard, and tomorrow at this time I want you to give him lap-briefs on your plans. I don't expect you to have all the answers, but make your briefs as tight as you can because, if you know Devil, he's going to rip them apart. You guys need to look him in the eye with confidence. Just don't bullshit him, or you're dead—then I'm dead!"

The men chuckled as they took CAGs words to heart. Facing the Venezuelans would be easier than the wire brush they would experience from Devil.

"And guys, this might be accelerated, we might flex to operating around Cuba—who knows. So get your people ready, groom your aircraft, stand your alerts and *Semper Gumby*."

The commanders left and proceeded to CVIC. Wilson's folder was big, and, as he sifted through the satellite imagery of the aimpoints and expected threat locations, he knew he needed help to divvy up element responsibilities. He thought of the launch sequence, the tanking plan, the EW suppression plan... details that depended on where the ship was going to be, details he needed answers for now. He would have to drive it and hope he was supported. Some forty carrier aircraft—and big wing bombers, SEALs if he needed them. And he had less than 72 hours to plan and execute.

Shane walked up with a chart of Venezuela covered in acetate. It was marked with the known SAM threat rings. Before handing the chart to Wilson, she mumbled, "Sir."

Wilson took it and said, "Thanks, Shane."

"Yes, sir," she said over her shoulder.

"Shane?"

"Yes, sir," she answered, turning around to face him.

"Please take a seat."

She did as she was told and sat down across the table from her CO. With a forlorn look on her face, she waited for him to initiate the conversation.

"Shane, we are spinning up big time, and I'm leading a huge strike with double the number of aimpoints I've ever seen. I need help, *your* help, to make me and the rest of the squadron smart on their threats, their level of training, the weapons they employ."

"Yes, sir."

"We need you to teach us. Today. No time to lose."

Shane struggled as she formed an answer. "Sir, I can't face them. They've all seen me naked! And my own roommate told them. Please don't make me stand in front of them. I'll get the information you need, and..."

"Ensign Duncan, *knock it off.*"

Shocked by Wilson's abrupt rebuke, Shane looked at him with wide eyes.

"Are you a naval officer? Are you a warrior? Are you a woman, or are you a whiny schoolgirl? We are going into combat, in days, and we need your help. I don't have time for the high-school Mickey Mouse about photos that *you* posed for. I don't have time for who said what to whom. I'm commanding a strike-fighter squadron, and you are my Intel Officer. I am *ordering* you to give my squadron an order-of-battle briefing on

Venezuela, and it had better be good. See Lieutenant Commander Armstrong and schedule it. Today. You've got hours to prepare. Now go."

"Yes, sir!" a chastened Shane answered as she got up.

"We'll revisit your concerns after this operation is over, but you're in the big leagues. People can be hurt by real bullets."

"Yes, sir!" she nodded as she turned to leave.

At that moment, the 1MC sounded; *"Ding, ding...ding, ding...ding, ding...*Rear Admiral, United States Navy, arriving."

Wilson checked the PLAT monitor on the bulkhead and saw the outline of a C-2 appear from the right side of the screen. It stabilized in the crosshairs as it made its approach to *Coral Sea*, hook down. With a thud it trapped aboard. The steel braided cable screeched as it was pulled from its housing and the turboprops went to full power. When the aircraft stopped, the prop pitch changed to idle, and the 1MC sounded again.

"Ding."

Devil Davies was aboard.

CHAPTER 42

(USS *Coral Sea*, south of Puerto Rico)

From his stateroom desk, Wilson felt the ship roll in the long swells. He thought of the exchange with Shane and the tough love she had needed to snap out of it and to move forward. Once things spun down, he and Annie would follow up with Coach and Macho.

War with Venezuela was less than 72 hours away. He surmised they were already at war—undeclared, of course—but if any American unit encountered a Venezuelan ship or plane, it would be declared hostile in minutes.

A real shooting war. Weed and his band of "misfit" aviators were in an undeclared shooting war, a one-sided summary execution with no warning. For Wilson, there was no love lost for the poor smugglers on the boats or planes, and the rich Americans who participated in the destruction of their own society earned special contempt. But it *was* unsettling, the high-tech manner in which they were hunted and essentially shot in the back with no warning. *Just tell them,* he thought, wondering why the United States didn't warn the druggies that, if caught on or over the high seas, they would be blown to bits. Even the Germans had done that during the world wars: give the merchant sailors a *chance* to look out for the U-boats—or stay ashore.

Weed was right. The media's fifth column would take the side of the downtrodden smugglers "just trying to make a living," while glossing over the drug lords who laundered billions in Panama each year and continued to feed a steady supply of poison into North America, poison that took down droves of kids each day… that could even take Derrick someday. Wilson's guilt returned. How he wanted to be home with his son, to pick up a baseball glove and play catch, to listen to him, to be there for him.

Mary. He wondered what she was doing. He hadn't received an email from her in days, which was unsettling. With the media reporting the Russian flights and the saber rattling in South America, it was strange he had heard nothing from her. Was she burned out dealing with the kids, with the Navy…or with him? *Was she cheating on him?*

The *Firebirds* of VFA-16, who made up his current "family," were not hitting on all cylinders. Trench was off the ship and maybe down forever. Macho preoccupied, his intel officer also distracted. And Coach was a wild card. He needed to get everyone focused on the real enemy they would be facing in hours.

He heard a knock. "Come in."

Annie stepped inside and closed the door. "Hey."

"Hey, what's up?"

"Just got through looking at my strike plan. Mining the port of Río Salta."

"Wow. We aren't screwing around."

"Yeah, it's the day after your strike on San Ramón. You need to take out most of the newer SAM sites, and we should be able to get underneath the older stuff and AAA. We'll bottle them up in port...or keep people out."

"Okay, we'll do our best. Who's gonna help you?"

"Stretch and Macho are on my strike planning team. We've got sixteen jets and a dedicated fighter sweep. We're taking no chances that you guys will have shut down everything."

"Well, happy mining. I just had a chat with Shane."

"Yes?" Annie asked.

"Told her we need her game face. She's been hurt, she's been wronged, it *is* wrong, we'll deal with it—but later."

"Gossip happens—*we're* gossiping," Annie smiled.

"Maybe. I'd like to think we're assessing our people. Besides, the bullshit is inversely proportional to the threat, and the threat here is as high as anything in CENTCOM."

"Concur. She's a kid, and she'll get over it. She's moving into one of the *Arrow*'s staterooms for the time being."

"Good. You ready for this?"

"Yep. Wonder what those guys are thinking down there."

What does he want? Daniel thought as he looked out at the blue Caribbean through the sound-treated windows of his observatory. With Annibel and the girls at the pool, he took a call from Ramirez on his secure line. He needed to always show confidence. *Smile,* he thought.

"Eduardo, I hope you are well."

"My friend, I hope *you* are well because Ramos is losing his ass in the Pacific, and he knows why."

"What do you mean?" Daniel asked.

"The *yanquis* are not only mobilizing their army to attack us, they have stepped up operations in the Pacific. Ramos has lost all his shipments in the past four days, and he *knows why*."

Daniel listened.

"You told us, Daniel, that the Americans would concentrate on the Venezuelan military once your puppet general rattled his saber. Jail a diplomat. Have the Russians fly in a provocative manner. Well, you were right! They are off our shores now! And they've shut down the canal, and Ramos' Pacific shipments are going missing—with no trace, like yours two weeks ago. Seems you just transferred your problem to him."

"And you, my friend, how are your supply lines?"

"I've shut down. I'm weathering the storm until it passes. But the shipments are the least of our worries. The American banks are using their Internet people to stop money transfers and freeze our accounts. Ramos is going to kill you."

Daniel froze for a moment, knowing that Ramirez spoke the truth. *Confidence.*

"We will see about that, but why do you tell me this, Eduardo? Don't you stand to gain from my death? Or if I engage Ramos in a turf war? You'll be the one standing. You'll own everything."

"My friend, if you are out, then Ramos is focused on *me*. Even if *both* of you are dead, the whole world focuses on me alone."

"Buy the Americans off!"

"Daniel, *you* could not buy the *Colombians* off, which is why you live in my country now! No, I want you and Ramos, my friends *and* enemies, close to me in this *ménage a trios* of convenience. So I warn you, my clever friend, to call off your stooge in Caracas, give the damn Americans their limp-wristed diplomat back, and stop the Russians from scaring Washington to death. Do you know that Raul has armed men surrounding their torture chamber at Guantanamo?"

"Yes, I've told my man to provoke but not to attack."

"Your man is a military fool, unaccustomed to thinking, taking orders from milquetoast politicians who themselves get it wrong."

"He's the top general of the *Fuerza Aérea Venezolana!*" Daniel raged. "There's no one higher!"

"He's a *fool*, Daniel! Did he communicate with the Russians and Raul? If he did, they have overplayed their hand, and the Americans are bringing the thunder! Did *you* communicate with the Russians and Cubans to coordinate what *you* wanted?"

"*Of course not!*" Daniel shot back. "There can be no trail, and these military details are not of my concern!"

Ramirez laughed. "These *details* will kill you, Daniel. You asked your man to stir up the Americans to take the pressure off—so he did! They now think Guantanamo is going to be invaded, and the Russians are going to start World War III! And you had them take a worthless diplomat..."

"*I did not!*" Daniel sensed he was losing control.

"You *did*, Daniel, because you didn't spell it out for the fools who work for you. You asked them to bring you a rock, and they did! Just not the rock you wanted. And now the excited American *cowboys* on their battleships are going to attack us, and I think they are really going to do it! Do not forget that they fight for their *flag*, you idiot, not for the riches you throw at your medal-covered generals and perfumed princes in Caracas...who have proven themselves inept!"

"You overreact."

"Do I? I'm the one bringing you word about Ramos. I'm the one husbanding my resources. While your beauty queen of a wife is in Caracas spending all your money and you are in your gilded prison bouncing up and down on your silicone *prostitutas,* the Americans have a satellite looking at you right now. And, if you don't move fast, they are going to send a guided missile into your glass observatory. And the last thing they'll see before it blows up is your bare ass!"

Furious, Daniel looked at the phone and resisted the urge to hurl it against the window. Outside the window was a view of Trinidad, lush and inviting. Surely, he could swim across the gulf to answer the island's invitation to *escape*—to be free of Ramos, free of the triangulating Eduardo who *deserved* to die, of Annibel, of business headaches, and of the damned Americans and their smart bombs. He could see the island, could reach out and touch it. *It can't be fifty kilometers away. It's right there.* While growing up, he had swum in the Pacific surf. In an instant, Daniel listed *swimming to Trinidad* as an option. He would miss the girls...Julianna would take it especially hard. Ramirez snapped him out of his daydream.

"Daniel! *Daniel!* Do you hear what I am telling you? If you don't have your fools bow and scrape before the Americans *right now,* and put the genie back in the bottle, you are dead. And if you don't pay reparations to

Ramos *right now,* you are dead. You may already be a dead man walking, but, remember, I warned you!"

Daniel heard a click as the line went dead. How he wanted to strangle Ramirez with his expensive silk tie, to rip that moustache off his lip with the fingers of his clenched fist. Daniel had grown accustomed to having his wishes fulfilled with a casual wave. Did he, once again, have to do the thinking, too? Did he have to do it for Hernandez, a *mayor general?* Daniel realized his *thinking* was getting him into trouble. Regardless, no more safe house frolics for Hernandez. *Bad dog.*

Ramirez was right about one thing. With few exceptions, the Americans fought for a flag—the damn stars and stripes! Who said it? Napoleon? *A soldier will fight long and hard for a bit of colored ribbon.* Would the American sailors and airmen also fight this way? Risk their lives for nothing, for their own inept politicians? *For a piece of colored ribbon?*

Daniel knew he had to find the exceptions, the traitors who would give up their country for a new jet ski, or simply to get attention. America had such men—and women—in their military. He would find them.

Ramos. Daniel stared at Trinidad as storm clouds gathered to his west but thought of Ramos instead of the island's luscious trees.

CHAPTER 43

Devil Davies wasted no time gathering his warfighters and gearing them up for a fight. Less than an hour after his arrival aboard *Coral Sea,* he received a perfunctory ten-minute "turnover" brief with a shell-shocked Meyerkopf.

Davies dutifully shook hands with him and then had Browne summon the "Warfare Commanders" and squadron COs to flag plot. Matson sent one of his *Sierras* to pick up the captain of *Gettysburg*, the Air Warfare Commander, and bring him to the carrier. He was the last one to arrive in the packed space. Squadron COs such as Wilson and Billy, two of the more junior officers in the room, stood along the bulkhead as the higher ranking officers took seats around the small table. The chair at the head was reserved for Davies. From above them the *hmmmm* generated by propellers of the turning COD resonated throughout the room.

With all assembled, Browne entered and announced, "Gentlemen, the Admiral." The room sprang to attention.

Davies followed Browne into the room. "Seats," he grunted as he took his chair. Davies' aide set a cup of steaming black coffee in front of him. Only one woman, a commander IT officer, was present at this gathering. Davies got right to business.

"Gents, we are spinning up to strike the Venezuelans. Captain, I want us to get into the Atlantic to a position one hundred miles northeast of Barbados in 24 hours. I want you to blow through the Sombrero Passage and let the world see you doing it. *Gettysburg*, you are riding shotgun. Who the hell is the destroyer commodore?" Davies then asked, scanning the room for an answer.

"I am, sir," a surface warfare captain answered, preparing for a legendary Davies blast.

"I want two DDGs in a launch window north of Aruba and to defend from any BMs they may launch. Put them in the right spot. The Dutch have a destroyer down there, and the Brits have one getting underway

227

from Kingston. You are going to be the task force commander of this little flotilla, and I want you down there riding one of your shooters. Do they have hangars?"

"One does, sir. *Norman Kleiss*," the commodore answered.

"Fuck...okay. CAG? Where's CAG?"

"Here, sir," Matson answered.

"CAG, put anti-ship and CSAR helos on one small boy and a *Sierra* on the one with no aviation detachment, riding free. Load it up with ordnance. We're expecting a surface fight and SOF delivery." Davies turned to Browne. "And, Ed, we need some more rotary wing capability down there. Find me a solution in ten minutes."

"Aye, aye, sir," Browne said and eyed the staff operations officer who left to figure an answer.

Wilson was unnerved by Davies' dramatics and suspected the others were, too. No welcome, no "pep talk" from their new strike group commander. Just a routine board of directors meeting with one agenda item: *starting a war* with Venezuela. Devil was a warfighter, and the collegial niceties of an officer and a gentleman social conduct were not important. Meyerkopf had come across as a social recluse, and Davies seemed to act like Chesty Puller with wings. Wilson had never met the man, but his reputation had preceded him, and it appeared to be accurate. While Davies was studying a chart of the Caribbean, the 1MC sounded.

"Ding, ding...ding, ding...ding, ding. Rear Admiral, United States Navy, departing."

All heard the C-2 above them taxi out of its parking spot and toward the catapult. Wilson and the others took furtive glances at the PLAT as the white aircraft turned toward the bow catapults. Davies resumed.

"Gents, we are the first out of the gate with a strike on their air base at San Ramón. We are going to be in the Atlantic east of Venezuela in the open and away from the submarine threat. After we neutralize San Ramón, we are going to mine the approaches to Río Salta. We've got the eastern part of the country, and the Air Force is going to deal with the area around Caracas. And Aruba. The Dutch have asked for our help to defend it. *Theodore Roosevelt* is underway, but still days away from helping. And the Air Force also has to deal with GITMO. Once *TR* arrives, they are going to augment the GITMO force and Aruba defense force. For now it's us and the boys in blue who will knock their lights out and neutralize the FAV. CAG, who's leading the San Ramón strike?"

Matson motioned to Wilson. "Jim Wilson, sir, CO of VFA-16." Wilson nodded an acknowledgement.

Davies studied Wilson for a moment. "Yes, nice to finally meet you. What's your plan?"

Wilson was taken aback. He had a general idea of what he wanted to do but had checked none of the details with Matson. Despite that, he knew he had better sound confident.

"Sir, we are planning a large raid. About forty aircraft will simultaneously hit their integrated air defenses and target aircraft shelters and revetments. We'll need big wing tankers from the Air Force, some *Tomahawks*, maybe a SEAL insert, a big defense suppression plan. We've only scanned the requirements, and the strike planning team meets once we finish here, sir."

"Okay, CAG, I want the TLAM and SOF requirements ASAP, but Skipper, here's your new tasking. I want you to cut their runways. Leave their damn jets alone. If they come up, then shoot them down and get you a Silver Star. But leave them alone on deck. We want a force-in-being to maintain the balance of power in this region. If they're smart, they'll hunker down and not come up."

Stunned, Wilson worked hard to control his body language. "Cutting" a runway, or in the case of San Ramón, run*ways,* was a high-risk/low-reward proposition. The craters generated by weapon impacts could be filled with relative ease, which could necessitate a return mission to keep them cut. Or the FAV could just use taxiways for take-offs and landings. They could even use dispersal fields and highway airstrips when they saw the United States coming…which Davies just said he wanted them to see as the ship moved through the Lesser Antilles' chain. Maybe such a show of force would cause the Venezuelans to back down, but if Wilson did lead a strike, why pull the first punch?

Another factor was the delivery. A dive would be the best way to hurl the weapons into the runways with an even greater kinetic effect, but with the tradeoff was added risk to the aircrew. Would he have to *plan* a pulled punch, selling it to his experienced aviators as a smart use of tactical airpower? Would this become another half-hearted American military operation? Weed and his *misfits* were out there *literally* taking no prisoners, but now—in the current world spotlight—would he have to risk his people for the *image* of force that the Venezuelans could counter? Devil Davies was a warrior and no doubt knew what he was asking. No, *ordering.* This had to be direction from Washington. Devil had combat experience in Iraq in the '90s. He knew full well what a dive delivery into alerted defenses entailed. Had *anyone* up the chain pushed back?

"Yes, sir," Wilson answered, for the moment "living to fight another day," hoping that CAG could intercede for him. He had a sudden realization that he, too, would be seen by his lieutenants as not pushing back. Later, in private...he hoped.

Up forward, the C-2 props changed pitch, and seconds later all heard a faint thud followed by a *ziiiiip* sound as the C-2 shot down the track. The catapult shuttle crashed into the water brake with a *boom* as the aircraft took to the air and turned right off the bow.

A lone "ding" sounded on the 1MC. Admiral Meyerkopf was gone, heading for the beach. Without question, a new sheriff was in town.

CHAPTER 44

Sun Tzu said, "The line between disorder and order lies in logistics...." In the arcane vernacular of military acronyms and jargon, RFF (Request for Forces) is one acronym professional staff officers must keep in mind. Their job is not to fight. Their job is to provide fighters, like Wilson, with the tools, actual and supporting, the fighters need to do their jobs. If Wilson and the aviators of Carrier Air Wing SIX are at the tip of the spear, various logistics staffs are the shaft, tasked to deliver what military urban legend says is "the firstest with the mostest." This task involves hundreds and thousands of military personnel in and out of uniform who use arcane terms like OPORD, CONPLAN, and OPCON, to name a few. Thousands of miles from the action, these staff undertake a monumental responsibility when going to full-scale war against a capable enemy. *Time* is always of the essence. *Logistics* are indeed for professionals.

This concept was dramatically displayed during World War II, when the "Arsenal of Democracy" delivered to American and Allied commanders a *tidal wave* of American steel that the Axis powers had no answer for. Then, separated by two oceans and relatively safe, America had time to retool her factories while the military forces at her disposal held, and, in some cases, reversed Axis thrusts before fresh men and materiel appeared in the latter half of the war.

It was SOUTHCOM's job to coordinate the flow of materiel from the United States to the region, to provide the joint component commanders with the bombs and bullets, the fuel and lubricants, and the meat and potatoes needed to execute the Operational Plan, the plan in which Wilson and the others would soon be nameless and faceless cogs. From spare *Hornet* F404 engines to copy machine toner, the United States could not be caught wanting the "nails" required for victory. And the logisticians ensured they would not be.

A tenet of American military strategy since the Korean War is the concept of forward deployment, to include forces garrisoned in Europe and Asia. Expeditionary in nature, the Navy and Marine Corps live by it, routinely deploying from Continental U.S. bases for months at a time to spots of world tension such as the Persian Gulf and Western Pacific. In earlier times, it was the Mediterranean, North Atlantic, and even the Caribbean.

The Caribbean. Long ignored by Beltway strategists and politicians, the whole region, with the notable exception of Haiti, was a playground for the rich from all over the world. Cruise ships, resorts, green islands, near-perfect weather, megayachts, money. *Fantasy.* The delights and temptations of the flesh were everywhere in this warm-water paradise, an uncomplicated escape only hours by plane.

It was easy to dismiss the threat of illegal narcotics and the power of the kingpins and narco-states. After all, where was the threat? Most nation-states in the region were social and economic basket cases, with military capability that bordered on laughable. Content to *appear* to toe Washington's line, they were addicted to the aid dollars America dispensed to the "downtrodden." The swath from Panama to Venezuela was swimming in enough petro dollars and illegal drug monies to raise everyone's standard of living to heights unseen. But, at the behest of the kingpins, the politicians stoked the fires of American exploitation and resentment, banking on American guilt to keep the aid flowing and ensuring that the "War on Drugs" was waged on an ineffective simmer. The pretenses allowed everyone to save face.

At some point, even Daniel Garcia would have enough mansions and yachts, girls and planes. Where else were those dollars going?

In a bizarre arrangement of strange bedfellows, the kingpins moved cash into the hands of state sponsors of terror to help keep the United States off balance in the Middle East. At the cost of, say, a small and "manageable" Iranian footprint, if not for the "protection" afforded by a regime bent on world domination, the largely Catholic, secular, and pleasure-seeking South Americans could rest easy knowing the American behemoth was tied up elsewhere. In like manner, the Russians, cash strapped and with a sizable underclass seeking a drug-induced escape from their own miserable existence, could be depended on to build a submarine—for military use or cartel smuggling, didn't matter—and to fly nuclear bombers under the Americans' nose whenever the situation called for it. Everything had its price.

It appeared now that the Americans were tired of the game, and media cameras watching F-16s land in Puerto Rico and full battle-rattle paratroops load into C-17s in North Carolina confirmed it. While forces flowed to Caribbean staging bases and to the waters around Venezuela and Panama, the *tyranny of distance* ensured that the movement would take time. Unlike other conflicts that required the United States to defend and hold, time was now the enemy of a strategy that required the Americans to strike soon to preclude the Venezuelans from dispersing their assets. The media—and agents watching—confirmed that real airplanes and real soldiers were flowing into the region at a never-before-seen rate to augment the forces already present. For their part, the logisticians counted every stitch in the military whip the long arm of the United States was preparing to crack hard against Venezuela.

With the sun setting behind her, *Coral Sea* ploughed east through the waves to take up her position in the Atlantic, away from restricted waters and shielded from the diesel submarine threat. With a "bone in her teeth," she had spent the afternoon blasting through the Virgin Islands between St. Thomas and St. Croix, in sight of every manner of pleasure craft, merchant, cruise ship and fishing trawler. The warm, 40-knot wind whipped at the hair of excited nugget aviators perched on the swaying bow, observing the islands about them: the small "rock" of Sombrero Island twelve miles to the northeast, Dog Island to the southeast, Anguilla and Saint-Martin behind it. On deck himself to get some fresh air after dinner, Wilson ambled among the parked aircraft in the "corral" between Elevators 1 and 2. Looking south, he noted a sailboat a mile off, spinnaker flying as a *Whaler* MH-60R made another low pass over it. Davies wanted the ship to be seen, and the people on that boat were getting the full majesty of 100,000 tons of American resolve passing left to right against the dramatic western sky. Wilson figured the boat would soon be turning to avoid the large waves of the carrier's wake that would be on them in minutes. Closer to Saint-Martin would allow network coverage to send friends the photos they were snapping on their phones.

Wilson could see the kids up forward were excited, excited to be involved in a real world operation, ready to make history, ready to be *tested*. He, on the other hand, was apprehensive, not about his ability to lead them or about how to deal with the Venezuelan threat, but about the manufactured sense of urgency from Davies and, apparently, Washington. He soon became lost in his thoughts as he stared at the outline of Saint-Martin twenty or so miles away.

In two days, Wilson was scheduled to lead a deck-load strike to San Ramón. Looking around the flight deck, he was reminded of what that looked like. Almost every aircraft he saw, some forty aircraft, would be launched. It would take about an hour. The join up south of the ship, then finding and tanking from four KC-10s, would take another hour. They would then push out in a tactical formation, check in with the AWACS, and bump up the airspeed at the IP. They would avoid "neutral" Trinidad and enter Venezuela with a hail of defense suppression, and, if the FAV sent up fighters, a hail of missiles would knock them down. He didn't expect the FAV would fly at night, and if they did, they would be nearly *blind* compared to the Americans with Data Link and NVGs and FLIRs to augment their powerful radars. Wilson guessed by the time one of their rusty F-16 pilots got a lock, he would already be targeted by Wilson with a radar missile, only a trigger squeeze away. *Ducks in a barrel.* Wilson hoped, for their own sakes, they didn't come up.

He strode aft past the island and wondered, *What's the rush? Why not wait until* Theodore Roosevelt *gets here? And the Marine Expeditionary Unit and all the Air Force tac air? The bombers in South Dakota and the paratroops in Kentucky and North Carolina could be kept on alert.* Wilson knew it would take less than two weeks to raise a credible American hammer over Venezuela that would likely diffuse the situation. *A diplomat? All this over a diplomat?* Wilson thought.

And the tasking! Cut the runways? It was as if they were being ordered to punch with brass knuckles but land nothing more than a soft jab. Wilson had a recurring thought that made him uneasy: that the United States was again going to pull its punch—by design—while he and his pilots were facing real AAA and SAMs fired by an angry and determined enemy. Once the runways were cut, the Venezuelans could fill the craters in days, a week at most. It was a recoverable injury that made no sense when factored in with Annie's mining strike, which *would* shut down Río Salta. Mining a harbor was a serious military objective that took months to recover from, even if the Americans—knowing where the mines were dropped—helped sweep the area later.

Wilson tried to guess at the U.S. objective. Punish the Venezuelans for the drug trade run from their country? Remind them who's boss in the Western Hemisphere? Discourage their nascent relationship with Iran? Up the cost of their cozy relationship with Russia? *Maybe it's more. Maybe they have something we don't know about.*

He figured that had to be it. Why else attack a country that wasn't on their radar five days ago? *Faith.* True faith and allegiance. He and the *Firebirds* were going to man their jets and fly hundreds of miles to strike a sovereign nation on faith. Those before him had done it. *Ours is but to do and die.*

The JOs on the bow, far from unthinking automatons, would nevertheless launch and fly into the enemy defenses like generations before them because Wilson, their CO, ordered them to do so. Like Matson ordered him, and Devil Davies ordered Matson. No, Wilson and the other aviators each sensed the mixture of anticipation and dread in themselves and each other. *Washington might turn this off, but we've gotta be ready if they don't.* Deep down, Wilson knew he was excited, too, and that soon turned into a personal indictment of guilt.

Wilson navigated the tie-down chains between two *Rhinos* and stood at the flight deck round-down. For several moments, he watched the boiling, frothy wake generated by *Coral Sea*'s four giant screws. Nearly a football field wide, the wake extended all the way to the horizon, the red sun sinking into it as the wake met the sky. Wilson figured they were making at least 25 knots. On the other side of the *Super Hornet,* he noted a brown-shirted plane captain taking a picture of the sunset. He figured the girl to be a teenager, excited to see the beautiful scene, wanting to record a memory of it. Although Wilson had witnessed such sunsets many times before on other ships on other oceans, he was grateful to see this one tonight. Despite the wind whipping at his flight suit legs, he wanted to stay and enjoy it, but he had duties below, and, as a senior officer, couldn't be seen wasting *too* much time in reflection. He turned and headed to the island.

What new thing did the Venezuelans have? Was it a threat? Would he be leading his pilots into some unknown danger?

CHAPTER 45

(USS *Coral Sea*, Western Atlantic)

Wilson sensed the increase in the ship's roll when he awoke at 0620. He switched on the TV monitor and selected the inertial navigation screen that displayed numeric data on the ship's lat/long, course and speed: 17 41 North, 59 54 West, heading southeast at ten knots. In the Atlantic about 100 miles off St. Kitts. Wilson figured the ship would transit at an easy pace down the Antilles chain with some day and night cycles thrown in to keep jets and pilots sharp before the main event tomorrow night. His day would be spent in CVIC flight planning with Stretch and Coach. One of his nugget pilots, LT Conner Davis, "Irish," had been hovering about the planning team and helping with the suppression package. Wilson knew he wanted to go on this one. He would schedule Irish as one of the HARM shooters. Wilson looked at the PLAT to "see" outside. From the image on the screen it was sunny. A good day was in the offing. The rolling of the 100,000-ton carrier wasn't out of limits for his pilots.

On the eve of battle, Wilson wanted to give his squadron a talk, to inspire them, to calm them. He wanted them to focus on the reason it was important they were there. He was still troubled at how fast all this was happening. *Coral Sea* was featured in network newscasts with video of the ship transiting north of St. Croix yesterday. Just the way Devil wanted it. The military situation in the Caribbean was 24/7 on the cable networks, and Wilson was surprised the powers-that-be hadn't shut down the satellite link that provided it—and the email connectivity to home.

What should I say to them? Wilson thought. Nuggets like Irish and Macho were chomping at the bit to go, to *prove* themselves in combat. All Wilson had to do was point and Irish and the rest of the nuggets—even veterans like Stretch and Olive—would run to their jets, drop themselves in the cockpit, fire up the engines, and go. Annie, *Steady-As-She-Goes Annie*, would man her jet in a less excited manner, taking everything in stride as usual, and she would launch and fly to any target assigned and deliver any weapon assigned. In three days, she was going to lead a strike, a big one, to mine Río Salta. Wilson drew water in the sink to shave.

Venezuela had oil money *and* drug money. Would the Venezuelans risk an American attack that was going to shut down both lucrative sources of income? *Why invite it by jailing the diplomat and why accept it?* Wilson thought. Broadcast video of Venezuelan mobs protesting the impending American action resembled mobs in any number of Middle Eastern population centers, the difference being that, in Caracas, women protested alongside their men and showed more skin.

Venezuela was by no means friendly, in bed with any and all enemies of the United States, sworn or disguised. The country was a powerful narco-state that fomented revolution in the region, welcomed Iranian influence, undermined American initiatives at every turn, and had a modern air force that faced no regional threat. While Wilson couldn't explain their behavior, he was also at a loss to explain why Washington was moving so fast, not trying deterrence or economic measures before pulling the trigger.

Wilson reviewed the flight schedule: Blade on a test hop, Ripper and Jumpin doing 2 v 2 intercepts with the *Raiders*, Ghost on a sea surface search, Annie and Dusty on a night intercept hop, Olive and Macho providing intercept training for one of the strike group small boys before their night trap. Routine training hops. Tomorrow would be the real thing.

After a quick breakfast, Wilson checked on things in the ready room and went to CVIC to begin a long day of planning for his strike the following night. It was foremost in his thoughts: forty jets, dozens of weapons required to "cut" two parallel runways and a taxiway, the fighter sweep package, the radar suppression package with jammers and escorts, the command and control plan, tankers, all manner of radio frequencies, a night launch in order, the join-up, the weather, en route formation, the air threat, surface-to-air threat, SAR assets and positioning, the ship positioning, and a night carrier landing in the wee hours. Then, he had to plan to do it again the next night, and the night after that, striking *new* targets, each one designed to attrite the FAV and gain air supremacy. Tomorrow night he would have to settle for superiority.

The plan was for *Coral Sea* to operate southeast of Barbados, launch two hours after sunset, form up, tank, push south for 30 minutes, then turn west and accelerate for the run in to San Ramón. After they hit the airfield, they would come off south, regroup, and transit back to tank those who needed it and recover around midnight. Another strike was scheduled to launch at 0300 with a dawn, "pinky," recovery.

It was critical that Wilson's strike succeed in grounding the Venezuelan fighters in the eastern part of the country and preclude the FAV from transferring fighters to San Ramón to defend their port at Río Salta.

Wilson's jets would be loaded up with 1,000 pounders to produce large craters. At least his formations would be coming in high with a running start. Annie's mining birds would be carrying mines weighing well over 1,000 pounds. The mines had no nose cones: it would be as if Annie's pilots were lugging large trash cans under their wings. They would have to come in slow over the gulf to deliver them close to shore in the Río Salta delta. Because there was no way the mining birds' raid could succeed with a significant fighter threat nearby, Wilson's strike *had* to eliminate that threat.

Each strike built upon another, and the leads, having a working knowledge of the aimpoints and expected degradation each mission would achieve, had to make assumptions on the success of the previous strike. They also knew not to bank on it, knew they would have to have contingencies to deal with a stronger threat than expected. First in combat, Wilson didn't have to worry about *that*...but he was under no illusion that the Venezuelans would just roll over. They would fight back, and hard.

The launch sequence, the tanking, the weather...*every possible detail* had to be accounted for with dozens of contingency plans. Wilson had today and tomorrow to imprint them on this brain and to consider every *what if* with his team. He then had to brief it to CAG and Admiral Davies who would pepper him with questions on those details. Without their verbal okay the strike would not proceed. Not a good thing.

Wilson felt the ship pitch and roll and was reminded that they were pretty much alone in the open Atlantic, even with *Gettysburg* a few miles away in escort. He wished he had a "lily pad," in the form of a destroyer, to launch a quick reaction combat SAR if the situation arose. Somebody's louder voice had gotten the small boys sent to the vicinity of Curacao and Aruba, and he doubted the *Rustlers* and their MH-60 *Sierras* could use Trinidad as a forward base. He would ask, though.

As Wilson studied the tactical charts of San Ramón, other strike team members met him in CVIC to begin their long day of planning. Deputy CAG Kay was going with Wilson, flying on his wing, but Wilson's assistant strike lead was his Ops Officer Stretch Armstrong. Dusty Rhodes would fly on Stretch's wing. Representatives from all the squadrons were there, each with a responsibility in this lethal cross-functional team. DCAG Kay, though, was too senior to be part of the planning; he would show up at brief time tomorrow evening.

Shane brought the team an updated order-of-battle chart. F-16s were imaged at San Ramón, and tactical SAM launchers were spotted in the vicinity of the airfield, but the Venezuelans could easily disperse them. A fixed SAM site was located near Río Salta, and another one south on the

Orinoco River. Wilson saw that the "seam" from the radii of both sites fell near San Ramón. He shook his head in wonder that the Venezuelans allowed for such a thin SAM umbrella over their main fighter base in the east. It would allow the Americans to come right at it. He surmised they didn't anticipate an attack from the sea. For Wilson, the mobile SAMs and AAA of all calibers were threat enough.

By 1000, CVIC was full of aviators in flight suits grouped at tables, poring over charts. Billy Martin would lead a follow-on strike after Wilson to hit the naval base at Río Salta, and the following day Army logistics sites would be destroyed to preclude resupply of the port and oil terminal. Then Annie would come in. Meanwhile, Air Force bombers and Strike Eagles with F-22 escort would deal with the threat to Aruba and Curacao from the Caracas region, and *Theodore Roosevelt* was expected to help them in another three days.

Wilson was measuring the distance between the initial point and the roll-in when CAG entered and caught Wilson's attention, motioning him over. Wilson got up and right away noticed CAG's pained expression. *Oh, oh,* Wilson thought.

"Flip, we just got word. This strike is going tonight."

Apprehensive, Wilson blinked at Matson. "*Tonight, sir?*"

"Tonight.... Time on target in ten hours."

CHAPTER 46

Wilson couldn't believe it. "CAG, you gotta be *shittin' me*."

"Nope. You and Billy Martin are flying tonight, and we're moving everything up after that. Just us. No Air Force fighters. We think they have the *Yakhont* missile from the Russians, a supersonic sea-skimming ship-killer. We've imaged a possible launch site here on the Paria Peninsula, and they may have an air-launched variant. If so, they could have fit one to their *Flankers*, so we're running south now to a position northeast of Barbados, using the island as a shield. We're not going any further." Wilson knew this doubled his range to San Ramón, and the sheer magnitude of what had to be planned and briefed in the next ten hours—*no eight...less!*—was daunting. He tried to find a reprieve.

"CAG, ten hours from now is dusk. You want us to hit them at *dusk*? Too early for NVGs, flying into the sun. Why, sir?" Wilson knew he was whining, but dusk and dawn were the *worst* possible times on target. At least dawn would give him ten extra hours to plan.

"We are concerned about the *Yakhont*. We have to hit them tonight."

Not giving up, Wilson persisted. "*Dusk,* sir? CAG, please."

Matson's face tightened into a frown as he locked eyes with Wilson.

"The White House wants to go on national TV in the eight o'clock hour to announce the strike—after it happens. As soon as you go feet wet on the egress, the President informs the nation."

Wilson shook his head in disbelief and frustration. Now he had to inform his fellow strikers, his squadronmates, his *friends*, about this flawed plan, *his* flawed plan. He had to sell it to *their* disbelieving faces. Matson continued.

"Flip, if you had two days to plan you would take the full two days. If you had a week, it would take a week. An 81% good plan tonight, *executed with violence*, is better than a 95% plan in two days. Now, you have my word that my staff and I are going to support you fully. I'm going to the bridge now to run interference for you. *Whatever Commander Wilson needs, he gets.* What is your game plan?"

Wilson answered, "Three divisions of strikers, slick Mk 80 series bombs in a high dive to cut two runways and a taxiway. A dedicated sweep ahead of us, lots of HARM and jamming from the *Growlers.* Will we have signals recon with an EP-3?"

"Expect it, and AWACS."

"And big wing tankers, sir. Gotta have them to get all these jets down there. At least two, three would be great."

"Already working it," Matson said as he nodded.

"And *Tomahawk....* Request a TLAM strike to soften their defenses and degrade their comms."

"Will ask, and I think that's doable. But we need to keep *Gettysburg* close by to intercept any sea-skimmers."

"Yes, sir," Wilson replied. He then made another request. "CSAR. Can we stage some *Rustlers* in Trinidad if we need them?"

CAG shook his head. "That's a tall order for a couple of reasons. Getting diplomatic clearance is number one, Number two, it telegraphs our intentions. It's a long drive from here, even from our expected launch posit. You'll have to plan that it isn't available."

"If one of us goes down?" Wilson responded.

"Evade until we can get to you. You guys will have plenty firepower to handle the threat. Look, take a quick look at all this, assign tasks to your people, make a list of questions and requests and get them to my staff. I'm sending DCAG down here with orders to make your life easier. You've got all the senior firepower you need to handle any request of the ship. I'd get them to build the bombs ASAP."

"Yes, sir. Thanks," Wilson said, resigned to his fate. "When do you want us to give you a run down?"

Matson checked his watch. "Noon, with the admiral. I'm outta here, and I'm at your service. All of us are. Task us."

"Thanks, CAG, appreciate it," Wilson smiled. Eight hours to launch, six hours to brief. *Sonofabitch!* he thought.

He walked over to his planning team. They had seen him talking to the Wing Commander, and Wilson could tell they were uneasy. He took a breath.

"We're going tonight."

The aviators' faces fell as they absorbed the news.

"Twenty hundred time on target, three divisions of bombers, a fighter sweep, suppression element with jammers and escorts. Expect AWACS and big wing tankers. Probable on the EP-3 and *Tomahawk*. No CSAR. Day launch, night recovery. And expect 400 miles—each way."

The aircrew let it sink in. Thirty aircraft launched from 400 miles at sea, major tanking evolution, hitting a well-defended target at *dusk* for some stupid reason, then back through the tankers to the ship for a night trap. The silver lining was a day cat shot. Shane hovered in the background. She knew something wasn't right and wanted to help if she could.

As the boss, Wilson wouldn't give them the opportunity to bitch. Going around the table, he assigned tasks.

"All right.... Stretch, you've got the strike element plan and weapons delivery. Get Gunner Short to get the Ordnance Handling Officer up to speed on the load plan ASAP so they can start building. Dusty— tanking plan and launch sequence plan. I want you to be the fuel and timing expert. Get with CAG OPS to coordinate the tankers and get one of the catapult officers in here to help you with the launch sequence plan. Find our expected launch position. Get help." Wilson then looked at Irish and Shane.

"Irish, make us smart on the threat. Shane, help him with the enemy order of battle and EW frequencies, training, tactics, all of it. You've got ninety minutes. *Go*. Midol, comm plan. Pokey, fighter sweep element— want four *Rhinos* with four AMRAAM, two '*Winders* and bullets. Wizard, want your jamming plan—two jets and enough HARM shooters who can also escort the jammers. Get with Irish and Shane. *Go*."

The junior pilots nodded and got to work as Wilson continued issuing tasks to the rest of the planning team, pilots and aircrew who would be flying on this strike in mere hours. Wilson noted the forlorn helicopter pilot. Wilson knew he wanted to help, but, with no combat search and rescue option, he would be unable to unless one of the jets had trouble near the ship. Wilson took him aside.

"Chan, we have no lily pad." The young aviator nodded his understanding, but Wilson could see his disappointment. He then pointed to the chart.

"Except this island.... Look at Trinidad. Study it. Assess the distances from here and the distance from the island to the target. Tell me what's possible. Give me something for my back pocket."

The lieutenant smiled at Wilson. "Will do, sir."

Wilson slapped the lieutenant's back as he went to work. He then checked his watch. Seven and a half hours until launch.

Edgar Hernandez led his entourage through the blast doors of the aircraft shelter at San Ramón. The early model F-16A was painted in earth tone camouflage and loaded with four *Python* missiles. The canopy was up and the boarding ladder attached. The Group Commander was saying something about readiness in his ear. He hadn't shut up since he arrived, and Hernandez was growing weary of it. He had flown this very jet many times as a younger man, over the Gulf of Paria, over the Amazon basin, even to some of the Antilles islands. Adoring crowds came to the airport to gawk at the sleek jet—and the stud pilot climbing out of it. *Happier days.*

"Senòr General, we have eight *Vipers* on full alert able to get airborne with less than five minutes notice. Our early warning radars are manned 24/7, and, once the Americans are detected in *any* direction, the group's aircraft can be airborne to defend the Bolivarian Republic."

Hernandez was a realist. *We have no chance against the Americans,* he thought.

"Group Commander, why are no *Sparrow* missiles loaded?" Hernandez asked. He sensed the fearful eyes of the others, wondering how their group commander would react to the question.

"Because of the foresight of the leaders of the AMV and the abundant resources of the Bolivarian Republic, the *Flanker* interceptors will destroy the American formations well out to sea. Then we will engage any leakers that dare to penetrate our sovereign airspace. We have a supply of missiles that can last *days*—enough time for us to destroy all the American aircraft sent against us." The entourage now turned to Hernandez to gauge his reaction.

Hernandez glared at the man with disgust. "You said the *Flankers* would destroy the American formations."

"Senòr General, in the unlikely event any survive, we have more than enough airborne force to repel them." The man's face betrayed him. He realized Hernandez knew he was lying, so he gave the only answer he could in front of his subordinates. In the small, insular AMV, he and Hernandez had known each other for over 20 years. Lying to superiors was a way of life as the truth led to demotion—or worse. Now, after advancing up the ladder, they were lying to each other on a daily basis, as most all did as the Venezuelan society adapted to its new normal. Hernandez would lie to his superiors today, too; the only question was how many times.

"And your anti-aircraft defenses. How will you deconflict with our fighters once they are airborne?"

The Group Commander stammered as he tried to formulate an answer. Hernandez knew the answer would be a lie, so he threw him a lifeline.

"Let me ask you this then. Have your anti-aircraft gunners, fighter controllers, and pilots trained in point defense in a coordinated manner to avoid fratricide by anti-aircraft artillery or surface-to-air missiles?"

"*Sí, mí general!*"

"At night?"

The man looked at Hernandez with big eyes before answering. "Sí, mí general!"

"When? When was your last exercise at night, because we know that's when the Americans come. We can set our watches! When did you conduct this exercise, Group Commander?" Hernandez was impatient for an answer.

"Ah, it was some months ago, mí general."

"Some months ago, eh? When specifically? Show me the report. What did your group learn from it? What are your strengths? What are your weak areas?"

"We...met all required exercise objectives, mí general.... We...."

"Do your gunners have night vision devices? Do they know how to use them? Do they have fresh batteries? How often do you train with them? Are they coordinated with your target tracking radars? How often do you conduct live fire drills? Are your gun emplacements supplied with sufficient ammunition? Can your gunners tell the difference between an F-16 taking off and an American F-18 three miles up?"

Hernandez refused to be lied to anymore today and found his newfound focus on the truth to be refreshing, despite the answers to his questions, which he knew would be bad. Not waiting for answers from the now reeling Group Commander, he spun toward the nervous F-16 pilot standing by the aircraft ladder. He watched the Commanding General of the Venezuelan Air Force approach him with a determined scowl.

"You. What is your name?"

The surprised pilot snapped to attention and answered as Hernandez and the entourage moved toward him. "Capitán José Manuel Espinoza, mí general!"

"Capitán, when was the last time you flew at night?"

The young pilot glanced at his Group Commander for help, but Hernandez stopped him.

"I asked *you*, Capitán! *When was the last time you flew at night!*"

"Last year, mí general!" the flustered pilot answered, his lip quivering.

"*Last year*, you say. In the air defense exercise? With other aircraft in formation?"

The hapless pilot turned pale with fear, eyes darting between Hernandez and his Group Commander. "No, mí general! It was to calibrate the approach control radars!" All were silent as Hernandez bore in for the truth.

"I see. Did you fly during the daytime portion of the air defense exercise?"

The young man, beads of sweat on his forehead, did not know how to answer.

Hernandez continued his probe. "Are you aware of an air defense exercise conducted *some months ago?*" While waiting for an answer, he could see the young pilot was petrified. *I should go easy on him,* Hernandez thought. *He may have less than 36 hours to live. I may have less than 36 hours to live.*

"Mí general, I heard of one a few years ago!" the pilot blurted. The Group Commander jumped in.

"Mí general, the training gained from an exercise lasts for two years! We have conducted training in accordance with written directives!" The Group Commander, too, was beginning to tremble, which would cause a scene in front of his men. Hernandez glared at him, ready to put an end to the charade.

"*Come with me,*" Hernandez muttered and headed to the hangar entrance adjacent the flight line, the Group Commander trailing as if to the gallows. Some of the entourage began to follow, and Hernandez stopped them cold. "*Just him!*" he bellowed to the dumbfounded group.

Once on the flight line and out of earshot, Hernandez turned to the Group Commander.

"That *boy* is going to his death tomorrow night, and you've done nothing to give him even a *chance* at survival! You are paid to think about what could happen and prepare this group for any contingency and you've fucked around by taking supersonic joyrides over the jungle and chasing pleasure yachts in the Paria Gulf. Your group has lots of pretty pictures of yourselves flying your airplanes in show formation, but that does nothing to defend the Bolivarian Republic from outside aggression! Don't you know an American super carrier has been spotted passing through the

Lesser Antilles and into the Atlantic? Do you even know the expected threat quadrant?"

"Mí general, who could have forseen the Americans—?"

"*You,* dammit! Do I have to train your men for you? Seems I do. You are relieved of group command, effective immediately. That scared *kid* could do a better job leading *you* against the Americans, but I'm not letting you anywhere near a jet. *You* are grounded. I will lead him and the others tomorrow night, and you can watch us go to our deaths with honor. If you are lucky, an American bomb will fly right into your lying mouth. Then, you won't have to live the rest of your life in shame."

Shocked, the demoted officer pleaded with his former mentor. "Edgar, *please.*... Edgar, let me redeem—"

"No, and how *dare* you call me by my first name? Get out of my sight!"

Hernandez stormed back to the group waiting in the hangar as the cashiered Group Commander walked away in shame.

Hernandez spotted the Deputy Commander. "You. You are in command of the Group. I want you and your pilots airborne this afternoon, and again tonight, practicing forward quarter intercepts. We expect the Americans tomorrow night. Break out the air-to-air missiles, and *get your people ready.*"

"Sí, mí general!" the Deputy said as he popped to attention and saluted.

Hernandez, still furious, headed to his car, and his aide scurried behind. His beloved *Fuerza Aérea Venezolana* was not ready for the *tsunami* approaching from the north. Ultimately, it was all *his* fault—through *his* lies and through his disinterest while acting as a *courtier* in Caracas by day and being serviced by Daniel's call girls by night. Cashiering the Group Commander in front of the others had made a point and had given them hope, but sacrificing him was an act to save himself from shame, displaying an *act* of leadership. He felt a deep personal guilt about serving the corrupt politicians and the cutthroat Daniel before serving his men. Edgar Hernandez had little hope for the ill-trained fighter pilots of San Ramón in their elderly *Vipers.* At least he would die with them—with *honor,* honor he had just denied to his subordinate commander.

The only thing that could save them now was if the Americans pulled their punch...or if the two Russian "toys" hidden along the outskirts of the field lived up to their billing. He directed the driver to take him home.

CHAPTER 47

Approaching noon, Matson led his DCAG, Wilson and Stretch to flag plot for the lap brief with Admiral Davies. This was Wilson's "show," with CAG and Deputy in support. Stretch carried a classified folder of imagery and a chart of the target area that depicted the aimpoints and potential threat rings. Once inside, Wilson took the chart and laid it on the table, and Stretch thumbed through the photos to find a satellite view of San Ramón with the Designated Mean Points of Impact, or DMPIs, marked.

As they set up the conference room, and before eight bells sounded, Admiral Davies walked in unannounced. He didn't say a word.

"Good morning, sir," CAG greeted him. "You remember Jim Wilson."

"Yes, Flip, ready to go?"

"Yes, sir," Wilson said as they shook hands. "This is my OPSO 'Stretch' Armstrong."

"Ted Armstrong, sir." Stretch added, extending his arm to shake hands with Davies.

"Nice to meet you. Okay, gents, we're going to remain standing, and you've got five minutes. Skipper, let's have the overview," Davies ordered in an abrupt tone.

Wilson swallowed and got to the point.

"Admiral, our tasking is a mission kill of the runways at San Ramón. We are launching at eighteen hundred from our expected launch posit here, northeast of Barbados. Thirty-seven aircraft with a dedicated sweep, radar and comm jamming, and three divisions of strikers loaded with laser guided bombs we are delivering in a dive to cut two runways and one taxiway at San Ramón at twenty-hundred local time. It's a *Viper* base with one squadron assigned, but they have two fixed SAM sites in the vicinity of the field and one at Río Salta. We launch, join up south of the ship in elements, then head south to rendezvous on two KC-10's. Once we get our gas, we push on timeline with the sweepers out front pretty much from the east, skirting Trinidad here, and avoiding the Río Salta defenses. We have a HARM suppression plan, two *Growlers* with escort, and two *Hummers* to augment one AWACS and one EP-3."

"Okay, lemme stop you. How about TLAM?"

"Sir, we've asked for TLAM to hit their early warning radars, C2 facilities, two 85mm AAA sites and the control tower. We've—"

Davies shook his head in disgust. "Why not the damn fuel farm?"

"We were refused, sir," Wilson replied.

"Who the hell refused you?"

"SOUTHCOM, sir. This is a mission kill on the runways, which will be out of action for several days before they are repaired, nothing more." Wilson was taken aback that Davies did not have a working knowledge of the tasking his aviators had been assigned.

Davies frowned. "Go on."

"Sir, we're going to come off left and circle back to the east to feet wet, then meet up with the KC-10 for another drink and back to the ship. About five hours total."

Davies was on a roll. "Where are the *Flankers?*"

"Imaged at Caracas, sir, and probably dispersed. We expect the *Vipers* to be dispersed. We've got plenty of firepower if the *Vipers* come up—and if the *Flankers* come over to help.

"What's the weather?"

Wilson drew a breath. "Not great, sir. Convective weather over the continent with high broken to overcast clouds in the vicinity of the islands. Winds at altitude are out of the east, which will help us on the run-in."

"When is astronomical twilight?"

"Sir, sunset is at 1821 local, so astronomical twilight is 1909 and night is 1936. The good news is we can affix our goggles as we approach the IP. The bad news is no moon tonight."

"When is your time on target?"

"Twenty-hundred local, sir."

"What time is that in Washington?"

"Nineteen-thirty, sir, thirty minutes behind."

Davies nodded as he studied the chart. "Combat SAR?"

"Sir, we don't have a lily pad, and the target is almost 400 miles from the launch posit. No, sir."

Davies nodded his understanding, unspoken between them that any downed aviators were on their own, at least for the night. Davies resumed.

"Thirty-seven aircraft. How many are going on the next strike?"

"A raid to Río Salta, sir, using SLAMs against the sub docks there. I think it's a division of strikers and a small suppression package. They've got lots of standoff and won't even go feet dry."

Davies studied the chart, breathing deeply. "Okay, what do you need from me?"

"Sir, do we have overflight rights for Trinidad?"

"No...yes," Davies said, grimacing. "We don't want to tip our hand and ask. Do what you have to."

CAG jumped in.

"Admiral, regarding the CSAR distance, we don't have a destroyer down there to keep a *Sierra* turning on deck, but what if we put one here?" CAG pointed to the island of Tobago on the chart.

Davies extended his thumb and middle finger on the chart to measure the distance between Tobago and San Ramón.

"That's about an hour's flight time, as the crow flies."

"Yes, sir, but it's better than nothing. What we need is fuel, and if we show up at this airport, Arthur Napoleon Raymond Robinson International with three or four SEALs to ensure the right attitude—and a bag of fifty dollar bills—they'll fill up the aircraft themselves."

"And if they don't?"

"We'll just take it, sir—and leave them the bag of money."

"So you want my SEALs?"

"Two CSAR aircraft with door gunners, rockets, and two SEALs each."

"With no dip clearance, no permission, a sovereign nation..."

"Yes, sir," CAG said.

"You gotta be shittin' me," *Devil Dog* answered. "Formations spilling over a fucking island is one thing, but Americans landing in a Banana Republic and taking their fucking gas at gunpoint?"

"Yes, sir. We'll pay for it, of course."

"You are serious?"

"Sir, with very little notice, my guys are being asked to fly down there in six hours in less than optimum light conditions, *damage some freakin' runways*, and fly back in a five-hour round trip with no CSAR. Just so the White House can announce it on TV."

"Dammit, Matson, I would get my ass handed to me in a sling."

"Sir, look at these pilots. *They* are going down there. Flip here just briefed you on this strike with a straight face, but I assure you he and his lieutenants know how screwed up this is. Jumping through our ass because of some artificial media timeline. If my recommendation is unacceptable, sir, then please get us a small boy as a lily pad. But yes, sir, please ask higher authority to cover you, to cover *them*."

Aware of the others watching them, Davies glared at Matson, taking his measure, surprised that Matson had confronted him in this way. Wilson was impressed. *CAG's doing battle with Devil for us!*

"Do not send helos *anywhere* until I give the word." Davies said, but with newfound respect. He was leaving the matter open to at least save face in the short term.

"Aye, aye, sir," Matson nodded, his backbone strengthened. Davies then turned to Wilson.

"Skipper, I expect you are able to lead a strike and cut a runway, that your sweepers can shoot down any bandits they send up, and that your HARM shooters know how to keep their heads down. What do you need in the next three hours?"

"Sir, I worry about the bombs being built and loaded on time, about the tankers being on station, about real-time ISR, about the ship launching us in sequence, and about briefing 60 guys in three hours, the comm lash-up with AWACS. The weather, sir.... What's the go/no-go on that?"

Davies pursed his lips. "This strike must hit the target on time, as close as you can. Do what you must. I'll talk to the Captain. Expect to get whatever you need. CAG, I'll call Miami. Stand by for their ruling on TLAM and CSAR, but, regardless, this is going."

"Yes, sir," Matson replied. Wilson and the others nodded their understanding.

"Good hunting," Davies said and left the way he entered.

CHAPTER 48

Time was slipping away from Jim Wilson, fast.

He was shocked at the speed with which it melted away as he and the others concentrated on each part of the strike. Wilson, as the strike lead, needed to be an *expert* on every aspect of the strike and needed to *know* where each aircraft was and what they were doing at any time during the five-hour mission, but he was overwhelmed. He wasn't *ready*. Everything had been rushed, and he wasn't certain that the yellow shirt directors had the launch sequence plan, wasn't certain the tankers would be where they planned with the gas, wasn't certain the TLAMs would hit on time. He was *uncertain* about the weather, and as he trudged up the island ladder in full flight gear with nav bag in hand, he felt *Coral Sea* rolling in the powerful Atlantic swell.

And he was late. Start time was in five minutes, and he had yet to preflight and strap in...and calm himself down. As luck would have it, Wilson's jet, 301, was parked farthest away on the bow, some 700 feet distant from where he undogged the hatch and stepped onto the flight deck.

His brief to the seventy aircrew and staff in a cram-packed Ready Room 5 had been disjointed. He had been able to concentrate on the "snapshots" of where everyone should be at a given time, and on the target area tactics, but that was it. The rest had been haphazard. He was not sure about the threat, not sure about support assets, not sure about the command and control. The good news was that, except for the Air Force tankers, it was an all-Navy strike. If the AWACS showed, fine. Wilson and the others knew they could manage okay with support from their own *Condors*, who would have an E-2 orbiting over the tanker track. They had covered the basics in the briefing—81 percent good—but, to Wilson, much had been left out for a strike of this magnitude. Training would have to make up for the lack of detail.

As Wilson strode forward, leaning into the stiff breeze, he surveyed the scene. Hundreds of sailors from fuelers to catapult maintenance crewmen prepared the ship and aircraft for launch, and all the jets, canopies up, were surrounded by squadron technicians and trouble-shooters. Weapons were still being loaded, and some jets had been towed into parking spots for start up. A launch of 30+ planes was big, most everything on the flight deck, and Billy Martin's aircraft were in the hangar bay waiting for Wilson's strike to go. The ship would then bring them up two at a time on the four massive deck-edge elevators. This was going to be a challenge as the ship was pitching and rolling such that the launch—and certainly the night recoveries—would be sporty. Low, gray clouds were scattered along the horizon under an umbrella of high overcast as *Coral Sea* pounded through the white-capped waves to her expected launch posit.

Wilson walked past Ghost as he strapped himself into the ejection seat of his jet, 310, parked over the Cat 2 jet blast deflector. The jet was loaded with HARM missiles the nugget pilot would launch against a fixed SAM site near Río Salta. *Ghost may have more than he bargained for*, Wilson thought as he continued forward. The young aviator flying his first combat sortie would need to join up, plug on the tanker, then deliver his weapons on time to suppress the site, at night. He would have to fly hundreds of miles back to the tanker and then find the ship for a night pitching-deck recovery—after some five hours airborne. *Varsity for sure.* All the strikers would depend on the HARM shooters using the call sign *Lance*, including this young pilot, to do their job so they could do theirs. It would be the same with the fighter sweep, using the call sign *Blocker*, and the jammers using *Volt*. All had to work as a cross-functional team with precise timing for the overall mission success of the dozen strike package jets led by Wilson, call sign *Slash*. Wilson again scanned the horizon and observed the deteriorating weather. How he missed the Caribbean.

After the main and element brief, Wilson had darted into the wardroom to make himself a peanut butter and jelly sandwich. He managed to cram it down before signing for the jet. In the ready room he checked out a pair of NVGs, a .45mm pistol, a blood chit, and took a call from air ops. *No, the strike can't launch any earlier!* After suiting up in the paraloft, he transited the length of the ship to the jet, taking furtive glances at the PLAT monitors whenever he could to gauge the weather. At every point, he felt the deck heave and roll underneath him.

All day the ship and air wing ordnancemen had built bombs in the magazines and loaded them on to the jets, loaded missiles, loaded chaff and flares. They were still loading as Wilson tramped between the bow cats against a forty-knot wind to the last jet on the bow, his jet. It was surrounded by maintainers, and a technician sat in the cockpit.

Oh, oh.

Chief Murrill met him as he approached.

"Skipper, we've had a minor crunch. A bomb cart hit the right stab."

"How bad, Chief?" Wilson asked him, concerned about both the jet and the time needed to fix it.

"A gash in the lower part of the stab. A bomb fin scraped it but didn't break the skin. The airframers say it's good to go, but the electricians are running flight control diagnostics tests to see if any maintenance codes are popped."

With Chief Murrill following, Wilson walked past the troubleshooters and over an electrical cord to see for himself. Crouching low, he saw a foot-long scratch in the bottom of the right horizontal stabilator. Somewhat deep, the gash exposed the black composite material. An airframes troubleshooter, Petty Officer Willen, hovered nearby.

"Petty Officer Willen, what do you think?"

"Sir, you can fly with it. We're gonna put speed tape on it, but we need to check that the jolt didn't damage the actuator. We're checkin' for codes now, sir."

Wilson frowned. The checks would take more time that he didn't have. Just then the air boss came over the 5MC loudspeaker. *"On the flight deck, aircrews have manned for the seventeen hundred launch. Time for all personnel to get into the proper flight deck uniform, helmets on and buckled, goggles down, sleeves rolled down..."*

As the air boss continued with the prestart litany and crews moved into position to start the engines of three dozen aircraft, Wilson leaned in so both Murrill and Willen could hear over the swirling wind.

"Okay, Chief, if your guys say it's up, I'm taking it. Going to do my preflight and get in, but we don't have much more time to troubleshoot. Make a call early, and I'll get into the spare. This is combat and I'm leading."

"Roger that, Skipper," Chief Murrill said. Willen nodded his acknowledgment.

As dozens of turbine engines around him sprang to life, Wilson did a quick preflight check. The ordies loaded the bombs, missiles, chaff and flares according to plan. An overworked sailor accidentally running a bomb cart into 301's horizontal stab could be dealt with. No one had screwed up on purpose. The accounting could wait.

Way up forward, mere feet from the deck edge, *Coral Sea's* pitch was pronounced. High winds buffeted him as Wilson ascended the ladder and lowered himself into the ejection seat where the plane captain helped strap him in. Perched on the forward deck edge, Wilson felt nothing but limitless sea beyond his left shoulder. Over 400 miles distant—and 2.5 hours away—was San Ramón. *Are they waiting? Do they* know*?*

Wilson sent the plane captain down with a smile as he closed the canopy to finish connecting himself to the seat in relative calm. Outside, the engines of the dozen jets parked on the bow howled as their pilots monitored their inertial navigation system alignments and entered waypoint coordinates. Wilson energized the battery and signaled the plane caption to begin the start sequence.

With his squadron troubleshooters and Chief Murrill watching, Wilson started the right and left engines and began setting his cockpit up for the flight. Off to the right, Petty Officer Willen stood ready to test the right stab, and Wilson gave him a thumbs-up. With that, Willen gave him the signal for back-stick. Wilson complied, holding it steady. No trouble codes were present on his flight control computer display. Willen had Wilson cycle the controls as other technicians near the stab watched it move. Satisfied, they gave another thumbs-up to Willen who relayed it to Wilson. *Firebird* 301 was an up jet.

Relieved, Wilson continued his checks. He soon noted an impatient yellow shirt director asking, via hand signals, if he was ready to taxi so they could begin to use Cat 2. With fifteen minutes to launch, Wilson knew he could finish his cockpit tasks elsewhere on deck—even airborne, if need be, heading to the tanker. The yellow shirt directed him to hold brakes as blue-shirted sailors ran underneath 301 to remove the tie-down chains. A moment later, the plane captain emerged with chains draped over his shoulders, giving his CO a salute that Wilson returned.

Wilson added a touch of power and crept forward as the yellow shirt directed him out of his spot and turned him aft down the bow. Twelve minutes to launch and the ship was still knifing south into the wind. A *Hummer* with folded wings and spinning props was parked behind the Cat 2 jet blast deflector. Wilson taxied past it, and the dozens of squadron troubleshooters, with care. The E-2s and tankers would be launched soon, and he needed to conduct a roll call on the strike common frequency.

"Ninety-nine *Broadsword*, radio check. *Slash* one-one."

"*Slash* one-two," Dusty responded in turn.

"*Slash* one-three," DCAG transmitted.

"*Slash* one-four," Stretch continued in order.

The rest of the strike package checked in: the *Blockers, Volts, Lances, Condors,* and the *Super Hornet* mission tankers, call sign *Arco*. The flight deck was a jumble of aircraft as the yellow shirts lined them up behind the catapults, and Wilson could see the deck was doing a good job of shooting them according to plan. He and the others in each cockpit continued with their checks—or just waited, lost in their thoughts. Wilson glanced at Ghost next to him. The nugget pilot was on his first combat mission, and, to Wilson, he appreared confident.

On the horizon, *Gettysburg* knifed through the waves in escort, a wisp of spray flying over her bow. As the strikers joined up on the Air Force tankers, she would launch a volley of TLAM to soften up San Ramón before Wilson's *main battery* arrived with the hammer.

Looking up at the island that towered above him, Wilson saw FOXTROT flapping hard in the breeze. *Coral Sea's* large battle flag flew above it at full extension as radar antennas spun from nearby masts. Wilson and thousands of his shipmates were on a U.S. Navy aircraft carrier preparing to project national power—and will—against an enemy, as carriers had done for decades. *But Venezuela?* Even minutes from launch, Wilson was uneasy about what the United States was doing. *Didn't the diplomatic thing fade away? Does Venezuela really want a fight with us?* Everything had happened so fast, and he was not sure the politicians in Washington knew what they were doing, launching a series of pin-prick raids that Venezuela could recover from within days. *Like cutting a damn runway!*

Wilson was also uneasy because this complex strike was not *suitcased*, the details not thoroughly understood by all the strikers, including him, the strike lead. Having a comfortable four out of five strike details covered, meant that an *uncomfortable* one out of five was not. This strike required answers to hundreds of such details. They would have to make it up as they went, and Wilson expected there would be a time tonight where he would have to audible: *You do a buttonhook. You go long.* Not a preferred recipe for success.

From his warm cocoon, Wilson saw the deck crew brace themselves against the wind. He noted the ship was turning to align the wind vane with the ship's longitudinal axis. The early launch was now sending the *Hawkeyes* and *Rhino* tankers up to relieve some pressure off the crowded flight deck. *Blockers* were scheduled next, and Wilson saw they were spotted behind the jet blast deflectors to be hooked up and shot in short order into the gray sky.

Wilson happened to look up and catch the dark silhouette of a large aircraft with swept wings against the high overcast, heading south. Scanning the nearby sky, he saw another one a few miles in trail. He knew this must be the KC-10s, call sign *Shell*. Wilson was fascinated, never having seen mission tankers transiting to their station overhead the ship, and he was thankful for the real-time intelligence it provided him. *Two tankers proceeding to station as planned.* With their 400-knot ground speed, the tankers would arrive at their station before the carrier aircraft just getting airborne underneath them, but not by much. Sometimes things just worked out, and Wilson was relieved he didn't have to sweat how many hoses would be available to his thirsty jets. He caught the attention of Stretch who was parked next to him, awaiting his turn at the catapult. Wilson pointed at the tankers high above them and received a vigorous thumbs-up in response. Wilson watched the tankers recede and wondered if the AWACS and EP-3 were also proceeding to *their* stations.

Deafening waves of deep resonating sound from afterburning engines at max power continued to bombard the flight deck crew as aircraft went into tension on both the bow and the waist, pilots cycling the controls before saluting their readiness to launch. Wilson watched the heavy aircraft, loaded down with missiles and bombs, claw their way into the air and accelerate ahead of *Coral Sea* as it rose and fell on the eight-foot seas. Wilson always felt awed by the sailors as they moved about the screaming aircraft with purpose, communicating to pilots and each other with hand signals as they went about their dangerous tasks on the heaving and rolling deck, tasks they had spent years learning, tasks the Navy spent decades perfecting and handing down through trial and bloody error.

In the space of about twenty minutes, the crew had launched the majority of Wilson's strike package. He could see the jets pulling up in sharp planform seven miles ahead of the ship and disappearing over the horizon to join up on each other before continuing to the tankers now ahead of them. Wilson would be the last one off, and he was grateful for the extra time to set up his cockpit and to take extra looks at the San Ramón imagery on his kneeboard card. He wanted to imprint his aimpoint onto his brain. He would also do the combat checklist again airborne, and more than once during the two hours before time on target.

The seas were increasing now as he saw the bow bury itself before the next swell lifted it high again. DCAG went off ahead of him, and Wilson was ready to launch. He was now compartmentalized, thinking not of the strike but of the cat shot and the moving deck edge over a football field away. Ahead of him, the metal catapult track led down to gray water, then back up to milky white sky. The night trap in four hours was going to be demanding, but he put that out of his mind as he watched the yellow shirt director straddle the track as the shuttle was retracted underneath him. On signal, Wilson dropped the launch bar and soon inched forward, with a thumbs-up to the weight board held high by a sailor: 48,000 pounds, his aircraft gross weight. Three dozen sailors between the bow cats watched him in *Firebird* 301, the last jet to launch on the event. Even at idle power, his engines still produced an ear-piercing din for all around it. Wilson now felt late and wanted to get going, to catch up with the others he would lead into combat. That was all that mattered now. *Fly the brief.* The politics of *why* was left to Washington. Commander James Wilson's job was to hit San Ramón a certain way at a certain time—with no collateral damage and no losses. Nothing more, but more than enough.

As the catapult went into tension, Wilson popped the throttles into burner, and the troubleshooters lifted their arms high with a thumbs-up to signal ready. Wilson saluted the catapult officer to signal *his* readiness. The catapult officer returned his salute and watched the bow to time the shot. As the bow began its upward journey, the catapult officer touched the deck. Anticipating the shot, Wilson watched the bow lift and pass through the horizon just before bursts of superheated steam hit the catapult shuttle and propelled Wilson and twenty-four tons of airplane into the gray Atlantic sky.

Their work done for the moment, the bow catapult crews wasted no time watching 301 recede from view. They "wrapped up" the bow and went below to take a quick break before the next evolution. Sailors removed their cranial helmets as relative quiet returned to the flight deck, but abeam the island, a tractor chugged to life as it pulled a MH-60 *Sierra* from its parking spot nestled against the island. Another tractor pulled another *Sierra* from its spot. Once the helicopters were spotted on the waist, the crewmen spread their rotors. Eight SEALs emerged from the island and divided into two groups of four. One group entered the cabin of each aircraft as the pilots and aircrew prepared them for launch.

From his chair on the flag bridge, Devil Davies watched the SEALS go through their checks and contemplated his next move.

CHAPTER 49

Staying low on the water, Wilson lifted his *Hornet* skyward at seven miles off the bow. He then rolled left to join his wingmen on a prebriefed radial thirty miles in front of the ship. With his radar sweeping in range-while-search mode, he soon found the *Slashes*, three formations separated by altitude. Wilson's formation of *Firebirds* was at fifteen thousand feet, *Angels 15*. As he leveled off to join on them, he picked them up as three dots on the gray horizon. Above he saw the other formations in their lazy turns, positioning to follow the lead gaggle at 15K once Wilson got aboard. The other package formations were to get to the tankers on their own.

In practiced motion, Wilson got on the left bearing line of the lead *Hornet*. While maintaining altitude and airspeed, he slid closer and closer using radius of turn. He soon saw that he was joining on Stretch who had DCAG and Dusty on his wing. Wilson eased up the bearing line as Stretch watched him. Once stabilized on his left side, Wilson added power and, through hand signals, took the lead from Stretch. Rolling out of his turn, Wilson steadied the formation on a heading of 180 to rendezvous on the tankers 150 miles ahead. Dusty slid under and joined on Wilson's left wing in silence. Craning his neck right and left, Wilson saw the other two *Slash* formations high and behind. He added power to climb to the briefed rendezvous altitude of 25,000 feet.

Good.

The weather had become a major factor. They faced a high overcast with convective buildups and squalls scattered about. Wilson weaved his formation through ragged layers of broken clouds, and on his radar he could pick out the returns of small isolated rain clouds below them. The sun, a soft light behind the gray, was low to the west. It would sink below the horizon in an hour, but, with the cloud cover overhead, darkness would approach much earlier. They would join on the tankers during "daylight" but would not complete fueling until after the sun had set.

Below the American formations, merchant ships ploughed through powerful waves as they lumbered north and east toward Europe. With the high overcast, alert lookouts on the vessels could see the specks of fighters heading south in V formations, unusual on the open ocean. If anyone on a ship's bridge was so inclined, a satellite phone call could report them. Wilson noted the time: an hour and twenty minutes to go. He figured the chance of a merchant sailor even being on a weather deck outside, much less looking out for anything, had to be remote.

Fuel. All carrier pilots obsessed over it, and the aviators took repeated glances at their fuel states, monitoring their engines and fuel flow and groundspeed against prefigured fuel "ladders" that served as checkpoints to gauge where their fuel levels "should" be. As last off, Wilson was "ahead" on fuel by a few hundred pounds, equal to a few minutes at his current airspeed. Ahead of all the carrier jets were the two *Shell* tankers. The fighters were scheduled for two—and by the end of the night, maybe *three*—stabs at a basket to take fuel in an effort to remain aloft for nearly five hours. He still couldn't believe he had seen them from the flight deck and was reminded that anyone on any vessel below them could also see them. The radio crackled.

"*Slash* one-one, *Condor*. *Shell* is on station at your one-seven-five for ninety."

"Roger, *Condor*, looking," Wilson transmitted on strike common frequency as he acknowledged the E-2 vectors.

"Roger. *Blockers* and *Volts* are about fifty miles in front of you."

"Roger, *Condor*, thanks," Wilson answered his shipmate monitoring a radar screen in the E-2.

With the big wing tankers on station, Wilson and the *Slash* formations would join on them in 10-15 minutes. They were in no rush as, by design, the *Blockers, Volts* and *Lances* plugged in first, aided by the FA-18E hose multipliers. Each KC-10 had refueling pods on the wings for a total of four hoses, and the *Rhino* tankers, call sign *Arco*, were probably on them now to fill up in order to transfer gas to the strike package aircraft once they showed up. The orchestration of flowing fuel across eight hoses to some thirty strike aircraft—in tight formations four miles up at 300 knots—was a huge timing and logistics challenge with many fallout plan contingencies. Carrier Air Wing SIX was going to do it *twice* in less than ideal weather conditions, and the second time at night. It was on the tanker things sometimes went to worms, and Wilson had to be ready to flex to plan B, C, or D with no notice. As strike lead, it was his call.

Wilson's tanker was *Shell* 02, stepped up above and behind *Shell* 01 at 24,000 feet. Inside forty miles, he locked it and, aided by his targeting FLIR, could see the specks of four *Blockers* refueling on one of them. Each fighter was fragged to receive 6,000 pounds upfront and 6,000 on the backside once the strike was complete. Wilson watched the rendezvous geometry build on his radar and counted the little dots around the larger aircraft, his eyes scanning the horizon for unseen traffic. He entered the circle with care so as not to run into wayward aircraft joining on the wrong tanker.

Wilson held an easy left turn as *Shell* 02 flew five miles in front of him with the four *Blockers* and the two *Volts* in tow. Smooth on the stick, he maneuvered onto the bearing line and glided his three wingmen closer. In trail, one of the *Arco* FA-18E tankers had a *Rhino* plugged in and receiving. Below, the rest of the *Slashes* were joining on *Shell* 01. Three dozen aircraft were in tight quarters, all within 1,000 feet of each other, as the KC-10 pilots did their best to avoid broken cloud layers and scattered buildups. Sliding closer and closer to the *Rhinos* waiting in line, Wilson thought of the time and fuel and sunlight. And of San Ramón, two hundred miles away.

Fueling complete, the *Blockers* and *Volts* slid away from the KC-10 and soon disappeared to take a holding position. The *Slashes* eased, two at a time, behind the black rubber hoses trailing from the pods, one on each wing. The gray KC-10 was a big airplane, and Wilson noted McGUIRE painted in yellow letters over a blue band on top of the vertical tail. Jersey boys, and maybe girls, were inside the tanker. Painted on the nose of the aircraft he saw nose art that resembled graffiti found on a Camden railroad car. On closer inspection, Wilson read WAR LORD.

Gliding as one, the aircraft took their turns on the baskets, with Wilson crossing under to the right and Dusty taking position behind the hose on the left wing. They extended their refueling probes into the slipstream to their right and stabilized behind the baskets that were bouncing a bit in the turbulent air. The pilots added power to "plug" them and push the hose forward as a green light on the store indicated good flow. Despite being up a common frequency, nothing was said as the aircraft plugged in order. Wilson took glances at the formations all about him. He was on time line as he waited for his wingmen to take on fuel. The tanker occasionally popped through wisps of cloud it could not avoid, but the KC-10 pilots held steady while receiver jets were on their baskets. *Thirty jets coming back here at night is going to be varsity.* Wilson put the thought behind him.

Wilson and Dusty finished on their hoses and slid over to the tanker's right wing. As the *Hornets* took their fuel, the sun slipped lower and lower in the sky until it was hidden behind a ridge of clouds. On the surface, the sun had set forty minutes earlier, but, at altitude, the western sky was a dramatic pink framed by gunmetal gray clouds and highlighted with distant strands of yellow stratus. The clouds were heavier to the west, the direction they would soon be headed. As he waited for Stretch to finish tanking, Wilson saw the lights of another merchant ship below. He turned his position and formation lights on, and Dusty, next to him, mimicked his action. Below and ahead, the four *Blocker* FA-18s edged away from their tanker to their briefed holding point. Wilson noted the time: 1903. Less than an hour to go.

Edgar Hernandez sat in his VIP quarters, alone, filled with regret.

Tomorrow night the Americans would come, and there was a good chance that tomorrow morning's sunrise would be the last one he would ever see. He could hear the sounds of jet engines on the flight line as the young pilots prepared to fly on a training sortie—on what was likely *their* last night on Earth. He would take the place of one of them. *Which one?* Was there a married pilot with a large family and a good wife who loved and supported him, an honorable man with a bright future? There were dozens of such men in the AMV. He was once one of them. *Once.*

Daniel had brought him rank and power, money and privilege. And sex. *Lots* of it, with big girls who resembled child toys, who serviced him with giggling smiles. He knew nothing about them, not even their names. He never asked, and they never offered. He and the girls were both there in the employ of Daniel; he for high level influence, they as payment for services rendered. Once he passed out in middle-aged exhaustion, the girls disappeared, never to be seen again. Which was fine with him. He did remember the girl with hair down to her waist, stoned out of her mind like the others. Girls…with parents. Who loved them, or once did.

His own wife of 27 years had long ago become a lifeless shell with joyless eyes, *knowing,* but not daring to complain. Resigned to her existence, she functioned as an acceptable hostess at Caracas receptions and asked no questions, living apart from her husband even though they were in the same house. Daniel saw to her comfort, too, and so long as Hernandez didn't embarrass her, all would be well. Daniel ensured there would be no embarrassment. Daniel took care of everything.

Hernandez stepped to the window, now darkened by the twilight, and saw two *Vipers* with twinkling anti-collision lights prepare to taxi out of the line. When the landline phone rang, it surprised him.

"Mayor General Hernandez," he answered.

"Mí general, this is the Group Commander. We think the Americans are preparing to attack!"

"Yes, I know, dammit! You better prepare your people tonight to meet them tomorrow!"

"No, mí general…tonight…within the hour!"

Hernandez froze for a moment as the message sank in. *"How do you know this?"*

"A cargo ship in the Atlantic called the dock master at Rió Salta and reported formations of planes high overhead. Who else but the Americans could do this?"

"Early warning radar? What do they see?"

"Nothing yet, mí general, as there is a line of heavy storms to the east. But we are receiving both electronic bearings and signals intelligence on a bearing that corroborates with the merchant sighting."

"Where was the ship when it reported?"

"A position ninety miles southeast of Barbados, in the middle of the ocean, mí general, and the airplanes were heading south."

Hernandez's mind raced. *Where are they going? If this sighting report is true, it could be Rió Salta. Or the oil rigs offshore. Here!"*

"Meet me at the command post at once!" Hernandez barked into the receiver. Fear and foreboding building in his mind, he summoned his aide to bring the car. This wasn't supposed to happen tonight. He had planned to have tonight to prepare to die, to write a farewell letter, *to repent to God.* He was now afraid to man a fighter and spare the life of one of his pilots—and afraid not to. His breathing rapid, he needed to know more, but dreaded knowing more, and Daniel was nowhere in sight. Maybe the flimsy report from the merchant seaman was all wrong. Most initial reports were. He watched the F-16s taxi for takeoff with a sense of urgency. *Is the boy Espinoza piloting one of them?* he wondered.

He grabbed his cell phone and punched in a number. A familiar voice answered.

"Hola."

"They're coming! *Now!"* Hernandez growled.

"We know."

CHAPTER 50

(*Slash* 11, Western Atlantic)

His tanking complete, DCAG backed out of the basket trailing from the left wing pod and slid under the KC-10. As he continued under the other three *Hornets* in his formation, a waiting *Rhino* took his position behind the basket. This FA-18E was carrying an in-flight refueling pod the aviators called a "buddy store" on its centerline station. It would stay with the KC-10s for now and trail the strike package if anyone needed emergency fuel once they returned feet wet near Trinidad.

With gentle pressure on the stick, Wilson turned away from the tanker, his three wingmen flying form on his right wing. Almost an hour after sundown on the surface below, it was getting dark. Wilson took them to a point thirty miles away where they could hold and save fuel before beginning their run in to San Ramón. The *Blockers* were about five minutes away from their push, and as Wilson neared his holding point, he saw the anti-collision lights of one of the other *Slash* formations. The strikers would push out individually and then ease together en route to form a gaggle, with the *Blocker, Volt,* and *Lance* formations on their own in support of the *Slashes*. The four *Blockers* would lead the airwing aircraft into the target area and knock down anything that came up to oppose them. The aviators noted lightning flashes to the west, and, as element lead, Wilson had the responsibility to avoid them. All the formation leaders did.

"*Slash* one-one? *Nightlight.*" Wilson was relieved knowing the AWACS was up, another potential disconnect averted.

"*Nightlight, Slash.* Go ahead," Wilson responded.

"Your signal, *stepladder.* Over."

"Roger, *stepladder.*" Wilson responded. This code word was their briefed word to continue. In thirty minutes Wilson and the others would roll in on the dual runways of San Ramón to put them out of action—for the time being. He then asked, "Picture?"

"Picture clean. Looks like you have some weather en route."

Wilson rogered and kept a wary eye to the west. Fifty other sets of eyes did the same, all knowing that, right now, a thunderstorm was a greater threat than Venezuelan fighters or AAA. All saw the distant flashes and hoped the storms were isolated or small enough to fly over. The high overcast made it darker than normal and only a pink glow could be observed to the west/northwest, but this glow was enough to prevent Wilson from donning his NVGs just yet. His thumb mashed down on the mike.

"*Slash*, any alibis?"

He listened for any from his wingmen, and after a few seconds one did.

"*Slash* two-four. Only got half my load."

Wilson acknowledged *Slash* 24's call. "Roger that. Stick with your aimpoint."

"Roger," *Slash* 24 replied. Just then, *Blocker* lead transmitted on strike common.

"*Blockers* pushing."

"*Nightlight* copies," the AWACS controller answered.

They were committing now, and Wilson didn't *know* if he had *Tomahawks* inbound to soften up San Ramón, didn't *know* if he had signals intel in the form of an EP-3, didn't *know* if the Venezuelans were alerted. He did know there was weather ahead, but he didn't know if it would pass or get dangerous. And he could guess that the White House press corps were monitoring their watches as they prepared to cover the President's address to the nation in less than an hour.

Wilson led his formation in an easy left-hand turn. As he watched his preplanned run-in speed align with his planned time on target, he felt a sense of progress. He had ninety degrees to go before he pushed the *Slash* formations on course behind the *Blockers*. Above and below were lone twinkling anti-collision lights that marked the *Slashes, Volts,* and *Lances* as they, too, waited to push out along the planned track. The others in formation were unseen in the darkness. Wilson could make out some position lights a mile or two away. Soon he could don his goggles.

"*Slash* one-one, pushing," Wilson transmitted.

"*Slash* two-one, pushing."

"Three-one, pushing."

The twelve *Slash* strikers rolled out on a heading of 250 and accelerated toward South America, with Wilson in front and the other two division formations on his left and right. Wilson tried his goggles, but the faint, yellow-gray glow was still too much for the light intensifiers. He could discern a line of storms ahead and commanded his radar to air-to-ground mode to get a look at it.

His radar display depicted a ragged—but solid—line of return, almost perpendicular to their track seventy miles away. With his naked eye, he could see lightning ahead of him, small pops of light. Some were sharp but most seemed muffled as they zipped from inside one cloud to another. At this speed, the strikers would be on the storms in eight minutes, and the *Blockers* before that. He saw that the line extended along the horizon in front of him from Tobago to Guyana. That made it *hundreds* of miles in length. They couldn't go around it, and going under it was a nonstarter. *We'll go over it.*

Wilson elevated his antenna and saw the return was not much different. Even the horizon line on his HUD was cutting the tops of the cumulus clouds. He was climbing the formation ever so slightly, but in the high twenties, knew that their heavy bomb loads would prevent a much higher climb. It would be impossible, at these weights, to get up to the forties. He had to keep climbing, looking, thinking, and *hoping*.

Flying into a thunderstorm required him to break a cardinal rule of aviation, and, with eleven bomb-laden wingmen hanging on to him in formation, the stakes were ratcheted way up. He wondered what the *Blockers* were doing ahead and called lead.

"*Blocker* lead from *Slash.* How does it look?"

"Pretty solid line, but we found a saddleback we can go over."

"Above forty?"

"Affirm."

Now Wilson knew at least the *Blockers* could get over the line at 40,000 feet, but there was no way he could get up there, even in burner, as heavy as they were with bombs *and* full fuel tanks. With the faintest twilight glow behind the line he could detect anvil-topped clouds south of their track with the anvils also pointing south, which showed the high-level winds from the north were shearing them away. Even in the clear, airplanes near thunderstorms could be pelted, with no warning, by hail thrown up from inside the churning clouds. The fact the anvils pointed away from them gave a degree, albeit small, of comfort.

Level at 30,000 feet, and close to 500 knots ground speed, they floated closer to the line as the flashes increased in intensity. Wilson scanned the line up and down to determine the strongest segments, the tallest clouds, and the thickest concentrations of energy. Far to the north and south—almost 100 miles in either direction—the line's strength did not seem to diminish. Wilson had to lead the formation through it or turn around.

DCAG—his immediate senior—was right next to him and, so far, had not offered any guidance. Wilson knew Devil Davies was watching his airplanes approach the solid line of weather, as were the controllers aboard the AWACS who transmitted the picture to staff officers in Miami and Washington. It appeared no one was going to jump in and make Commander Wilson's decision. The line now loomed just off his nose. Inside the base clouds, in the teens and low twenties, muffled bulbs of grayish yellow light pulsed on and off. From this bubbling caldron of energy rose a wall of dappled gray, a shadowy and foreboding tapestry of dark cloud. And jagged veins of electricity shot from cloud to cloud in front of him. A thin stratus layer above obscured what little starlight was available to measure the tops of the serrated "mountain range" now less than forty miles ahead.

Wilson was glued to the radar display, hoping, praying for a break, praying for a call from above, wishing that someone *would* jump into his cockpit and direct him what to do.

"*Slash, Blockers* have punched through, in the clear. May have some weather in vicinity of *Bullseye*."

Wilson rogered the call as he struggled with his decision. Fly two dozen jets with live weapons through the weather? Or abort? The *Blockers* could abort. *Nightlight*, the *Volts* and *Lances* could abort. He knew the aircrews in the aircraft, knew their faces, their young inexperienced faces. *All* could abort *now,* and, with weather reported in the vicinity of the target, it was a reasonable call, the *right* call. It met the go/no-go criteria they had briefed. *Wait, did we brief it?* Did this scenario fall through the cracks in their haste to launch? What would Washington do if they turned around? How would Devil and CAG react? The big question remained. Should they risk the jets to hit San Ramón on time line, or live to fight another day?? The CNO wasn't an aviator. *Who advising the President was?* Did Washington even *know* or care about the fine details of fuel, time, and distance, or the perils of thunderstorm penetration? Wilson concentrated on his radar as his wingmen concentrated on him to lead them, to *take care* of them. He continued ahead, delaying the decision to the last minute—the final minute. He continued ahead, praying for deliverance.

A magnificent burst of energy lit up the wall of cloud in front of him, a metallic flash with bright streaks of horizontal lightning stretching for miles. It outlined the details of the cumulonimbus clouds forming the barrier he had to either penetrate now or avoid by turning around. The warning was clear: *Don't come in here*. With twenty minutes to the target they had no time to hold and wait, no fuel to spend making decisions, and

Wilson knew what lay before him wasn't going to dissipate in the next minute. The *Blockers* were already past it. *Good.* They reported more weather en route to the target. *Bad.* What to do?

"Looks like a seam to the right," DCAG transmitted.

Wilson saw it, too, a somewhat clear area between two angry thunder cells of heavy radar returns. The clouds went up 10,000 feet above them...no way to get over them.

Wilson was the strike lead, and it was his call. Grateful for Not-o's veiled encouragement and implied approval, he swallowed hard, then keyed the mike.

"Ninety-nine *Broadsword*, find a seam and punch through. *Volts*, if you have us in sight, take trail. Snuggle up on your leads. *Slash* two-one and three-one, take altitude sep."

One after another the element leaders rogered him while their wingmen slid close to their leads in parade formation. Wilson knew the human hearts in two dozen cockpits were now beating faster as they approached the line of storms. *No turning back now.* Bolts of gnarled electricity shot between the clouds in front of Wilson as he led the *Slashes* in an easy turn to a course that was *bad* compared to *really worse* on either side. It was now dark, but the aviators kept their goggles stowed. They would have to concentrate on flying formation in the roiling clouds, which meant the wingmen would see nothing but a wingtip position light in the gloom.

Wilson rolled out, eyes locked on the radar to lead his four planes into the storm wall. He positioned his rear view mirrors to see his wingtips— and the *Hornets* flying tight form next to him. Below them, the cells boiled in disconnected flashes that illuminated the silhouettes of the formation aircraft. In the next two minutes, Wilson would be leading *three* aircraft, not thirty-three, and the clouds reached out to *Slash* 11 and pulled him and his wingmen inside at 500 knots.

At once the jets were buffeted by rain and gusty winds. Wilson fought to hold his jet as steady as possible for the sake of his wingmen. Dusty was welded to his right, and DCAG was holding position on the left as the rain lashed at them in driving sheets. Glancing at his mirrors, Wilson could barely make out the shadows of the *Hornets* until an explosion of lightning nearby lit up DCAG and Stretch next to him, who then disappeared into the darkness as suddenly as they had appeared. Wilson had been there himself, muscles tight and tense, *squeezing the black out of the stick* and fighting to hang on to the only reference he had, a green or red light some ten feet away bouncing in the turbulent clouds with blurred streaks of water running down the canopy, holding on, *hanging on*, praying that they would punch through soon. None of them was even thinking about the reception waiting for them at San Ramón less than twenty minutes away.

Trying to ignore the constant rivulets of water that obscured his vision, Wilson was concentrating on his attitude pitch lines when he saw wispy threads of electricity expand on his nose, run across the windscreen, and move aft down his canopy. Though harmless, it was disconcerting to watch *St. Elmo's Fire* envelop his jet with its electric massage. He tried to see if his wingmen were similarly affected but could see nothing on Dusty's nose.

A bolt materialized ahead, and before Wilson could process its presence, an arc of electricity slammed into his nose with a deafening *crack.* A painful shock caused him to release the controls. His heart jumped into his throat as the cockpit went dark. *Fuck!* After what seemed like an eternity, Wilson regained his grasp on the stick and throttles, and the green cockpit lighting and computer instrumentation of his returned. Noto transmitted on their tac freq.

"You okay?"

"Okay. Lost everything for a second."

"A long second."

"Affirm." Wilson replied as he continued through the embedded storms, leading them only by radar and instinct. The rain pummeled the aircraft with no let up.

Wilson flinched as a thunderous bolt exploded off to their left and, for an instant, turned night into day. His already tense shoulders fought to hold his aircraft steady. Then, a sound like a shotgun blast went off next to him as the sky again burst into light. He checked his left mirror.

"Think I took a hit," Stretch transmitted.

Wilson shifted his mirror but could not see beyond the faint outline of DCAG's jet. "You still with us?"

"A-firm. Still running. Ears ringing." Stretch answered. Wilson responded with two mike clicks.

With muffled flashes all about, Wilson's radar display showed a reduced level of return ahead—with less than ten miles to clear air. He wanted his goggles and felt for them in the console. Once this formation popped into the open, he would don them first thing.

The visual and aural tension of the rain subsided, and, after blowing through a wisp of cloud, the formation burst into clear air as if they had flown out of a wall into a room. Thirty miles away on the dark surface below was the island of Trinidad with its brightly lit towns and settlements.

Wilson's three wingmen opened up as soon as they could, drifting away from him and the tension of his position lights. They were all grateful for a break, if only for a moment. After the electric shock his aircraft systems had taken minutes earlier, Wilson did a careful and thorough recheck, deselecting and reselecting his weapons switches and completing another combat checklist. He then latched his goggles into place on his helmet, turned them on, and allowed his brain to absorb the greenish panorama of South America ahead of him. He saw the *Blocker* formation ahead, just a single light at this distance, and craned his neck to see the others in the strike package. "Let's goggle up," he transmitted, and reset his external lights. He looked toward San Ramón, and, with the last bit of luminance on the western horizon, detected tall clouds hovering near the field.

Their route funneled them into the Columbus Channel and along the southern coast of Trinidad. While descending the formation to their roll-in altitude, Wilson could make out the yellow flare stacks of offshore oil rigs in the distance, their flaming tongues flickering over the black velvet water. With the lightning ahead and the flares burning below, the view could have been a scene out of Dante's Inferno. Wilson craned his neck to look for the others, abeam and behind, and saw some formations. After the confused cauldron they had just emerged from, he had to find out if his strikers were intact.

"*Slashes*, any alibis?"

He received no response, a good sign in this instance. He queried the others.

"*Volts, Lances*, you okay? Any alibis?

"*Volts* up. No alibis."

"*Lances* up. No alibis."

Amazed at their good luck, Wilson breathed a sigh of relief. Could San Ramón throw anything at them that would be worse than the line of storms they had just survived? Looking north, the weather seemed to curve away and appeared reduced compared to this brutal segment, and Wilson would take them through the sovereign airspace of Trinidad to avoid the heaviest stuff on the egress. *Screw 'em if they don't like it*, he thought. *We'll ask for forgiveness.* Devil—and Washington—owed him that. After punching through the thunderstorm line, after jumping through flaming hoops to get off the deck—and doing it all on time—their leadership owed them a lot.

When the elements fanned out into position as they neared San Ramón, the *Blockers* started chattering about an airborne contact on their nose. The target was fifty miles away, and Wilson noted increased lighting flashes in its vicinity. On closer inspection, he realized the flashes were not from lightning. They were from AAA.

CHAPTER 51

At 100 feet and lights out, the *Seahawks* sped over the waves, gunners at their mounts, and scanned the horizon for trouble.

The crews, and the eight SEALs, aboard the two aircraft had received twenty minutes notice to pack a change of socks and a dopp kit. They received orders to launch for a one-way trip to Tobago. Once there, they would fill the aircraft gas tanks and stand by for tasking if any fighter went down from Skipper Wilson's initial strike, or from Skipper Martin's strike later in the night. One of the squadron mechanics volunteered to go in order to help service the helos, and the mission commander was handed a wad of cash as well as a letter from Devil himself that requested they be given "all assistance" from the local authorities. The SEALs were there to help rescue any downed aircrew and to convince, if necessary, the airport fueling personnel to cooperate. Before launch, the ordies had delivered another miracle, arming each *Sierra* with two *Hellfire* missiles and a pod of rockets, as well as full belts for the door gunners.

Devil Davies was taking a gamble, hedging that SOUTHCOM would approve this covert, no-notice action to make Tobago an impromptu lily pad for *Coral Sea* strike aircraft. He ordered the aircraft to launch for the two-hour run to the airport at Crown Point on the island's southern tip. From there, the helos would be gassed and available for tasking. The aviators and SEALs were ready for anything, and SEAL Lieutenant Rich Keller was overall mission commander. LT Sean Sullivan, as the senior aviator and pilot of *Flintlock* 612, called the shots for the helos.

Staying well out to sea, the aircraft avoided Barbados to their west and did their best to stay away from any surface craft. Twenty minutes ago they had come upon a sailboat, which appeared out of nowhere in the darkness, requiring evasive action to avoid the mast. In the vicinity of Tobago they dodged the surface craft they encountered, but once they made the left-hand turn to the southeast, small craft were everywhere, even at night. Now, with five minutes to landing, the aircraft had to ignore them.

Sullivan led the helos to a position south of the runway at Arthur Napoleon Airport. Through his goggles he saw the fuel farm, the bright lights of the terminal behind it. A small turboprop commuter was the only aircraft of significance on the ramp, and there were a handful of general aviation aircraft parked on the far side of the runway. The fuel farm was on the south side, and once he led the *Seahawks* abeam it, he would initiate an easy buttonhook to the left and slow to a run-on landing on the narrow access road. The gunners and SEALs were locked and loaded, and the pilots did not radio the tower to ask for permission.

Sullivan keyed the ICS and turned toward his co-pilot, LTJG Pete Sanders. "Sandy, ready to turn in?"

"A-firm," he replied.

"Okay, here we go…. Holding about 30-degree angle of bank. Rising terrain. Surf line."

"Visual. Palm trees at our nine o'clock, coming to ten. A bunch of them, about 75 feet tall."

"Okay, visual. See any airborne traffic?"

"Negative."

The graceful *Sierras* rolled out on the road and flared their noses high to bleed airspeed as the pilots placed them as close to the fuel farm as they could. One of the gunners reported seeing airport ground crew on the ramp, but the crew didn't seem excited. No rotating lights of police. No headlights of any kind heading their way. No one seemed to know they were there.

Once the wheels touched, the SEALs jumped out to take perimeter positions. Sullivan keyed the AWACS orbiting in the vicinity.

"*Flintlock* six-one-two reports *beach blanket*," he said, transmitting the briefed code word for *Safe on deck, Crown Point*. Within minutes, the message was reported to Davies in flag plot.

The aircraft idled, rotor blades whipping through the moist air. While the SEALs secured their perimeter, the pilots stretched their legs in their cockpit seats to relieve the tension of the last two hours. Sullivan checked his watch. Skipper Wilson's strike was to be on target in five minutes. According to his nav display, the target was over 100 miles away on a direct line over Trinidad. After they got gas, they would have at least 200 miles ahead of them to avoid Trinidad and go feet dry on the planned ingress route of the strike aircraft. If any of the jets went down, Sullivan's helicopters were at least two hours away from helping them. The aircrew were exhausted, but they all had the same thought.

First fuel, but before that…a candy bar.

As Hernandez stepped into the bunker, the watch captain approached him with a troubled look. Outside, he heard the sound of two of his F-16s in burner as they, one after the other, thundered down the runway for takeoff.

"Mí general, we have large formations of aircraft to the east, about 100 miles. They're coming at us."

"One hundred miles! You've had no earlier detection than that?"

"Mí general, they've come out of a line of storms! We cannot see through thunderstorms. *They flew right through them!*"

Hernandez was amazed. Flying through such a line was suicidal for an individual fighter, and the Americans had done it *in formation? They can ignore the forces of nature?*

"How many planes?" he asked.

"It looks like three or four formations, mí general. We do not know yet how many planes are in each formation. One is in front."

"That is their fighter sweep, dammit! Where are you sending our boys?"

"To intercept that formation, mí general!"

Hernandez fought to remain in control. The watch captain had never seen such a formation, and inside 100 miles, he had only minutes to scramble his fighters. In their "training," they had intercepted just one contact: a low/slow flyer, in clear air, daylight hours. Not three dozen fighters—a formation the size of the entire AMV fighter force! A formation coming at them with multi-mode sensors and long-range missiles and flown by the *Americans*, the finest in the world! Sending his *Vipers* into that buzz saw was suicidal.

"No, you idiot, that formation is ready for them! Send them south—to draw the Americans away from here. Maybe we can come in from their flank."

"Sí, mí general!"

In the darkened control room, Hernandez watched the scope as the cursor rotated to illuminate the heavy radar return from the east. He paid special attention to the blips emerging from the storms. The controller at the console was talking to his fighters on the radio, and the communication was piped in through an overhead speaker. Hernandez heard his nervous pilots acknowledge the instructions as they maneuvered to intercept.

Employing their heat-seeking missiles required them to see the target at close range.

They didn't have a chance. Hernandez couldn't bear it.

"Turn them south! Now!" he fumed.

"Sí, mí general! We have radioed the instructions!"

Hernandez heard the excited pilots transmit that they had contact on the Americans and were turning to engage them over the Columbus Channel, fifty miles east. He saw the blips turn left into the maw of the American missile envelopes.

"*South! Now,* I say!"

After lifting his MASTER ARM switch to ARM, Wilson transmitted to the *Slash* divisions. "Tapes on, *Armstrong.*"

Up ahead, the *Blockers*, a tactical formation of transonic *Super Hornets,* saw the two bogeys turn left and south at thirty miles. It appeared to be a strategy to pull them away from San Ramón. Chasing down the bogeys—declared by *Nightlight* as bandits—would cause the American formations to bunch up in the vicinity of the airfield with an increased chance of a blue-on-blue engagement. A disappointed *Blocker* lead had to skip this opportunity for an air-to-air kill.

The job of the *Blockers* was to shoot down anything in front of the strikers, which would allow them to offset left and roll in on the runways to the right. This gave the strikers the shortest and most direct line back to the relative safety of "feet wet," despite the proximity of Río Salta. Pulling off target with a bag of knots, the strikers would quickly skirt the heavily defended port

Then, the bandits turned back into them, and the four *Rhinos,* in eager anticipation, sorted and locked them inside launch range. Three of the four aircraft fired radar-guided AMRAAMs, and, from miles behind, Wilson watched tiny points of light separate from the *Blocker* aircraft and rise on their profile toward the Venezuelan jets. They now knew the Venezuelans were ready and fighting back. And over San Ramón, they saw AAA mixed in with the lightning.

In the far distance, as one of the *Blocker* missiles found its mark, Wilson saw a flash followed by a jagged and descending trail of fire. Another distant explosion to the southwest produced excited cries from the *Blockers.* "*Splash two!*" they transmitted as another curling trail of light fell earthward. The *Blockers* had knocked down the bandits. They had done their job.

Now, approaching the initial point, Wilson and the *Slashes* had to do theirs.

With high altitude winds at their backs, they were now over 600 knots of ground speed and would be at their roll-in point in minutes. Wilson's senses were becoming overloaded. His Radar Homing and Warning gear was *booping* and *deedling* in his headset which meant enemy radars were watching him, *illuminating him*. To his left, he saw the fiery trails of HARMs fired by the *Lances* arc high overhead. Their purpose was to home in and silence the enemy emissions as the *Volts* jammed them. Disconcerting, however, was another cloud.

It was a stationary thunder cell, one they could avoid by going around or over. The problem was it was parked at the point in space from which Wilson needed to lead the *Slashes* to attack on San Ramón's runways. The plan was offset left, roll-in right, but, with two minutes to go, the cloud was *right there*. Wilson watched it on the radar, hoping for rather than sensing any motion, knowing he needed to make a call— soon. "*Come on!*" he muttered. Wilson knew the others could see the same electronic blob on their cockpit radars. This was a contingency they hadn't briefed, and Wilson had to make up a play and hope everyone understood. You *do a buttonhook*. You *go long*.

"*Slashes*, we need to go mirror image, offset right, roll-in left. Repeat; offset *right*, roll-in *left*. Come off northeast, and get feet wet ASAP!"

His eleven wingmen, in order, acknowledged the transmission as they set themselves up on Wilson's right side, all of them breathing deep as adrenalin pumped through their bodies. The long chute of jets would roll into a steep dive, one by one, and line up on their aimpoints—just like the dive-bombers and attack jets of yore. The 20th-century weapon delivery would send a political message to a 21st-century adversary in a new and undeclared conflict that, one week ago, was on no one's radar. Wilson and the eleven jets next to him would do this for Washington. It was their job, their oath, and they followed orders, even stupid ones *to cut the frickin' runways*. And, if required, they would come back to recut them. Venezuela needed to be taught a lesson, and if they dishonored some damn diplomat—never mind the societies they destroyed by the poison they mass-produced—they would get theirs.

None of that mattered in the twelve *Slash* cockpits. To them, the *reason* they were there was the last thing on their minds. They were now in tactical formation over dark and hostile territory, watching their FLIR displays build and sweetening their aiming diamonds as the briefed landmarks and reference points came into view. The *Blockers* were off right, at the moment heading north toward Río Salta, and the *Lances* were lobbing HARMs into the boiling kettle of San Ramón's defenses. They saw lightning to the southwest, AAA bursts in front and below. The bright booster rocket of a SAM burst from its launching pad. When Wilson heard cries on the radio that one of the *Slashes* was spiked and breaking formation to evade, he continued to count down the range, count down the seconds, check wingmen positions, and watch AAA shells rise single file into the sky. Despite another lightning flash to the left, everything was silent in the *Slash* cockpits—except for clipped radio transmissions, the hum of electronics, and their own deep breaths and elevated heartbeats.

Ready.

Wilson picked his aimpoint, the western end of the north parallel runway. The four aircraft of his division had that runway, the *Slash* 21 jets had the other runway, and the *Rhinos* in *Slash* 31 had the taxiway. There was no easy way to deconflict twelve diving strike fighters into twelve separate aimpoints in an area of less than two miles wide. The *Slash* 31 division was going to take the worst of the AAA as the last down. The nugget pilot assigned to *Slash* 34 had watched Wilson with wide-eyed attention from the back of the ready room four hours ago, a pilot who now would be *Tail-End-Charlie* on this strike. Wilson had seen him around the ship but didn't know his name. He found it on his kneeboard card. *Kid*. His call sign was Kid, and he looked the part. This was his first time at sea away from the familiar Virginia Capes operating area. The VACAPES, an area mariners called *The Graveyard of the Atlantic,* was home for Wilson—and Kid.

On timeline almost to the second, Wilson flew his *Hornet* tangent to the imaginary cone he would intercept to begin his dive. After he went, Dusty would follow, then DCAG, then Stretch, each with three heavy bombs to drop in a stick with exact spacing, to penetrate the concrete and then explode a huge crater, rendering the runway inoperable. They would be followed by two more divisions of strikers to cover all available concrete. None of the aviators wanted to come back here, and they would work hard to identify their aimpoint and not screw it up. They *had* to get the bombs off. Pulling off target still lugging an extra two tons of deadweight was not career enhancing, and they would be easy prey for the gunners. If the gunners could see them...the aviators were lights-out on their NVGs, enjoying almost daytime situational awareness. Did the gunners have goggles, too? Or did they rely on radar to aim their fire—or the rumbling noise of 24 jet engines—to put a barrage of lead into the sky and hope one of the Americans ran into them.

At thirty seconds to first impact, and with flashes from lightning and AAA off his left wing, Wilson transmitted, "*Slash* one-one's in." He pulled his jet hard left, then overbanked down as he banged out some chaff and craned his neck to pick up his aiming diamond through the HUD. Stabilized in a dive, he rolled out and pulled his nose onto runway 28R of the Venezuelan fighter base at San Ramón.

CHAPTER 52

(*Slash* 11, over San Ramón)

Like his attack against the yacht, in what seemed a lifetime ago, Wilson was again hitting a target under a thunderstorm.

The storm was now south of the field, and, with the *Slash* formations attacking from the northeast, there was a ledge in the clouds they could get under to visually acquire their separate aimpoints. Wilson rolled out and, by instinct, checked Dusty in position before returning attention to his displays. On his FLIR, Wilson designated his aimpoint, right on the runway centerline tire marks, and, on his HUD, aligned his jet with the steering cues for release. He was in a steep, high dive, airspeed building and San Ramón growing larger through his windscreen. Fiery balls of 57mm rose up to him and then rocketed past as he plunged toward earth. Wilson fought to ignore them—they were close but missing above him— and returned his concentration to the FLIR. His eyes flew from the HUD altitude box to the steering to the FLIR display as he kept his scan going the same way he had trained for years. He fought to ignore the distracting lights of AAA that zipped by in his periphery. The release cue was dropping down, fast, and Wilson put his thumb on the pickle for release.

Without warning, his cockpit went dark. *What the fuck!*

Stunned, Wilson waited for the cockpit to return to life and realized with horror that it wasn't happening this time. Fear burst into his brain as he yanked back on the stick. *Did they hit me? Another lightning strike?* He was under five g's and the airplane's nose was moving up but not fast enough for Wilson. *I'm in MECH!* He was now in a black cockpit and struggled to recover from the dive in manual flight control mode. Using the cable and pulley backup system to fly the jet, his heavy jet, the goggles affixed to his helmet were his only sensor or instrument.

Wilson realized he still had his bombs attached and, knowing he was right over several enemy gun emplacements, he let off on the g and, in the darkness, found the EMERG JETT switch and pushed it. Nothing! As he turned to the right in his desperate flight to safety, he pushed it again and waited in vain for the familiar lurch of jettisoned bombs and fuel tanks.

AAA rounds were all about him now, and he flicked on his gooseneck flashlight to see altitude on the cockpit backup display. Under 10,000 feet, his nose was breaking the horizon as the g pushed down on his goggles in his struggle to fly the airplane and escape with his life.

In frantic fear, Wilson cycled the battery switch to get basic electric power. *Nothing!* He cycled the number two generator in another vain attempt to restore power. With *total* electrical failure, the flashes from bomb impacts below him, the lightning behind him, and AAA whizzing by next to him produced eerie shadows in his dark—and quiet—cockpit. Now deep in the caldron of Dante's Inferno, Wilson saw a *Hornet* pull off to his right a few thousand feet above him.

Fly the airplane. Wilson began to repeat to himself the first axiom of aviation, and, with his goggles, he could see the Columbus Channel—and safety—beckoning. Another *Hornet—DCAG?*—flew away high off his right. His ordnance was still attached, and repeated depressions of EMERG JETT were having no effect. Wilson sensed he was slow and shoved the throttles to MAX. On his steam gauge airspeed indicator he was doing 400 plus. He wanted to double that.

Wilson shot a glance over his right shoulder at San Ramón. In addition to the blinking of AAA guns, he could see clouds of smoke on the field from the numerous *Slash* hits. Breathing through his mouth, he concentrated on getting fast and maintaining a slight climb. Bright fireballs of AAA shot by him in groups of three and four, orderly trails from low to high. His body was tense, ready for impact.

He felt and heard the thud behind, on his right.

Terrified, Wilson twisted his body in the ejection seat to see what he could, pushing his helmet and goggles with his left hand to see over his wing. Through the narrow field of view of the goggles, he sensed flickering behind him. He then felt the airplane yaw right. Both were signs he had lost thrust on the right side.

Sonofabitch!

Squeezing the stick with his right hand, Wilson secured the right throttle with his left. He then reached across to lift the protective cover and punch the right fire light button. He now had to step on left rudder to keep the aircraft in balance and twisted his neck again to see if securing the right engine had had any affect. He still saw flickering from behind the right wing. That was evidence enough for him, and he pushed the fire extinguisher ready button and dropped the tailhook as part of the emergency action procedure he knew by rote memory. With zero electrical power, he didn't know if any of it would work. *Zero!*

Río Salta, also sending streams of AAA skyward, was passing down his left side, and he figured he had about 20 miles to feet wet. He was flying. It had been over a minute since he had felt the impact and secured his engine, and he could navigate visually. He saw the faint outlines of more *Hornets* passing over him high to his right. Most of all, Wilson wanted to get feet wet, but he also wanted to tell them he was still flying. With his left hand, he unzipped the pocket on his vest and pulled out his CSEL survival radio, a brick-shaped radio with an attached battery and a collapsible antenna. He flicked it on and popped off one of his mask fittings to stuff the earpiece in his ear. He then realized they hadn't briefed a discrete Combat SAR frequency! It was one of many items that had fallen through the cracks. He selected GUARD and transmitted, mindful that the Venezuelans could also monitor that frequency. Unsure about how long his jet could stay together, Wilson decided he had to let his wingmen know he was with them. He depressed the push-to-talk switch.

"Mayday. Mayday. Mayday. *Slash* one-one on GUARD. Still with you. Total electrical failure. Switching squadron tac." Wilson only had to wait a few seconds for an answer, but it felt much longer as he struggled to fly his stricken jet toward the water.

"Roger, *Slash* one-one. Switching!" Wilson didn't recognize the voice—maybe it was DCAG who, by his seniority, would run the CSAR as on-scene commander. But Wilson didn't wait. He switched to A and began to punch in the squadron tactical frequency.

Without warning, his nose pitched up.

Wilson pushed the stick forward. *Nothing!* As the nose continued to rise higher and higher, he saw nothing ahead of him but the band of stars making up the Milky Way. He deflected the stick left. *Nothing!* In a panic, he jerked it back to the right. The stick was dead in his hand.

Now the jet, with its nose parked high, was in danger of stalling due to lack of airflow over the wings. With a burst of adrenalin, and his mind in overdrive, Wilson stomped on the left rudder pedal. The *Hornet* obeyed and yawed left, the nose knuckling down to the horizon. As the airplane fell through on its side, Wilson stomped on the right rudder to try and hold the nose steady in a shallow climb toward the coast. Although it was sluggish, the nose responded, and Wilson pulled the left throttle out of burner to hold the attitude. How he wished he could lose those bombs and tanks weighing down his jet!

The airplane rolled off to the right and full left rudder did not stop it, so he helped it along with full right rudder. When his jet rolled inverted and nose down, Wilson stood on the right rudder and reengaged the left blower to recover. The nose came back through to the horizon, and Wilson released the controls. He was heading toward another storm that sat off the port along the coast. He wasn't sure he could roll away from it and hoped to stagger past using only rudder and differential power on his one operating engine.

With no pitch control, he had to keep the jet rolling, and with each roll he lost altitude. He was now in the low teens making progress toward the coast, and the storm.

Lieutenant Junior Grade Mark "Kid" Webb, the wide-eyed nugget flying *Slash* 34, Tail-End-Charlie, had a visual on Commander Wilson in *Slash* 11.

Low and to his left, he picked up the gray planform of a *Hornet*, lights out, rolling toward the coast. He figured the jet had to be Skipper Wilson, who the lead *Slash* division had reporting missing before the skipper came up on GUARD. Five miles from feet wet was good news, but it appeared the stricken aircraft was flying into a thunderstorm off to the north. The *Slashes* were clear of the heavy AAA over San Ramón, and the radar warning gear had also quieted down. He kept his eyes on the aircraft that was rolling in such an unusual manner. He noticed a small light on it—aft of the wing line from what he could tell—and sang out to the others.

"*Slash* three-four has a visual on a *Hornet*, midnight. Heading east into that cell north of us."

"Kid, where away?" responded his lead in *Slash* 33.

"About my nine o'clock low, two miles. Looks like angels twelve."

Eyes in the strike aircraft snapped north toward the cell, but only Kid in *Slash* 34 was close enough to see the jet. DCAG jumped in.

"Stay padlocked on him, *Slash* three-four. Are you both feet wet?"

"Almost… He's rolling toward the storm, and he may be on fire!"

"Stay with him, and say your state."

"*Slash* three-four is seven-point-five."

"Three-three is seven-seven."

With fewer than 8,000 pounds of fuel and the tanker nearly 200 miles away—through more convective weather—the *Hornets* didn't have much time to stay. And, even if the runways at San Ramón were out of action, the FAV could have *Vipers* inbound from dispersal fields, even *Flankers* from Caracas.

However, they would not abandon one of their own just yet.

Wilson was heading toward the thunderstorm in his path, one that was strengthening and forming an anvil top high above him. The storm was the least of his worries.

As he approached the safety of the coast, still using the rudder to control his jet, the glow from his right side was becoming more pronounced. Wilson knew he was on fire. The jet could explode any minute. He could get out now with a chance to live—and be captured. The storm was in his path, but it was worth entering if it got him feet wet into the Columbus Channel. Although he had no CSAR to pick him up, he had a better chance at rescue in the water. Since two or three more rolls should get him there, he prayed his dying jet could hold on a bit longer.

Knowing he would have to get out soon, Wilson ripped the goggles off his helmet and dropped them by his feet. When, with both hands, he began to stow his radio in his vest pouch, he was thrown up against the left side of the cockpit by an explosion from behind. The tearing of metal caused the jet to roll hard right. The negative G-force pinned his hands up, and the radio flew away and slid down to the windscreen. He had to get out *now,* but he couldn't. He couldn't reach down to the handle.

Wilson was out of his seat from the negative G, hanging in his straps as *Firebird* 301 rolled faster and faster as it picked up speed. Unknown lights spun in front of him and blood rushed to his head. Wilson tried to push off the top of the canopy with his left arm but the force was too great. Shocked that he could not move, he struggled and cried for help even though he knew there was no one in his cockpit. He was pinned, *helpless,* in a corkscrewing jet with airspeed building.

Pushed up against the canopy, Wilson could not move from his position. With all his might, he tried to reach down to the handle—and couldn't! He began to panic, whimpering, straining, praying, fighting for life. *Help me!* The violent spinning was causing him to choke, and he feared he would pass out any moment.

Jim Wilson's life flashed before him. Hitting a home run during a boyhood baseball game. Mary holding newborn Derrick. Weed sitting next to him on a liberty boat. *All* of it flashed by in an instant. The sharp point of a single coastal light below became a blur. Pinned.... *Helpless....*

Wilson gave up struggling. It was going to happen. It would be painless. No chance. Even if he could reach the handle, an ejection would probably kill him. Why fight anymore? He had given it a good fight. But South America...hadn't thought it would end here.

Then, deep inside his soul, a raging defiance burst forth, and with it a volcanic explosion of superhuman strength he didn't know he possessed. He tensed his body, closed his eyes tight, and bellowed.

"NO!"

CHAPTER 53

Wilson awoke to cold—and pain.

Hanging in his straps, his helmet and mask gone, he realized that he was out—and alive. The pain grabbed him immediately. His left arm was immobile, and his shoulder hurt like hell. He felt moisture on his neck. *Blood?* With his right hand he felt it and figured it was rash caused by the nylon straps. Wilson lifted his head and saw the parachute canopy above him. *Four-line release.* He felt for it, but the pain made him lose interest. With his good hand he found the beaded ring and pulled, and, with a loud *whoosh*, his survival vest inflated around his neck and waist. The minor exertion caused his body to go limp with exhaustion and pain.

Sharp pain dug through his right thigh. Wilson tried to move his leg and couldn't. One arm and one leg out of commission. *They must be broken*, he figured.

His flashlight was gone, ripped out of its grommet snaps by the force of ejection. He sensed something next to him...a wall, a milky wall. Wilson realized he was in more trouble when a sudden flash lit up the wall. *He was next to the storm.*

A *boom* from inside stung his ears and caused him to flinch. He was regaining his senses. *How did I get out*? he wondered, having no memory of even touching the handle. He looked for his jet below. Nothing. *What happened to it? What happened?*

In the ambient light he could detect the clouds reaching out toward him. He was over the coastline, and the winds at altitude would push him back over land. He had been so close—if only his *Hornet* could have survived another roll. Then, he felt his pouch. His survival radio! *Gone!* Lost like the flashlight in the ejection. He now had no way to communicate with potential rescuers. He tried to come to grips with this dreadful development. Severe injuries and no radio. No way even to call the rest of the *Slashes* to tell them he was alive. He tried to see and hear any of them. Nothing.

Feeling the cold moisture on his face, Wilson entered the cloud and lost all bearing in the milky darkness. At least he had his gloves. Even though he had no depth perception, he felt as if he were climbing, not falling, and realized he was caught in an updraft. A rumble from inside the cloud reminded him of the danger he was in.

He was hanging from a parachute inside a thunderstorm.

Ice crystals pelted his face from below, and he raised his hand to shield his chin. Soon they became marble-sized balls of hail that, on the way up, bounced off his inflated life vest and the soles of his feet. Wilson looked up at his parachute canopy, and it appeared to be full, still undamaged.

Another frightening rumble came from nearby. Then, blasting the air with the sound of a rifle shot going off in his ears, a horizontal tube of translucent electricity, rectangular, appeared out of nowhere in front of him. Wilson recoiled in terror, feeling close enough to touch it. The intensity of the light was blinding, and he felt its power down to his marrow. The lightning bolt disappeared as quickly as it had come, but Wilson's ears continued to ring in pain. He knew he was in deep trouble.

Hail shot past him, going up, up, up. Wilson sensed himself turning, *feeling* it in his only flight instrument, the seat of his pants. As raw fear enveloped him, he remained braced for the next bolt of energy. Every hair on his body seemed to stand up as positive and negative electrons worked him over. He kept one eye shut and squinted with the other to defend them from the blinding flashes.

The twisting increased, and Wilson felt nauseous again. He became fearful the chute would collapse from the interaction of the turbulence and the barrage of hail from below. Wilson shivered with cold.

A thunderous bolt from behind almost knocked him unconscious, and he realized he had lost control of his bowels. He was amazed to see hail floating, just floating in front of him. Then, as the hail—and Wilson— reached the apex of the climb, they began to fall. As if caught in a runaway freight train of air, he and the hail were now riding the downdraft in the very middle of the storm. More rumbling, constant and muffled flashes. Wilson could feel the parachute's nylon cords vibrate from the hail pounding the top of the canopy as the surrounding air became even colder. How could he escape? When would this end? Powerless, and damn near freezing, he wished he were on the ground, even if it meant having a Venezuelan soldier pointing a rifle barrel at him.

WHAM! A dazzling bolt materialized and then disappeared in front of him. A flash of heat from the main stump cast off jagged saplings of electricity. *Oh, God, please!* Even wearing his nomex gloves, Wilson was losing the feeling in his fingertips from the bitter cold. His ears, wracked with pain from the booming lightning bolts, were painfully cold. He felt he could reach out and touch the lightning, but he didn't dare. His working arm and leg were drawn inward, in fear and because of the cold.

Wilson sensed he was climbing. He then realized he was caught in the cycle of the storm, caught inside a giant washing machine of charged particles, ice, and speeding air molecules. Wilson was in the middle of them as they shot up through the storm. Once the spinning started again, he vomited. The vomit went up into the storm with him, as had everything else.

Let death come, Wilson thought. Surrounded by the rumbling of the unpredictable evil that would hit him the next time, he was freezing. As he drifted in and out of consciousness, he could see the frost on his vest and gloved hand. He knew he could not last much longer.

Down. A hailstone smashed into his bare head, then another. *Cold.* Breaking the relative silence of flowing air, ice particles beat on the parachute—and Wilson. A booming crack sounded behind him. Further away but *damn close!* Wilson hung in his straps in misery. Beyond caring, he waited for the end to come.

Rain. Another deafening rifle shot next to him turned night into day. Tingling. Drenched, cold skin. Pain—everywhere. Weakness. Resignation.

A light. A point of light someplace below. Wilson picked up a slow rotation. *There's water.* He saw a dark land underneath. Venezeula…his enemy, his foreign enemy. Wilson checked for his .45 pistol and was relieved that he had it. Rain, instead of hail, beat on his body. Warmer. Out of the washing machine. Another crack behind, then one in front. From the light, Wilson could detect trees below, a forest. Another spin. *There's the coastline again.* So close to safety. *What hit me?*

Wilson licked at the rivulets of water flowing down his face. He was thirsty. With luck, he would have time to drink from his canteen before the soldiers showed up. He could drink three canteens.

Wilson scanned for vehicle lights below. *None.* He saw a settlement in the distance, and, using the line of storms to the east as a reference, he determined the settlement was northwest. A smaller one was located to the southeast. A bolt illuminated the ground. *About 1,000 feet to go.* Wilson deployed his seat pan which fell away with a painful jolt. *Four-line release.* He found it on the risers. *Who knows what the surface winds are*, he thought, *but it doesn't matter.* He pulled the release.

Lighting was striking all around Wilson, and one bolt exploded into a treetop below. He knew he was falling at seventeen feet per second. He would hit the ground hard, as if he had jumped off the roof of a one-story building. *Proper body position, bend the knees, eyes forward, hands on risers. Five-point contact.*

The lightning lit up the ground below, and Wilson could see he was heading into a forest that covered rolling terrain. He made out a ridgeline to the south and, maybe, a small clearing to the east. Now he was concerned about getting caught up in one of the trees. The dark had returned, along with a light rain, and Wilson knew he would go into a tree in seconds. He put his good leg against the other one as best he could. With his right hand, he pulled his elbow in tight and protected his neck. He felt the seat pan hit something.

Here it comes.

Branches ripped and clawed at him as he fell through the tree, and Wilson cried in pain as a branch pried his good arm away from his body. His body jerked to a halt as the parachute caught up in the tree. Then, with twigs tearing at his face, he continued down, pulled by his own weight, until he crashed in a heap on the muddy ground.

Wilson lay there for a few seconds to collect his wits. In excruciating pain, he rolled onto his good leg as he undid his Koch fittings. He felt for his canteen in his g-suit pocket. The pocket was open, the canteen gone— most likely lost in the violence of the ejection. He was exhausted, but he had to have water. He kept a small flask in his vest and retrieved it.

Then the sky opened up, and a band of rain beat down on the trees and foliage. Even under the canopy of tree branches Wilson was soaked again by the deluge, but unlike nature's washing machine minutes ago, it provided warm water. Using a nearby fern branch as a funnel, Wilson pulled the tip to his mouth and drank his fill of fresh rainwater and then refilled his flask. Grateful to be alive, he sat there in the pouring rain, fingers feeling the mud of solid ground, and tried to regain his bearings.

Wilson looked at his watch: 2035. Thirty-five minutes had elapsed since he had rolled in on Runway 28R. He then realized that, at that very moment, the President was speaking to the nation. *Mary. Are you watching? I need you, baby.*

Wilson felt again for his radio, and with dread confirmed that it, too, was really gone. Pain returned, and pushed into every part of his body. He couldn't walk, but his .45 was firmly attached to his chest. Would he fight if they came upon him? The steady rain, even the bolts of lightning coming down around him, gave him a reprieve from capture for the moment. He sat under the tree breathing, thinking, recovering.

He was an American fighting man. His duty now was to evade.

CHAPTER 54

(Group HQ, San Ramón)

Hours later, after the world had watched the President of the United States speak about his surprise attack on the Bolivarian Republic, Hernandez made a report to Caracas.

The directed energy weapon seemed to have worked the way the Russians had said it would. But it required a radar handoff to track multiple targets, and the Americans had delivered effects on them the AMV controllers had never seen. The runways at San Ramón were cut in several places and would be out of action for some time. It could be weeks until construction crews could clear debris and fill the deep craters. They had paid a high price with the loss of two *Vipers* to American sweep fighters—and before the *Vipers* could even attempt a missile shot on the attackers. On the bright side, the Russians had night vision goggles and were able to acquire and track one airplane and disable it. Gunners firing barrage AAA into the air then managed to shoot it down with several eyewitnesses on the coast. An hour ago, a piece of wreckage was found, the wing on an American F-18 with the number 301 on a flap surface. Hernandez had mobilized search helicopters with Bolivarian Army commandos and armed patrol boats to find the pilot, whether he was dead or alive. There was no indication yet of an American rescue attempt, but intercepted American communications revealed they thought the pilot was able to get out of the stricken aircraft. Hernandez promised his leadership that he would find the pilot before they did. An American pilot would be an invaluable prize for the Bolivarian Republic—and a bargaining chip for Hernandez.

After the attack on San Ramón, the Americans hit Río Salta with no fighter opposition, the port suffering moderate damage. Because they could expect the Americans to return tomorrow night, he would truck the *Vipers* at San Ramón to dispersal fields and have the *Flankers* out of Caracas fly barrier combat air patrols to defend the capital. Not counting air-to-ground close air support aircraft and high performance trainers. He could maybe get 15 fighter aircraft into the air.

At the moment Hernandez finished his report, he learned of American attacks on the capital. The Chief of Staff ripped into him, asking Hernandez if he could hear the sirens and thumps of American ordnance through the phone line, blaming him for the inept performance of the AMV in defending the Bolivarian Republic from attack. How could he accuse Hernandez of not defending the Bolivarian Republic? One of the American aircraft carriers was more than twice as powerful as the entire AMV! He didn't deserve blame for this mismatch. Generals always blamed everyone but themselves. But, on a higher level, Hernandez knew he deserved it. If he were in Caracas, he would have already been cashiered—or worse. One way or another, he had only days to live, Hernandez knew he must now be one of those who got into the cockpit of a *Viper* being trucked to a dispersal field and attempt takeoff on a narrow highway strip. If he survived that, the flight controllers would vector him to a one-way meeting with an American formation that could out-stick him with missiles and flood his sensors with electronic jamming such that he would have no idea what was going on. At least he would die with a shard of honor.

Unless he could deliver the downed pilot, alive. That prize, and Daniel's help, could save him. Once his report to Caracas was concluded, he ripped into *his* subordinates. Finding the American pilot alive was job one, and to make a point, he removed his sidearm and discharged it into the ceiling. He now had the full attention of his astonished and fearful staff, and they set out with renewed vigor—one group to find the American, the other to disperse the intact assets of San Ramón.

Aboard *Coral Sea*, Admiral Davies was waiting for LTJG Webb in CVIC. It was nearing midnight, and Kid had already boltered on his first pass before getting aboard with a lucky 4-wire on his next attempt. The recovery of the first strike was winding down, and the jets from the second wave would be here in an hour or so. *Coral Sea* was pitching and rolling as much as the new guys had ever seen, and it was *black* outside. Davies knew they had to go back tomorrow night and wondered if the untested aviators in Carrier Air Wing SIX were up to it.

CAG Matson and DCAG Kay also waited with Davies, who was becoming impatient.

"He trapped ten minutes ago. Where the hell is he?" Devil snapped at Matson.

Without being told, Kay picked up the J-dial phone and contacted Webb's squadron, the *Hells Angels* of VFA-54 in Ready 6. He was waiting for an answer but cradled the receiver when the young pilot walked in still wearing flight gear that reeked of perspiration. Kid's hair was matted down with sweat, and mask lines etched his face as he hoisted his helmet bag. Seeing the heavies when he walked into CVIC—all of them looking at him—caused his night-adapted eyes to open wide even in the bright fluorescent light. Matson spoke first.

"Admiral, this is Lieutenant JG Webb."

Davies took two steps toward him. "Where have you been, son?"

A nervous Kid answered, breathing through his mouth. "They shut me down at the top of the bow, sir. I came here straight from the flight deck."

"Okay, did you see Skipper Wilson get out?"

"I think so, sir. Coming off target, I saw a *Hornet*, lights out, in the teens, heading northeast. I was maybe a mile away from it when we were approaching the coast. It was rolling...weird, like barrel rolls, not jinks. I think it was on fire someplace aft. Then, it started a pretty steep descent, and soon there were two flashes. I think it was breaking up, and there was a trail of fire as it went in."

Matson nodded, visualizing the ejection seat sequence and the parachute opening. "Sounds like the first flash was the motor of the seat rocket firing and the second the parachute spreader gun. You were on goggles?"

"Yes, sir. I was turning toward it."

"What altitude was it?" Davies asked.

"I'd say low teens, sir."

"Where?"

Kid studied at the chart of Venezuela on the planning table and pointed. "We were about here, sir, coasting out feet wet. DCAG led us east around a storm, then north along the line we had to punch through on the ingress."

"Where you hit by lightning?" DCAG asked him.

"No, sir, but I was on Mikey's wing, and I think he was. My whole fuckin' field of view lit up. Ah, sorry, sir!" Kid answered, embarrassed that he let loose with a profanity in front of the admiral.

"No worries," Davies said as he concentrated on the chart. The area pointed out by the nugget pilot was in a marshy flat covered in mangroves. A little spit of land led into the Columbus Channel, an area full of tiny estuaries. Satellite imagery confirmed it was little more than glorified swampland, and a downed aviator would have a challenge *surviving* in it, much less evading a determined enemy.

"Let's see your tape," CAG said. When Kid retrieved it, Commander Hofmeister took it to a nearby monitor to play for the admiral.

The grainy, green infrared image of San Ramón came into view. Kid's aimpoint was on the taxiway, and the men watched as he slewed his diamond over it. In the background, they could hear clipped transmissions from the other strikers, including Wilson's "in" call. The picture built frame by frame, and as the runway complex came into greater focus, they could make out small blips of light crossing the screen left to right—AAA.

"Was the AAA heavy?" CAG asked him.

"Don't know, sir," the young pilot replied. "Never seen it before." His response caused the senior aviators to smile.

The image rotated as the aircraft rolled in, and rows of impact explosions erupted on the runways from the bombs of the *Slash* 11 and 21 divisions. Runway 28R had three cuts across it, not four. Wilson's aimpoint was missing, evidence that he didn't get his bombs off—at least not on target. Minutes passed as they watched the tape. They heard Wilson's strained MAYDAY call, then nothing. DCAG gave a summary.

"Admiral, I was down the chute behind Flip, and while I was concentrating on my aimpoint, on the pull off he just wasn't there. No flashes from AAA hits, and no evidence of impacts from his bombs. Kid here saw a *Hornet* on the egress—"

"Are you *sure* it was a *Hornet?*" Davies queried, eyes narrowed.

"Yes, sir. Twin vertical stabs."

"And you saw him get out?"

"Yes, sir, I think so, right next to a thunder cell. But I couldn't make out a chute."

"Have you seen an ejection before? On goggles? Ever?"

Kid held his gaze. "No, sir."

"Could you have seen an airplane exploding?" Davies continued, unconvinced.

"Could be, sir."

CAG stepped in. "Kid, thanks. Great job tonight. You get out of your gear, and we'll see you in the debrief. Thanks." After the lieutenant departed, he turned to Davies.

"Admiral, we heard Flip on GUARD reporting a total electrical failure and switching to the squadron tactical frequency. While circumstantial, it seems something happened to him over the target area, and he was trying to fly the jet over the water.

"Maybe the frickin' Venezuelans were spoofing us."

"Sir, the strikers, including Not-o here, recognized Flip's voice, and he said he was switching to squadron tac. The enemy isn't going to know that frequency, not a minute after he goes lights out. We also have a fellow aviator who saw a struggling *Hornet* on the egress and light patterns that indicate an ejection."

Davies shot back. "Dammit, Matson, that boy can barely shave!" Matson stood his ground.

"A few hours ago 'that boy' was over the beach, sir." He pointed at the chart. "*That* beach, a place you and I haven't been. He's qualified in my book, and I think Flip got out and is in those mangroves."

Davies considered the chart, breathing through his nose. "I agree," he said.

With his fingers, Davies measured the distance from Tobago to San Ramón. He rubbed his chin as hr thought.

"We've got two armed *Sierras* with a squad of SEALs in Tobago, about a hundred miles away. But they need an escort, and we need to find Wilson's posit before I send them."

Hofmeister spoke up. "Admiral, national assets will show us where an ejection occurred, which narrows the search. Imagery of the thunderstorm at that time can help, too."

"Yes, please get it. And my staff will get with the Air Force. Maybe they can help. We'll send a report to SOUTHCOM." Davies then turned to CAG.

"Is Wilson married?"

"Yes sir, his wife's name is Mary. My wife is friends with her. They have two kids."

Davies nodded. "Okay. Get word to the wing commander in Oceana. It's midnight in Virginia Beach, but we need to tell her he's missing. *Do not* screw this up."

"We'll get word to the beach, sir. I'll contact my wife and give her a heads up."

"I want him back, CAG. We've gotta figure out how."

"Yes, sir."

"And give Kid a shot of brandy, or whatever your doc has in his locker. All of the guys that flew tonight deserve it for the recovery alone. And, yes, dammit, I know there is *no alcohol allowed on a fucking navy ship.* You are authorized. Do it."

"Aye, aye, sir." CAG replied with a smile.

Davies then went back to the imagery, thinking about what *he* would do on the ground. They had to find Jim Wilson, *fast.*

CHAPTER 55

(Ready 5, USS *Coral Sea*)

Annie Schofield surveyed the *Firebird* officers from the front of the ready room as they sat in their high-backed chairs. With Skipper Wilson missing, the command-by-negation military culture expected her to pick up the flag and lead. Her career had prepared her to lead, but she didn't want to accept the standard this way.

Although their posture reflected a tight-lipped stoicism, their thoughts wallowed in the irony and the emotion of the situation.

Of all people, the skipper! Shot down!

Or was it an aircraft malfunction?

Either way, he was lost.

Maybe dead!

No contact!

Wilson's empty chair in the front of the ready room was an unnerving reminder of the unpredictable danger they lived with every day. And, for nuggets like Macho, it hit home. *This can really happen.* The uncertainty made it worse. *If he was shot down, how? Are they waiting to get me, too?*

Most of them had been up all night flying strikes or planning them for tonight. The rest were maintaining the jets and otherwise managing VFA-16 as a fighting unit. They were in full-combat mode, grabbing naps when they could between duties in Air Ops, on the LSO platform, in the ready room, and on the flight deck. As usual, the chiefs supervised the sailors that made it all happen, while the officers handled operations with the fully mission-capable jets handed to them. The next several days would be full of strikes—Annie was leading one this afternoon—but their next priority, job number two for the *Coral Sea*/Carrier Air Wing SIX team, was to rescue Commander Jim Wilson from the Venezuelan delta.

Killer, at the duty desk, gave Annie the word. "Ma'am, everyone is here."

Annie nodded and stepped toward the assembled group.

294

"Okay, good morning. We are gearing up for another big day and night, and from what ops is hearing, we'll be flying hard for at least the next 48 hours, working targets in the Río Salta/San Ramón area. We're going to mine Río Salta this afternoon, and the Air Force is working target sets in the western part of the country. *TR* is about 48 hours from being able to help us. When they do, we'll take a day off, and then get right back on it.

"This operation came up on us without warning. We were having a great at-sea period in the sunny Caribbean, bumping heads with the Colombians and reporting drug runners. Then Trench was blinded. We hit the guys who did it. Venezuela took our ambassador. The Russians messed with us along the east coast, and Castro mobilized near Gitmo. They are all in bed with each other, and last night we picked up the gauntlet.

"Skipper Wilson, the finest aviator with whom I have served, is missing. He's *missing*. We are going to find him, but I'm not going to give you all a lollipop and tell you everything will be okay. We are professional aviators, and we've been given a job to do. We are going to hit the assigned targets as briefed. That is our job. However, our other job—for as long as it takes—is to find Skipper Wilson. We are not going to abandon him, and we are not going to abandon *you*. We have no idea if he is dead or alive. So he's alive. We have no idea if he's evading or captured. So he's evading.

"We do not lose faith with each other. Our leadership trusts us to do our jobs, and we trust them to never give up on us, to back us, to *never* give up. I want you to know that as you plan and fly, as you reflect on this situation. I, and I'm sure CAG and the admiral, will not do our *best*. No, we will do *whatever it takes* to find you. Again, the ending may not be happy, but you have *my* personal guarantee that *I* will not stop until all of us are accounted for.

"We also look out for your families. We take care of our own.

"That's what I wanted to tell you. So let's get back to planning, sleeping, flying or eating. That's it. All else can wait. Anything for me?"

She looked around the room and was about to dismiss the officers when Dusty raised his hand. "Go," she said.

"XO, wha…what are we doing? Last night we conducted a major strike to cut some runways, and today we are going to hit some comm towers and drop mines in the water. A few weeks ago, everything was calm and now, as far as *we* are concerned, we are at war. It seems we are poking them in the eye while they fight back as hard as they can, and we *let* them continue to fight. What is the national goal of these strikes?"

Annie nodded her understanding of the question. She then shrugged her shoulders.

"I don't know."

The room was shocked by Annie's frank and unexpected answer. They saw in her calm demeanor that she meant it. This answer from their XO was disconcerting, and they waited for more. Annie did not disappoint.

"I don't know," she repeated. "What I do know is that I've been assigned a strike this afternoon that several of you will fly with me. Olive has a strike lead tomorrow, as does Stretch, and you JOs are going to be wingmen. We and the rest of Air Wing SIX are going to respond to tasking. And that may change. It may change this afternoon.

"When you sign for a jet, you trust that the maintenance department says it is 'up' and ready to go. When you taxi on deck under the control of the yellow shirt, they can taxi you from bow to stern and back again and you just do it. You trust they have a plan for you. If you bring the jet back with an overstress or prang it on deck with a hard landing, the troops have to fix it. If, over time, we find the assigned jet is not really up, or the yellow shirts are inefficient, or you have a repeated history of ham-fisting the jet, we need to take corrective action.

"Right now, I am a carrier aviator who works at the pleasure of the President, and he, through national command authority, has given me a task. As a military woman, I salute and I say aye-aye. This obedience does not relieve me of my duty to plan a smart strike and do everything in my power to take care of my wingmen—*you*—and to get guidance from CAG about how hard I should press over the target area, how much risk I should accept—*for you*. Once the political goal of this operation becomes clearer, and if I don't like the goal or the manner in which it is obtained, I can express my opinion up the chain to the Skipper, and if he's not here, to CAG. If I don't like the answer, I can either 'shut up and color' or resign. Any day I want I can turn in my wings—a step we all know is irrevocable. So, we decide carefully. Another way I can express my opinion is to vote this November for politicians who best represent my views—on this particular national security matter and others—a right all of you have as well and should exercise."

Annie took a few steps and addressed Dusty with a confident smile. "For now, I'm following orders as a fleet strike fighter pilot on this ship, not accepting stupid stuff, taking care of you in formation. I am free to stop anytime I want. I'm going to trust the chain of command until they lose my confidence, because I can think for myself. Just as your sailors trust you, as the yellow shirts trust you and you trust them on the roof. That sound good?"

"Yes, ma'am. Thank you." Dusty answered, ready to follow. Annie continued.

"So, what *we* are doing is hitting our assigned DMPIs with everything we've got, on time and on target with fused weapons. That is our job. We concentrate on that and on taking care of each other. *We* need to be as tactically smart as possible and not give an inch to their defenses. Like last night. If they come up to fight, we knock them down. If they sortie out of the harbor, we find them and sink them with no remorse. That is a message I hope they get from us—fighting back means certain death, so don't fight back. This will demoralize the Venezuelans and aid us in whatever Washington has in mind. And, again, I don't know what that is. Long answer, but if we hit the assigned targets on time and fight like hell to defend each other we are doing what is expected of us. We'll let Washington worry about the policy."

Dusty again nodded his understanding, still not 100% convinced, but willing to fight alongside Annie and his squadronmates. Annie was a warrior and was now the de facto leader of the *Firebirds*. She had earned their respect.

Annie dismissed the officers, and, as they headed out, she caught Olive's attention and motioned her over.

"Yes, ma'am," Olive said as they stepped to the pull-out charts.

"I know you are planning your strike for tomorrow. Where are you going?"

"There's a SAM site at the top of the Peninsula de Paria. We need to eliminate it for *TR* before they start working in the central part of the country."

"Okay, but please take an hour and try to reconstruct Skipper's track and where Kid last saw him. Winds at altitude, the terrain below, areas offering concealment, landing zones. Maybe we can ask for a recon mission to find wreckage, with a follow-on SOF mission to check an area of interest. We need to find intel on what the Venezuelans are doing, so get with Shane and have her do the legwork, and you direct her efforts. I'll ask CAG to give you some help from his staff."

"Yes, ma'am."

"I want you to lead your strike. *Then,* I want you to be the Skipper Wilson rescue officer, the go-to expert. You can fly wing on other strikes as required, but we need you to concentrate your efforts on helping us find the skipper...*after* your strike lead."

"Yes, ma'am," Olive acknowledged with a smile.

"Great, we'll touch base tonight after my hop."

"Yes, ma'am."

Part III

Amazing Grace, How sweet the sound
That saved a wretch like me
I once was lost, but now am found
T'was blind but now I see

—John Newton

CHAPTER 56

Wilson spent the night where he landed, miserable and wet, gnats buzzing about his head. The pain from his shoulder and leg shot through him each time he shifted his weight. Lying in his own filth, he was exhausted.

As the rain stopped and returned at intervals, Wilson had managed to unhook and roll out of his inflated vest, panting for breath from the exertion. With his right leg and left arm immobile, he found it difficult to maneuver out of his flight gear. He did manage to crawl a few feet through the mud to a tree trunk in order to prop up his back. It took most of the night to get out of his harness, and, during the process, he dozed a few times from fatigue and tension. Now that the sky had begun to gray to his right, he at least knew where *east* was, and the light would perk him up for what he knew would be a long day.

He knew the Venezuelans were out looking for him, and, injured as he was, he could not move ahead of them toward the coast, which he now knew was off to his left, north. Wilson saw a dead tree about 50 yards distant among the others of the forest. He would make for that before selecting another orienting landmark. *Fifty yards.* With dread, he realized that short distance could take hours.

During the night, Wilson had heard the sounds of tree branches snapping or small animals crunching on the forest floor. Each *snap* had been terrifying, not knowing if he was being stalked by a soldier or a panther. He thanked God for the light.

God. Wilson needed Him now more than ever and found himself praying for strength—and for the ability to make decisions that would deliver him from the evils that surrounded him. *Please help me, God,* he repeated over and over. He took a drink from his small pocket canteen and thought of Mary, Derrick and Brittany. He guessed Mary knew by now, but the kids? Eleven-year-old Derrick could comprehend all of it, and Brittany, at eight, could understand Daddy was in trouble, just by watching her mother. He said another prayer asking God to give comfort to his family.

I need a walking stick. Wilson looked about for a sturdy branch, something two to three inches thick. After a few minutes, he found a stick to get him to the dead tree, and wedged it next to him. Then, he alternately pulled with his right arm and pushed with his left leg, which allowed his back to slide up the trunk of the tree. With determined effort, he managed to stand, and gasped for breath for the next five minutes to recover.

Earlier, after salvaging some seat-pan items and stuffing his vest pockets with them, Wilson had removed his flotation gear and harness and hidden them under a fern. He draped the vest over his back and pulled it around his left hand to fashion a makeshift sling. His mosquito net hood was a welcome relief as he placed it over his head. The sun now cast patches of direct light throughout the trees, and the warmth felt good. He hoped for a nice day.

He took his first step. Resting his right shoulder on the stick, he dragged his right leg over the forest detritus. He had to take a step and stop, take another step and stop, but he was moving.

He reached the dead tree in good time, less than an hour. He allowed himself to rest as he took a chug of water and read his compass. He figured a heading of 045 was as good as any until he got to another reference point or to a clearing from which he could assess the situation. He was alert to the guttural rumble of fighter engines above and had his signaling mirror in his pocket ready to go—if he could ID one of the jets as a *Hornet* or *Rhino.*

What had hit him? He had lost *everything* in the cockpit at once, the flight controls going into MECH as the jet dove toward the ground. It seemed to have been an electrical glitch, but one he had never seen or experienced. Directed energy? Was that it? Did the Venezuelans have such a weapon? Something that could fry every circuit in his highly vulnerable "electric" jet?

His mechanical watch, the one he wore only during combat, showed 10:35, and he looked up through the trees to see a lone contrail overhead. He traced it to its source and saw an airliner heading north. *That guy is way up there*, he thought. His *Coral Sea* boys wouldn't be back this morning, but probably this afternoon and tonight. He thought of Annie's strike and tried to remember if it was scheduled for this afternoon at Río Salta. He would get a ringside view if he could find a clearing.

Through a break in the trees, Wilson saw more trees in the distance, as if on a hill to the south, a quarter mile away. He could hear a stream gurgling and headed toward it to drink his fill and top off his canteen for the night.

Energized, he crunched along with his stick and one good leg toward the pleasant sound of the water. By a stream, he had to be careful of humans as well as animals, but needed to move by day. His game plan was to get near and then stay in the brush in order to watch and listen before approaching the stream as the sun set. Afterwards, he would find a place to hunker down for another cold and damp night. As he dragged through the forest, Wilson realized the stream was more east than north, but he had to have water—and he could follow the stream to the sea.

No helicopter sounds. Wilson didn't expect a rescue, but he thought the Venezuelans would have several helos up searching for him. And would have dropped teams of soldiers to search for him. *No shouts. No vehicle sounds.* He tried to remember from the briefing what the topography was like...*mangroves.* Flat. He found another break in the trees and looked south. He saw that the forest sloped up to a ridge. *Rolling hills? Where are the mangroves?* It didn't make sense, but the aeronautical charts he had reviewed in his planning were not detailed land navigation charts. He should have crammed one into his g-suit pocket...one of many omissions on this hurry-up strike.

After two hours of effort, he still could not see the stream. And it sounded no closer. Exhausted in the midday heat and humidity, he eased himself down. *Sleep. A short nap in the shade. Plenty of daylight left.* He would find the stream this afternoon, regain his strength, and be in a good position to traverse a fair amount of ground tomorrow. He was hungry, but not yet hungry enough to eat a lizard or large insect. That would come, though, according to survival accounts he had read over the years.

Weak and wounded, crawling through the jungle, evading and serving with honor. He thought of stories from the Vietnam War: Dieter Dengler. Lance Sijan. Bud Day. Downed American airmen who didn't give up. Of the three, Dengler made it to rescue. Starving, naked, weak from exposure and injuries from their ejections. Escaping from the enemy. Crawling inch by inch to freedom fighting jungle rot and disease. Incredible stories. Their examples were the performance bar Wilson and his generation had to meet. As the pain returned, he wondered if he would be able to even reach for the bar—with only one good arm and one good leg.

Wilson lay down in the dirt, shaded by a fern. *Just a few minutes*, he thought, *enough to catch my breath.* Resting on his stick, he focused his eyes on a hole in the foliage to the northeast. Through the leaves he could make out distant trees on another hillside almost a mile away. Another mile of rolling forested terrain.

Where the hell am I?

CHAPTER 57

(Columbus Channel)

Annie rolled out wings level and descended to her delivery altitude only a few hundred feet above the waves in the Columbus Channel. With Jumpin on her right wing in a loose tactical formation, she bumped up the airspeed and selected air-to-ground. She then designated her offset aimpoint on the southern tip of Agave Rock and slewed the cursors over it. The green steering cues on her HUD jumped, and she saw, on her tactical display, the "mine line" she would soon overfly to deliver two 1,000-pound mines across the mouth of Río Salta.

At Annie's seven-o'clock, a mile in trail, were Olive and Irish, and behind them was a division of *Raiders* from the two-seat *Rhino* squadron VFA-23. The eight aircraft were the mine-layers, call sign *Stream*, with Annie in the lead. Above her to the south, a division of *Arrow* FA-18Es formed a barrier combat air patrol, serving as a layer of defense from any FAV fighters dispersed from San Ramón or sortied from Caracas. Behind the *Streams*, a suppression package of *Growlers* and HARM shooters from the *Hobos* provided jamming and electronic attack against any SAM radars that may be painting them. At least the *Streams* could take comfort that, while they had their heads down working their targeting systems, no threat would come at them from the side or the back.

Coral Sea had moved closer during the night, but not so close that Annie's strike birds didn't require tanking from Air Force KC-10s before descending toward the Columbus Channel—and their target. With clear weather the Colombian early warning radars may have seen them come off the tanker and obtain a raid count. Now on the surface, the mine-layers could take added comfort that their jets, weighed down with heavy, drag-inducing mines, were able to avoid detection by enemy tracking and guidance radars, which the *Hobos* planned to suppress anyway.

AAA and hand-held SAMs, however, were always a problem. Even over the water they could be present on any of the dozens of small craft scattered about in the *Stream*'s path. Any knucklehead on deck with a popgun might get a lucky shot into a cockpit or into a vital area of the aircraft. As Annie led them into the Columbus Channel, they could avoid the small craft, all painted white, with mild heading changes, but in the narrow part it was trickier. And, once Annie designated and got on her steering line, she would be committed. The mines had to go in their assigned "holes."

Annie had three miles before she needed to turn right and get on the pickle switch. Ahead of her, dead in the water, was a small boat, maybe 30 feet, a typical Caribbean fishing boat with a small cabin up forward. Annie would fly right over it, and if anyone on deck saw her and wanted to, all they had to do was fire straight up and the fighter would fly right into the bullets. To avoid such a possibility, the *Streams*, under Annie's lead, could then select GUN and strafe the boat, keeping their heads down. This was war, and the unknown boat was a threat to her and those behind. With only seconds to struggle with the decision, she pulled up and left at the last moment. She then overbanked down and right to get on her steering. As she looked out the top of her canopy, she saw a man and a boy on the boat stare at the *Hornet* in awe as it thundered *past*. Annie had made the correct decision.

"Just popped over an innocent fishing boat. Ignore it," she transmitted to the others. Rolling out and leveling off again, she hit the initial point and turned right on course. "*Stream* lead is IP inbound, *Armstrong*."

Annie heard the *Magnum* calls from the *Hobos* and the *Comet* EA-18Gs, and saw the HARMS streak by high above as they looked for "trons" to home in on. The *Raiders* were in position and nothing had yet come up to challenge them. Roaring over the waves, with young Jumpin holding position on her right wing and her airframe moaning at the high airspeed, Annie saw another vessel in her path. This one was an oilfield service vessel, dead in the water along her steering line and inside Venezuelan waters. Approximately 200 feet long, the aft half of the boat was flat, and it had a superstructure forward. This boat could pose a threat to Annie and the others following her, or maybe not. Again, with only seconds to decide, she put her GUN pipper on it and pulled the trigger—holding it down.

A cloud of gun gas formed over her nose as she watched small tracers of 20mm explode away from her toward the boat. She concentrated on the forward superstructure and then kicked the rudder pedals to spray the length of the boat. From a mile behind, Olive saw the long, thin cloud of gun gas float behind Annie's jet and, moments later, the bullets made the water "boil" all around the service vessel on Annie's nose. Annie made a small jink and got back on heading.

"*Streams* one-one and one-two are in," she transmitted.

Shore-based AAA arced over the Americans and black puffs bloomed above them as the fighter pilots kept one eye on the steering cues and one on the shore watching for SAM launches. In the roadstead to Río Salta were two ocean-going tankers and several smaller coastal tankers—they would be "caught" by this minefield. Annie thought about the adage that you could drop bags of flour in the water and tell the enemy they were mines, and the enemy had a decision to make. A wrong bet would lead to catastrophe for the unlucky ship assigned to take the gamble. In this case, however, the Americans were not taking half measures. Annie and the *Streams* would deliver their heavy mines on time, allowing them to rest on the sea floor precisely where they planned. There the mines would lie in wait for an acoustic or metal signature, or both.

A half ton of high explosive came off Annie's left wing with a lurch, and her HUD steering then jumped to the next aimpoint thousands of feet ahead of her as the release cue marched down. Annie kept her thumb on the pickle switch as it did. Once the second mine fell away with a jolt, Annie pulled hard north as Jumpin's last mine came off, leading him and the rest of the *Streams* away from Venezuelan offshore rigs a few miles on their nose. Splashes of AAA shells on the surface were scattered about. Annie saw nothing over her right shoulder as she left Río Salta in her rear view mirrors—no missile plumes, no jets. Calling off, she lit the burner cans and accelerated to .95 indicated mach, cracking the throttles back into midrange burner so Jumpin could hang on inside her turn. She waited to hear the last of the *Stream* aircraft call off as they raced north through the Gulf of Paria. When she heard the welcome "*Stream* two-three and two-four off," she safed her switches and concentrated on leading her charges through the narrow five-mile passage between Punta Peñas and Chacachacre, edging her formation close to Trinidad as she did.

Within three minutes, she was approaching the *Boca de Navios* passage, a watery valley with the rising terrain of Venezuela and Trinidad on each side. All the *Streams* were aboard and egressing, no hung weapons. The *Arrows* were also egressing north, high over Paria, while the suppression element returned to the east. At mast-top height Annie blew by an expensive looking sailboat, the passengers watching in astonishment as Jumpin hung on next to her. Once the Americans were safe in the open Atlantic, Annie entered a graceful climb away from the surface in an easy right turn. Through the brilliant puffy clouds she led them toward the waiting tankers. They would soon head home to *Mother*, their mission accomplished with no losses.

Wilson heard the sharp crack of a fighter cutting through the air at high speed and the rumble of military jet engines. He heard them from the direction of the afternoon sun and craned his neck high to catch a glimpse of one of them. He caught sight of a contrail and was rewarded with the sight of a fiery pinpoint at the end of it. Right away Wilson recognized it as a missile and shouted, "Yes!" He listened for several minutes to the rumble of the engines, military and familiar. *Hornets*, his *Hornets*. *Is that Annie?*

He listened, and then realized he was facing south. From where he had ejected, Río Salta—if that was where Annie was going—was to the west. Maybe Annie had led them through the "back door," from the south. *Maybe that isn't Annie. Maybe these guys aren't attacking Río Salta. Maybe it's a Venezuelan missile.* He continued to listen long after the sound receded from his ears, long after the pain and exhaustion returned and reached a familiar peak. He had, maybe, four hours of daylight left, and he still hadn't found the stream. He needed water and rest. Tomorrow morning he would make his way north and to the coast. Sijan. Dengler.

I can do it. I have to do it.

At the same time Annie was leading her formation north, Daniel waited for Edgar Hernandez to answer. He caught a faraway glint of sunlight on the water as he stared out at the gulf. The southern horizon—and the Río Salta complex—seemed calm. He saw no evidence of the American attacks in this distance.

"Mayor General Hernandez, señor."

"Edgar, how goes the war?"

Hernandez didn't answer. Daniel repeated his question. "Edgar, are you there?"

"Si, señor." Hernandez answered.

"Good. Please bring me news of your progress."

Hernandez took a breath. "We shot down one of their fighters last night using our new toy. We believe it is one of their senior pilots, and he ejected along the coast. We are searching the area to find him, señor."

"Very good. He can be a valuable asset," Daniel said. Hernandez agreed, but for a different reason. He continued.

"The Americans just dropped bombs in the water near Río Salta, probably mines. This will bottle up our oil terminal trade, in and out. And last night, they disabled our base at San Ramón. It is unusable for the moment."

"Very well. Have you experienced losses?"

"Si, señor, two planes and their pilots last night."

"*Lo siento*, Edgar. Brave sons of the Bolivarian Republic defending the homeland from the barbarians to our north. Ensure their families are taken care of, and send me the bill."

"Si, señor," Hernandez answered, knowing he should have been in one of the cockpits. Tonight, when the Americans returned, he would be. Hernandez hated himself, and hated more that he had to spend his remaining precious minutes on earth talking with his tempter, this living devil, *Daniel*. The devil then asked him a question.

"Edgar, are the Americans going to invade the Bolivarian Republic?"

"Not this week, but they could—if they want to—in the next 30 days. First, they must mobilize an invasion force and send most of it by sea. They *are* sending such a force to defend their fortress at Guantanamo."

"The Bolivarian Republic is too vast to invade, even for the Americans."

Hernandez could not control his frustration.

"Señor, from a standing start they invaded a land-locked Afghanistan less than a month after *nueve-once*! Within *two months,* they had taken the country! Then, in only thirty days, they took Iraq! They can *do it*, señor. You saw them do it yourself in Panama, with nothing more than paratroops. My forces cannot hold, even with the Russian toys you supply us with to "zap" one or two of their jets. We cannot repulse the *tidal wave* coming down on us, but I will lead my forces to the death and take as many as we can…maybe even modest losses will be too much for the weakling American politicians to endure."

Daniel absorbed the outburst from Hernandez, an outburst that could be forgiven considering the stress Hernandez had endured the last few days. Before responding to his general, Daniel looked out at Trinidad, his lifeboat. He thought of Ramos.

"Mayor General Hernandez, thank you for your political and military assessment. I detect however, that you are going to lead the FAV into battle yourself, from the cockpit of a fighter jet."

Hernandez didn't like where this was going, but responded truthfully, *with honor.*

"I am, señor. I cannot ask them to give their lives while I am safe in a bunker. I have failed them and the Bolivarian Republic—and you, señor."

Daniel waited a long moment before he responded. He could sense the unease Hernandez felt on the other end of the line.

"Mí general, your service to the Bolivarian Republic, and to me personally, is not yet over. I need you. And dying an inglorious death in a burning airplane does not befit a man of your station. So, no, Edgar, I cannot allow it, my friend. I enjoin you to delegate this task to younger men, men of *greater honor than you*. They will do battle with the Americans, perhaps giving their lives in the process but surely taking some *yanquis* with them. I mean, the Americans conscript *women* to fight for them..."

Daniel then lowered his voice and became the icy street thug of his youth.

"And, Edgar, if you defy me...know that I will take your family— roughly—from your home. I will show video, *hours* of video, to your long suffering *mujer* of the ways you've betrayed her over many years with my party girls. I will have her watch as my men, filthy and diseased, rape your crying daughter, repeatedly. They will then tie a rope, with a stone at the other end, around the neck of your son. As he pleads for his life, I will personally push the stone into the Paria Gulf. All this in front of her. Your women, Edgar, will live their days knowing of the betrayal and pain that *you* inflicted on them. So, mí general, there will be no more talk of glory and honor from *you*, a man who has *none*, until you turn back the American attack. Or...until you bring me the American pilot. Bring me the pilot—who can serve as ransom for both of us—and then, Edgar, I will let you die with glory. I will keep your shame from your family. You have my *word* as a *man*. Unlike you, Edgar. Succeed in this task, and *then* I will let you die."

Hernandez trembled in horror at what Daniel would do to his family and how Daniel held his reputation, his *honor*, in his hand, a worse thought to Hernandez than dying. Either way, he was a walking dead man, and he figured Daniel would kidnap his family no matter what to ensure his obedience.

"I will bring you the American, señor."

"Good boy, Edgar! Good dog! Now get to work!" Daniel snapped out the words and hung up.

The deal Edgar Hernandez had made with the devil so many years ago had come due.

CHAPTER 58

After she recovered from the Río Salta strike and debriefed, Olive grabbed some food in the wardroom. She then met Shane in CVIC for what they both knew would be a long night. Olive was already mentally and physically spent from her four-hour brief and man-up, her four hours airborne, and the long post-flight debrief. With Skipper Wilson lost and XO's tasking to find him, she would run on adrenaline past midnight. Her CO was out there, and Olive, as the lead investigator, had to find out where.

Shane had the satellite imagery that marked the geographic position where the emergency beacon of the ejection seat was activated. Olive called Ready 6 and summoned Kid to meet her in CVIC. Within minutes, Kid arrived and walked up to Olive.

"Yes, ma'am."

"Kid, I'm trying to reconstruct where Skipper Wilson got out. I've plotted the lat/long from your mark after he ejected. Where were you in relation to him when he got out?"

Kid noted the position on the chart. "I was about at his two o'clock. I overtook him as we hauled ass out of there. About a mile. I tried to stay with him, but he was too slow. And he was rolling, like a barrel roll. It was weird. He was in a steep dive when he punched, and somewhere just above 10K."

"You were on goggles?"

"Yes, ma'am, the whole time."

"How could you tell the aircraft aspect?" Olive asked. "With lights out at night? No moon?"

"I was close enough, about a mile. And there was this cell behind him, to the north, that kind of backlit him with almost continuous cloud-to-cloud lightning. He was right next to it."

"There was a cell next to him?"

"Yeah, it was almost like he was going into it."

Olive checked the imagery time: The seat was activated 1932:34 local. The mark also showed Wilson got out over a small inlet leading into the channel. Another mile or two and he would have been feet wet with a better chance of rescue.

"What direction were you going when you saw him get out?"

Kid stroked his chin. "Northeast. We were all egressing northeast. Skipper was, too."

"Did you see a chute?"

"It's hard to say with the cloud background." Kid shook his head. "I can't say for sure."

On a nearby console Shane had the weather radar video and stopped it at 1932:34. "Ma'am, here's the radar showing the storms in the area. There's the one they had to avoid over the target."

Olive studied the image on the screen, noting the inlet and a large clump of radar return to the northwest of it. The clump had to be the cell Kid had seen. She brought the paper imagery over and placed it next to the screen.

"Can you fast forward please?"

"Yes, ma'am," Shane said. The radar return moved toward the northeast.

"Fast forward," Olive asked again.

The return moved across the channel into Trinidad. "Stop! What time is it?" The display time indicated 1958:20. Olive had a hunch.

"Shane, get with the guys in Metro. Find out what the winds at altitude were when the skipper got out—from 5K, 10K and 15K. See if you guys can overlay the weather radar display on top of the satellite imagery and synch up the times."

Even though he was a nugget, Kid followed Olive's line of thinking. "Ma'am, do you believe he went into that cell?"

"Yes. At least we have an area to search."

Hernandez stuck his head outside the open door of the helicopter as it approached the crash site and entered a hover. A crewman pointed to a piece of wreckage. It appeared to be a wing flap, painted light gray. He could see the Columbus Channel just beyond a small peninsula. Nothing out here. Not even natives in dugout canoes. Nothing but briars and muck, snakes and gnarled bushes. Hernandez detested this part of the Bolivarian

Republic. It wasn't fair. Trinidad was visible in the distance across these beautiful Atlantic waters, but the Venezuelan shoreline was unlivable from Paria to Guyana. At least the oil underground made up for it. The beaches of Caracas would have to suffice for Venezuelans. *Aruba.* The Bolivarian Republic should have kicked out the damn Dutch and taken Aruba. *We would have done it right*, he thought, unlike the Argentineans against the Brits 30 years ago. *That* was the war he wanted, not Daniel's foolish war against *the fucking Americans!*

The aircraft landed, and Hernandez stepped out with three of his officers. The *Hornet* was scattered about in pieces, few of them larger than one meter. The heaviest, the engines, were buried deep and circled by large crater rims made up of the spongy soil. *He must have been near supersonic when he went in,* Hernandez thought as he tromped in the brush, kicking at control actuators and pieces of aluminum. With the familiar smell of fuel oil in his nostrils, Hernandez took a moment to study one piece of gray aircraft skin stenciled with the words NO STEP.

The fuselage was buried deep...no way to know yet if the pilot got out or not. The pilot was one of their squadron commanding officers, James Wilson, highly decorated. *A TOPGUN.* Hernandez wished he had gone to TOPGUN.

Finding the ejection seat would confirm whether or not the pilot had gotten out. He prayed the seat would be empty, meaning the pilot *could* be alive. Conveying that news to Daniel would buy him time. Buy his family time. Chances were the seat, if the pilot did eject, was many kilometers from here. Still, they had to look.

Across the channel was Trinidad. *Freedom.* The Bolivarian Republic should have taken that, too: The English-speaking mongrels were no match for the AMV. Hernandez and his pilots could run up and down the island with impunity—like the damn Americans were now doing over his homeland.

Nearby, nervous perimeter soldiers scanned the sky for more Yankee angels of death. A call came in, and Hernandez got back in the helicopter. They flew only three minutes northwest before the pilot again lifted the nose high to land in a small clearing. The ground was stable as they strode to the tree line. Once there, a soldier pointed to a mangled piece of metal, one Hernandez recognized as an ejection seat.

It was empty.

CHAPTER 59

AS Davies stepped away from his chair in flag plot, he caught himself watching the recovery on the PLAT, a mindless time waster from his younger days. He needed to decompress, to stretch, but he could not allow himself to be seen doing so by the watch standers. Río Salta mined. San Ramón out of action. The Bolivarian Navy staying in port. Aruba defended, and the Marines facing down Castro's brigades along the fence line at GITMO. The Russians staying away. The Air Force was doing good work in and around Caracas, and *TR* was passing the Bahamas, en route with more carrier airpower.

All was going well for SOUTHCOM, except for the one downed pilot in Venezuela, *Davies's* pilot, and he wanted Wilson back more than any of them. He looked at the monitor of CNN and saw Wilson's wife being interviewed and pictures of Wilson in his service dress uniform. His missing pilot was all over the media, the "war" Davies was fighting now a sideshow. While it was good that the public cared, the calls from Miami were coming every 30 minutes. *Have you found him yet? Have you found him yet?*

What was he supposed to do? Just send a helicopter full of SEALs some 400 miles to the Venezuelan coast and *hope*? He needed something more than "He ejected here…" from his wing commander before he risked more of his men in that dense, swampy brush. Was Wilson alive? Already captured? Davies needed SOUTHCOM's national asset help *now*. *Tell me where he is SOUTHCOM, and I'll go get him. Hell, just give me a 25-square-mile area to start from!*

Davies walked into the vestibule and stretched his arms and back out of sight of the others. He then returned to his seat and took a sip of cold coffee from his porcelain mug.

Tim Matson walked up to him with a tall woman, one of his pilots, in tow. He could see Matson's fatigue, but everyone was exhausted. Stress and overwork was a staple of shipboard life, especially in the throes of combat.

"Admiral, may we have a word with you in the ops spaces?"

"Yes." Davies got up and led them to the conference room next door. Matson introduced him to LCDR Kristin Teel of the *Firebirds*. All business, Davies gave her a perfunctory handshake and said, "Okay, whatcha got?"

Spreading a chart on the conference table, Olive began. "Sir, XO Schofield asked me to spend some time investigating Skipper Wilson's ejection. We have eyewitness evidence that he may have ejected here at 19:32:34 local, and we received a transponder hit that corresponds to an ejection at this exact spot. That and the eyewitness account are pretty solid pieces of evidence that he ejected over Venezuela."

"Concur," Davies growled, wanting Olive to get to the point. She sensed that she needed to be faster and funnier.

"Yes, sir. We then took satellite imagery of the weather over the target area at that time and overlaid it on this chart, and then the radar imagery." As Olive overlaid the translucent imagery slides over the chart, a thunderstorm with heavy return was next to the lat/long of the first transponder hit. "And, when we include the winds at altitude, the winds were out of the south, southwest."

"Keep going," Davies said, more interested.

"Now we overlay imagery at five-minute intervals," Olive said as she placed slides over the chart and waited, then again and waited. Like a slow cartoon, the thunder cell transited across the Columbus Channel and crossed over Trinidad. The imagery showed it took approximately 20 minutes to do so. Davies was quick enough to see where Olive was going.

"You think Wilson's in Trinidad?"

Olive stood up straight as she answered. "Yes, sir. There are accounts of aviators who have ejected inside storms and 'ridden' them for miles—and survived."

"You just said he ejected outside the storm."

Olive was ready for this one, and laid a schematic of a typical thunderstorm on the table. "Yes, sir, but storms pull in air from the bottom. We think Skipper Wilson got out in the vicinity of 10K. He could have been sucked into the storm, and the winds at altitude would have helped by giving him a push."

"Why hasn't he called us?"

"Sir, he may have lost his radio during ejection. The strikers heard him on his survival radio moments before, and he was observed rolling his jet out to sea before it went into a steep dive. He was probably trying to recover the aircraft and may not have had time to stow his radio in his gear."

"He could be captured."

"Yes, sir, but he *could* be in Trinidad."

"Okay. Then why doesn't he contact the locals?"

"Sir, he could be anything from injured to captured to dead. But we have no imagery, no visual signals that prove he is on the ground in Venezuela. Nor do we have any intel that the Venezuelans have him. We *do* know the jet impacted in Venezuela and that the Venezuelans are at the crash scene."

Davies studied the chart. The storm track imagery she laid out crossed over the southeast tip of Trinidad. It could have deposited him on the island. It could have carried him and dumped him out to sea. However, with SOUTHCOM breathing down his neck, and being inclined to action, as were his aviators, he made a decision. *Why not?*

"Okay. Tim, get with my Ops, and get your guys on Tobago spun up. Have them fly this track to see what they can see."

"Yes, sir. Shall we get dip clearance?"

"No, fuck 'em. We can apologize later, but we can't shut them up when our birds lift off from their frickin' air patch. They'll know something is up, and the Venezuelans will know it, too."

Matson nodded. "Yes, sir, and I'm going to launch two *Hornets* to hold offshore to be called in if needed."

Davies nodded his approval. "Yeah, make it happen." Turning to Olive, the admiral said, "Commander, what do you go by?"

"Olive, sir."

"Olive. Nice job, Olive." Davies said and spun for flag plot to inform SOUTHCOM of his new plan—for now, his best and only plan.

CHAPTER 60

Wilson got to the stream before sundown and lay in the mud as he drank his fill of fresh water. After he topped off his water bottle, he tended to a wound on his left wrist. During his fall through the trees, a branch had scraped it and drawn blood. The intense throbbing in his hand caused him to fear infection.

Wilson considered his situation. He faced another night in a damp flight suit, shivering as he tried to conserve energy. He had water now, but needed food to keep up his energy, *and* he needed to keep warm. But what food? As the light receded, he looked around for berries and found some red ones. He took a taste and spit out the bitter fruit. He wasn't *that* hungry, and didn't need a stomach infection to add to his woes.

Wilson crawled to a spot near a fern and was able to fashion a crude bed from the large green leaves of nearby vegetation. Puffy buildups hovered above, as they always did in a clear sky. He could detect no rain, either by sight or smell, and he could hear no rumbles of thunder. He would sleep here and keep going. Wilson removed his left boot but found he could not remove the other boot from his swollen foot. He feared trench foot—or worse—was developing.

As the stars appeared and he lay on his back, he again thought of home and Mary. He wanted to be safe and secure in her arms, warm, at rest right next to her, at peace. What was she thinking and doing now? He imagined Karen Hopper and Gail Martin, Billy's wife, at her side with the rest of the *Firebird* spouses. Accustomed to looking to Mary for leadership, they would be holding her up in support. *Derrick and Brit.* Both were now old enough to *know*, and Derrick old enough to know *why*.

Wilson's entire body ached: broken bones, insect bites, dampness, chill, the discomfort of his own filth. How much longer to the coast? Once there, how could he signal? He'd have to develop a plan on the fly. He shivered and knew, with the sun just setting, he was in for long hours of the same. *If I could just sleep....*

It hit him then that he was in real trouble. Did Dengler and Sijan know they were in trouble? If so, they showed incredible will: the standard he had to uphold. Bud Day nearly made it to freedom. Even after being captured, he had had the fortitude to endure five years of prison and brutal torture. *Medal of Honor*. Wilson tried to imagine being imprisoned that long. In *five years*, Derrick would be driving a car.

He had to stop thinking like this, but it was a struggle not to in his dire predicament. As much a struggle as it was to stay warm and to get as comfortable as possible so sleep would come. The underbrush crackled nearby, another disconcerting reminder that he was not alone.

While trying to will sleep, Wilson came to grips with the fact that he needed human help and that exposing himself to the Venezuelans might be the only way to save his life. He would have a *chance* at survival at least. The United States was engaged in military action with Venezuela, but would it be for five years? He couldn't remember if Venezuela had signed the Geneva Convention. He kicked himself for not knowing for sure. *No excuse*. But it didn't matter. It seemed every signatory was on their own program anyway, and American airmen could always expect the harshest of treatment.

Wilson needed help. From the time he had fallen through the tree, he had prayed to God for deliverance, asking for and expecting to receive— praying and *hoping* for—the sudden appearance of a *Seahawk* overhead that would lower a SEAL with a rescue hoist to pluck him from his living hell. He had asked for strength; he had received, instead, increased weakness. Deep down, he knew that an occasional prayer was not going to get him through this ordeal.

He huddled under the fern, his weakened body again shivering in a reflexive effort to stay warm. Looking up through a break in the trees, he saw the three stars of Orion's belt. *The Hunter*. Now, Wilson was the hunted. The fact that he hadn't yet had to avoid Venezuelan soldiers tramping through the bush to find him, or hadn't yet heard FAV helicopters searching overhead, was little solace. He rolled, as best he could, to his left side. Exhausted, he craved sleep, but the discomforts he felt in every part of his body prevented it. For a moment, he saw the shadow of a soldier who stared at him as he smoked a cigarette. Wilson froze. Maybe the soldier hadn't seen him. Wilson tried to focus on the soldier, but as he faded away, Wilson realized he was just a mental image. *Hallucination*. At that point, part of him would have welcomed capture— the part Wilson now had to fear: a malfunctioning mind.

The night dragged on. Every ten minutes seemed like an hour. He couldn't get comfortable: pain, covered by itching from dirt and insects, all covered by a blanket of cold. He could feel his foot tightening in his boot. He would have to cut the boot off—tomorrow. *Too exhausted now.*

Wilson heard a far-off mechanical sound, a faint, throbbing hum. He turned his neck to hear better…a helicopter. He sensed it was coming from the east. He tried to find the North Star, Polaris, through the trees to verify the direction, but he could not. The sun had gone down on his right. This noise was coming from the east. *Doesn't matter. A helicopter, finally.*

Maybe they could blow down the trees and land right next to him. The SEALs would then come to him with a stretcher, while Mary and the kids followed carrying an apple pie. After an acupuncturist fixed his leg, they would go to the beach, camp out with a fire, and roast marshmallows. Then ride a jet ski. Like they did back home, when they were young…and free.

The *whup, whup, whup* of the rotor blades grew louder. As Wilson strained to see the craft through the dark branches, the noise, rising and falling in pitch, continued to get louder. *Is that a* Seahawk? Wilson asked himself, and struggled to match the sound with the familiar sound of the helicopter he had spent his entire career around. He reached for a flare but hesitated. What if it was FAV? *Do it!* he thought. *This is what you wanted! Deliverance!* But he could not. Even as human beings drew closer, his training and his instinct—not knowing what *kind* of human beings they were—told him to evade. Wilson was surprised by his sudden surge of mental strength.

The helo drew closer, fast, and the rotors seemed to tear at the treetops. He could then make out the background whine of the jet engines, but his ears picked up the sound of *another* helicopter in the distance, also closing fast. He couldn't see it, but it was coming right at him. *They must have my position!* he thought and let out an involuntary *"Yes!"* as the aircraft barreled toward him. The sound of the rotors cutting through the air just above the trees was deafening, and it registered with Wilson: This was a big helicopter, a *Seahawk!* And the sound of another helo nearby confirmed, in his mind, they were American military aircraft.

Wilson struggled in the darkness to find his pencil flare. In a frenzy, and despite the danger, he placed the flare in his teeth so he could screw in the launcher with his one good hand. *Hurry!* The vibrating roar of the aircraft was right on top of him. *Oh, God, please!* He had to fire the flare straight up to get their attention, but, if it was too close, it would scare the pilots. *Fuck that*, Wilson thought. His real worry was that he would hit the aircraft or its rotors with the flare on a lucky—or unlucky—shot.

As Wilson lifted the pencil flare and aimed at Orion's belt, a speeding black mass roared over. The rotorwash shook the trees and swirled the debris on the forest floor into a confused cyclone all around Wilson. Dust drove into his mouth and nostrils, and pain stabbed into his bad arm as he tried to steady himself. The thunder receded, along with the screaming of the jet engines that propelled the lights-out MH-60 along its course.

"*Stop, dammit!*" Wilson cried amid the din.

The flare was now useless, if shot *behind* the speeding aircraft where none of the aircrew could see it. Wilson shot it anyway, hoping the wingman *might* see it. The miniature rocket shot from the launcher and careened off a branch and back into the trees where it quickly extinguished. An opportunity had presented itself and was lost, all in a matter of seconds. *Fuck!* Wilson cursed his hesitation, writhing in pain as he thrashed about in the dirt, beating himself up mentally if not physically. He collapsed into frustrated tears when he grasped that rescue—*deliverance*—had come and gone. As the aircraft had continued on course, he had heard no indication of a turn. *Sonofafuckingbitch!* he cried out loud. He would not get another chance like *that*, and realized he was not ready, the fault his and his alone.

Breathing hard, he strained his ears as the *Seahawks* faded away. After five minutes, he could no longer hear the rotors, and the multiple miseries of his resting spot returned. He lay looking up at Orion, *The Hunter*, so named by ancient men, ancient men who, no doubt, were fighters.

Flying *Flintlock* 612 from the left seat, Sean Sullivan eased the helicopter to 100 feet as he crossed the surf line. "Comin' left," he said on the ICS to his co-pilot, Sandy. Behind them, 614 maintained position. Sandy checked in with them on the radio.

"Six-one-four from six-twelve. What luck?"

"Negative, twelve," the pilot in the trailing *Sierra* responded. Neither aircraft had seen any sign of Commander Wilson.

Leaving four SEALs in Tobago, the *Rustler* aircrew had split the others among two aircraft. They had seen and heard nothing on their high-speed dash over Trinidad, and before Sean got near the offshore rigs a few miles on his nose, he initiated the turn into the Columbus Channel. Venezuela was ten miles south, the bright lights of the Río Salta complex clearly visible. With Sandy monitoring the altitude and tight angle of bank, the door gunners stayed alert. Sean rolled out on an easterly heading to fly south of the island as Sandy transmitted *bookcase,* the briefed code word for "Mission Complete." The E-2 orbiting offshore then relayed it to *Coral Sea* and to Davies. With no previous transmissions from *Flintlock*, all knew this mission to find Wilson, or any clues about his fate, was a failure.

Staying a few miles offshore of Trinidad, the pilots conversed with each other and their crewmen as they conducted an informal debrief of their mission. All were on night vision goggles as they had been since they left the ship.

"Guys, did you see *anything*?" Sean asked the gunners over the ICS.

They both responded negative as Sean eased the aircraft a few degrees to the right to give greater clearance to an oil rig on the horizon, standing out on the water as a cluster of dazzling lights and flare stacks.

Sandy added, "Nothing, and there weren't a whole lot of clear areas for pickup either. Just some scattered huts.... Guess everyone in them is awake now."

"Yeah, wonder what they do down there," Sullivan said, more to himself than to the others. He then added, "Okay, we've got about another twenty miles before we can breathe easier and make the turn to the northeast. Remain armed up and keep your heads on a swivel."

"Aye, sir," the gunners answered.

Sean's mind wandered back to the high-speed run they had just completed, covert and low level, *varsity* for sure. He was relieved to be out over the water and clear of obstacles but wondered if they would have to return.

CHAPTER 61

Wilson awoke after another restless night, catching some sleep only as the sky lightened to the east. He knew what lay ahead: a dash, as best he could on his one good leg, to the sea and rescue. With an opening on a deserted beach, he could use his signal mirror and his flares if another helo happened by. The sea, and the chance of freedom it represented, would also be good for his mental outlook.

Get up! Wilson thought as he grabbed his water bottle.

He pulled himself to his feet and decided to keep the boot on his injured foot for one more day. After getting his bearings, he put the sun on his right shoulder and began to move along the stream.

Breathing through his mouth in the twilight, Wilson moved with his crutch, one slow step after another, the gurgling stream as his company. He dreamed of a beautiful Caribbean beach just ahead: palm trees, azure water, and white sand. This part of the forest was as thick as he had seen it. As he crunched along in pain, he saw no breaks in the canopy above him, which prevented the sun from warding off the morning chill. As least he was moving, and sweating. Cold with perspiration was not good, but at least he wasn't freezing.

He took several breaks as the agonizing morning wore on, but, when the sun peaked at noon, he was exhausted. He was also discouraged, despite the fact he had caught glimpses of sea birds all morning. Trying to see ahead, all he could make out was forest, and craning his neck to hear the distant surf, he heard only the buzzing of insects. *A sea breeze!* He could feel it, and he could smell the salt water. He moved faster, hobbling on his painful foot, sprinting to the finish. *Just a little farther!*

His fatigue soon caught up with him, and he lowered himself to the ground, out of breath, hurting, *dying.*

Wilson was sure he was dying. The infection was getting worse, and the foot was no longer as painful, a fact that scared him. His wrist also concerned him, and his intestines had developed sharp pains. His heart raced like a jackhammer. *Day. Sijan.* He *had* to keep going, he was an American fighting man, and this was his fight now. *Dengler.*

Wilson got up, took several steps and fell. He let out a loud cry that he knew could be heard by anyone within earshot. He was spent. *Let them come*, he thought and closed his eyes.

Mary and the kids.... How are Mary and the kids?

"Please, God, help me," he mumbled as the insects buzzed around his face. *I'm sorry, God. I'm sorry.*

Wilson opened his eyes and realized he was still on the ground in the forest, the sun lower in the sky to his left. His foot had begun aching again, but he now didn't have the strength to cut the boot off. Guessing an afternoon rainstorm would appear at some point to add to his misery, he looked for potential shelter,

He then heard a sound...*words*...singing. A man was singing. He strained his ears to the east. *English* words. *Another hallucination?* He concentrated and listened...*what do...sailor...way, hey...*

Energized, Wilson got to his feet by concentrating on the source of the sound more than his debilitating pain. He crossed the stream...*put him...*and tried to identify what the man was saying. The words came with an accent, and, after taking a few more steps, he identified it. *Irish!* Wilson staggered toward the sound. *What the fuck?* Soon, he saw faint movement through the trees. He drew closer and saw a man in a shaded clearing. The man seemed to be singing to himself as he was moved to and fro. He was wearing an undershirt and appeared to be exercising. Wilson soon comprehended the lyrics.

What do you do with a drunken sailor?

What do you do with a drunken sailor?

*What do you do with a **drunken sailor**, er-lie in the mor'nin?*

Wilson thought he was hallucinating. An Irish drinking song, sung by some guy out here. *In Venezuela!* He got to an opening in the trees and stopped, propping himself up on a tree trunk. He could now see a clapboard cabin about 30 yards away, smoke coming from the chimney. He felt for his .45.

Put him in a longboat till he's sober!

Put him in a longboat till he's sober!

*Put him in a longboat **till he's sober**, er-lie in the mor'nin!*

The man was elderly, balding, salt-and-pepper hair on the sides. He wore a white t-shirt and dark trousers. He was swinging his arms, doing deep knee bends and rotating his torso as he sang. He then started kicking ahead of him, hitting his outstretched hand. He switched to a new song he sang between breaths.

*Glorious, Glorious, one keg o' beer for the **four** of us!*

Singin' glory be to God that there are no more of us...

Just then a vehicle drove up the dirt road, an American-made sedan. Wilson crouched low as it pulled alongside the house.

There's the highland Dutch and the lowland Dutch,

*The Rotterdam Dutch and the **Eye-rish!***

Wilson watched as a woman, slight, with black hair, stepped out of the dusty and rusty vehicle. She shouted to the man in English, with a voice that had a Caribbean lilt. "Father, what are you doing outside half naked?"

"Hello, Monique!" the man replied. "Just exercising on this *glorious, glorious* day!"

"I brought you dinner, if you will get properly dressed to eat it!"

"Thank you, lass. You run inside, and I won't be much longer!"

Now God made the Irish. He didn't make us much,

*But we're a heck-of-a-lot better than the **Gosh-darn Dutch!***

The woman shook her head in mock disgust as she hoisted a basket of groceries out of the back seat and took them inside. The man stopped his singing and his exercising and looked around, up at the sky through the trees and then off to his right, away from Wilson. Wilson watched as the man stepped over to a tree stump and retrieved his short-sleeved gray shirt, shook it once, and put it on. He then reached down and put something around his neck.

A collar!

The man adjusted the collar and walked to the door, humming the same ditty he had just been singing. *Father...the man was a priest!* A Catholic priest in Venezuela? Wilson surmised he was a missionary. The woman couldn't be the man's daughter, so Wilson pegged her as the housekeeper.

Wilson stayed down and crawled to a spot where he had a better view of the door. He sat there for hours, wondering what to do. He needed help, but now that an opportunity had presented itself, he was hesitant. Once alerted to his presence, soldiers could be here in minutes. After all he'd been through, was a rifle butt across the jaw from an angry Venezuelan soldier worth it? Could he hold out another day and evade to the sea? *It must be nearby. One more day.* Wilson assessed his boot and his hand.

Hours later, with the sunlight fading, the woman came out of the house, got in the car and drove off. Wilson watched the cabin, and, from time to time, he saw a shadow move past a window. After a while the man came outside, and Wilson saw him go into the outhouse. The priest moved with a sure gait, but Wilson knew he could kick and that he seemed to be in decent shape. Wilson, on the other hand, was armed, but he was also weak—and maybe closer to death than he figured. With his head pounding from stress and dehydration, all of his body in pain, Wilson had to make a decision, *fast*.

The man came out of the outhouse and headed for the cabin. Wilson had the pistol in hand, breathing hard with fear and uncertainty. He dropped the pistol and got up, lifting his good arm in the air as he took a deep breath.

"*Father?*" he croaked in a whisper.

CHAPTER 62

Annie Schofield was exhausted. After three days and nights of operations, the pace was getting to her and everyone aboard *Coral Sea*. During this time, Carrier Air Wing SIX had degraded the San Ramón and Río Salta complexes: their defenses, the supply depots, the key bridges, as well as the facilities themselves. In the eastern part of Venezuela, the FAV was not flying fixed wing, and the Bolivarian Navy remained pier side. The Americans did not attack the moored ships, or even the parked airplanes, many of which remained visible in revetments or on parking aprons.

The Venezuelan forces around the capitol remained strong, however, and one FAV *Flanker* had downed a F-15E *Strike Eagle* during the night and escaped to tell the tale. The *Mud Hen* crew was able to steer their stricken aircraft out to sea before they conducted a controlled bailout near a Dutch destroyer and were rescued. Despite the fact there were hundreds of combat sorties about the Bolivarian Republic, the shoot down of a *second* American fighter made world news. Venezuelan anti-ship missile batteries were being attrited by the Americans with stand-off weapons. One Venezuelan missile had attacked that same Dutch destroyer which, in turn, was able to successfully spoof the missile and make it guide on something else: a coastal merchant that was in the wrong place 12 miles away. The missile worked as advertised and broke the 350-foot Panamanian-flagged and Brazilian-owned ship in half. The stern sank in minutes and took most of its 30-man crew with it. Emboldened, the Bolivarian forces conducted night and day raids on the Dutch protectorates of Aruba and Curacao, only 14 and 36 miles away from the Venezuelan coast. The local police forces were no match for armed helicopters and light infantry.

The conflict was threatening to spin out of American control. Despite the success of the destroyer using standard NATO countermeasures and tactics, American naval leadership was cautious and kept their ships well outside the known surface-to-surface threat rings, an action that angered the Dutch who *did* accept that risk—and had the rescued American aircrew to prove it. Colombia and Panama demanded the Americans cease fire, and the Cubans continued to reinforce their brigades around Guantanamo. The American air-bridge resupplied GITMO as best they could, flying contorted approaches to remain clear of Cuban threat fire.

Trinidad and Tobago, watching the conflict play out all around and above them with several known airspace violations, and probably more unknown, expressed their dismay with a belligerent Washington. At its closest, Trinidad was less than *ten miles* from the military and human colossus of the Bolivarian Republic, and some of its offshore oil rigs were even closer than that. The Venezuelans, attacking them with little more than Boston Whalers and small arms, could cripple their economy and punish them for any cooperation with the Americans. And Port of Spain, sandwiched between Venezuela and the Americans, went to great lengths to ensure Caracas that they were not.

Theodore Roosevelt was positioned south of the Dominican Republic, from where it could support GITMO when required and conduct CAP and strike sorties in the Venezuelan Op Area, in order to placate the Dutch by defending the "ABC islands" of Aruba, Bonaire, and Curacao. Each theater was roughly 400 miles away from *TR* and needed more airborne fuel than could be provided by its own carrier-based tankers. USAF tactical airpower based in Puerto Rico depended on big wing tankers to strike Bolivarian targets 500 miles south, and the suitable concrete to base KC-10s and KC-135s in the region was limited. The *tyranny of distance*, therefore, applied to American operations even in these restricted waters, and with the eastern portion of Venezuela somewhat neutralized, *Coral Sea* was an invaluable asset that could move where required.

While the islands of the Lesser Antilles offered concealment for the carrier, which made the Venezuelan targeting problem more difficult, Devil Davies and Rick Sanders weren't too keen on operating *Coral Sea* in restricted waters. They had to make a tradeoff, and it was decided that *Coral Sea* would move into the Caribbean near Dominica, affording it coverage of most of the Venezuelan coast. If the Air Force could then dedicate one tanker to them, the carrier's in-house tanker assets could serve as hose multipliers to send waves of tailhook jets to the continent— and catch them for a drink on the return—in cyclic operations lasting all day or all night. *Logistics.*

Annie checked the PLAT video monitor. *Coral Sea* was steaming hard for the Dominica Passage and, according to the expected track, would transit the passage after midnight. The *Firebirds* and the rest of CVW-6 had stood down from flying for the night, but the aircrews were hard at work planning tomorrow's strikes. Annie had a late afternoon time-on-target. She would lead eight jets to deliver six standoff land attack missiles against a Caracas missile site, an hour's flight from the expected launch posit.

Daydreaming, she noted the bright sun and sharp horizon on the screen. She felt the ship rise and fall as it maintained a 28-knot speed of advance. Someday, she would like to return here with Mark and their boy in an ocean-going sloop. Annie was a romantic, like most naval officers, and the power and majesty of the high seas held a place in her soul. In Mark's, too, and together they would teach their son lessons in navigation and attention to detail, lessons he would keep in his heart forever. Once this pop-up *war* was complete, and after her CO tour, they would return to enjoy this beautiful part of the world. She would retire at twenty, three more years.

Olive sat down next to her. "XO, got a minute?"

"Yeah, go."

"Ma'am, I know the helo didn't find anything on their run over the island, but I still think the skipper is there."

Holding Olive gaze, Annie pressed her. "Why?"

"Shane is doing a good job coordinating with the ship to get SOUTHCOM to share the signals intel they are getting. Seems the Venezuelans have the ejection seat, but they don't know where he is either."

"How do you know he didn't go into the water in the channel? Or, if he *was* carried by the storm, couldn't he have been deposited on the other side of the island—in the Atlantic, at night?"

"Ma'am, I don't know, but I have a hunch. We've been flying all over the channel, and we've seen nothing. But the storm we think he got caught up in weakened after it transited the island."

Annie wasn't buying it, but didn't want to shoot down Olive's passion—just yet. "So then, do we ask CAG for another helo run over Trinidad?"

"No, ma'am. We know Trinidad is spun up about that and bending over backwards to stay neutral in this. But we have an embassy there. We have agents. Send them down to where the storm crossed the island and see what they can learn. Quietly. Covertly."

"Venezuela has agents, too."

"Yes, ma'am, and they may have already figured this out, although Shane has no reports that they have. So, we have to act. Meanwhile, may I get back on the flight schedule?"

Annie smiled. "Can't keep a *Hornet* pilot out of the fight for long. Sure, get with Stretch. And ensure Shane keeps a close eye on the intel dispatches."

"Yes, ma'am," Olive replied with a smile.

Daniel could feel the pressure in his chest. Events *were* spinning out of control. Ramos was coming for him. He knew it. And the Americans were not reacting to type. He had never believed they would *attack* Venezuela— relentlessly—day and night. Now they were moving their operations to targets in and around Caracas, not stopping short as they always did elsewhere. Did they intend to conquer the Bolivarian Republic? March troops into the capitol?

With the Americans and Europeans monitoring every square meter of the Caribbean, nothing was moving on the water, and the mules were fearful to try any shipment of product. They even rejected the offer made by Daniel's traffickers, double the money, and then hid to escape their wrath. The Americans also had shut down the Panamanian money laundering and had increased their maritime forces in the Pacific, all of which put a big dent in Ramos's supply chain. Only a trickle of product had made it to *El Norte* in the past two weeks from any of the cartels, and nothing to Europe. Dealers could operate off a small warehoused supply of product in the short term, but, for Daniel and the cartels, the money flow from interrupted supply lines was felt all the way up the chain. For the first time in years, Daniel had to monitor his own supply of cash.

The secure phone rang. The dog Hernandez. *He better have good news*, Daniel thought as he picked up the receiver.

"Yes, mí general."

"Señor, the American pilot may be hiding in Trinidad."

Daniel gazed across the gulf at Trinidad. His lifeboat.

"Why do you think this?"

"The Americans flew their helicopters over the island last night. Port de Spain knows and is upset about it. My people are feeding the media, and it should be public soon. We are listening to them, and we know they listen to us. I will instruct my people to report on our tactical frequencies that we have captured the American, which will sow confusion and buy time."

"Do you have people in Trinidad?"

"Not my people, señor. Caracas has agents, of course ,but I do not control them. Do *you* have people, señor?"

Daniel did, and he could see where Edgar was going. Daniel's agents would save Edgar's hide. And his own hide.... For a moment, he hesitated and sensed Edgar fidgeting as he waited for an answer. If he could catch the American with this information, Edgar would no longer be necessary.

"I have.... Trinidad is a big island, with many people. If the American lives on it, he could be anywhere."

"We think the southern coast, señor, a place called The Devil's Woodyard. This is where their helicopter flew."

The Devil's Woodyard, Daniel thought as he studied Trinidad in the distance. He liked the name.

"I will take action, Edgar. Tell me, how goes the war?"

Daniel could hear Hernandez swallow on the other end. "Señor, the Americans have rolled back our defenses to the east and are now concentrating on the capitol. We have missiles to attack their ships, but it is difficult to find them. They stay far away, near the islands, and send their planes to attack. We are doing our best, but we do not have the forces to resist them."

"You shot down one plane. Can you not hit others?"

"We did shoot down another, but the Dutch rescued the pilots on the high seas. After the first night's loss, the Americans changed their tactics, señor. They are using stand-off precision weapons they can fire from many kilometers away, and they are picking off our assets, one by one. We tried to hit one of their warships, but the missile was deflected by their defenses and sank a Brazilian cargo vessel. They stay hundreds of kilometers away, señor. They even attack us with bombers based in the United States! Their reach is longer than ours."

Daniel listened and took in Hernandez's grim military assessment. "How long can you hold out, mí general?"

"They must put boots on the ground to overrun us, señor, and our forces are much larger than what Panama had when they overthrew Noriega years ago. They have shut down Río Salta, they have air superiority over the Bolivarian Republic, and the politicians are nervous the people will revolt."

"Then they should string up some people!"

"Sí, señor." A chastened Hernandez agreed.

Daniel knew he needed the downed American pilot as a bargaining chip to save his own skin. He could see his life here was coming to an end; his business empire for sure and, maybe, his actual life. Where could he go? *Mallorca.* The Spanish dialect was different, but there he could hide from Ramos and the world. One hundred million was all he needed. He had survived on much less. Annibel could be replaced easily enough...but he would miss Emma.

"Edgar, we need this American pilot. I'll do what I can, and I know you are doing all you can. Maybe your pilots will deliver us another American today. That chance is worth sending them up to defend the Bolivarian Republic to the last man—except you, of course. You are *much* too valuable.

Reminded of his fate, Hernandez waited a moment to respond. "Sí, señor."

CHAPTER 63

Father Dan Cody peered into the bushes along the tree line. He saw a man emerge, filthy and weak. The man looked fearful and appeared to be seriously injured. No threat.

"Yes, who are you?" Father Dan asked and stepped closer.

"Commander James D. Wilson, U.S. Navy." Wilson whispered, again feeling lightheaded as he struggled to stand.

"Indeed…. Are you hurt?"

"Yes, right leg and left arm. I think the leg is broken."

Wilson stepped from the bushes into the open as the priest drew near. "Do they call ya Jim?" Father Dan asked.

Wilson stopped and caught his breath. "Yes, some do."

"Well then Jim…are ya hungry?"

"Yes, Father. What is your name sir?"

"Dan Cody, from County Cork. I'm a Maryknoll Missionary priest."

Wilson offered his dirty right hand, and Father Dan took it. "Nice to meet you, Father. I need help, please."

Father Dan went to Wilson's right side and lifted Wilson's arm over his shoulder so he could help him to the cabin. Wilson grimaced as they hobbled to the steps.

"How did you get here?" Father Dan asked.

"I was shot down a few nights ago. I'm a pilot."

"Yes, I can see your jumper looks like something a pilot would wear."

"It's a flight suit."

"Yes, of course. Regardless, it could use a wash. I'll ask Monique to take care of that for you."

Struggling up the steps, Wilson hestitated. "Monique? Who is that?"

"My housekeeper. She was here earlier today, but she's gone to town. Doubt she'll be back…but mebbe."

Wilson grew concerned. He was placing his trust in this priest, who may or may not be *trust*worthy. The townswoman he had seen here a few hours ago, *Monique,* would probably take one look at him and shriek with horror—and go right to the Bolivarian Army.

Father Dan led him inside the one-room cabin and put Wilson on his freshly made bed. Wilson protested, but the Irishman insisted. "Bedspreads can be washed."

Wilson collapsed on the mattress, grateful for the first comfort he had felt in days, and knew he could sleep for hours.

Father Dan gave Wilson some water and turned toward the stove. When he brought a plate of food over, Wilson perked up and began to scoop the rice into his mouth with dirty hands.

"Easy, lad, even we Irish use this thing called a fork," Father Dan said. Wilson took the fork and attacked the chicken and green vegetables. Within minutes, he was cleaning the plate with his tongue.

Sated, Wilson fell back in bed, breathing hard from exertion and pain. At least, now, when they came to take him prisoner, he would have had a good meal. *Cold leftovers have never tasted so good. Sleep.* If he could only sleep before they came for him…. But this priest wouldn't shut up!

"So, my boy, you're a military pilot?"

Wilson berated himself for admitting it earlier when he said he was shot down. Said he was a pilot. *Dammit.* Maybe he would be smarter now that he had some food and drink. "My name is Commander James Wilson, U.S. Navy."

"U.S. Navy you say? What are you doing on dry land then? Was your ship shot down?"

Wilson assessed the priest as he struggled for a way to answer him.

"Are you Catholic, my boy? Do you know you can trust a priest with confession? Do you have something to confess? A little white fib? Making war and not love? People confess the sins of both, you know."

Wilson's stress level increased. *Can I trust this guy?*

"How old are you, lad?"

Wilson considered the question. Date of birth. Innocuous enough. "I'm forty," he replied as he settled back onto bed.

"Forty. Yes, *life begins at forty,* they say. Me, I'm seventy-four…be seventy-five next month. Forty, eh? You are certainly no lad…but you are to me. I was ordained…. What? *Ten years* before you came along to dirty a diaper. Where are you from?"

Wilson kept his eyes on the ceiling. Was this an interrogation? He didn't answer.

"When I was forty, I was in Formosa. Called Taiwan now. I spent twenty-seven years there. We converted a good few to Christ. They send us out to *spread the good news*. Alone and unafraid, eh? Do you believe in Christ Jesus, Jimmy?"

Wilson nodded.

"Good, good. My work here is done, eh? Catholic or no, we are all on the same team, are we not? Here, let me help you out of those dirty rags. Can't the Americans afford better?"

Wilson was concerned about his foot. "Father, I can't remove the boot. We'll have to cut it. Are you able to cut it?"

Father Dan inspected the boot and the surrounding skin swollen tight against it. "Yes, and it looks like your shin has seen better days, too. I have some medicine."

"Are you a doctor?"

"I am!" Father Dan replied with a smile. "Of theology—and philosophy, mebbe. Never took my finals because they sent me off on another mission. Doesn't much matter to the Chinese peasants bent over picking rice in a paddy, now does it? No, I'm not a medical doctor, but I know enough about medicine and penicillin to administer it. Are you allergic to anything?

Wilson shook his head.

"Good! We'll have this leg back in no time. Looks like you may have some trench foot going on here."

Wilson winced as the priest cut away the boot laces and removed the boot. The room reeked of his rotting flesh. "Oh, goodness gracious, lad, even a fishwife would faint dead away with this smell! Let's get some soap and water and some bandages to fix you up."

As the priest administered to him, Wilson noted the shadows had grown longer. "Father, I need to get back to American forces. Can you take me to the coast?"

"Yes, the American Navy, they'll be waiting for you out there, eh? Well, we'll have to go in the morning, but it's not easy to get to. You know, Christopher Columbus landed here in 1492, *after sailing the ocean blue.*"

Wilson gave him with a puzzled look.

"Yes, lad, Christopher Columbus himself. About fifteen kilometers as the crow flies."

"Father, the Venezuelan army is looking for me. I need to get to the coast without being spotted."

Father Dan turned toward Wilson with a puzzled face. "Well, I...I imagine they are. But I've never seen any Venezuelans here. Don't think you have to worry about that."

Wilson was incredulous. "No Venezuelans?"

"No, they keep to themselves down there, and the people here don't visit. Because of the language barrier for one thing."

Wilson sat up, eyes wide, trying to comprehend. "Father, where am I?"

"They call this place *The Devil's Wooodyard*. Heh, they sent me *here* to evangelize. Guess I've got nowhere to go but up."

Wilson touched the priest's arm to stop him. "No, Father, what *country* are we in?"

The old man studied him for a moment. "Trinidad, my boy."

CHAPTER 64

(The Devil's Woodyard)

Wilson let the information sink in. It made sense now. After he ejected, he had been pulled into the storm, and it had carried him across the Columbus Channel and deposited him here, in *Trinidad*, a neutral country. He should have known by the topography. *Trinidad.* Venezuelan troops were not going to swoop in and take him away. He was safe...for the moment.

"Where did you think you were?"

Wilson lay back in relief. "Venezuela."

"Oh, yes, the *Bolivarian Republic,* as they say. Godless and spoiling for a fight. So you obliged them, eh?"

Wilson didn't answer.

"Looks like they got the better of you. How many of them did you kill?"

Wilson shot him a look. "I didn't.... I don't know. My target was not people." Wilson caught himself before he went any further. *Shut up, you idiot!*

"Doesn't matter, really, now does it? Washington and Caracas have a disagreement, and they send you to kill Venezuelan boys. Guess it's like shouting to win an argument. They kill; you kill. Someone will eventually stop shouting, and the other is declared the winner. He who shouts last, eh? Will defeating Venezuela make you happy?"

"No, it's a job."

"Well, then. It seems you are dedicated to it. I mean, it sounds like you've cheated death once, and you were on the brink of it again—until you stumbled across my little slice o' heaven. Would ya give your life for this job? How much do they pay you?"

Wilson looked out the window.

"Not enough, I should think. They don't pay me but a few shillings, either, and I've lived in the forest for decades, with the cold, the heat, and disease, and with no medical treatment. Fifty years. Most of my mates

334

have gone on to their reward, yet here I remain, in the mud—blessed by God."

"Thanks for serving mankind, Father."

"Oh, don't mention it. It's my job to save souls this way. You...you seem to save them another way."

Wilson winced from the barb, and the pain, as he shifted his weight.

"You are a filthy mess, and we need to clean you up. I have a bathtub over yonder. I'll draw some hot water and put you in for a soak. Then, we'll have some tea."

After Father Dan set a bucket of water over the wood stove to boil, he used a hose to fill the tub halfway with water held in a cistern above it. Wilson struggled to remove his flight suit but needed help. Although his foot was swollen and painful, it could bear some of his weight, and he could still wiggle his toes.

Removing the last stitch of Wilson's clothing, Father Dan led him to the tub. The hot mixed with cold made for a perfect temperature as Wilson lowered his body into the water. He felt an immediate melting away of tension and pain.

"Here, you can scrub your neck with this," Father Dan said as he handed Wilson a flimsy washcloth. "And here's some soap. You'll probably need the whole bar."

Just then a vehicle drove up. Alarmed, Wilson sat up, his eyes darting from the window to Father Dan.

"Don't worry. It's just Monique back from town. She won't be a moment."

Wilson lowered himself in the tub as he listened to Monique's footsteps. She walked up to the door and knocked.

"Come in, lass."

When she opened the door, Monique gasped with fear as she saw Wilson in the tub. Embarrassed and vulnerable, Wilson looked back at her with wide eyes.

"Monique, this is Jim. He's an American. Had some trouble with his airplane a few days ago and is in need of a bath and clean clothes. Can you take his jumper and underwear and wash them for him?"

Monique was still in shock as she noted the torn, mud-covered flight suit. Afraid she would run screaming and tell who-knew-who that he was there, Wilson gave her a weak wave and said nothing. He wanted the American Embassy to rescue him, not the local gendarme or some other stranger he couldn't trust. And he still wasn't one hundred per cent sure he could trust Father Cody. *What have I done?*

Monique spoke first. "Father, what have you done now? Why are you helping this *soldier*?"

"My dear, haven't you been paying attention? That's what I do, and I can assure you, after speaking with him a while, this man *needs* help. *Big time* as they say."

Averting her eyes, Monique busied herself and gathered up Wilson's clothing and the soiled bedspread. She took them to the vehicle and returned with a load of Father Dan's clothing, neatly folded. She set the stack on his dresser and then placed a bag of dry-cleaned clothes in his small wardrobe.

"Monique, could we trouble you for his clothes by morning? Our guest may not be here too much longer."

Wilson remained as inconspicuous as possible in the cooling water of the tub.

Having finished her tasks, Monique grabbed her keys and stepped to the door. "Father Dan, you stay here and out of trouble. And no more soldiers!" She glanced at Wilson with a combination of fear and disapproval as she left.

"Good night, my dear. See you in the morning. A basket of your mother's cinnamon rolls would be a special treat for our guest—and yours truly."

"You be good, Father!" Monique scolded from outside. Wilson heard the car start and pull away into the twilight to return the ten miles to town.

"She's gone, lad. You can get out now. Here's a towel for ya, and I think we can wrap you in blankets till she returns tomorrow."

Wilson, in his weakness, realized with dread that the woman had his flight suit—with his ID card in it. Father Dan noticed the wave of fear that swept over him.

"What's the matter, Jim?"

"She has my ID card. It's in the pocket of my flight suit. It's important and I need it back."

"Well, you'll get it back tomorrow. It may be a little soggy, but she'll bring it back. Monique is trustworthy, and she's much more than a scrubwoman. She's a big help to me serving my little parish out here, doing things for people I cannot. You have nothing to fear, Jim. You are safe here. Be not afraid. You'll like Monique when she gets to know you better. You must admit, a half-dead soldier is a fearful sight. Most of the people of Trinidad are followers of Jesus Christ, but they keep voodoo in their back pocket, if you know what I mean."

The priest helped Wilson out of the tub and helped to dry him off. He then offered, as clothing, his own robe and gave him a glass of water. Wilson, still exhausted, lay down in the bed and started to think about Mary and the *Firebirds*.

He soon drifted into a light sleep and awoke to a rhythmic voice. He opened his eyes to get his bearings and realized he was in the darkened cabin. Father Dan was murmuring in his Irish brogue.

...Holy Mary, Mother of God, Pray for us sinners,
now and at the hour of our death, amen.

Wilson listened for a while as Father Dan recited the same prayer over and over from his chair on the other side of the room. *Hail Mary.* A "Hail Mary" touchdown pass. He could use a *Hail Mary* right about now.

He listened closer as Father repeated the words and then drifted back into unconsciousness.

At the laundromat in town, a nervous Monique pushed the flight suit into the top load washing machine with Wilson's underwear and socks. She had never seen this fabric before, covered in mud as it was. And stinking to high heaven. She wanted to wash the load fast and get out of there. Could she put this fabric in a dryer? She decided to take the chance.

"Monique, how is our good Father today?" asked her friend Mariella across the counter.

Monique turned with a start. "Oh, he's fine. Ate all his food. He's fine." She returned to her laundry.

"He needs to pray for us. The Americans are making war everywhere over our heads. They will bring evil to us. All so they can take our oil!"

Monique kept her head down and ignored her.

"I can hear their warplanes and bombs in the night. What kind of men kill like this? They are *monsters!*"

Monique kept at her work. She wished Mariella would shut up.

"At least they are not here in our peaceful country. If they want Venezuela, they can have it."

"They may be here," Monique said.

"Here? You think they are here?"

"Maybe…"

"Have you seen soldiers out there, an army to attack us? Is Father all right?"

"Father is fine. The soldier…I'm not so sure." Monique regretted her slip.

"An American soldier! Here! With Father Dan! More will come. We must tell the sheriff!"

"No, Mariella. Only one, and he is sick. Father is helping him. He is a Good Samaritan, and we must be, too."

"Trouble will come!"

"Mariella, it will not come if you keep your big mouth shut! Promise me you will not tell! *Promise!*"

Mariella's eyes darted about in fear. "Men with guns will come! How can Father do this?"

Monique walked around the counter and grabbed the woman's arm. "Mariella, you must *promise me*, and you must trust in God!"

Mariella looked at her and nodded. "I promise," she whispered, fear still covering her face.

"Good. He will be gone soon. I will see to it."

As the women resumed their work with their laundry, a man outside the door flicked a cigarette butt into the street. He walked, in no hurry, to the center of town and sat on a bench outside the post office, which was closed for the night. He picked up his cell phone and punched in a number.

CHAPTER 65

Annie awoke as revile sounded. With her strike brief scheduled in six hours, she needed to print the kneeboard cards and check the weather over Caracas. Blade was her assistant strike lead, and Macho and Killer would fly on their wings. The plan was to launch SLAM-ERs off the coast of Caracas and guide them into the targets south of the city. Macho and Killer would deliver the weapons at altitude, and she and Blade would guide them in the end game. The *Raiders* would also launch weapons from positions over the ABC islands, and divisions from the *Hobos* and *Arrows* would act as fighter sweep and defense suppression, respectively. While two EA-18Gs from the *Gremlins* jammed enemy emitters, a single *Condor* E-2 would provide the required early warning and command and control. Day launch and pinky recovery in calm seas with a moon. *Could be worse.*

Coral Sea and Carrier Air Wing SIX had settled into a routine. The combat learning curve had been steep, and routine launch and recovery, formation, radio comm plan and tanking details could be "glossed over" in the brief with no loss of preparation and execution. The aircrews, even nuggets like Macho, were experienced now, allowing more time spent on target area tactics and aimpoint study. And "*switchology.*" A precision weapon like the SLAM-ER, delivered in a two-plane coordinated attack amid alerted defenses, required a high degree of preflight planning and briefing.

After lunch, Annie met with her team in CVIC. They learned there had been a skirmish during the night along the western fence line at GITMO: a trade of automatic weapons and RPG fire. No Marine casualties, but SOUTHCOM was spooked. They knew *TR* was not going to give any more help down south as it moved closer to GITMO. *Coral Sea* got a short break during the transit through the Leeward Islands, but the aviators were gearing themselves up for near 24-hour operations.

Annie's strike planning team put the finishing touches on the cards and briefing slides, and Annie went through it once, her team offering critique and addressing contingencies. They would be 300 miles from their launch points, and each strike division would have a dedicated *Rhino* mission tanker for upfront tanking en route and could expect another tanker to drag any low-state fighters back to the ship. This mission was "high-all-the-way," which allowed the jets to save fuel. Also, they had a "lily pad," USS *Independence*, a Littoral Combat Ship hovering off Grenada, cloaked from enemy targeting radars by the island and able to dash and launch a *Sierra*—a combat SAR was required. With stand-off precision weapons, dedicated tankers, face-to-face briefing with all the players, and a lily pad, if need be, Annie and the team were confident.

The howl of jets launching one deck above them permeated the space as CAG strode into CVIC and walked up to Annie's planning team. One of the lieutenants saw him and sang out, "Attention on deck!"

They rose to their feet as CAG raised his hands. "Seats, seats. Please continue. How's it going, XO?"

"Good, sir," Annie replied as she motioned to the chart. "We've got *severe clear* over the target area, and the jets are loaded. After a bite to eat, we'll brief it in Ready 5 at noon. Care to join us?"

"I'd like to, but duty calls. How are you going to hit these guys?"

"We're going to tank en route to a point about 100 miles north of the target. From there, the *Hobos*, call sign '*Whisk*,' are going to zorch out in front in a sweep right at Caracas. When they get near the coast, they will then tac-turn west. If the FAV comes up, it will be into the teeth of the Hobos, or they'll glom onto them as they transit along the coast. We'll have a clear lane and a back-up plan to deal with any that don't take the bait."

Matson nodded his understanding and tacit approval.

"The *Firebirds* are the easternmost launchers and the *Raiders* the west. Our targets are the missile launchers, and imagery has them in clearings south of the city. We will run in right up to the edge of their tactical SAM and AAA threat rings and release, egressing hard over the water. Our control birds will then guide them in the end game from a position well behind. By the time the weapons impact, we'll be near the coast and will run out of there the same way. All this time, the jammers, call sign '*Jelly*,' will be doing their thing by lobbing HARMs in there to suppress the defenses."

"What's your call sign?"

"The SLAM birds are '*Lumber*,' sir. Gonna lay the wood to 'em."

CAG smiled. "Good, because the admiral and SOUTHCOM are watching closely. Gotta knock out the anti-ship threat ASAP so we can get closer. Our Air Force buddies aren't flying today, and *TR* is moving closer to GITMO. Going to be an all-Navy show. Your show."

"We're ready CAG. We took advantage of the break yesterday, and we're all up to speed."

"Looks like it. Well, good hunting down there, and we'll see you when you get back."

"Thanks, sir."

One of the lieutenants again sang out, "*Attention on deck!*"

"Carry on, please," CAG said as he walked to the door.

At that moment, Edgar Hernandez focused on the command post screen as his Intelligence Officer briefed him.

"Mí general, the Americans moved one of their carriers, the *Coral Sea*, through the Dominica Passage last night, and we think it is near Dominica this morning. At that location, their planes are in a position to attack the Bolivarian Republic. However, for some reason their Air Force is not flying today, and their other aircraft carrier, the *Roosevelt*, is still off Hispanola and moving closer to their illegal prison at Guantanamo Bay. Gunfire along the fence line was exchanged last night and was probably started by the Americans, mí general. They keep one of their aircraft carriers nearby. With this development, we can expect only one to three waves of American attacks from this one carrier off Dominica, allowing our forces a better chance to repel them."

"How many planes do we have today?" Hernandez demanded.

"Almost twenty, mí general. Eleven *Flankers* and seven F-16s."

"Not even two squadrons.... Can't we get more?" Hernandez asked his wing commander.

"Mí general, my people are working around the clock. We have one *Flanker* and one *Viper* down for high-time engine changes and—"

Hernandez exploded. "Dammit! This is not time for scheduled maintenance! Must I do *everything* myself? Get those jets back in flight status! Without them, we may not have an AMV or a Republic tomorrow!"

"Sí, mí general!"

Hernandez calmed himself and moved on. "What intelligence do we have today on the American intentions?"

"Señor, we see the same familiar pattern they use in Arabia. Roll back the enemy defenses and soften up the battlefield. Their amphibious ships could be anywhere."

Hernandez narrowed his eyes. "Do you really think the Americans will land a few thousand troops on our shore days, or even weeks, from now?"

"No, mí general, but they can reinforce Aruba or wait in the northern Caribbean for more forces. They used that type of reinforcement tactic both times they invaded Iraq. And they have airborne forces and air-delivered forces, commandos that can take and hold harbors and key nodes, all with tactical airpower delivered from several bases in the region and their carriers. This is a much easier supply problem for them."

Hernandez stroked his chin. When would they come? Where? With San Ramón out of action and Río Salta mined, the Americans had seemed to lose interest in the eastern part of his country. He believed they would come to Caracas today and tonight, and this aircraft carrier movement seemed to confirm it.

"Mí general, the Americans also have one of their warships near Grenada, and our shore agents observed a helicopter fly out to it and land."

"Don't *all* the American ships operate helicopters?"

"Sí, mí general, but we believe this aircraft had SEALs aboard. They could be using it to rescue downed aircraft as a precaution."

"Where do you think they will attack?"

"I think the capitol tonight, mí general, and I think they will come for the long-range anti-ship and anti-aircraft missile batteries in the hills south of us. They like to attack at night and have the weapons and training to do it, but they need daylight hours, too, in order to maximize their effectiveness."

"Today? Within hours? Here?"

"Sí, mí general."

Hernandez studied the screen again. If the Americans came into his engagement zones, he could get lucky. A concentrated effort of fighters could yield another downed American—maybe two. Overwhelm them and make them bleed. Their own press would make it seem worse. Hit them from every direction, high and low. Maximum effort *today*.

"How is your missile supply?" he growled at the group commander.

"We can last a few more weeks, mí general. Lots of heat seekers."

"Very well. Load up every station, and top off all the jets with fuel. I want all loaded weapons expended today and tonight. Send up everything you've got and *defend the Bolivarian Republic!* Fly the damn pilots until they collapse. I want them to bring the jets back empty. *Everything you've got!*"

"Sí, mí general!"

CHAPTER 66

(The Devil's Woodyard)

Wilson awoke to bright sunlight streaming in from the window above him. He lay there a few moments, confused, before he realized where he was. *The cabin...I'm in the cabin.* Father Dan sat reading in his chair, and, when Wilson moved again, the priest turned to him.

"Well, Jimmy, you were sawin' logs all night, ya were. Sweet dreams?"

Wilson winced as he propped himself up. "I was out. What time is it?"

"Oh, it's already half past eight. I've said the Rosary and done my daily prayers. Monique should be 'long now any minute with breakfast. Are ya hungry?"

"I have to contact the embassy."

"Yes, she'll bring a phone with her, one of those modern handheld gadgets. I don't have one. All I've got is a wristwatch, so I'm not late for mass."

"Do you have a chapel?"

"Yes, down the driveway, a short walk from the main road. A football pitch or two away. Oh, sorry, that's *soccer* to you Americans"

"Father, it's important the Americans get me back. You'll be rewarded."

The priest smiled. "I am, Jimmy, already. I am blessed to be able to help you and any other wayward travelers."

Wilson sat up. "I need to go to the outhouse, Father."

"Yes, of course. I'll help."

Father Dan gave Wilson a pair of slippers and helped him stand. He then held him steady as they moved, one step at a time, to the outhouse.

The priest waited outside for Wilson and looked up at the sky, thankful for a clear blue day. *"Thank you for this day, Lord,"* he whispered. *"Please grant me the grace to serve others and to make disciples."*

When Wilson opened the door, Father Dan reached out to help him. "Sorry we don't have an indoor loo, Jimmy, but we're off the beaten path here. I'm sure, when you get to Port of Spain, they'll have nice facilities."

"I'm fine, Father, and I appreciate your kindness." Wilson answered him as he grimaced with each step, which was more of a hop.

"How's the leg? Looks like the swelling has gone down."

"Does look better. Still hurts though."

"I'll brew some tea. We can chat for a while before Monique gets here."

Father Dan deposited Wilson in his chair and set about brewing the tea. Wilson craved coffee but was grateful for anything. *What day is it?* he thought. Was this his fourth morning or only his third?

"So, Jimmy, why are you at war with Venezuela?" Father Dan asked as he filled the kettle with water, not making eye contact.

Still not sure he could trust the priest, Wilson took time to formulate his answer.

"I'm an American fighting man, and I follow orders."

"Indeed, you risk your life for your country and your president. Commendable. But you are a man of forty you say, married. As Kipling said, you ain't no bloomin' fool, now, are ya? Yet, you go wherever your President tells you and blindly kill?"

"No. Our orders come from National Command Authority. They are lawful, and we carry them out with the minimum force required against military targets."

"Minimum force? Why not use maximum force and get it over with? When I was a schoolboy in Cork, I got in a scrap with Evan, and I must say I didn't hold back! Funny thing is, we became fast friends. He died last year of the cancer."

Wilson listened but said nothing.

"I mean, the United States could just blow Venezuela to kingdom come. Just like you did Hiroshima years ago."

"Destroying Hiroshima ended the war quickly and saved lives. The Japanese knew they could not continue."

"Yes, so what's the difference here? War is war, right? It looks to me like *you* are in the midst of a war. Why not end it—*and become fast friends?* If anyone is still alive."

"Proportionality."

"Proportionality you say? Ah, yes, *jus bellum iustum*, the teachings of Saint Augustine. Just War Theory. You know this theory?"

"I've been exposed to it," Wilson said.

"Obviously. Are you fighting a just war?"

"Yes."

"Of course, or you wouldn't be here. So, your President declared war?"

"Yes, actually our *Congress* must declare war."

"I see. Did you hear your President declare war?"

"No, I was flying—" Wilson stopped short.

"Yes, like the Japanese at Pear Harbor, eh? Like when I got the first lick on Evan, don't ya know? He didn't see it comin'. Knocked him on his keister, I did!"

"To minimize harm to us, we attacked with surprise. It's a valid tenet of warfare."

"Yes, yes. Well, why did you attack Venezuela in the first place? What forced your President to send you?"

"They kidnapped our ambassador." Wilson could see where this was going, and he knew he had a weak hand.

"*Kidnapped* him? Well, I should say, then, we've been lucky not to have *endless* war here in Trinidad with all our kidnappings. And I'm sure they happen on the continent on a daily basis."

"He's our sovereign ambassador. It's *different* with countries. You just can't go doing that."

"Yes, like Tehran in 1979, eh? But as I recall all your countrymen were returned safely. Not justifying it, mind you."

"And we've been in a state of quasi war with them ever since," Wilson answered.

"Yes, and, from what I can see, Venezuela, too. What is it about Venezuela you don't like? Socialism?"

Wilson drew a breath. "Venezuela harbors narcotraffickers who produce drugs and then ship them to the United States and Europe. They are killing our kids with this stuff."

"Yes, drugs. I've heard of this *War on Drugs*. Been going on for some time now, hasn't it? Are you winning that war?"

Wilson didn't answer.

"Didn't think so. Why does Venezuela want to destroy your country, to kill your kids as you say?"

"They don't want to *destroy* it. They…" Wilson stopped, and turned away to exhale.

Father Dan smiled at Wilson as the pilot realized what he was about to say.

"Yes. Destroying your country would be bad for business, now, wouldn't it? Who would buy the cocaine, the marijuana? Supply and demand, is the key. And there's certainly demand in the United States and in Europe, now isn't there, Jim? When I was a young man visiting Boston, years ago in the sixties, the demand wasn't there. But soon it was. *Lucy in the Sky with Diamonds* it was. The Summer of Love it was. Aye, dreamy times. No one had a care in the world. If it feels good, do it, and I think there was a lot of *doing it* going on then, Jim, before you were born. And then there was *Women's Lib*. Why not act like a man? Indeed, why not? So you can *make love,* as they say, with no consequences. Just take this little pill, and, if *Heavens to Betsy,* a wee one comes along—a *mistake* as they say—you can kill it. *Just kill it,* legally now. Millions and millions of innocent babies. You can *take care of it,* they say."

Wilson absorbed the truth of Father's words.

"So, the upshot of all this.... People delay getting married and delay having a family. Or they ask, why get married at all? There's *time* of course, time to have fun, and the girls are offering their bodies with no strings. So, *why not?* Everyone has a little fun, and no one is to blame. *Freedom,* they call it. And, if we are not happy all the time, we can divorce, and the state can take care of the wee ones. And, speaking of the state, we can't have any favoritism, so we'll banish prayer and moral teaching from the schoolhouse. That way anything goes—freedom of expression, separation of church and state and all that. So kids grow up without parents, and they devalue life, devalue women. After all, naked girls are only a few clicks away on the Internet. And we can play songs about killing each other or ourselves on the radio or cheat each other to gain money and power. And God is nowhere in sight, is He now? We have no peace, nothing but anxiety and worry all the time. No prayer for healing. No forgiveness. No trust. No love. And no gracious mercy from God because no one seeks it."

Father Dan got up and stepped to the stove. "I must say, Jim, I'd probably stick a needle in my arm, too, if I had to live that way."

"That is *not* how our country is," Wilson growled, perturbed. Father Dan continued to work at the stove, preparing the tea.

"No, you're right. I mean, *who am I* but an old Irishman in the Caribbean woods preaching the Gospel? Oh, there's sin all over the place here, too: gossip, jealousy, promiscuity, greed. It's no different here than in the states. But people here *do* for each other more. They don't have little gadgets in their faces all the time, and they are happy with what they have. And, for the most part, they are good parents for their children, even though they have little. Yes, they marry and have children, and they bring their wee ones to church to worship God. Like I saw in the United States fifty years ago."

Wilson sat with his head down, reflecting on Father Dan's words of indictment. Wilson knew he was right.

"So, what do we do, Father? Are we doomed? How do we turn ourselves around?"

"Well, do *you* go to church?"

"No," Wilson answered, ashamed.

"Well, then, *go to church*, and pray, and take your family with you. Lead them in prayer. Live your faith. Ask for forgiveness. That's all you have to do. Now, if you were a Catholic, we have some more requirements involving things like confession and days of obligation. But for now, *until you become a Catholic*, all you have to do is lead your family to church. I should think they need men like you more than ever."

While Wilson considered the priest's words, a car drove up. His face strained with apprehension, Wilson struggled to look through the window.

"Ah, Monique—and breakfast. And some clean clothes for ya." Father Dan said.

CHAPTER 67

(Paria Peninsula)

"Trinidad!" Daniel exclaimed to Hernandez on the other end of the phone line, stunned and pleased by the news that the American may still be alive—and not yet safe.

"Sí, señor. Last night, one of our operatives heard some loose talk in the town of Guayaguayare, to the southeast. The American may be in the nearby hills, harbored by a missionary."

"How did he get there?"

"We do not yet know, but we need a team to investigate."

"Then send one!"

"It is not that easy, señor. The American combat air patrol will see a helicopter the moment it gets airborne, and, once it's in the open, they will shoot it down. And all of my fighters are now in and around Caracas to repel the expected American attacks today."

Exasperated, Daniel exhaled in disgust. "Then, what do you propose, *mí general?*"

"Señor, your team from Paria could fly across the Dragon's Mouth, stay clear of Port de Spain, then fly down to the expected location in the south."

Daniel had two *Jet Rangers* and four military-trained men, equipped with automatic weapons, who could do this job—either in broad daylight or at night. They could swoop in and kill those harboring the American—*a missionary?*—and return the pilot to him to use as a hostage for bargaining with the Americans or with Ramos. Of the two, Ramos, his ticket out of Venezuela, was top priority.

"Where do I send them exactly?"

"We are obtaining that information, señor. My operative is following a woman, a scrubwoman, who will lead us to the missionary and the American."

"Then do it, Edgar, and do not fail me on this one—or your son will be dead by noon tomorrow!" Daniel barked as he threw down the receiver.

349

He nodded to Alphonse, his number two, who had been listening on another phone.

"Put a team together, and *bring me this American!*"

"Sí, Daniel, you'll have him standing before you by midnight."

Daniel nodded and looked out to sea at Trinidad. It was happening the way he had feared. But would Ramos want the pilot? Would he want to risk the full fury of the American Army? Would the Americans even negotiate with him? In his experience, *everyone* negotiated. Surely they would want this pilot back at any cost and would allow Daniel safe passage out of Paria to Mallorca.

The Americans don't want me, Daniel thought. *They want the Venezuelans, Hernandez. Yes, let them concentrate on Hernandez around Caracas while I snatch the pilot and negotiate a separate peace.*

Daniel's plan was coming together.

Annie smiled at her sailors as she headed up the flight deck. Her jet, 302, was parked over Cat 2 on the bow. *Coral Sea* was making bare steerageway as it maintained her expected launch position and it was a pleasant afternoon with a light breeze. A high overcast had formed, and there was a squall line to the west that would be a factor for launch. Behind Annie, on Cat 3, a *Hummer*'s props turned in preparation for the early go, and, to her left, a *Sierra* was also turning to take station as plane guard.

Annie's strike brief had been well received by the 40+ aircrew in attendance, and, over the continent, the weather was the usual: afternoon buildups with probable scattered thunderstorms. She would have to assess run-in lines and make a weather audible once they were down there. The threat was high, and the *Whisks* were likely to have their hands full as they skirted the coast and the SAM rings. The chance for an air-to-air kill got everyone excited, but the aviators had to temper this excitement and not follow a contact into a SAM threat ring that could bag them with an unseen shot.

Annie got to 302 and returned the salute of 302's plane captain, Airman Davidson, a lanky kid from Tennessee.

"Afternoon, ma'am."

"Afternoon, Davidson. How's your jet?"

"Good to go, ma'am! Topped off. Good pressures. Power hooked up."

"As usual!" Annie responded with a smile as she bounded the ladder to stow her Nav Bag. When she got back on deck to begin her aircraft preflight inspection, Shane Duncan, wearing a float coat and cranial helmet, stood in her path.

"Ma'am, there's a development. The embassy in Trinidad got a call that Skipper Wilson is hiding there. We think the Venezuelans believe the skipper is in Trinidad."

"What have you learned?" Annie's eyes peered at Shane from under her dark visor.

"National assets intercepted cell phone conversations that lead us to believe the Venezuelans know he is being harbored in the south of the country, right where Lieutenant Commander Teel said he might be. He may be receiving help from a missionary."

"Are we going after him?"

"There is a team from the *Flintlocks* in CVIC now with CAG and Commander Hopper. They are adding on a late afternoon CSAR. Two helos from here and one that's already on the lily pad off Grenada."

Commander Hopper, Annie thought. *CAG is pressing him into service. Good.* She then thought about the tactical environment they would soon face.

"It'll be dark by the time they get down there."

"Yes, ma'am," Shane replied, unable to offer more than that.

Hers is not to reason why, Annie realized and shifted gears. "Great. Thanks for letting me know, Spy. Good intel."

Shane smiled, and as she turned to go below, Annie grabbed her arm.

"You're making a difference out here," Annie shouted near her ear.

"Yes, ma'am. Thank you, ma'am," Shane nodded with an appreciative smile as she turned to leave the flight deck and go below.

Annie's mind wandered as she continued her preflight. *There's a good chance Flip is alive and still evading. Maybe Weed and the helo guys will get him tonight.* Annie knew the dusk light condition was not ideal for a rescue, and that her strike would be 200 miles west as they egressed for home, and that straight-line distance meant an overflight of the Paria Peninsula. Annie wanted to help—200 miles could be covered in fewer than 30 minutes—but Weed and his team could do it. There just wasn't enough gas in the air to support all the jets hundreds of miles south of *Mother.* Still, she was glad Shane had delivered this real-time report.

Annie bounded the ladder again and dropped into the ejection seat as Davidson followed to strap her in. The other aircrews were in their cockpits, including Macho next to her. Annie tried to assess Macho's mood as she watched her set cockpit switches in preparation for engine starts. Macho didn't seem nervous as she readied for the long-range strike. Her first step would be to launch with a heavy weapon hanging from her left wing, an asymmetric load the nugget was capable of handling. Then, if they encountered FAV fighters at delivery range, Macho would get a crack at one if they leaked through the *Whisks*. A lot was about to happen in the next two hours.

Annie finished her preflight checks and had just taken a breath when the familiar voice of the Air Boss came over the 5MC.

On the flight deck, aircrews have manned for the 1530 launch...

CHAPTER 68

(The Devil's Woodyard)

Wilson was glad to be back in his flight suit and reunited with his ID card. His right boot was off, and he wanted to see if he could put it back on his foot and bind it with a cord or rope. The medicine Father Dan had given him seemed to be working, but the foot was still swollen.

He was also worried. Where were the embassy guys to rescue him? Did Monique call the right number? The right office? It was midafternoon, almost 24 hours since he had revealed himself to Father Dan. He had to get back to the ship, to the *Firebirds*, to Mary…to God.

"Here you go, Jim," Father Dan said as he handed Wilson a baloney and cheese sandwich. "Not the kind of feast Monique would make for us, but beggars can't be choosers, eh?"

Wilson thanked him and waited for Father Dan to join him.

"They say the *finest chefs in the world* are men, but most of us men, for decades, have depended on the good graces of women to keep us fed. Haven't we, Jim? Who does the cooking at home? You or your wife?"

"My wife."

"Yes, common I'm told. Is she a good cook, your wife?"

"Yes, the best."

"Well, then, you are truly blessed."

Wilson was growing impatient. "Father, how far is Port of Spain?"

"Oh…well, it depends, of course. I should say two hours by car. Weather is clear, so yes, roughly two hours. Let's give thanks now."

Wilson listened as Father Dan said grace. Once he was finished, Wilson took a big bite of the sandwich. His strength was returning, despite his crippling wounds.

"So Jim, in the few hours we have left, I do want to know. Why do ya fight?"

Unsure if he was being set up for another attack, Wilson eyed him with suspicion. *Just let me eat, Father.*

353

"I'm not trying to be difficult. I just don't know many soldiers, and certainly no pilots. Now Ireland doesn't have much of an air force, ya know. Why *do* you?"

Wilson took a drink of water and gathered his thoughts.

"Father, the world is dangerous and it's governed by force. I love my country and the people of my country—and the freedoms we enjoy. I took an oath to support and defend the constitution of the United States against all enemies, foreign and domestic. There are countries, and Venezuela is one of them, that want the United States weakened, if not destroyed, so they can subjugate their own peoples, and peoples around them, in a quest for power or money. I believe my country is the last best hope for freedom on this earth, that we are given freedom from God, and we have a responsibility to free people."

"Yes, but by killing them?"

Wilson appreciated the hospitality of the priest, but could not take his sarcastic body blows anymore.

"Father, we try to *deter* war by showing strength and will. We talk— *Lord, do we talk*— and try to sway countries from courses of action that will lead all of us to ruin, and if they do not cease in attacking us, or otherwise cease in aiding and abetting our enemies, then, yes, I am *legally ordered* to take action. *War is politics by other means*, isn't it Father? We warn and warn and try not to escalate, but they don't believe us. And, at some point, when they force us to act, they almost welcome it."

"Who forces you to act?"

"Venezuela, for crying out loud! *They* are the ones shipping the drugs that kill our kids. *They* are the ones who took our damn diplomat. *They* are the ones who foment revolution in the region, and this "revolution" is really a totalitarianism that saps freedom. *They* are the ones giving a resurgent Russia and terrorist Iran a stronghold here. Sure, they offer bread and circus carnivals and baseball games to placate the masses, but their government is not good and we are doing everyone a favor if we remove them."

"Like you did in Iraq?"

"Yes, Father! I fought there. Even before 9/11, I was fighting there! You and the rest of the world didn't know it, but we were. And Saddam was killing his people and threatening the region with more death. Isn't that part of your Just War Theory, Father, to act only when inaction is worse?"

"So you believe in your vocation?"

Exasperated, Wilson answered. *"Yes*, and I'm doing everything I can to hit my assigned target with precision, *precision* my country has spent trillions of dollars on in our effort to spare civilians, even when our enemies kill civilians all over the place and, frankly, are rewarded for it. We could blow Iraq or Venezuela or Iran off the face of the earth, but we don't because we don't indiscriminately kill. Instead, we accept risk for our own people, like me. We stop the drug lords from shipping to my country, and we pray our kids won't start using and frickin' *adults*—if you can call them that—stop. But that's a much heavier lift, so, stopping the supply is what we're left with!" Wilson paused and changed his tack.

"What about *you*, Father? Is military force *ever* justified in your perfect world? Do we just have to pray that our enemies will change their minds before they gather around us and kill us? As their drugs poison us under our noses? Before they take *you* away, Father, and prevent you from spreading the Gospel down here? I say no. And, yes, I'll get back in a jet and come down here again to prevent them from doing so. We are the *good guys*, Father, and our guns *prevent* wider war. And don't even put me on the same level as them!"

Father Dan sat expressionless as he absorbed Wilson's blast. Wilson regretted losing his temper.

"Well, Jim, you certainly have a passion for what you do. You may even think you are saving souls. *Destroy the village to save it,* and all that. Myself, I choose to save souls through the message of the Gospels, and to show love to my fellow man."

"As *I do* Father, but I live in the *real world*, with plotting, evil men. And there are times I am called on by my country to stop them by force for the greater good. I only wish my country would allow us to *win*—win something, *anything*—and actually free people from tyranny and defend ourselves from harm instead of just *managing* bad behavior, and managing it poorly."

Father Dan answered Wilson. "So, ya think I've not seen evil up close? Corrupt officials? Theft? Murder? Even the deep hurt of slander and jealousy? You think evil is only countered by all-out warfare and once the evil—*Venezuela* in this case—is destroyed, all will be well? Won't the evil men in your own country go elsewhere to find the drugs they need to get rich while destroying your society? I do not condemn the soldier and what soldiers must do. I guess we should be glad we have soldiers—and there was the good soldier at the foot of the cross—but I choose to arm myself with the *shield of faith* and the *sword of prayer* handed down from God. Mighty armies He has laid low, and the Gates of Hell shall not prevail against his holy church."

Wilson nodded. "Yes, Father, we need all the help we can get. I'll serve as an instrument in this struggle here on Earth, and please pray for my country, and my family…and me."

"Oh, I will, Jim, and you can pray, too, ya know. It's good to pray for these things, and let the hand of God do His good work."

Wilson checked his watch. "Father, I really need to get back to American control."

Father Dan smiled as he stood. "And miss another night of Monique's porridge?" He then looked out the window and stopped smiling. "What is that?" he said to himself as much as to Wilson.

Alarmed, Wilson peeked over the sill and saw a man moving among the trees. His heart jumped to his throat, and he lunged for his pistol.

"Do you know that guy, Father?" Wilson said as he staggered to a position near the door. Adrenalin pumping, he began to breathe through his mouth in fear.

"No, my visitors come up the driveway.

"Where's Monique?"

"Don't know. Thought she would be back by now."

Wilson sensed he was girding for battle against an unknown force that did not wish him well. He had two ammo clips and could see outside through windows on three of the four walls. He needed to know what was going on behind the cabin, near the outhouse. *How many? Who?*

He peered out the window, careful not to be seen himself. He saw no movement at first, but then a man darted between the trees and crouched behind one to get a better look at the cabin.

"He doesn't know we've seen him out there. Don't think so anyway." Wilson then noted Father Dan standing in front of the window. "Father, get down! Get away from the window!"

"Why? What have we to fear?"

"That guy doesn't look like a friendly neighbor. Please, Father!"

Father Dan stepped away but did not seem concerned. Wilson took another peek and saw the man was still watching the cabin. He scanned for other movement but saw none.

"Father, look down the driveway. Do you see anything?"

The priest stepped to the side window and searched outside for a moment. "No, nothing there."

Wilson turned back to the window and watched, chest heaving. In pain, he grabbed the pistol with his left hand and chambered a round with his right, making an audible click. As he did, Father Dan opened the door.

"*Father!*"

The priest stepped out onto the porch and peered into the woods. Wilson's heart was about to burst out of his chest. *What is he doing?*

"Come out. Come out, lad. What do you want?"

"*Miguel. Aqui.*" Wilson heard the man shout the words from the woods. *Could be a bluff,* Wilson thought. Who was this guy *not* in uniform? And speaking Spanish. Not good.

"Come out now. My name is Father Dan. Are ya hungry?"

"*Dammit, Father, don't invite him in!*" Wilson said under his breath.

"I won't, lad. Just sending him on his way," he murmured back.

Just then Monique drove up. Father Dan and Wilson kept their eyes on the woods to gauge a reaction. When she parked the car, she saw Father Dan on the porch looking into the trees. "Father, what are you doing?"

At that, the man revealed himself and scrambled into the open, 9mm pistol drawn. "*Mujer, alto! Aqui, alto!*"

Monique shrieked in fright and froze by her car. Wilson watched and waited, heart pounding.

"Monique, it's okay. Stay where you are," the priest said with outstretched hand. "This man means us no harm."

"*Donde esta el Americano?*" the man demanded. Wilson could see he was muscle: black clothing, close-cropped hair, sunglasses, thin mustache. He looked in the woods for further signs of movement.

"*Miguel!*" the man shouted, drawing closer to Father Dan, pistol pointed at his head. Monique's eyes were wide with fear.

"*El Americano? Esta en el casa?*" the man demanded. Father Dan played dumb.

"I'm sorry. I do not understand. *No hablo.*"

The man, face now contorted in fury, pointed at the window and fired into the cabin. Bits of broken glass peppered Wilson as he crouched below the window. Monique screamed, and the man bolted to her and grabbed her arm. Her screams continued. "*Quíete!*" he barked at her, and Monique, eyes wild with fear, was reduced to whimpering as he shoved her around under his tight grip.

"Leave her be!" Father Dan commanded with raised voice, but the man ignored him.

"El hombre! *Ahora! Aqui!*" he bellowed. Monique was hysterical with fright.

"I don't know what you mean! Stop hurting her!"

The man fired in the air as Monique screamed in terror under his grasp. "*El Americano! Ahora! Miguel!*"

Father Dan put out his arms to calm the man who was seething with anger. "I do not have an American. You can look inside," he said as he motioned to the door and stepped aside so the man could pass. Wilson understood Father Dan was allowing the man inside so Wilson could take a clear shot from his vantage point along the wall.

Father held his hands up to show no threat as he stepped further from the door. With Monique yelping, the man pulled her up the steps as he trained his pistol on Father Dan, who held his hands higher. The man put his left arm around Monique's shoulders as he pressed against her back. He pushed the open door wide with the muzzle of the gun, and listened. Father Dan remained motionless with his hands up, and the man slowly led Monique inside.

The moment Monique's torso passed into the room, with her attacker pressed against her back, Wilson fired from three feet away

The bullet entered the man's right side under his ribs and ripped him away from Monique and slammed him into the door. Monique fainted flat on her face. Wilson grabbed the .9mm and safed it as Father Dan entered the room. The man was dead in a heap on the transom, blood pouring from a gaping would on his left side where the slug had exited and lodged in the door.

"Monique!" the priest cried.

"I had a clear shot, Father. I think she's okay."

Father Dan went to Monique and rolled her over. He noticed a knot on her forehead but saw only a spot of blood from a cut lip. Looking back at the man, he saw a growing red stain moving along the seams of the wooden boards to a nearby rug. He got up to move it before the blood ruined it.

"Father, you told a lie," Wilson said with a relieved smile, still trying to control his breathing.

"Yes, I did, and I'll have to ask for absolution."

"A man is dead, an *evil man*. You helped me save our lives."

"Who do you think he is?" Father Dan asked.

"Venezuelan agent, maybe a local tough looking for a ransom. And if there are any more out there like 'Miguel,' the three gunshots are going to bring them here soon. Can you handle a pistol?"

"Never fired one," Father Dan said.

"*Never*, Father?" Wilson said as he rolled his eyes. "Well, you might today."

"Oh, no, I won't. I *will not* do that."

"We'll see, Father, because I think we can expect more trouble from more evil men—soon. I'm going to need your help."

"Well, at my age, I'm not much help."

"But you *can* do something, Father, and the time for theory is over. We have to fight."

Monique stirred, took a look at Wilson, and shrieked.

"Monique, it's okay. You're okay," said Father Dan. "Jim here saved you."

She looked at the dead man, now lying in a bright red pool of blood, and shrieked again. "Father! We must leave this place!" she pleaded. "More men will return! This *American* will be the death of us!" She looked at Wilson with trepidation.

"Did you talk to the embassy? Who did you talk to, Monique?" Wilson demanded, beyond impatient with the woman. She recoiled in fear as Wilson continued.

"Who, dammit? Who did you talk to and what did they say?"

"I talked with a woman…and told her you were here. She said they would come for you today,"

"Well, the day is almost over! What was her name?"

"Ms. Dove, she said, like the bird!"

"Okay, Ms. Dove. Do you have a cell phone?"

"No, I used the pay phone in town."

Wilson shook his head in disgust. The whole *world* had cell phones, except this forsaken place!

"There is no coverage," Monique added, reading his thoughts.

Wilson exhaled in frustration. The dead man, armed, had been searching for Wilson and would have killed Father Dan and Monique once Wilson had been captured.

"We must move him," Father Dan volunteered.

Wilson agreed, and, with Father Dan doing most of the work, they were able to cover him and drag him on a sheet to a corner of the room until help arrived. Monique would have no part of it, but provided rags and paper towels for Father Dan to clean up the mess by the front door. The blood would be a permanent stain until the boards could be sanded down.

Wilson had to use the outhouse but decided not to risk going outside. He used, instead, a cooking pot to relieve himself. Monique was shocked and averted her eyes in disgust. Wilson didn't care.

It was nearing 5 p.m. "Father, we have to watch," Wilson said as he peered outside. Nothing in the driveway. Nothing in the woods.

As Wilson turned from the window, a pane of glass exploded next to him.

CHAPTER 69

Annie keyed the mike. "*Lumber* two-zero pushing with four."

From three miles away, she heard the other division lead of VFA-23 *Super Hornets* key his mike. "*Lumber* three-four pushing with four."

"*Condor*," acknowledged the E-2 controller coordinating the strike.

Ahead of the *Lumber* divisions, and beyond Annie's visual range, the four *Whisks* from VFA-54 were sprinting for the Venezuelan coast at a transonic airspeed. The American fighters were over four miles up, above the late afternoon buildups. However, they were close to, and unnerved by, a high overcast that had not been forecast. It highlighted the aircraft silhouettes to surface observers. As strike lead, Annie had little choice but to live with it. This far out to sea, they were safe for the time being.

Macho maintained tac wing position on Annie as they increased their run-in speed. In fifty miles, she and Killer, not quite in formation but near enough for mutual support, would sprint ahead to deliver their SLAMs. Once the two junior pilots released the missiles and cleared to the northeast, Annie and Blade would pump once and follow them in, controlling the weapons into the target. It was a delicate operation that required detailed coordination and clear situational awareness, but one they had practiced in training.

On her linked display, Annie could "see" the *Whisks* ahead and the *Jelly* suppression division behind her. Blade and Killer were a mile to her right, and the four *Rhinos* of the other *Lumber* division were mere specks beyond them. They were all heading south. Annie could make out the coast on her nose. The clustered metropolis of Caracas, at her two o'clock, was cloaked in buildups with towering cumulus above the southern mountains. In five minutes, Macho and Killer would sprint ahead to deliver their weapons as Annie and Blade did a tight one-minute turn to build separation.

Showtime.

The radio sprang to life. "*Whisk* one-one. Single group, *Bullseye* one-two-zero at ten. Hot."

"*Condor* copies, and second group *Bullseye* two-three-zero at twenty. Nose cold."

"*Whisk* one-one. *Condor,* declare the eastern group."

"*Condor* declares both groups hostile."

This call from the E-2 electrified the American cockpits. The Venezuelans had two groups of fighters in the vicinity of the SLAM targets, one of them hot. Annie referred to her timeline and noted the *Whisks* would be making their western turn in three minutes—unless they committed on this eastern group that was now nose hot on the American formations. The *Whisks,* no doubt, had their radars looking at them to sort the enemy formation and get a raid count.

Annie scanned the horizon, trying to determine an avenue of clear air, a *canyon* through the cloud buildups. Too far away to determine. Once Macho released the weapon, it would fly a programmed track. Annie would "grab" it via data link in the end game, and she figured it would be below the scattered buildups by then. *Hoped* it would be. The radio blared again, and her heart skipped a beat.

"*Whisk, Condor*, third group orbiting *Bullseye*. Hostile."

"*Whisk* one-one looking. Clean there."

"Look low!" the E-2 shot back.

Wow, Annie thought. The Venezuelans have a significant opposing force airborne. *Did they have tipper info? Should we pump and let the* Whisks *deal with them—and avoid the risk of fratricide?* She rejected that notion. They didn't have a cushion of fuel—*they never did*—and this was a contingency they had briefed. Annie and Killer would have to flex to air-to-air if any leakers got through, and they would have to deal with them before they released the SLAMs. The tension level had spiked for everyone.

Annie mulled the options over in her mind as the formation closed at nine miles per minute.

"*Whisk* one-three, single group, *Bullseye*, cold, five thousand."

"That's your group," *Condor* answered him. "Hostile." *Whisk* 11 then took charge.

"*Whisk* one-one committing on the eastern bandit group. *Bullseye* one-zero-zero at twenty, nose hot, fifteen thousand."

"*Condor*."

"*Condor, Whisk* one-three committing on the bandit group orbiting *Bullseye*, nose hot now, five thousand."

"*Condor*."

"*Condor* from *Whisk* one-one. Monitor the western bandit group."

"Roger, *Whisk*, western group two-one-zero for twenty, nose cold, appears to be orbiting."

"Roger. Watch him."

From the radio calls, Annie built a "picture." The *Whisk* division was going to engage the bandits over the SLAM run-ins, a train wreck of turning and missile-firing fighters the Venezuelans had planned—or stumbled onto. In less than two minutes, she and Macho would take separation, placing Macho at greater risk. Killer, too, but each would have the other a few miles away if the situation became dire. They were feet wet, another advantage. She made her decision and keyed the mike on the auxiliary radio.

"Macho, Killer, we're gonna continue as briefed. *Armstrong*."

Macho had never felt such a high stress level in her cockpit.

The FAV was up and waiting for them. The *Whisks* sounded concerned and realized they had more bogies than they could handle. In coordination with her XO, she had to deliver, alone, a weapon she had never delivered before. She was unsure of what to do if things went to worms, which they were well on their way to doing. However, she had an AMRAAM on her right wing and two *Sidewinders* on her wingtips to deal with any bandits. And she had bullets. Once she released the SLAM, her job was to egress hard with Killer, rendezvous with Annie and Blade at the briefed get-well point, and then head back to the ship.

Macho's mouth was dry as she designated her aimpoint, the HUD symbology jumping to the new geographic coordinate. On her displays, she could make out the coastal chart and the positions of the *Whisks* and the bandits, positions which would be merging soon.

"*Lumbers, action*."

Macho pushed the throttles forward and bunted her nose to increase speed for her run-in. She saw Annie in a knife edge left turn above her, and, far to her right, she noted Killer in his run. The *Whisks* were clobbering strike common frequency with their running commentary on the three bandit groups they were juggling. The late-afternoon sun played across her visor, and, catching herself, she raised the MASTER ARM switch to ARM. Her radar warning receiver began to display symbols, and, in her headset, those symbols manifested themselves as aural *boops* and *deedles*.

Sensory overload.

Taking quick glances at Killer, Macho spent most of her time "heads down" in the cockpit acquiring her target as she sped toward the coast at 500 knots. Through the puffy buildups she could see the ridgeline, and her missile launcher was on the northern face of it. On the FLIR display, the designated aimpoint was clear of distracting returns; that could be her target, but she wrestled with uncertainty. She had miles to go before release but saw some clouds ahead and maneuvered to avoid them and give Annie every advantage in controlling the weapon. The targeting comms of the *Whisks* and *Condor* filled her headset.

"*Whisk* one-one, sorted left on the eastern bandit group one-five thousand."

"*Whisk* one-two sorted right!"

"Fox Three from *Whisk* one-one on the lead bandit eastern group."

"Fox Three from *Whisk* one-two on the trailer!"

"*Whisks* crankin' right!"

"*Condor.*"

On the horizon, Macho caught two faint tendrils of white smoke, and one of them had a visible light—the rocket motor—as the AMRAAMs rose in altitude to home in on their prey. She couldn't see the specks of the *Whisk* aircraft as they moved off to the right and west, or the bandits even farther south. Over the city, she saw glints of light in the hills behind it and soon realized the glints were AAA bursts. Breathing through her mouth, Macho swallowed hard. Ten miles to release, and she still couldn't make out her target on either the FLIR or the radar.

Shit!

"*Whisk* one-two. Pop up contact in the eastern group! Untargeted and beaming east—gimbals!"

"*Condor* from *Whisk* lead. Watch him."

"*Condor.*"

"*Whisk* one-one. Splash the eastern bandit, eastern group!"

In the distance, Macho saw a black puff in the center of her HUD, with a fiery trail corkscrewing down below it.

"*Whisk* one-two. Splash the western bandit, eastern group!" the exuberant fighter sweep wingman cried out. Macho saw another fireball erupt on the horizon.

The *Whisks* were now two sections, with the Number 3 and Number 4 aircraft running down the western group that was luring them over Caracas. The lead section, who had just dispatched two bandits in the eastern group, Macho's left, were flowing west behind the other *Whisks* according to plan. *Condor* was monitoring a leaker and another untargeted group over *Bullseye*.

With under a minute to release, Macho approached the coast, trying to find the target, trying to make sense of the intercept comms. *Armed up! Find the damn target! Don't get shot!* Frantic to find her target, Macho slewed the FLIR diamond left, then right, and found some return. Allowing the picture to build, she identified the launcher obscured by a stand of trees. *That's it!*

She bumped the castle switch to lock it and transmitted, "*Lumber* two-one captured!" She heard Annie's familiar voice roger her call.

AAA detonated in black puffs ahead of her, and, over the city, she saw SAM plumes and heard the anxious calls of the *Whisks* who were in the middle of everything. *Condor* was intoning about bandit contacts nearby, the *Jellies* were shooting HARMs somewhere behind her, and an emergency beeper was going off in her headset. *Where is Killer?* Macho was task saturated, and Annie's calm voice broke through the confusion.

"*Lumber* two-zero has control. Release it, Macho."

Annie's use of Macho's personal call sign snapped Macho out of her funk, and with one last check of symbology, she mashed her thumb down on the pickle switch. Over 1,500 pounds. of weight fell from her wing, and Macho rolled up left to see the SLAM-ER fall earthward. A second later, its wings deployed, and the turbojet engine lit off.

"*Lumber* two-one, rifle away!"

"Roger," Annie answered.

Macho heard Killer release his weapon, but the strike common frequency was clobbered with threat calls and intercept comms to the *Whisks*. Then, Macho heard *Condor* talking to *her*.

"*Lumber* two-one. Leaker, one-eight-zero at fifteen. Seventeen thousand. *Hot!*"

A bandit was running on her, and maybe on Killer, who was now trailing her as they egressed northeast. Annie and Blade, with their heads down controlling the weapons, were vulnerable. Macho looked over her right wing to the south, then whipped her head left to find Killer. She saw nothing.

"Killer, you with me?" Macho asked on the tactical freq.

"Negative! Dump some gas!"

Macho reached down and energized the fuel dump switch for a second, seeking section integrity with Killer despite the fact that the bandit would also see a cloud of fuel and get an early tally on her.

"Visual! I'm at your left, seven long! Check north!" Killer directed.

"*Lumber, Condor*, your bandits are retreating south."

Deliverance! Macho thought. As she rolled out of her turn, she saw Killer joining on her left wing and saw Annie in her southbound run, controlling the weapon. *Condor* said the bandits were retreating which implied south, and Annie and Blade were heading south. They would need help.

"Annie, Macho has a visual, six clear," Macho transmitted, informing her flight lead that she had eyes on her. They were three miles apart.

"Roger. Blade is in spread with me. You guys join up, if you can, and sanitize ahead of us."

"Roger!"

With this audible, Macho and Killer pulled hard across the horizon, plugging in the burners and pointing to a position in front of their leads to intercept. Macho's radar cursor bounced back and forth on her right display screen as she pulled her nose through the low afternoon sun, and both pilots listened to the *Whisk/Condor* commentary to regain situational awareness.

The *Whisks* were now two flights of two in lead-trail and separated by five miles. Both flowed along the coast, outside of the multiple threat envelopes in Caracas. The FAV seemed to be opposing this strike to a much greater degree than the Americans had seen before. Annie's *Lumber* division was pretty much one gaggle as she and Blade concentrated on flying the missiles into their target launchers, while Macho and Killer joined on them to sanitize the airspace ahead. The FAV fighter—they didn't know which kind—was running south from the Americans and was, for now, no factor. Macho knew, though, she would have to watch it.

"*Lumber* two-zero, five miles…" Annie transmitted, and Blade followed in sequence. The senior aviators were tracking their targets and, via data link, would fly the missiles into them. About thirty seconds to impact. Macho was now on Annie's left wing.

Flying the airplane, monitoring the radar, avoiding a midair with her wingmen, and trying to make sense of the fighter comm, Macho froze when a contact popped up on her screen.

Inside twenty miles! And hot!

Her responsibility.

CHAPTER 70

The pop-up contact entered Macho's radar search volume from below, like a shark attacking prey on the surface. Although surprised, and for a moment speechless, Macho recovered.

"Annie, contact on our nose, twelve miles! Angels ten! Hot! Egress now!"

With no time to ask *Condor* for a declaration, Macho bumped the castle switch and was rewarded with a lock. The bogey was coming right at them, and Annie, in the closer aircraft, was vulnerable.

"Three miles!" Annie transmitted, almost protesting. *So close!*

Macho put the bogey in her HUD field of view and saw a speck against the green background of Venezuela. Just then Macho saw a missile plume shoot out ahead of the "dot" in the target designator box. Horrified, she keyed the mike.

"Smoke in the air! *Annie, break left! Chaff flares!*"

Macho pulled the trigger, *hard*. With AMRAAM selected, she waited for the launch sequence to begin, and, for a moment, she wondered if the missile was hung on the fuselage station. Then the missile shot ahead with a rumbling *VROOOMMM* that she heard in the cockpit. Macho was mesmerized as she watched the white plume billow in a graceful arc up and then down as the fiery rocket accelerated ahead of her at twice the speed of sound.

"*Fox three. Annie, break now!*"

Everyone seemed to be talking on the radio at once, but Macho's frenzied comms got through Annie's end-game concentration. Annie rolled and pulled inverted, spitting out expendables, her data link momentarily losing the SLAM-ER—which was now seconds from impact.

Above her, Macho pulled hard left and picked up the enemy missile trying to follow Annie. Macho could now identify the bandit as an F-16 *Viper*. She saw it break hard right to avoid the AMRAAM missile she had fired at it.

The missile's warhead exploded just behind the Venezuelan, and, for a moment, Macho thought the *Viper* had survived. Then a flame burst from the empennage, and black smoke poured from the tail as the fighter continued in controlled flight to the east. The enemy missile tracking Annie had burned out. It seemed Annie's last-ditch defense and flares had caused it to drop lock or to lose the energy needed to catch her.

In her defensive maneuver, Annie had reacquired the target on her data link display and, with seconds to spare, slewed the SLAM-ER into the air-surface missile launcher and guided it in. She did not know if her missile had destroyed the target. *No time to worry about that.* Blade keyed the mike.

"*Lumber* two-two, time out on the western launcher. Egressing north. Visual on one and two."

As the *Firebird* division of *Lumbers* egressed north, Macho jinked into the burning F-16 to put it in the HUD field of view. *Evidence.* She then reversed back and overbanked down to join Annie and the others, all hightailing it to the get-well point. *Lumber* three-four was doing the same, and Annie hoped at least three of the four targets were destroyed. Just then she heard a cry.

"*I'm hit!* Whisk *one-two is hit!*"

Annie snapped her head left and saw a speck of flame trailing black smoke about ten miles away and north of the city. It appeared the jet was feet wet in a slow turn to north.

"Get it out to sea!" *Whisk* lead commanded, but it was no use. The stricken *Rhino* seemed to corkscrew, and soon a wingman sang out with a welcome report. "Good chute! *Whisk* one-two is down approx 10 miles north of the harbor!" The Americans could see the blinking lights of numerous AAA batteries along the coast, their black puffs hanging in the air above Caracas. They also saw the plumes of a few unguided SAMs hoping for a lucky shot against the Yankee fighters.

Annie swung into action. "*Whisk*, mark the posit. Keep him in sight. Say state."

"*Whisk*, low-state eight point five!"

Roger, *Whisk. Lumber* two-zero assuming on-scene command. *Jelly*, what is your playtime?"

The suppression element lead replied with a 9.3, which equated to roughly 40 minutes until they would have to depart for the tanker. Not enough time, but Annie was going to buy them more.

At forty miles north of the coast, Annie slowed to max-endurance airspeed and assessed the situation. The *Whisks* were standing off and trying to monitor the survivor as best they could. The *Jelly* EA-18Gs were also orbiting away from the threat. *Condor* was reporting the FAV back on their CAP points and not a threat to the Americans.

The CSAR helo on the LCS off Grenada was over an hour away, and all the fighters would be out of fuel by then. They needed gas in the air, and they needed it *now!* Annie took charge.

"*Condor*, this is *Broadsword* lead in *Firebird* three-zero-two. *Whisk* one-two is down, *Bullseye* three-four zero at forty-five, good chute, *Whisks* monitoring. Get *Mother* to launch the alert CSAR, and we need gas down here now. Send the mission tankers you have our way and have them launch the alert *Texaco*."

With *Mother* over 300 miles away, Annie had to lead the SAR effort and delegate/direct who stood the watch over the survivor and who got gas. There was not enough airborne gas for all the fighters at one time, and Annie formulated a plan.

"Blade, you and Killer RTB. Make a report to *Strike* and, once on deck, debrief CAG. Macho and I are going to get some gas and conduct a RESCORT of the CSAR helo."

"Roger, Annie. Wilco." Annie could detect the disappointment in Blade's voice, but there was only so much gas available.

She directed one *Jelly* element—a *Growler* and two *Rhinos;* a section of *Lumber* three-four; and one of the *Whisk* wingmen to come with her in search of the fuel en route to them from over 100 miles away. They would have to join on the tankers, sort what was available and who would get it, and leave enough for those remaining on station near the downed pilot. She sensed she had too many airplanes and not enough gas. She directed the other section of SLAM-ER *Super Hornets* to stay on scene with the *Whisks* as long as they could and to go back to the ship when they reached a RTB fuel state.

As Macho flew formation on her wing at 20,000 feet, Annie set her power to max-range cruise and hit altitude hold. Head down in the cockpit, she flipped over her kneeboard card and jotted down what she had and what she needed. The downed pilot was a nugget they called *Lemur*; Annie didn't know much else about him. She had two *Whisks* nearby, and, while she took the rest with her to refuel, she also had a *Growler* and four *Rhinos* that would remain on station

Coming down from the north were two tankers, 105 and 401, with six and four thousand pounds of "give," respectively. She had 10K to split between herself and Macho, the other *Growler* and escorting *Super Hornets*, one *Whisk* FA-18E, and two more *Lumbers* flying two-seat

Rhinos. The ship was launching an alert tanker that could give another 10K when it arrived, in about 30 minutes, at best. She conducted a roll call and got everyone's fuel state. At the moment, she was leading eight jets to find fuel and leaving six on station in the vicinity of *Whisk* one-two. Their task was to monitor and suppress any Venezuelan effort to capture Lemur who was now floating in his raft about 15 miles off the coast and talking on his survival radio. Those six jets would need fuel in approximately 30 minutes, and Annie needed her gaggle to expeditiously tank and get back down there to relieve them.

Never enough airborne fuel!

"*Condor,* from *Broadsword* lead," Annie transmitted. "We need gas down here. Get *Mother* to send another *Texaco* and two alert fighters to relieve on station." Annie was aware of preps for a large night strike, but with a downed airman and active SAR effort, the strike could wait. Annie needed their jets.

Annie finished scribbling on her kneeboard and took action.

"*Lumber* three-six and three-seven, sorry, not enough fuel. You guys RTB. *Jelly* four-four flight, I want you at max endurance and wait for the en route *Texaco. Whisk* one-four, you stay with us and take 2K with me on one-zero-five. Macho, you take 4K on four-zero-one."

With this plan, Annie would get three jets, and the *Jelly* suppression element, back in the fight some 15-20 minutes later. They would then relieve the aircraft holding on scene near the survivor so they could find another tanker in order to do one of two things: tank to relieve them or RTB. With no guarantees, they all had to hope that the helo was airborne and en route. After Annie coordinated the tanker rendezvous 75 miles away, she moved everyone over to the briefed CSAR frequency.

"*Flintlock, Lumber* two-zero. You up?"

"Affirm, *Lumber.* Just departed the lily pad, en route."

"Roger. *Whisk* one-two is down. I'm the on-scene commander. We have good comms with him, approx fifteen miles off the beach." Using base number code, Annie relayed a rough lat/long coordinate to the *Sierra* crew to enter into their navigation computer.

"*Lumber* lead from *Flintlock,* expect base-time minus twenty." By referencing the briefed base-time, Annie determined they were fifty minutes away from the datum. Annie rogered him, and asked *Condor* to give the ship a status report. She needed to concentrate on finding 105 and taking on 4,000 pounds of fuel, enough for almost an hour of "playtime" at max endurance.

As she searched for *Raider* 105 ahead of her, Annie could relax a bit. Two tankers and the CSAR helo were en route. Everyone knew their roles, and the ship was informed. She could join on a tanker and take fuel in her sleep. Once complete, in some 20 minutes, things were going to get intense again. At a safe altitude, she flicked off a mask bayonet fitting and took in several lungfuls of air in an effort to relax.

Annie found 105 on the horizon, locked it with her radar, and turned to intercept.

You can do this, she thought.

CHAPTER 71

(The Devil's Woodyard)

Monique screamed in terror as the bullet shattered the glass next to Wilson.

There was someone in the woods, he thought as he fell to the wooden floor and eyed his .45 pistol. Father Dan crouched low and looked at Wilson, now the de facto leader in Father Dan's cabin. Outside, they heard a man shouting in Spanish—one man.

"Father, slide the pistol to me," Wilson said. Father Dan remained frozen, but acquiesced when Wilson nodded that he meant it.

Wilson took the pistol and dropped the clip out. Four rounds left. He popped it back in and chambered a round.

The man outside continued to shout. *"Ven afuera! Ahora!"* Monique was beside herself in fear, curled up in a ball on the floor.

"Father, I need—*we need*—your help! That man is going to kill us."

Father Dan was unsure about what to do. He had never dreamed he would be in such as situation: *asked to kill,* self-defense or not. He considered his options. Wilson was almost pleading with him to help. The morality of it all pulled at him. Monique whimpered on the floor with her hands around her ears. She needed protection, but how was he to offer it? Pray? Go out and confront the man as he had with the first? *Pull the trigger on a handgun?*

"Father!" Wilson growled. "Is there any opening where you can see behind the cabin?"

The priest nodded, and crawled, his elderly body showing its age, to the log bin by the fireplace. For the first time, Wilson noticed it had a door. Father Dan opened an inside door and then, inch by inch, an outside door from which he could see the tree line behind the cabin in a 30-40 degree cone. *Better than nothing,* thought Wilson.

"Can't see anything or anyone out there, Jim."

"Good," Wilson said at the same moment the man outside changed his tactic.

"*El hombre Americano!* No kill! *Dame el Americano…solamente.* Padre, you okay! *Santa Maria digo la verdad.* Truth."

Wilson could understand the man's pidgin English enough to know what he meant. Hand over Wilson, and he would let Father Dan go, invoking Saint Mary that he was speaking the truth. Wilson considered it. *He* was the cause of their danger. Father Dan smiled at Wilson and shook his head. "Don't worry, Jim."

Wilson eased up to the windowsill and peeked over it. *Nothing.* He was exhausted, and his injuries made it difficult to move, much less move well.

"Father, I need your eyes," he whispered and motioned to the windows.

Father Dan crawled to the side window and raised himself up to peer over it, then lowered himself back down. He shook his head. Nothing.

The man fired, and, with a *crack,* the slug buried itself in the board above the door. *Ahora,* he shouted, and Monique's whimpering increased in pitch.

Wilson then heard other voices in the distance. The man outside answered them in Spanish. *Dammit!*

A peek over the windowsill revealed two men darting among the trees.

Sonofabitch, Wilson thought. Three men could surround the cabin. Set it on fire and smoke them out. With his injuries, Father's advanced age, and Monique's emotional paralysis, an escape was out of the question.

Outside, the sun was lowering. *Where are the damn embassy guys?* Wilson fretted. No matter. He would have to hold out as long as possible. And he did have two pistols and, if he could only motivate them, two additional sets of eyes. Monique appeared to be a basket case, and he didn't think he could trust her to report what she saw with accuracy, even if she could peer out a window. Maybe she could move furniture.

"Monique," Wilson called out in a low tone. "Move the table to the window. Put some cushions on top of it." Monique looked at him in confusion. "*Now!*" Wilson barked at her in an effort to snap her out of her stupor.

Staying low, she pushed the table to the window under Wilson's direction and crawled to retrieve cushions from a couch and easy chair. With Father Dan's help, she made a soft spot where Wilson could lie prone and shoot through the space where the window pane had been blown away by the bullet. They added a small stool and stacks of books to give Wilson added cover and helped him up on the table. From this position Wilson had a 30-degree line of fire. Father would have to be his eyes elsewhere in the cabin.

Wilson had nine rounds left in the .45, another ten in an extra clip, and four in the other pistol. Twenty-three total rounds. He knew he would have to expend some to keep them honest out there and slow their movements. He waited, motionless, looking at the trees down the sight of the pistol. Father and Monique stayed low, watching him watch the trees.

Wilson saw movement and pulled the trigger. The deafening report filled the cabin and Monique screamed. The round sprayed bark from the tree it hit, and one man darted away as the others fired at the house. One bullet shattered another window, ricocheting off a ceiling beam as glass peppered Wilson's back. After several seconds of wild firing, one of the men shouted a command to stop. Wilson sensed they didn't want to waste ammo either.

"*El Americano,* now!"

Sundown was in an hour, an advantage for the men outside. Wilson had an idea.

He had three pencil flares left, and cocked the launcher before he screwed one into the firing tube. Setting the pistol down next to him, he stretched out his arm, thumb on the release mechanism, and waited for movement. After a long minute, he saw a silhouette dart among the trees and fired.

With a whoosh, the flare shot ahead through the window and into the woods. It then ricocheted off a tree, bounced off the ground, and slammed into another tree. The alarmed men shouted and scrambled away from the wild pyrotechnic as Wilson picked up the pistol and fired two rounds. A man shouted and in Spanish Wilson heard the word *ayudame!*

At least one—Wilson still didn't know how many were out there—recovered enough from the surprise to fire off four rounds. The shots came from the southwest corner of the cabin and broke a side window. The men cursed and screamed at each other in Spanish as the spent flare came to rest. Wilson's hope for a fire went unfulfilled, but he was sure he had wounded one of his attackers. Someone was now whimpering in pain for help.

"One man is hurt in the leg and bleeding," Father Dan said.

"Do you know Spanish?" Wilson asked him.

"Enough," Father Dan nodded.

The rapid *thump, thump, thump* of helicopter rotor blades could be heard in the distance, and they seemed to be getting near. Again, Wilson wasn't sure what *kind* of helicopter it was, and, as he listened, he kept his eyes on the spot where the wounded man crouched behind a tree. Motioning to the side window, Wilson asked Father Dan to take a peek.

"Nothing. Can't see anyone," he replied.

The rotor blades were beating heavier, and Wilson strained to identify the sound. He wanted it to be a *Sierra*, but couldn't be sure it was. And he heard the sound of only one aircraft. How he wished he heard two, a better chance that it was a rescue party. As the men outside shouted over the din of the rotor blades, Wilson kept watch. The wounded man no longer seemed to be involved in the firefight.

The helicopter flew over, and Wilson heard it turn as it did. It was *their* helicopter, whoever they were.

"Father, what do you see?"

A bullet smashed through the window above the priest, showering him and Monique with glass. The petrified woman drew her legs up and hugged them. She appeared beyond help.

"Well, someone is out there, Jim."

"Yeah, that answered my question. Stay down."

The helicopter returned overhead and seemed to enter a hover to the north of the cabin, along what Wilson knew was a road. Reinforcements, but whose? He wished he could take a peek.

"Father, go to the other side and look out the window. Can you identify what kind of helo it is?"

"Helo?"

"*Helicopter!* What kind? Color? Anything." Wilson had to fight to remain calm.

Father Dan scooted over to the other side as another bullet smashed into the clapboard. Through the trees he could make out a helicopter. "I'm not much of an airplane nut, Jim. Not sure what kind that is."

"Color? What color?"

After a moment, Father Dan answered. "White...part of it blue."

That was a clue for Wilson. Not military. It *could* be Americans from the embassy, a security team. *More wishful thinking,* he surmised. Soon, he knew that to be true as he heard Spanish shouts from the road as the helicopter took off.

"They've sent more, Father."

Wilson needed to somehow *redefine the fight.* But how? With the added men, they would soon be surrounded and stormed. He had another idea.

"Father, take this flare. This is the 'day' end. Pull the top just like the old soft drink cans and stick the end outside through the log bin door in the back. It will smoke heavily. You can let it fire, but don't expose yourself. And try not to let it fall outside. We can use the other end later."

Bewildered, Father Dan took the flare and crawled to the rear of the cabin. Outside, the shouts increased.

"What are they saying, Father?"

"They are moving to surround us."

"Yeah, that's what I'd do, too. Monique...*Monique!*"

The woman jerked her head at Wilson in surprise.

"Water, I need some water. Please, Monique." Wilson smiled at her.

Monique nodded and crawled to the sink. Grabbing a glass from the counter and staying as low as possible, she set it under the tap as she turned the lever. She then scooted over to Wilson and handed it to him. Wilson downed the water in one gulp and smiled again. "Thank you."

He then looked behind him. "Father, crack open the bin door and pop the flare!"

Father Dan pulled at the flare actuation device. As Wilson watched him, a round smacked the stool Wilson was hiding behind, and other slugs thudded against the cabin walls. The men were showing no signs of slowing their fire.

After some more fumbling, Father Dan actuated the flare. "Oh!" he cried as pink smoke billowed out from it with a loud *whoosh.*

"Hang onto it, Father. Just stick it through the opening!" Wilson shouted. In seconds, he could see the bright smoke wafting in front of him and floating into the woods. The men outside shouted to each other in Spanish.

Wilson kept the pistol aimed at the tree. If the men were coming to the aid of their stricken mate, he would shoot. He heard shots hitting the back of the cabin. "Father, make sure you keep your hands inside."

"Oh, I dropped it!" Father cried. *Fuck!* Wilson thought. He wasn't sure what he would have done with the night end of the flare, but he had wanted to keep it. Now it was on the ground outside and too dangerous to retrieve.

Pink smoke was everywhere, and it rose into the air above the trees. Wilson had sent a signal in a last ditch effort to draw the attention of local law enforcement. With any luck, American embassy personnel, or even Trinidad military if they were in the area, would see the smoke. Rounds continued to slam into the cabin.

Hope the good guys see this.

CHAPTER 72

Edgar Hernandez nodded to his colonel. "Do it."

The American was reported in Trinidad and pinned down by Daniel's muscle, but he was holding out, harbored by a missionary priest! Hernandez thanked his good luck. From San Ramón, a quick reaction force of twenty men could be flown to the position in Trinidad in less than thirty minutes. "*Capture* him. He is of value only if alive," he added.

The men were far from elite forces, and they were not combat proven, but they were all he had with such short notice. He wondered if the Army could get three helicopters airborne! With the sunlight remaining, they could get in and at least secure the perimeter from nosy locals before a snatch and grab team from Caracas could get there in the morning. Maybe he would get lucky and his men would capture him tonight.

The American strike near Caracas had yielded some good news: A *Super Hornet* had been downed by one of his *Vipers*. With the pilot in a raft not too far offshore, the Army and Navy were doing everything they could to capture the pilot. The Americans, however, had fighters orbiting nearby, and they were doing all *they* could to rescue him first. It was a race against time to capture the two downed pilots separated by over 300 miles. With the Americans concentrating on their downed airman off Caracas, Hernandez felt sure he could get his helicopters across the channel and into Trinidad unmolested by enemy fighters. He called Daniel to give him a status report.

Hernandez found it ironic—in a very pleasing way—that two Americans would guarantee his safety.

Pink smoke rising above the wooded expanse of The Devil's Woodyard drew attention, the kind that Wilson wanted. A U.S. Embassy special agent and two Marines were in a Ford Explorer en route to pick up Wilson from

377

the cabin of the mission priest. Special Agent Gillian "Jill" Fischer, a 12-year veteran of the FBI who grew up in St. Croix, rode shotgun in the vehicle with two Marines and the staff physician. By the time they had gotten the word on Wilson, it was midmorning, and the traffic getting out of Port of Spain was heavy. Then, although Father Dan's cabin was several miles inland, they had made a wrong turn and headed to the coast.

"See the pink smoke?" she asked the driver, a Marine.

"Yes, ma'am," he replied. "That's the kind the *airedales* use when they are signaling."

"Guess he knows we're coming, but how?"

They drove along in silence for another minute, the route taking them to the vicinity of the heaviest smoke concentration. "Pull over," she commanded.

The Marine pulled over, and Jill lowered her window. "What do you think?" Doctor Larry Woodruff asked. She lifted her hand and listened for a moment. In the far distance she heard a gunshot, with its echoing *pop*.

"Hear that?" she asked. After several seconds, they heard two more pops in rapid succession.

"There's a firefight out there, so get ready. Let's go. *Chop, chop.*"

The driver accelerated as Jill listened through the open window. The weapon reports were from pistols. Were they stumbling on a drug turf war? Was Wilson involved in it?

"Stop here," she commanded while looking at her GPS. Around the bend was a driveway, but Jill wanted to go the rest of the way on foot. The firefight could be heard right through the trees.

"Let's get out and go on foot. Doc, do you have a sidearm?"

"I do."

"Good. Smith, Garcia, lock and load. Not sure what we're going to find here."

The Marines broke out flak jackets and helmets from the rear of the vehicle. One picked up an M-16, the other a BAR. Armed with her .9mm, Jill wore a Kevlar vest. Woodruff had his .9mm at his side and a medical bag. "Doc, stay with me and behind me," Jill ordered.

They entered the tree line, separated into two groups, and crunched, as quietly as possible, through the woods, listening and looking. After a few minutes they came upon a man who sat with his back against a tree. He had a pistol, but appeared wounded. He was shouting, and they could hear two others answer him in Spanish. Shots rang out beyond them. Through the trees, Jill could make out a cabin. She turned to Doc Woodruff.

"We've stumbled onto a firefight, and the pilot Wilson is probably involved. Call the office and have Captain Carpenter, the attaché, call the Pentagon first. Then, tell the *chargé d'affaires* to call Washington. We need backup *now!* Head back toward the vehicle and monitor the radio." Jill handed him a walkie-talkie so they could communicate near real time. She then turned to the Marines.

"You two, take sides on me and fan out, keeping sight. And stay *out* of sight."

As Woodruff placed the call, the other three spread out and crept ahead, listening to the shots and shouts.

"*El Americano, ahora. No muerte.* No kill."

Jill then heard a voice shout in pidgin English. "Weel-son! Why you risk? *Ven aca*—leave them free. You man? Hide *con mujer.* Afraid man?"

"Wilson is inside, I know it," she said. "Probably with the missionary, and there may be a woman, too. Do you see the wounded man by the tree?"

The Marines nodded.

"Okay, he doesn't look too good so let's go around him. The others are to the south. Take out the active shooters when you get a bead on them with the BAR. Then we'll capture the wounded guy."

"Got it," Smith answered.

They crouched and scooted through the trees, around the wounded man. He appeared delirious and no threat. They continued south, and then east toward the gunfire until one of the Marines saw a man. "Tallyho. Guy in a black shirt. See the big tree. Look about three feet up the trunk to the right."

Jill did and saw movement. "Yep, there's one. Sergeant Smith, take him out."

"Yes, ma'am."

With Jill keeping watch, the Marines moved behind the trunk and set up the BAR. The light was receding; they had to work fast.

"Eighty meters," Garcia whispered to Smith as he looked through the sight at the man, who was hiding behind a tree and watching the cabin.

"Concur."

"Take him."

Garcia squeezed a burst, and Smith saw the man fall.

"Got him."

"Okay, let's move out!" Jill said.

They heard another man cry "Jose! *Jose!*"

The trio moved 20 yards and crouched down, looking and listening. They heard nothing but the sound of gentle trade winds through the trees.

"Throw a rock," Jill commanded Garcia.

He picked up a stone and threw it high into an opening between branches. They heard it fall and waited as Smith aimed his M-16. Nothing.

Light was now becoming a real factor. Then, they heard rotor blades.

CHAPTER 73

From 14,000 feet, Annie backed out of the basket as *Whisk* 14, a *Super Hornet*, waited his turn with his refueling probe extended while flying on the *Rhino* tanker's left wing. The pilot inside was a lieutenant and went by Woody. The sun was about 20 degrees above the horizon, and it would set in 33 minutes.

Both Annie and Macho carried two *Sidewinders* and bullets, plus two empty drop tanks. The *Whisk* FA-18Es had similar loads, and two of them had AMRAAMs left. The air-to-air missiles were all but useless in an air-to-surface attack. All of Annie's wingmen had full drums of 20mm, and that forward firing weapon would keep the Venezuelans' heads down until the helo could arrive, with one, maybe two, *Hellfire* missiles, and its own door guns. However, guns required getting up close and personal, and the Venezuelans on those boats had guns, too—and, likely, handheld SAMs.

Coordinating with *Condor,* Annie learned the *Flintlock* CSAR bird was 40 miles away and en route to the datum. With the *Whisk, Lumber,* and *Jelly* sections either on station or en route, Annie would have to manage their fuel and direct aircraft to tankers or back to *Mother,* all while finding and escorting the *Flintlock* to the scene and defending it as it moved in for the rescue. *Whisk* 11 reported a large flotilla of small craft were five miles away and closing fast. They would be upon Lemur in about ten minutes. The jets on scene could hold them off – they would have to.

Woody backed out of the basket with his 2,000 pounds, the basket whipping a little as it came off the probe. He retracted the probe and slid under Annie, who called Macho on auxiliary frequency.

"Macho, how you doing?"

"Another thousand to go," Macho answered, holding her position in the basket.

"Roger, have a visual on you. When you are done, come off east, and we'll direct your eyes on us."

"Roger."

Annie signaled the tanker pilot to retract the basket, and, when it was reeled into the store, signaled *good stow* with a thumbs-up. She then opened her hand to signal they were detaching and banked her formation away as the tanker, with no more to give, secured the refueling store prop and banked the opposite direction, heading back to *Coral Sea.* The pink glow to the west reflected off the aircraft's tactical gray paint.

Annie saw Macho detach east. "Macho, we are at your right three o'clock. Two miles."

Once Macho had a visual on Annie, all three jets took a course to intercept the *Flintlock* coming down from the Littoral Combat Ship off Grenada. Annie descended her formation through two columns of buildups and, with her radar, scanned the surface to find the MH-60 which was heading southwest at 100 knots. The geometry resembled an isosceles triangle, with Annie leading three jets to intercept and escort the CSAR helo on one side, then turning 90 degrees right to intercept Lemur's position on the water.

She leveled at 10,000 to conserve fuel and picked up the *Sierra* at her 10:30 low, on the water heading southwest.

"*Flintlock, Lumber* two-zero. Visual contact. We're high above now."

"Roger, *Lumber.* Proceeding to the last known datum."

In a lazy right turn, Annie led the mixed section of *Hornets* southwest and into the sunset, a brilliant red horizon with the yellow orb still visible above it. She raised her dark visor to see inside the cockpit and adjusted the lighting. Now with 45 miles to go, she sanitized the sea below with sweeps of her radar and eyeballs from three cockpits. The puffy, scattered clouds, turning gray in the low light, could conceal a vessel, and the aviators had to look around each buildup to ensure *Flintlock* could ingress unmolested, even though a fully armed *Sierra* could take care of itself. The low light on the darkening water made it a challenge.

The fighters could make up the distance in minutes, and they would have to.

"*Lumber* two-zero from *Whisk* zero-one. We're approaching bingo fuel."

"Roger, *Whisk.* Can you give us ten more mikes?" Annie responded and waited for an answer. It finally came.

"We don't have much of a cushion now. The go-fasts are about five miles away, and we are going to roll in on the lead boats, one run and off. *Condor* from *Whisk*, do we have permission to engage?"

Annie sensed the answer would be a long time coming.

"*Whisk* lead from *Lumber* two-zero. If the go-fasts are a threat, you are cleared to engage, on my authority."

"Roger, ma'am." The lead *Rhino* replied.

The *Super Hornets* were holding west of Lemur's posit as they watched the boats. Lemur's sea-dye marker aided them with relative distance, but the low light would soon obscure the growing patch of fluorescent green. Lemur would then be almost invisible in his gray raft on the gray surface.

From 5,000 feet, *Whisk* 11 put his flight into combat spread and tac-turned them out of the sun and toward the boats. The geometry called for a crossing shot, and each fighter had to estimate how much lead to take. The boats were coming in clusters and singles spread out over miles of ocean, and a big one was in the lead.

"I've got that big guy up front," *Whisk* 11 broadcast to the others. "Aim for one and hit it, be sure to lead them, and save expendables until you pull off. *Armstrong!*"

Annie listened as she strained to see what she could over her nose. The datum was over 20 miles away and obscured by the ubiquitous buildups.

"Lead's in," *Whisk* 11 transmitted.

Annie continued to monitor the UHF comms to try to build a tactical picture in her mind as she and Macho closed in. *Whisk* 12, Lemur, was in his raft and talking with his flight lead on his survival radio. If the boats heading from the south reached him, it meant certain capture. The *Whisk* and *Lumber* formations were rolling in from west to east, out of the setting sun, to strafe the boats and keep them away from Lemur. The *Super Hornets* were running out of fuel, too. Annie transmitted to give them some situational awareness.

"*Whisk* from *Lumber* two-zero. Be there in five mikes."

"Roger, and we'll have to bingo then. We'll leave all our ordnance here."

"Roger," Annie acknowledged.

She heard the jets call in and off like they would in routine weapons training. She also heard reports of muzzle flashes from small arms on several of the go-fasts. The Venezuelans were fighting toe-to-toe. They wanted Lemur as much as she did, but they weren't going to get him. She continued to listen.

"Okay, the big guy is dead-in-the-water, but the swarm is still moving at thirty, forty knots."

"Yeah, I'd say the lead boats are inside five miles."

"Watch for hand-held! Flares!"

"Two's off. Safe, Winchester, five-point-four."

Inside ten miles, Annie picked up several wakes, then more, all racing north to Lemur somewhere ahead of them. She couldn't yet see the raft. The *Rhinos* capping over him were low on fuel and out of bullets, and *Flintlock* was at least fifteen minutes behind. It would be dusk by the time they got there, and Annie's other *Lumber* section would not be there to help before the helo came in. Even with her low fuel state, she and her two charges would have to hold off the swarm of boats. All they had was bullets. And will.

"*Lumber* two-zero from *Whisk*. We are bingo for the tanker. Do you have us in sight?"

From 3,000 feet, Annie could make out one dark *Super Hornet* planform pulling hard as it came off a run. The boats were scattered, two were smoking, and she could make out the twisted wakes on the surface as the craft evaded American fire. They kept coming for Lemur, and she wondered if they had him in sight. Annie keyed the mike.

"*Whisk, Lumber* lead on station with three. Visual on one of you...now two. We've got the go-fasts to the south. *Whisk* one-two, you up?"

"Affirm, *Lumber!*"

"Roger, looking for you. Shine your white lens flashlight north." After several seconds, Annie saw a glint below her.

"Okay, gotcha! *Whisk* one-two, we've got a visual. *Lumbers*, he's at my ten o'clock low, about a mile."

"Two's visual," Macho answered.

"Three's visual," their add-on *Super Hornet* wingman, Woody, answered.

The boats were now on Annie's left shoulder for three miles and boring in on Lemur. She saw spray around the lead boat as the last *Whisk* pulled off. The boat stopped, but another took its place. More were streaming in from the south to help, and Annie estimated twenty, strung out over several miles. As she passed near Lemur, she marked the position on her Nav display as a reference.

"*Lumber* from *Whisk*. We're bingo! Sorry we can't stay!"

"Roger, *Whisk*. Nice job. We've got it."

"Yes, ma'am," the *Whisk* lead replied. He then added, for Lemur's benefit, "Hang in there, buddy!"

With its dazzling orange glow to the west, Annie realized that the low sun would now highlight the jets if they came out of it. As the *Whisks* climbed to the north, and their waiting tanker above her, she elected to turn her formation right and set up an east-west circle. They could see each other as the light lowered, and she instructed them to keep their external lights off. *Flintlock* was twelve minutes out.

She would be bingo fuel by then. *Dammit!*

The Venezuelans were minutes away from Lemur. Looking over her shoulder, she saw one of them getting too close.

She pulled the jet hard right and armed up the gun. "*Lumbers*, take trail and set up a wagon-wheel from east to west. I'm in hot on the lead boat. *Tapes!*"

Annie pulled away from the others and down to begin her run. She sensed Lemur somewhere below her as she lined up on the lead boat, a go-fast bounding north. Passing 3,000 feet in a shallow dive, and using "Kentucky windage" to aim, she put the pipper on a patch of water ahead of the boat. She watched her altitude decrease, airspeed increase, and dive angle build. She couldn't get too steep.

"Lead's in…" she transmitted.

The boat veered hard right to evade. Annie repositioned her nose and squeezed the trigger.

Tracers flew out from over her nose as the gun barrels cycled under Annie's command. A a low, guttural *BRRRRRRRRPPP* sounded in the cockpit as dozens of 20mm rounds raced ahead to the patch of water the boat would cross in seconds. Annie was still firing when the first bullets found their mark. The water erupted into geysers around the 50-foot boat as she observed a few flashes on the hull. Annie yanked her nose up and left and decided against expending any flares to escape detection. She saw the boat slow and wallow to the northeast, out of action. More continued in behind it.

Macho was next in line in an effort to keep an American gun on the disorganized flotilla at all times.

Macho pulled right and assessed that a boat to the west of the group was the near threat. As she rolled in, she sensed right away that a left pull off to the east would put her directly over the main group of boats and coming off right would highlight her. In an instant she decided to come off right and into the sunset, counter-circle from Annie and Woody. Despite her momentary loss of concealment, the maneuver gave the Venezuelans a longer crossing shot problem for their gunners on the bouncing decks. She lined up on the boat, more a skiff, took lead, and waited for the IN RNG cue. To her left, as she passed right to left in front of them, she saw "winking" from several boats, small but bright muzzle flashes.

They see me! They are shooting at ME!

When the mission computer rewarded her with a cue, she pulled the trigger and kicked a boot of right rudder to ensure her bullets were leading the boat. She saw it turn into her and slow as it did. Fountains of water bloomed on the sea where it would have been. *A miss?* She pulled off and overbanked right, and, for a moment, she could look underneath her. She saw the boat resume toward Lemur. *Damn!*

"I missed him!" she cried on the radio.

From one of the boats a bright light bloomed and shot ahead toward Macho, a handheld SAM. Woody was on it immediately. "Macho, *break left!* Missile at your left seven! *Flares!*"

At her wingman's direction, Macho broke hard into the missile and expended flares while pulling the throttles to idle as she whipped her head left to acquire it under the crushing g. The left turn also brought her into the sun, which was too much IR energy for the seeker head, and it went stupid. "Reverse to the right," Annie called to her when she was clear of threat fire.

"Three's in hot on the leader," Woody transmitted. Annie watched him overbank and pull down, rolling out west in a familiar shallow dive. He was lined up on the leader's starboard quarter when he let loose a massive burst. A thin cloud of gun gas from his 20mm cannon marked his flight path as he continued in. The water frothed white around the cigarette boat and impact flashes were noted on it, followed by black smoke as it slowed to a stop. Woody came off right.

"Sierra Hotel! Nice job three," Annie called in encouragement. She was now in trail on Woody, with Macho north of them looking for a hole to enter the circle to continue strafing. Annie picked out a skiff on the eastern periphery of the group, tight on her position with small arms flashes visible. She pulled down into it, spraying it in a short burst as she jinked in a level right turn away from it and expended flares. All the aviators now knew handheld SAMs were a threat they had to honor.

Woody was in position to fire next, and, as he rolled in, Annie noted the range from her to *Flintlock* on her display. Ten miles…roughly five minutes.

They were going to run out of bullets—and fuel. Where were the other sections to relieve them?

"*Lumber* three-one and *Jelly*, say your posit."

"Jelly flight is eighty miles."

"*Lumber* three-one is ninety-five." Annie knew both sections were at least ten minutes out. Maybe the *Jellies* could cover the distance in eight minutes.

"Roger, *Jelly.* Your signal is *buster.* Need you now. We've got our hands full."

"Roger that. *Jellies, gate.*"

Macho took her place in the irregular "circle" of fighters and picked out a ski-boat bouncing on the waves at high speed. The sun was sinking below the horizon and visibility was deteriorating. None of them had a visual on Lemur, and the twilight condition was making it more difficult to pick out the small craft, even with their distinctive wakes.

The Americans continued to cull the herd as they approached Lemur's raft. In the low light, the Venezuelans could not see the survivor either. They counted on sending overwhelming numbers to comb the area—and hoped someone would come across him. Once they got him aboard, the Americans would stop firing. The setting sun was a worse problem for them, knowing as they did the Americans' superior ability to acquire and prosecute targets at night. Both adversaries were in a desperate race against the clock, and the boats were closing in on Lemur.

Annie squeezed the trigger, and, after a few rounds, the gun stopped firing. Out of bullets. *Winchester.*

CHAPTER 74

"*Lumber* two-zero is off. Winchester." Macho and Woody acknowledged. Fuel states were dwindling, too. Woody rolled in on the boat Annie had missed and peppered it. As he did, he noted a few small lights zip past his canopy. *Small arms!* A lucky bullet could ruin his day.

As the Americans flew in tighter and tighter circles to keep a nose pointed at the threat, the airspeed decreased under the g they were maintaining. Whenever they extended away to regain airspeed, they gave the enemy a momentary "sanctuary"—and expended fuel they didn't have.

Annie had no choice. She would have to make cold runs, as would the others when they ran out of 20mm, keeping pressure on. Then she had an idea.

Recalling a story from the Vietnam War, she selected *Sidewinder* and caged the seeker head. The missile seeker growled in her headset as she pulled around to the right to find a target. She picked out a cabin cruiser, a small yacht that was easier to see at range. She maneuvered to place the boat in her HUD field of view and inside the seeker head circle. She got a high-pitched tone, and, once she uncaged the missile, the circle remained on the boat. *Yes!* she thought and pulled the trigger.

The *Sidewinder* shot off the left wing with a sharp bottle-rocket *whoosh* and twitched in flight as it bore in on the yacht. Small arms flashes from several watercraft were visible all around her as Annie pulled up and peered over her nose to assess the effectiveness of her attack.

A bright flash popped next to the yacht as it continued ahead for a moment, then veered left to the west. The yacht then slowed as other boats raced past it. Annie must have damaged it, despite the absence of flame or smoke. She keyed the mike to tell the others.

"Use your '*Winders*. Keep their heads down. Go for the northernmost boats!" Macho and Woody rogered in order.

"*Lumber* two-zero, *Flintlock*. We see the enemy boats. Looking for you."

Annie, maneuvering hard at the moment, scanned the horizon for the *Sierra*. She didn't have an exact position on Lemur floating on the darkening water. Maybe he could see the helo.

"*Lumber* one-two, lead. Do you see *Flintlock* coming in from the northeast?"

"*Condor.* Pop-up contact. One-seven-zero at ten. On the deck. Hot." The E-2 controller transmitted.

"Negative on *Flintlock*. Flash external lights!"

The *Sierra* pilot energized the anti-collision strobe lights of the helicopter and flashed the searchlight before dousing them both.

"*Whisk* one-two has a visual! Check right ten!" With Lemur directing, the helicopter swerved right ten degrees to bring it over him.

The *Hornet* pilots still didn't have a visual on Lemur. Their hands were full prosecuting the boats.

Macho rolled in on a boat and tried to lock it—no joy. In a dive, and with range decreasing fast, she uncaged her missile and immediately got a tone. She fired the AIM-9 from inside a mile and pulled up hard among the muzzle flashes. The missile's rocket motor was still firing when it slammed into the go-fast boat. In their race to the north, none of the other boats came to the aid of the go-fast as it stopped in the water and began to burn.

As Macho pulled off left and did a belly check to the right, her heart skipped a beat. About two miles away, a lone fighter, low on the water, was barreling down them on from the south. She only had time to blurt out a disjointed warning to the others.

"*Bogey coming in from the south! At my three o'clock! On the deck!*"

By instinct, all the American aviators looked south. Annie and Woody both picked up a gray object with a small light—*burner plume!*–at fifty feet over the waves coming right at the lead boats. Appearing supersonic, it stayed on course with no indication it saw any of the Americans, including Lemur. Annie snatched her jet back to the right, over the winking boats, as the g-suit grabbed her legs and torso. In the low light, she identified it as a *Flanker,* lights out. By habit, she searched around the bandit to spot any wingmen.

"*Condor*, we got a bandit out here!" Annie radioed with dismay.

"Affirm, merge plot! *I've been trying to tell you!*"

Woody was at his roll-in point when the jet appeared at his one o'clock low. "*Tallyho!*" he cried as he tried to put his nose on it and shoot, but it was too close and fast. The enemy fighter shot down his right side and maintained course. *That guy doesn't see us!* Woody thought.

Then, Woody realized he *had* as the *Flanker* pulled up into the oblique through northeast, unable to pull hard with its excess airspeed. Though he tried, Woody had no chance to turn and run it down.

Macho did. Although slower, she saw the *Flanker* flash past her six o'clock from a few miles away, and reversed left. All she had left was a *Sidewinder* to fight the bandit arcing up and zooming into the sky, still in burner, at her eight o'clock high. She lit the cans and squatted her jet, selecting BORESIGHT on the HUD to get a lock as she placed the *Flanker* above her and pulled.

The radar and missile locked on with a screaming tone, and, with no time to assess range, she pulled the trigger in a desperate attempt to hit the fighter as it extended away. The missile shot off the rail, a rabid dog chasing the hot point against a cold sky. Because of the speed differential, it was a tail chase, and Macho didn't have the airspeed to go up with it. She had to depend on the missile to find its mark. If the bandit saw it and broke, chances are the *Sidewinder* wouldn't have the energy left to track it.

The FAV pilot must have seen Macho's missile come off the rail. He broke down and right and deselected burner, which made him "invisible" against the eastern twilight. Macho still had a radar lock and had little choice but to pursue. She called to the others.

"*Lumber* two-one engaged with a bandit. Twelve o'clock high, passing through east, nine thousand! I'm *Winchester* missiles!" The Venezuelan extended further away to the southeast with Macho in lag pursuit, tracking him on radar and FLIR.

The *Flanker* was a threat Annie had to honor, but, with the helo about to enter a hover to pick up Lemur, she couldn't abandon him. Between the three of them, Woody had an AMRAAM and a *Sidewinder*. In an instant, she directed them.

"Woody, Macho, commit on the bandit to the east and sanitize south. I'm staying with *Flintlock*. Copy that *Condor*? *Lumber* two-one and *Whisk* one-four are stripping on the bandit to the southeast."

"*Condor* copies."

Annie was now alone over the angry little armada, and, with the lowering light, could see the faint arcs of bullets climbing into the air from the pitching and rolling hulls. Their fire was unguided small arms, but a lucky bullet could find its mark. She had an AMRAAM and a *'Winder* to hold them off. First, she had to know where Lemur was on the darkening waves below her.

"*Whisk*, one-two, *Lumber* lead. Do you still have *Flintlock?*"

"Affirm, check right another ten."

"*Whisk* one-two from *Flintlock*. Get your IR strobe out."

Annie picked up the gray helo fuselage as it came upon Lemur from the northeast. Since she couldn't see the raft, or the IR strobe, she had to guess where he was. She would use *Flintlock* as a reference. Anything south of the helicopter was fair game.

She pulled around to the north, lights out and invisible to the boats. Annie could make out nothing but wakes on the water and picked one to expend her last AIM-9. She saw *Flintlock* slowing in front of her, and to ensure the *'Winder* didn't guide on the helicopter, she had to get past it before firing. The boats were almost on top of them.

Annie got a tone and squeezed the trigger, and a dazzling blaze of fire shot from her right wing. The missile twitched up and then down into a speeding 30-foot yacht, holing the fiberglass hull with its warhead fragments. As the yacht slowed to a stop, scattered rows of faint lights rose above Annie. Even though they were small arms, she had to keep her distance. With her eyes now padlocked on the helicopter, she called to Woody for an update.

"Woody, what luck?"

"We're chasing it down, but it's approaching the coast."

"Well, if it's in LAR, shoot it!" Annie was losing her cool under the growing pressure of her race against time. Just then an aural warning sounded in her headset. "*Bingo. Bingo.*"

With only 4,500 pounds of fuel and the *hope* of an inbound tanker still 100 miles away, Annie—as well as Macho and Woody—had to leave soon. The *Lumber* and *Jelly* sections were still 5-10 minutes out. Annie was alone with her unplanned wingman, *Flintlock*. The helicopter radioed a command to Lemur.

"*Whisk* one-two, pop smoke!"

"*Whisk* one-four, Fox three on the bandit heading southeast seven thousand," Woody cried.

Annie pulled her jet around to the east as the tiny swarm of boats closed in on the helicopter. In the twilight, she could make out the curling smoke from Lemur's flare. She could also see the gunner on the *Sierra's* left side belching bursts of flame at the nearest boats to hold them off. At best, they need two minutes to pick up Lemur. Spray billowed up below the helo as it slowed over Lemur.

Annie was Winchester, but maybe she could draw some fire. With her mind working overtime, she had another idea. *I have two drop tanks.* She could come in low and drop one to cause confusion among the boats and keep their attention away from *Flintlock*. A diversion. She needed the others back to help her, and within minutes they needed to climb to the tanker. Two more minutes…. They could make it.

"Woody, Macho, if you haven't splashed that bandit, get back here!"

"Five seconds!"

"*Lumber* lead, *Flintlock* dropped a swimmer, and we're circling around for pickup."

"Roger," Annie answered as she set up for her run. She selected her drop tank on Station 7 first. She would come in on a shallow dive out of the east, get down to below 500 feet and estimate lead as best she could for a tumbling, empty drop tank. She set her radar altimeter bug to 250 feet. She would be right in their face—and their bullets in hers.

"*Timeout-kill* on the bandit heading one-five-zero. Angels six!" Woody crowed, which elicited a sigh of relief from Annie. *They're okay. They can come back to help.* She whipped her head left for an instant and saw a flickering light descending to the southeast—the *Flanker* in its death throes.

Using the faded smoke as a reference—Lemur and the swimmer were down there somewhere—Annie overbanked and pulled down toward the water to find another target. Muzzle flashes came from scattered points all over the waves, and, as the helicopter circled, bullets turned the water into white froth as the helo door gunner worked over the boats he selected. Annie picked a wake and saw the dim boat that made it, what she identified as a center-console fisherman with muzzle flashes visible. A dozen small lights flashed past her left canopy in an orderly row. She bored in on the boat, with crisp movements of the stick to correct for lead, left index finger on the SELECT JETT button. Watching the picture build, she sensed more tiny light streams around her and listened for Woody, *Flintlock, Condor.* Annie did not think about what she was doing, she just did it, by reflex. If not her, who?

The boat was visible through her windscreen, two muzzles flashing on the bow as she roared over it at 450 knots. She pushed the button and felt her tank fall away as she pulled up and left to the south, behind the lead boats. Almost at once, she heard an aluminum punch and felt a slight shudder in the airframe—along with a sharp, metallic *clank* behind her.

From three miles away, Macho saw a small stream of flame arcing over the vicinity of the rescue. None of the aircraft had anti-collision lights illuminated, but the stream allowed Macho to boresight lock the object on her radar. Her FLIR showed an image of a *Hornet* with bright white heat cascading down its left tail above the stabilator.

Annie knew she was hit and could sense the flame aft over her left shoulder. Within a second, the left fire light illuminated and *"Engine fire left. Engine fire left."* sounded in her headset. Macho's frantic call followed.

"Annie, *you're hit!* We'll be there in thirty seconds. Get outta there!"

Annie yanked the left throttle around the detent and pushed the fire light over her FLIR display, which was filling with aircraft caution indications. She had to ignore them as she trimmed out the yaw and craned her neck to keep sight of the *Sierra* and the smoke. The boat was continuing in, and *Flintlock* was now stabilized in a hover to pick up Lemur and their swimmer.

From two miles away, Macho watched her XO roll in from the south, trailing flame that attracted the attention of gunners on every boat. On her FLIR display, she could see the sudden dashed lines of bullets zip past the stricken *Hornet* as it rolled in over them. Filled with sickening dread, she watched the jet struggle to turn, taking fire now from all quadrants. "Annie, you're taking heavy fire!"

In her cockpit Annie, acknowledged the anxious call of her wingman. "Roger. Dropping my centerline on them. Left engine secure. *Flintlock,* status?"

"On the hoist now!" the aircraft commander replied.

Annie picked a boat and came in from the stern, hoping to be unseen, but, trailing a tongue of flame, she was the center of attention as the Venezuelans shot everything they could in an effort to bring her down. While the *Flintlock* M240 gunner hosed the nearest boat from 500 yards away, the co-pilot watched the burning *Hornet.* Stabilized in a dive among the criss-crossing boats, with their guns blazing into the air, a determined Annie pounced on them yet again—even as they smelled blood.

As she concentrated on her target, finger on the jettison switch, Commander Jennifer Schofield had her lone engine in afterburner to give her staggering, burning jet at least 350 knots in the dive. Impatient to release her last store, she hoped she could do it in time. It was all her, no computer-aided system, no ballistics, no real chance of hitting anything. But it was *something.* And it was all she could give at the moment Lemur's rescue was in the balance.

Annie watched the boat disappear under her nose and heard the supersonic snaps of bullets outside. She then heard and felt another aluminum punch on her left side. Hand gripping the stick hard and standing on her right rudder pedal, she shouted into her mask. "*C'mon...come on!*" Behind her, a MANPAD was shot from its launch tube on a bucking speedboat and sped toward her.

As Annie pushed the jettison switch, an explosion behind her caused her to lose control. The airplane corkscrewed ahead as the *Flintlock* co-pilot watched in horror a half mile away. From a vantage point behind her, Macho saw Annie's jet flash and tumble near the water.

"Annie, get out!" she cried.

Annie's arms were pinned against the canopy as her jet rolled out of control. She was unable to stop the roll, unable to reach for the handle. The horizon spun into sensations of lights and negative G-force, choking, bewilderment, and confusion. Then clarity. She thought of her boy, and Mike, and her mother. The horizon spun again and revealed a dim whitecap in front of her.

She wondered if she had made a difference.

CHAPTER 75

(The Devil's Woodyard)

Wilson listened as the sound of the helicopter drew closer. The automatic weapon he had heard outside was new, and it puzzled him. *Now what?* The rotor sound was coming from two helicopters, and, again he tried—and failed—to identify the aircraft type.

Through the trees, Jill and the Marines saw the *Super Pumas* come in from the south and circle to land. They could make out the yellow, red, and blue markings on the tail boom. Venezuelan.

"Shit, they're gonna be here in a minute," she said.

"We can keep this guy down, ma'am." Garcia said with a confident nod.

She knew they had to hole up in the cabin. Damn, she shouldn't have left Doc alone!

"All right, let's circle back and get Doc. Then we go into the cabin!" The Marines were skeptical.

"Is the pilot going to shoot us? And what about the wounded guy?"

Jill also needed answers to those questions, the sooner the better.

"First, let's get back to Doc. Then, we'll identify ourselves to the pilot. We'll also keep a bead on these guys, especially the wounded one in front."

They scrambled over the forest floor toward Doc Woodruff as the rotor blades got louder. Like the cartel helicopter, the *Super Pumas* were setting down or fast-roping soldiers off near the road.

"Doc, where are you?" Jill shouted.

"Here!" the nervous doctor yelled back. "Are they ours?"

"No! *C'mon!*"

They moved toward the cabin and again saw the wounded man against the tree trunk. He appeared delirious, but the Marines kept their weapons pointed at him as Jill raised her voice to shout over the rotor din 100 yards away.

"*Slash* one-one. Can you hear me?"

Startled, Wilson turned his head.

"*Slash* one-one, this is Special Agent Fischer of the American Embassy. We are on foot and not with the helicopters. *They are Venezuelan!* We need to come inside and help you. Hold your fire."

Wilson didn't know what to do. *This* wasn't textbook. A woman, who spoke with a Caribbean lilt, who knew his tactical call sign. Could this be a trap? The rotor blades whipped at the air in the distance.

Drawing a full breath, Wilson shouted back. "What's the number of the day?" He had to verify this woman was friendly, but he also needed help.

Fortunately, Jill Fischer had done her homework.

"*Five!* It's five! Now hold your fire. I have three armed men with me."

Dammit, Wilson thought. Was this a trap? He peered over the sill and saw the wounded man, no threat.

"Show yourselves!" Wilson demanded.

Jill raised her hands and stood, motioning for the others to do so. The aircraft were now idling on the ground, and soldiers would be on them in minutes. Uneasy and vulnerable, they watched the trees.

"What's the letter of the day?" Wilson shouted again, seeking another correct answer to authenticate them.

"*Juliett!* Now hold your fire!"

Wilson sighed in relief. "Come in. Come in," he yelled. He then turned to Father Dan. "Americans are outside to help us. The helicopters have soldiers. It's going to get hot again."

Father Dan chuckled. "*Again,* you say?"

Flying *Hunter* 407, Weed led a flight of three *Super Hornets* high over the dark Paria Peninsula as the sun set over his right shoulder. Beyond the gulf, the island of Trinidad awaited, with bright offshore flare stacks dotting the waters around it. The lights of Port of Spain shone off his left nose.

Pressed into service, Weed was glad—and honored—to have CAG's trust to lead a CSAR to save his friend. Both knew Weed was not Matson's first choice, but CAG's strike leaders were busy and/or exhausted and needed relief. And Weed was available.

Once clear of Venezuelan airspace, he would descend and find the two MH-60 *Sierras* that had sortied out of Tobago. They had eight SEALs aboard, ready for anything.

The intel guys said Flip was holed up in a shack on the island's southern shore—with a priest! Thankful that Flip was okay, Weed smiled to himself, but he wouldn't relax until Flip was in a *Rustler* aircraft and on his way to safety. With Venezuelan agents reported in the area, the combat SAR was to serve as backup to the embassy pickup crew sent from Port of Spain to an unpopulated area of the island.

Now over the gulf, Weed chopped the power and led his wingmen, Dog in 404 and Cisco in 405, down to 10,000 feet. He needed to find the *Sierras* visually and escort them to the briefed lat/long where they would find the cabin and Flip.

Weed took a heading of 120 to join up with the helos over the island's eastern shore. A reflection of pink from the west washed both the gray cumulus columns that dotted the gulf and the cloud concentrations over the island. A purple thunderstorm, loaded with lightning flashes, floated north of the capital. Once Weed got them below 10,000, the sun would be down. but it would still be too light for their NVGs—and would be for at least another half hour. His radar searched ahead down low, and he saw no enemy radar warning indications from Río Salta, just 40 miles away.

"*Hunter* lead, *Rustler* six-one-two with you. Flight of two. *Bullseye* zero-two-zero at fifty. Sixteen souls. Four times M240 7.62."

Weed keyed the mike to answer. "Roger, *Rustlers. Hunter* four-zero-seven flight of three. Eight minutes out with two by two missiles each and twenty mike-mike. Thirty minutes of play time."

"Roger," Sean Sullivan replied. After days of camping at the airport in Tobago, he and Pete Smith were more than ready to affect the rescue and go home. They all were, especially the SEALs, who were missing the action in Venezuela.

A sudden call from *Condor* increased the tension of the pilots in each cockpit.

"Ninety-nine *Hunters.* Expect OPFOR on scene. *Paradise* reports."

Weed looked over his nose at Trinidad. American ISR assets were reporting an opposing force. Hadn't the embassy team secured the site? Weed knew the diplomats didn't have a proper radio to talk to him, and since Flip hadn't come up on his survival radio, he didn't expect he would now. But the *Rhino* jets *could* monitor certain mobile frequencies. Weed needed info, even if it were only one side of a conversation. He had an idea.

"*Condor* from *Hunter*. Can you get *Paradise* to talk with the embassy team—if they are on scene?"

"Roger, *Hunter*, we'll try.... And, *Rustlers,* bear one-one-zero for sixty."

Weed rogered him, and his radar searched to find the helos as he worked the coordination through *Condor*. What kind of opposing force? Where? How many? *Has Flip been captured?* Weed needed answers, and, by glancing at his fuel, he knew he had less than thirty minutes to get them.

Below, Trinidad was green and wooded, with rugged hills. *Diplomatic clearance? Sorry*. They were there to get one of their own. The embassy pukes could make apologies later. The two *Sierras* were holding east of the island and waiting for their escort to arrive. With *Mother* over 250 miles away, they couldn't reach her. To preclude upsetting the West Indians further, they would have to take Wilson first to the LCS off Grenada, and from there to *Coral Sea*. *Condor* broke in with a call.

"*Hunter, Condor*. Switch base freq minus 65.250."

"Roger, *Condor*."

Using the briefed base frequency number as a foundation, Weed switched up the frequency on the auxiliary radio and listened. After several seconds, he heard a female voice.

"We are with the subject inside the briefed cabin and need backup!"

Weed listened, unable to transmit, unable to ask questions. He nudged the stick to the right to avoid a cloud buildup as his radar continued to search for the helos ahead of him.

"Yes, dammit, a priest and a woman. Estimating twenty enemy outside!"

Weed was monitoring the embassy side of the conversation, and, as the formation continued to descend—they were now passing the briefed cabin location, thirty miles to the south—he built a picture. *Inside a cabin with a priest.* That made sense from the brief, but the woman's voice was not American. It sounded Caribbean. Weed needed clarification, and got *Condor* to come up on the freq. After listening some more, Weed asked.

"*Condor, Hunter* four-zero-seven. Who are we listening to?"

"Stand by, *Hunter*."

Weed then saw some return on his display and bumped the castle switch to lock it. After a few seconds, the symbols stabilized and showed a low and slow contact on his nose for 25 miles, heading south. Weed asked them to verify.

"*Rustler, Hunter* four-zero-seven has a radar contact. *Bullseye* zero-six-zero at forty. On the deck, heading south."

"That's us, *Hunter.*"

Weed now "had" the helos, and soon they would be "holding hands." He nudged the stick again to intercept and called *Condor.*

"*Condor, Hunters* are joining on the *Rustlers.* What luck?"

The E-2, orbiting 150 miles away, also had some good news.

"*Hunter*, the woman is IDed as an embassy employee. They are inside with *Slash* one-one."

Weed was relieved, but only for a moment. Flip was okay, but he—and the people with him—were somehow trapped by an unknown opposition force. With 25 minutes of fuel before he had to bingo, Weed had to get them going, fast.

"*Condor* from *Hunter.* We are going to push ASAP. Find out who is outside."

"Roger that, *Hunter.*"

As he passed a gray column of cloud, Weed's FLIR display picked up two white helicopter silhouettes. Weed turned to put them in his HUD field of view and soon saw them as they hugged the coastline, dark dashes against a gray sea.

"*Rustler, Hunter.* Visual at your right three high. Five miles. Ready to go?"

"A-firm, *Hunter*," Sean, in *Rustler* 612, replied.

"Roger. Expect an OPFOR when we get there."

"Roger, *Hunter.*"

So they wouldn't be detected by the local populace, Weed directed the *Rustlers* to go feet dry along a deserted patch of coastline at the "heel" of the island. As the helicopters turned west, the fighters overflew them at 5,000 feet. They were able to keep their eyes on the helicopters against the dark green forest while the sun sank deeper.

"Cisco, stay here at angels five. We're going to three," Weed radioed the message to his wingman as he continued down with Dog. "This is going to be opposed. *Armstrong.*"

The *Rhinos* weaved in a figure-eight pattern to stay above the two combat-loaded helicopters. They were sprinting through the twilight gloom at 120 knots toward the cabin—and trouble.

CHAPTER 76

(The Devil's Woodyard)

Jill and the others burst through the door as the Venezuelans stormed up the driveway and fanned out along the tree line. They fired their first shots at the cabin as Garcia took a position at the side window to Wilson's left, busting out a pane to get a clear field of fire.

The other Marine trained his weapon on Father Dan and a terrified Monique who were crouched near the stove. "They're okay! They're friendly!" Wilson barked at the young lance corporal who ignored him.

"Commander Wilson, my name is Special Agent Jill Fischer." Jill showed her credentials as she introduced herself.

"Have him take his weapon off them!" Wilson shouted, concerned that *he* was the cause of real danger to these two innocent people.

Jill motioned the Marine to the other side window, turned back to Wilson, and pointed at the doctor. "This is Doctor Woodruff. He can help you with your injuries." In pain, Wilson rolled off the table and eased himself to the floor.

Slugs ripped into the clapboard from automatic weapons, and Garcia had trouble picking targets in the low light.

"El hombre *Weel-son*, venga aqui. Ahora!" blared a bullhorn.

"Who are they?" Jill asked Wilson as she punched buttons on her phone.

"You tell me." He winced as he shifted his weight under Woodruff's guidance. "We were fighting drug thugs. Don't know who these guys are."

"Here they come," Garcia muttered.

"Weel-son, *surrender!*" the voice on the bullhorn sounded again. Their helicopters were idling on deck down the road, rotor blades adding white noise in the background.

Jill heard commands in Spanish. "Garcia, can you understand what they're saying?"

"Ma'am, I'm from Boston. The only Spanish I know is my last name," the Marine deadpanned as he sighted in a target.

Jill looked at Wilson. "Can you shoot?"

"Yes, I've been holding them off. Have most of this clip left, and that's it."

"Okay," Jill said. "Get back up there. Doc, help him." She turned to the Marines and gestured toward the side windows. "You guys have the flanks. Talk to each other!"

"May I offer a prayer?" Father Dan volunteered.

Jill nodded. "Yes, please do!"

"Heavenly Father, please deliver us..."

A tear gas canister crashed through the window above Garcia and knocked him down. It then bounced on the floor in front of Monique who screamed in fright. Smith grabbed the canister and tossed it out the open window in front of Wilson. As gas wafted through the room, they fanned it from their faces, and those who were able covered their mouths with whatever they could reach. "I can't see anything! Not enough frickin' light!" Garcia grumbled in frustration, his eyes tearing.

"Then do your best and shoot!" Jill commanded. "If you can see the helos through the trees, hit them!"

Wilson, back at his perch, peered outside for any sign of movement. If this was his rescue party, they were woefully unprepared. Bullets thudded the cabin from all sides as Jill and the Marines returned fire. The BAR Garcia fired had, no doubt, drawn attention, and he was hosing the trees with burst after burst. How much ammo did he have? Another tear gas canister bounced against the cabin and landed on the porch, the gentle wind carrying some of the noxious smoke inside. They all struggled to function.

A shadow burst from the trees and rushed to a cover position by the vehicle. Wilson squeezed the trigger, and the silhouette was knocked back as if pulled by a rope.

A spotlight was directed on the cabin, and the Venezuelan gunners corrected their aim. Bullets broke out the rest of the glass and hit the walls inside, knocking objects off the shelves. Garcia was driven back by a fusillade of fire, and one round knocked the BAR from his grasp and holed its barrel, rendering it useless.

"*Fuck me,*" he cursed as he reached for his sidearm.

Jill peered out the back as the Venezuelans poured fire into the front of the cabin. Lying prone, she scanned the tree line for movement and saw none. With her left hand, she pushed open the bin door to open her field of view.

A hand grabbed Jill's wrist from below. When she yelped, another hand stuck a pistol through the opening and fired two shots. The weapon's deafening report and its hammer blow to her clavicle stunned her, and she went limp. Through the noise of gunfire and Monique's screams, Wilson turned to see a soldier stick his head through the opening. Their eyes met in the dim light, and Wilson saw the sharp South American features of a young man. His murderous eyes focused on Wilson as he pulled his pistol up.

With Monique just outside his line of fire, Wilson squeezed off another round.

The young man was propelled back through an explosion of red mist and into the darkness beyond the open door. Woodruff jumped up and grabbed Jill's ankles to pull her away from the opening. The woman was unconscious, and with the amount of blood flowing from her neck, all feared the worst. The doctor saw that the bullet had hit the edge of her vest by the clavicle. Because most of the force was absorbed by the vest, the bullet left only a superficial wound when it fractured her bone. Woodruff bandaged her while she was still unconscious, assisted by Monique who was grateful for the task.

Weed designated the briefed lat/long on his nav display, and the FLIR slewed to the position. Nothing hot, just the outline of the forest. He opened his field of view and got some white hot return to his right. He slewed the aiming diamond over it and selected NARROW.

Weed saw helicopter rotor blades spinning as the aircraft sat on a road, and faint smoke wafting through the trees to the south. As he waited for the picture to build, he heard a man's voice.

"We've got an agent down, and we're low on ammo! Yes, alive."

Weed didn't have positive identification for anyone involved—except Flip. He didn't *know* what was going on down there, but he guessed that Flip and some others—locals or embassy types—were holed up in the cabin. He had to find it and make sure. His training precluded him from going in guns blazing, but it appeared to him that this situation required just that. He looked over the nose to try to discern anything with his naked eye and saw no anti-collision lights from where the helos were located. The absence of lights was an indication of covert behavior.

"*Condor*, can you get some clarification as to what's going on? Can you *declare*?"

"Stand by, *Hunter*."

"*You stand by!*" Weed shouted in frustration as he pounded the dashboard. Always hurry up and wait, but the fuel wasn't waiting. And his friend was in trouble. *Calm down,* he told himself.

Weed veered away from the site as the helo bored in, five minutes out. He wanted to hold away and above any small arms. It was almost dark...he couldn't take it anymore...and keyed the mike.

"Goggles."

The three *Super Hornet* pilots reached up to remove their helmet-mounted systems and donned their night vision goggles, a delicate operation as they maintained loose formation on one another. With their anti-collision lights and position lights secured, they used formation "strip" lights on the fuselage to determine the aspect of the jet next to them. They squinted from the light intensification coming from the western horizon, but, being on goggles now was better than not using them.

Drawing closer, Weed identified the helicopters on deck as *Pumas*, rotors turning at idle. He continued to listen, impatient for an answer from *Condor*. He keyed the mike.

"*Condor, Hunter*. We need to get this show on the road."

He saw muzzle flashes through openings in the trees and was able to pick out the cabin in a small clearing. The building had electricity, but, as he watched, it was cut.

"*They just cut the power!*" cried a male voice on the cell phone. Weed also heard a gunshot in the background.

Weed sensed he need to act—*now*. Circumstantial or not, the evidence was overwhelming that Flip was inside with some embassy types, and they were attempting to hold off an attacking force that he guessed came from the two *Pumas*. The *Rustlers* didn't have much more of a fuel cushion than he did, and the word from *Condor*, who was talking to the ship, who was talking to Miami, could take all night as the staff weenies covered their sixes. Who were the attackers in these military helos? Trinidad? No, the embassy was here. Drug guys? No. The two identical aircraft screamed military, and Venezuela had *Pumas*.

"*Condor*, from *Hunter*. The aircraft are *Pumas*, and the friendlies in the cabin are taking fire from outside. We've got a visual. *Request clearance!*" Weed transmitted.

"Stand by, *Hunter!*" the harried Tactical Coordinator replied from his station inside the E-2 "tube" far away.

"*Hunter* four-zero-seven from *Rustler* six-one-zero. We've got a tally on the LZ."

"Roger, six-one-zero. We've got two *Pumas* turning on deck north of the cabin and small arms fire observed north and west of it."

"Looks like one guy is lifting," Weed heard the *Rustler* pilot transmit.

The lead *Puma* lifted up and transited to forward flight, turning north away from the firefight. Weed was over him and could reverse his turn and pull down to pursue him.

"*Tallyho*," he transmitted. *Pumas* were not armed gunships, but if the aircraft circled back toward the cabin, it could pose a threat. Weed wanted to stay with it, but had to lead the Rescue CAP and get Flip out of there.

"Cisco, detach and shadow the bandit helo turning through north. If he turns back to the cabin, engage."

Cisco, in 405, acknowledged and pulled away from the formation. He took a position behind the *Puma* that was reversing left to the west. For all Weed knew, Flip could be inside that aircraft, which, at the moment, was not a threat. The aircraft on deck was another matter. Not knowing if it carried soldiers or would be the vehicle to pluck Flip from the island posed a problem. Flip could be inside it or, if captured, could be led to it right then. The *Rustlers* and their SEALs could deal with the threat, and Weed would be overwatch if the aircraft became a threat to them.

"*Rustler, Hunter.* You've got about two miles to go to the contact of interest. There's a clear area next to it on the east and it is surrounded by trees on all sides. Fire still coming from the north and west."

"Roger, *Hunter.* We've got a tally. We're going to make firing passes on the tree lines and circle back to land our GRE boys."

"Roger. *Condor,* you copy that?"

"*Condor* copies."

"*Rustler* lead's in hot," Sean transmitted in calm control.

Weed and Dog circled high above as the two *Sierras* took trail and offset north to roll in left. Without slowing, they flew by the *Puma,* and Weed watched a band of M240 fire rain down on the aircraft's tail boom. Flashes from bullet impacts riddled the boom and the tail rotor slowed.

Perfect, Weed thought. *That helo isn't going anywhere!*

Rustler lead then reversed and allowed the opposite M240 gunner to open up on the western tree line as the aircraft roared over the cabin, spitting a stream of fire that ripped through the trees. The trailer came in next and covered the northern tree line in 7.62 fire as the left-side gunner fired over the cabin into muzzle flashes from the south.

"*Holy shit!*" Weed heard the caller say.

CHAPTER 77

Wilson and the others listened to the approaching rotors with dread. *Reinforcements.* Keeping his flashlight beam concealed, Wilson checked his clip. *Three rounds left.* In the corner he heard Father Dan murmuring to Monique as the two Marines, frustrated and fearful, let go with a continual stream of curses from each of their positions, When the Americans ran out of ammunition, they would come, and the able-bodied Marines—and maybe all of them in the cabin—would be summarily executed. He sensed, though, he would be captured and held for ransom. He would be the cause of six deaths, two of them innocent, a fact that would weigh on him the rest of his life.

A ricochet hit Garcia in the forearm. *"Mother fuck!"* he cursed. In the shadows, Wilson saw him holding the arm as he writhed in pain. *One* able-bodied Marine.

"Smitty," Wilson bellowed. "Take Garcia's spot. It's heavier there. Doc, pick up a weapon and cover us as best you can to the south."

The men complied, and the doctor left Jill with Father and Monique. The helo rotors grew louder and louder, and soon Wilson heard a loud *brrrrrpppppp* to the north followed by shouts outside. The helicopter seemed to be right on top of them when a deafening series of staccato *pops* filled the air. As the automatic guns tore at the trees outside, the human beings behind them screamed. One helo roared over, and then another, with more sounds of high-caliber guns that once again ripped into the trees and the earth around them.

"What the fuck!" Garcia cried as they heard the shouts and wails from outside. Wilson listened, too, and realized the firing had stopped.

The helicopter sound was now to the south, and Wilson sensed they were turning back to them. *Were they American? Who else would fire into the trees at these guys?*

A shot fired and the bullet exploded into the clapboard, followed by another. Excited shouts outside were unintelligible except for one word: *"Weel-son!"*

"Sir, here they come!" Smith shouted. If the helos were American, Wilson needed them to come back, *now*.

Having to lie prone, Wilson could not move about the cabin. "Doc, can you help Smitty?" Wilson barked. Just as the doctor joined Smith at his window, the helos returned and the sound of their rotors and the hum of their engines got louder.

Smith fired off three rounds, and then his pistol clicked. "*Dammit!*" he cursed. "Sir, I need ammo!" he shouted. The sounds of men outside came closer.

"Here!" Wilson offered, and Smith bounded through the darkened room to retrieve Wilson's .45. He returned to the window and took a bead on a soldier crouching near the car. The report of the .45 was deafening and flashed in the room. Smith crouched low to avoid the fusillade of bullets that followed. As the aircraft drew near, Wilson sensed them slow into an approach. A gun burst again ripped through the air and sprayed the trees near the cabin, close, dangerously close. They heard a scream outside, and Smith peaked over the sill to see if the man was still near the car. He couldn't see anyone there, but he did see a soldier fire into the air.

The soldier was then shredded by a rapier swath of hot lead from the M240. The thunderous zipper-like sound exploded in their ears as the helicopter entered a hover over them, its downdraft generating a hurricane of swirling leaves and debris. To further the chaos, high-pressure rotor wash also entered the cabin through the busted out windows. Monique screamed again and bullets flew everywhere.

Outside, Wilson heard someone shout. "*Capitán!*"

The darkness inside the cabin had turned objects and people into faint silhouettes. Easing himself down, Wilson returned to his spot on the floor near the door and wished he could make eye contact with Father Dan. Continual noise was pounding into his brain: the sounds of the helicopter engines and rotors, the automatic weapons, the shouting, the gunfire outside.

Wilson then heard the crunch of boots, followed by a click.

A miniature sun seemed to explode in the room near Smith. Wilson was at once blinded and stunned.

Weed noted his fuel. Ten minutes. Comparing states with Dog and Cisco, the three of them had the same. Cisco followed the *Super Puma* until it crossed into the Columbus Channel and headed toward San Ramón.

Once satisfied it was no longer a threat, he returned to join his flight lead overhead.

With his wingman Dog trailing a mile behind him, Weed had his eyes padlocked on the cabin. The *Rustlers* had torn up the tree line, but he could still see sporadic resistance. The first *Sierra* set down near the cabin, and he watched four objects—the SEALs—scramble clear while the door gunners covered them. The helicopter remained on deck as the other orbited in overwatch. To the east, a few miles away, he saw headlights on the road. *Oh,oh.*

"*Rustlers* from *Hunter.* You've got a vehicle comin' down the road from the east." He saw a flash from inside the cabin. *Fuck,* he thought. *Hope Flip is okay.*

At the same time, Cisco came up on SAR common. "Ninety-nine SAR players, we've got multiple slow movers inbound. Twenty miles south!"

Weed snapped his head south. Across the dark body of water, the Venezuelan coastline was devoid of light and barren, except for Río Salta to the west. Further inland, he could make out the San Ramón complex, but saw no aircraft lights. He turned his nose in their direction and let the radar work for him as the data link display was empty. Within seconds, he had formed a plan and transmitted it to the others.

"Cisco, roger. Get a raid count if you can and get above them. Break, break. *Rustlers,* you've got responsibility for the vehicle to the east about a mile. *Condor,* you monitorin' this?"

"*Rustlers,* roger all," Sean transmitted.

"Affirm, *Hunter. Condor* has multiple slow movers on the deck. Two-zero-five for eighteen. Heading zero-three-zero."

"*Hunter,* break. Cisco, do you have a VID yet?"

"Helos. Looks to be six, maybe more. Lights out. Radar contact, one-eight-zero for twelve."

Twelve miles! Weed thought. They could be here in five minutes. His radar scanned low and locked something on the nose for fifteen miles. The aspect vector was hot, heading northeast, with an airspeed of 150 knots. His FLIR slaved to the contact, and Weed saw a sleek, thin helicopter coming at him. He selected WIDE and saw many other similar returns.

A formation of helos coming up from Venezuela. *Fuck!*

Cisco then made a report. "*Hunter* lead from four-zero-five. We've got a flight of ten. Appears to be eight *Hinds* and two *Hips.*"

This alarmed everyone. The Venezuelans were flying those aircraft in an apparent assault to take back the cabin and its precious treasure—

Wilson. Coincidence or not, eight *Hind* gunships posed a serious threat to the *Sierras* and to the SEALs on the ground. Weed and his two other *Rhinos* had two *Sidewinders* each and guns. With no time to lose, Weed keyed the mike.

"*Condor,* declare!" he demanded.

"Stand by, *Hunter.*"

Dammit! Weed thought. *Ten freakin' attack helos coming at us and no declaration?* He went to military power and selected AIM-9. With a visual on Cisco a few miles southwest, he turned left and climbed.

"*Hunters,* taking angels five. Dog follow me up. *Condor,* the *Hunters* are setting up for slashing attacks on the gorilla of helos. *To the southwest.*"

"Roger, *Hunter.* Stand by," *Condor* replied, working the coordination as best they could. Through his goggles, Weed could now see the faint objects moving in a large formation toward the island, and, five seconds later, Weed had his answer.

"*Hunter, Condor.* You are cleared to engage the bandit group. Two-two-zero at five, but *only* once they've gone feet dry. Acknowledge."

"*Hunter* four-zero-seven, roger. Acknowledged. Break, break: Cisco, take position west of them, and, after Dog and I are off, come in. Take the lead aircraft, whatever it is. *Rustler?* How are you guys doing?"

"The boys are securing the site, and we expect to have 'em aboard momentarily."

"Roger."

Both formations of American aircraft had their hands full: Weed and the *Hunters* with the ten *Hinds* and *Hips* and the *Rustlers* with troops hiding in the trees and an unknown vehicle on the road, the helos and the SEALs sanitizing the area to pick up *Slash* 11. Complicating matters, the distance from the coastline to the landing zone was 2.5 miles, about a minute of flight time for the speedy gunships. Weed knew by *Condor*'s caveat that wreckage landing in Trinidad had political value. He maneuvered his jet to be in his dive, radar locked on a *Hind* with a good missile tone, just as it crossed the surf line.

"*Hunters, Armstrong,*" he transmitted on SAR common.

"*On yer belly! Hands behind yer back! Everyone!*" the voice shouted inside the cabin. Before Wilson could move, hands grabbed him and forced him to the floor. In agony, Wilson cried out in pain, and he heard Monique wail again. "Hands behind yer back! *Now!*"

"I'm an American doctor," Woodruff protested.

"Shut the fuck up! Hands behind your back, dammit!"

The voices were American, and the heavy footfalls and rough actions of these men told Wilson they were SEALs.

"Mikey, take that window! Pete, *the door.*"

"Rog-o!"

Wilson felt a man use a twist-tie to secure his wrists and heard Garcia protest. "All right, man! *Ow!* All right! I'm fuckin' wounded, you stupid squid!"

"Fuck you," the SEAL shot back.

Standing over him, Wilson's SEAL asked him a question. "Sir, state your name, rank and social."

"James D. Wilson, Commander, U.S. Navy, 123-45-6789. *Slash* one-one."

"Roger, sir. Where's your ID card?"

"In my flight suit, left breast pocket." Wilson heard Father Dan groan.

"Don't hurt the man and woman. They helped me." The sounds of gunfire, shouting, and helicopter engines continued in the background. The SEAL rolled Wilson up and fished inside his pocket until he felt the card.

"What about this woman?" the SEAL asked.

"She's embassy, took a ricochet to her clavicle."

The SEAL flashed a light on the card to inspect it. "We got him, boys. Let's get 'em in the bird."

"Roger."

As Wilson felt the SEAL roll him back, a wave a relief came over him. *Deliverance.* They would make it. The lieutenant then cut the twist-tie, and Wilson was free.

"Okay, skipper, we got a bird outside. Can you walk?"

"With help. My left shoulder is hurt and right leg broken."

"Roger, sir, we gotcha."

"Where you from?" Wilson asked, detecting an accent.

"Staten Island. I'm Lieutenant Joe Rovelli. We gotcha, sir."

Soon, everyone's twist-ties were cut, and SEALs' flashlights gave enough light to see the shaken look on Father Dan's face and the numbed blankness on Monique's. Outside, occasional gunfire was heard, and the sound of helicopter rotors filled the air. Rovelli listened to a transmission in his earpiece, and Wilson heard him mutter.

"*Fuck.*"

"What's goin' on?" Wilson asked.

"We're gonna have company. Let's go, you guys! *Now!*"

CHAPTER 78

(*Hunter* 401, over The Devil's Woodyard)

Weed pulled his jet across the horizon, his *Sidewinder* growling, and bumped the castle switch to auto acquire. A dashed-line circle appeared in his HUD, and, as he overbanked, he pulled it to the helicopter closest to him and rolled out.

The *Sidewinder* tone screamed in his headset as he watched the planform of a *Hind* about to move across the breakers on the beach as the range counted down. *Close enough,* Weed thought and squeezed the trigger.

A white streak shot from his left wing with a *whoosh* and flew straight as an arrow into the lead gunship. The aircraft exploded, and the fireball plunged into the vertical cliff face. He picked up his nose and selected GUN as he led another *Hind* in a high deflection gunshot with a radar lock. With less than 1,000 feet in range, he pulled lead and squeezed the trigger again, bright tracers flying out of the gun barrels with a sharp *buuurrrrppp*. He pulled up and left, and looked down at his target—which continued on unhurt.

Dammit! Weed thought to himself. *Too much lead!*

Dog rolled in and followed Weed's example, putting a *Sidewinder* into a near, and then a far, *Hind*. The second lost its tail boom which caused the fuselage to rotate out of control and career into the trees. Two aircraft in one run—a feat probably not accomplished since World War II—but Dog pulled off out of missiles *and* at bingo fuel.

Cisco rolled in from the opposite direction and targeted a *Hip*. The Venezuelans could not see the Americans, but they now knew they were there and began to expend flares. The lucky *Hip* expended a band of flares just as Cisco's missile was tracking it, and the seeker head glommed onto the flares and exploded harmlessly. He strafed another helo and scored hits, turning it out of formation to the east.

Four down, six to go. And they were approaching the LZ.

Weed ignored Dog's fuel plight and was back in with his second missile, his target a hot *Hind* against a "cool" backdrop of forest. From inside a mile, he fired. The missile wiggled as it accelerated and blew the rotor disk off the aircraft, which rolled flaming into the trees and was followed by a large fuel-air explosion. He then aimed for the farthest aircraft when a band of bullets shot in front of him and caused him to pull up hard. Horrified, Weed realized he could not keep the attackers away from the *Rustlers*. He had to warn them.

"*Rustlers*, we're trying, but some are going to get through! Do you have everyone?"

"Survivors coming inside now, sir. Shit, looks like more than we thought!"

"Well, the gunships are going to be there in less than a minute!"

Cisco rolled in for a second time—Weed didn't have track of Dog— and another helicopter, a *Hip*, was shot out of the sky. *Five down.*

"Dog, where are you?" Weed snapped on radio.

"I'm bingo, sir. Holding max endurance!"

Weed lost his patience. "Get down here and keep firing until you're Winchester!"

"Aye, sir!" the chagrined pilot answered.

The Venezuelans were splitting up. Weed could now see one *Sierra* on deck near the cabin and another orbiting to the east.

"*Rustlers*, they're coming from the south. Doing our best to pick them off!" Weed warned. He rolled in on a *Hind* and blasted it with 20mm, leading it better this time, and saw flashes pop up all around the fuselage and rotors. Another enemy helicopter pulled away to the east, wounded but still airborne. Weed ignored it. *Four left.*

"Here they come, *Rustlers!*"

"We see 'em," Sean transmitted back. He saw the wounded *Hind* that one of the *Super Hornets* had winged and determined it no factor. Behind it was another one, and he swung his *Sierra* low over the trees and down the right side of the *Hind* to get behind it. It then occurred to him one of the fighters could confuse him for enemy, and he transmitted, "*Hunters, Rustler* six-one-two is rolling in on a *Hind* southeast of the LZ, trailing the one you guys drove away."

"Tally! *Visual!*" Cisco sang out, and turned his attention to another gunship—one that posed a direct threat to the *Sierra* getting ready to load survivors near the cabin.

In 612, Petty Officer Second Class Mark Ryan, a rescue swimmer manning the left door M240, saw the same enemy threat that Cisco did. Inside 1,000 meters, he noted the enemy flight path converging on him with little drift. He looked over his right shoulder at Sean in the cockpit right seat. "Sir, I've got a *Hind* at our nine-thirty, about 500 meters!"

Sean, his "bucket" of situational awareness overflowing, concentrated on the *Hind* in front of him and keyed the ICS. "Open fire!" he blurted out as he maneuvered above the tree tops behind *his* gunship—a target that did not know Sean's *Sierra* was behind it.

Mark energized the weapon and, with adrenalin coursing through him, squeezed the trigger hard. The 7.62 rounds flew out from the *Sierra* under the rotor arc as he assessed lead, while tracking his target five football fields away. The *Hind* ahead of Sean rolled right, maybe warned by the guy Mark was shooting at, and, as Sean reacted, Mark's round flew high over the *Hind*.

"Fuck," Mark cried over the ICS.

Just then, *Rustler* 610 radioed, "Fucking A, Sean, your gunner hit that guy comin' for us. He's smokin' and heading west!"

"*Sierra Hotel!*" Sean answered, then keyed the ICS. "Way to fuckin' go, Petty Officer Ryan! That's your kill!"

A surprised Mark smiled under the plastic screen that protected his face from windblast. The *Sierra* lurched again, and Sean had another job for him.

"All right, Ryan, we got a *Hind* ahead of us, eleven o'clock, about 800 meters! You have a tally?"

Mark swung the gun to the forward stops and stuck his head outside. On his goggles, he could see the thin silhouette of a gunship in a slight left turn.

"Tallyho!"

"*Open fire!*"

Mark squeezed the trigger again as Sean maneuvered the *Sierra* above and behind the *Hind* to lag it and give Mark a clear shot. Mark aimed for the tail rotor of the armored gunship, the weakest part of the airframe, and unloaded on it with short bursts. Sensing the threat from behind, the *Hind* reversed hard right.

Sean saw an overshoot coming. "Petty Officer Young, get ready. *Hind* comin' out our one o'clock. Three hundred meters!"

"*Tally!*"

"*Open fire!*"

The right door gunner unloaded, from near point-blank range, a long burst from his M240 into the *Hind* as it turned hard and traversed down the *Sierra's* right side. Through their goggles, the aircrew saw scattered impact flashes along the fuselage and rotor arc. Sean lifted his aircraft into a high yo-yo to stop the overshoot and to give his door gunner the best field of fire. Now looking *down* on it, Young poured fire into the top of the wounded gunship. Within seconds it was out of control and exploded as it went into the trees.

"Splash one *Hind!*" Sean crowed on the radio. "Nice job, guys!" he added on the ICS.

When Weed saw the gunship explode to the east, he figured the *Sierra* trailing it was 612. But he was losing situational awareness, The *Rustler* on deck near the cabin accounted for one of the *Sierras*, but the other was now mixed in with three—*Or is it four?*—enemy gunships. He had to get SA back, *fast.*

Two enemy helos bore down on the LZ, and none of the fighters were in a position to stop them. The gunships were in a stepped up tac wing formation and were right on top of the site. Weed's heart was in his throat as he transmitted, "*Rustler* six-ten. Two are right on top of you!" The *Hinds* could shred the *Sierra*, the cabin, and everyone in them in one pass. He pulled his *Rhino* left to track the lead aircraft, which appeared to be a *Hip.* He winced, expecting multiple bands of killing fire to explode from the gunships in a slashing attack. To his shocked surprise, the helicopters shot past without firing. Maybe they missed the site or were unsure.

A reprieve.

Weed was filled with professional admiration for the Venezuelans, men with little combat experience or representative threat training, who came in against heavy odds. However, he had a job to do, and more brave men would have to die for him to accomplish it.

Bingo. Bingo.

The passionless voice of *Tammy* sounded in Weed's headset. Mission fuel was gone, but he had no choice but to stay. *Fuck it!* Weed thought. They would land in Port of Spain or Grenada if need be. The Venezuelans split, and Weed took the leader turning through northwest.

"Two's in on the lead!" Dog called, back in the fight.

Concerned, Weed scanned the horizon for his wingman…and could not find him. He then craned his head up and, in one motion, pulled up and right before his heartbeat could even increase from the shot of adrenaline pumped into it. Coming down like a safe next to him was Dog, who, concentrating on the *Hip,* had lost track of his lead and not done a belly check. But for Weed's defensive driving, both aircraft would have occupied the same piece of sky. An unnerved Weed pulled off the *Hip*.

"You better shoot him, Dog!"

The *Hip* was zipping along the treetops in a left-hand turn with Dog high and to the inside. The young pilot had to make another high-deflection crossing shot—in a dive—and had to keep altitude in his scan to avoid flying into the ground. Dog was diving, tracking, and turning as the *Hip* pulled hard into him. Dog squeezed a burst, then another and saw no impacts on the fuselage or blades. The aircraft grew larger in his HUD and he couldn't miss...

"*Watch your altitude!*" Weed shouted on the radio. Dog snatched his jet up at over eight g's. The *Hip* survived, and the nugget pilot escaped 100 feet over the trees as he pulled up and away. His heart pounded when he realized how close he had come.

"Dog, come off right. Lead's in. Cisco, can you take the other guy?"

"*Which is which!?*" the confused lieutenant shot back. He had lost SA in this free-wheeling rotary-wing shell game.

Weed came at the *Hip* head on and hosed it as he passed one mile in range. Sparkling flashes appeared on the nose and rotor disk as Weed steepened his dive, keeping one eye on altitude so he would not make Dog's error. His gun stopped firing—*Winchester!*—and Weed pulled off left as the wobbling and burning *Hip* staggered into the trees and exploded.

One left, a *Hind*. And it was circling back to exact revenge on the most vulnerable American asset.

CHAPTER 79

(The Devil's Woodyard)

Rovelli and another SEAL helped Wilson as the Marines and Doc Woodruff dragged Jill into the *Sierra*. Two other SEALs and the door gunners covered them with fire into the tree line. Wilson noted the familiar *Seahawk* airframe, and, when the M240 fired, it illuminated the USS CORAL SEA stenciling above the cabin door. Rotor wash swirled dust and leaves about them, and, without earplugs or a helmet, the roar of the helicopter engines and spinning rotors overhead was deafening. He saw the pilot motion for them to hurry up, and the SEALs picked him up to carry him, rather than help him, over the ground.

They pushed Wilson inside, and he sprawled on the cabin floor next to Jill. His pain returned as the SEALs shouted, fired, and jostled for position inside the cabin. Numerous 7.62 rounds exploded from their barrels on either side of him, and he sensed the change in the whine of the high-pitched engine and felt the airframe lurch amid the confused noise and swirling air. He wasn't strapped in and realized he didn't care.

In the cockpit of 610, Lieutenant Justin "Oscar" Meier heard the fighters' crosstalk on the radio about a *Hind* circling to the southwest and posing a threat. He figured it was the same one that had over flown their position minutes ago. He didn't know why the Venezuelan gunships hadn't fired as they roared over and didn't want to know. He picked up the attack helicopter through the trees at his two o'clock. Moving right to left in front of them, it was turning left and would soon come back. *Frickin' jet guys!* It was their job to keep the threat away*! What are they doing?* he thought. *They need to shoot that sumbitch!*

"They're all aboard, sir!" the door gunner sang out over the ICS. Two metal punches were heard from somewhere behind them in the tail boom. "Get us outta here!" he cried as he hosed down the tree line near the priest's shack.

"Okay! Hang on! Comin' up." Oscar answered.

With a death grip, he lifted the collective and felt the aircraft rise. He also *felt* the extra weight of thirteen souls in back and fed rudder to keep the aircraft aligned as he pushed the cyclic forward while increasing collective. The *Sierra's* nose pitched down as the rotors dug into the air to propel it forward. On the climb out, Oscar picked up the *Hind* inside a mile, rolling in for another run. He keyed the mike.

"*Hunters, Rustler* six-one-zero lifting with fifteen souls and a *Hind* on my nose!"

"Roger. Visual. Tally!" Weed radioed back. "Cisco, Dog, *shoot it!*"

Oscar heard the desperation in Commander Hopper's voice and sensed he could not depend on his escort fighters to help. Sean was not in a position to help, and while his own M240 pea-shooters were not designed to bring down an armored helo, they were something. The two helicopters were going to a merge, and, for now, his only chance was to defend himself.

With his mind racing, Oscar increased speed and charged at the threat. At the same time, he keyed the ICS to direct his co-pilot, Lieutenant Junior Grade Alison "Cheese" Kirkman.

"Cheese, lase him! Target the *Hind, now!*"

Head down in the cockpit while Oscar flew, Cheese brought up the laser designator on the nose and slewed it toward the approaching aircraft. At the same time Oscar tapped right rudder and informed his left gunner.

"Petty Officer Sackheim, we got a *Hind* on the nose at eleven-thirty. *Open fire!* Bringing it down the left side!"

With the sound of a chainsaw, the M240 spit a stream of bullets ahead of the *Sierra* and toward the nose of the onrushing gunship. "*Are you lasing him, dammit?*" Oscar cried to Cheese.

"Yes, shit, *yes!*" she blurted back.

Both pilots were anxious as they flew at the growing menace. The gunners behind them detected in their pilots' voices, and of the two, only Sackheim on the left door gun really knew the danger they were in.

Flickering light appeared on the *Hind's* nose, flame from the muzzle flash of the twin Gsh-23 cannon barrels slung under its nose. The horrified aviators flinched as the bullet stream passed below them. Sackheim continued to pump 7.62 rounds into the flying tank coming at them and heard himself release a primal scream as if any second a cannon round would take his head off. It went against every one of Oscar's instincts to keep themselves "skinny" by flying at the threat. However, looking down their barrels presented the enemy gunner with the least amount of rotor cross-section to hit and allowed Oscar to close the distance and thereby escape their cone of fire as quickly as possible. The enemy rounds were missing right and Oscar heard Sackheim's gun go silent—Winchester. He then pedaled left to give Petty Officer Souza, the right gunner, a clear shot and avoid flying into the 23mm buzz saw. The gunner got off a few bursts as Cheese worked to keep the laser on the enemy cockpit. Oscar lifted the aircraft to get above the *Hind* and restrict its field of fire. He felt an explosion next to his right shoulder.

In the cabin, Wilson felt the aircraft lurch this way and that as the door gunners blazed away at something. Despite the violent maneuvering, it didn't faze Wilson that he wasn't strapped in; he was surrounded by bodies. In the low light, he saw Rovelli's impassive face. Powerless to act, Rovelli stared ahead at nothing, knowing that worry could not make the situation better. It was up to the aviators now.

Something hit the aircraft, *hard*. A spray of small fragments entered the cabin and caused everyone to flinch. Amid the profane cries, Wilson heard someone shout, "*Hoist!*" and the firing continued from the gunner on the right. He noted that Rovelli made the sign of the cross and closed his eyes. *Not a bad idea,* Wilson thought.

Up forward, Oscar noted the *Hind* drifting left—*The laser may have dazzled him or blinded him!*—and continued left to keep his nose on. The enemy cannon rounds were missing well left, and Oscar was able to roll in behind the gunship. Remembering some *Hind* variants had their own door gunners, he didn't press it too close.

"Okay, I'm falling off right. Keep lasing as long as you can, Cheese. Cease fire, Souza. And maintain a tally, Sackheim." They all acknowledged him on the ICS. As quickly as the threat had appeared, it had receded.

Weed watched from 2,000 feet above, and saw Cisco come in to hose down the *Hind*, but the *Sierra* following it was too close. *Dammit,* he cursed to himself as he pulled off to get a better angle.

The Venezuelan formation had only one helicopter left to cause trouble. Unsure if it was in control, Weed's fighters, out of bullets, monitored it going east. The helo pulled up right, then rolled left in a dive. It wavered back to the right, then overbanked, and the pursuers could see it was doomed. It flew into the trees upside down and exploded two miles from the cabin.

Oscar and Cheese watched the struggling gunship the whole time, both sickened when it rolled on its back. They knew the pilot was somehow incapacitated—*probably blind*—and they were the cause of it. It was kill or be killed over The Devil's Woodyard, and they were victorious. But Oscar was surprised by his subdued reaction; he felt no "victory roll" bravado, no need for a fist pump. He keyed the ICS. "We got him, guys. He's down.

We're outta here." Oscar heard grateful shouts from the cabin as the word passed around. He rolled left to the northwest and home.

Weed gathered his wingmen in a running rendezvous to the northwest. They had to abandon the slower helicopters, and the fighters were well below bingo fuel. He didn't bother with Trinidad airspace restrictions as he climbed up between the buildups into the clear sky above—*big sky, little airplane*—and called the ship. A tanker was going to meet them southwest of Grenada, and, if they couldn't plug, they could duck into the island to land and get fuel. It would be close. It always was. He wondered if Flip was okay and keyed the mike.

"*Rustler, Hunter.* You got *Slash* one-one?"

"Affirm, sir. Got him."

"Roger," Weed answered as he let out a sigh of relief. His friend was okay.

Wilson heard that the threat had passed and they were heading home. As he came down from his adrenalin high, exhaustion swept over him, as did the pain, not the least of which was the pain caused to his eardrums by the screaming whine of the engine turbines above and the jackhammer thump of the spinning rotors. As if reading his thoughts, a crewman helped him don a cranial helmet which provided some relief and served as a better "pillow" than nothing. The SEAL corpsman took his wrist to assess his pulse and keep him comfortable.

Sleep. *Just sleep.* It was over, and he was alive. Three days in the woods, or was it four? He had made it. *Father Dan!* Wilson lifted his head to find him and saw the profile of his head. He raised his left hand, and Father Dan grasped it. Wilson closed his eyes, and drifted off. He was still surrounded by bodies, twelve stunned and gasping human beings crammed into the cabin. Most of them were strangers, people he had never met, strangers who had risked everything for him.

Edgar Hernandez waited in the command post. His life had come down to this: depending on the Army to snatch and grab the American pilot from an old priest. He had to give them their due. Crossing the channel was something they had never done before, and the Google Earth image of what everyone *thought* was the cabin and copies of some aviation sectional charts were all they had to go by. These kids were young and scared. Venezuela had supplied them with Mi-35m2 *Caribes*, the best helicopter gunship in the world, better than the American *Apache*, no expense spared. But the crews were ill-trained, even worse than his *Viper* pilots. They didn't know how to fly their machines to the limit and knew even less about mutual support. The *Super Pumas* had gone ahead without an escort! And he and Daniel now expected them to pull off a miracle and get Wilson before the Americans did. Two minutes ago radar at San Ramón reported a formation of American fighters over Trinidad. "Dammit," he swore under his breath.

Twenty minutes passed, and the command post received only broken radio transmissions from the *Caribes*. Then, excited cries.... *One down. Two.* They see the cabin and are returning! *Yes.* Then long minutes of nothing.

After ten minutes of unnerving silence, a young voice called the tower at San Ramón for clearance to land. "Dammit, I want a mission report from that aircraft!" Hernandez fumed.

Another minute passed, and the pilot transmitted again. "All lost.... American *Hornets. Seahawk....* No success.... Injured. One engine out."

Hernandez understood the meaning of the disjointed transmission. *Failure.* And imminent death. For him, his wife, and his children. Daniel would not forget. It might not happen this week, but Daniel would act before the month was over: a brutal execution of his family one-by-one while Hernandez watched. When the other American was plucked from the waters off the capitol, his back-up plan had been dashed as well, despite the loss of another American fighter whose pilot reportedly rode it in.

He shuddered at the thought of what he had to do.

He met the Army *Hind* crew on the flight line as they climbed out of their damaged helicopter and inspected the jagged holes where American cannon punctured the aluminum skin around the boom. The Plexiglas of the nose gunner's canopy had two impact marks on the left side and another on the skin under the door release; the gunner had been saved by armor plate. The aircraft and its crewmen were lucky—they and the *Super Puma* that escaped before the fight began were the only survivors. Twelve helicopters were sent and two returned...and Hernandez knew that if the Americans had really wanted these two aircraft they could have had them.

The Army pilots were wide-eyed in bewildered shock. The four soldiers they had carried in the cabin, weak from airsickness and fear, accepted the shots of brandy handed to them by the doctor. The pilots were uneasy with the fact they were alive and feared they would be shot. They feared more, though, the stigma of not having died honorably against the enemy. They begged to go back and share the fate of their dead countrymen. Hernandez had known from the beginning it was a long shot to send these men. His aide walked up and told him the initial count was *fifty-nine* dead or missing, mostly soldiers in the back of the aircraft who had a zero chance of survival. These young pilots would be haunted by this night—and the faces of their mates—well into old age, as would Hernandez. He took a shot of brandy when he thought no one was looking and downed it. Dozens of other shots remained on the tray…unclaimed by the dead.

Who knew how many seamen had died trying to capture the downed American off Caracas? Even though the Americans had again snatched one of their own from under the noses of the Venezuelans, the effort had at least claimed another *Hornet* whose pilot did not get out. However, one dead American pilot and two downed *Hornets,* compared to numerous destroyed surface-to-surface missile sites, a half dozen fighters and ten or more helos, was no comparison at all. The Bolivarian Republic could not sustain these losses, not even one more day. This was their maximum effort, and it had all ended in failure. Capturing *one* American alive would have made the toll worth it—but it was not to be.

Buoyed by a second shot of liquid courage, Hernandez summoned his aide. "Prepare a *Viper*, wingtip missiles only, and full twenty millimeter." The reluctant aide went off to do as he was ordered while Hernandez scanned the flight line, now quiet, nearly empty of aircraft. He looked up at the moon and studied the way the silvery backlit clouds to the south clung to the mountains, the mountains of his childhood.

The taxiway was the runway least damaged by the initial American raid, and the repairs were complete. It allowed plenty of concrete for Hernandez, and he suited up in silence while forming his plan. Expressionless, he strode to the jet, conscious of the crewmen who snapped to attention in an orderly row. His aide appeared, face full of sorrow. "The aircraft is prepared, mí general."

"Good," a stoic Hernandez replied as he preflighted the jet. The crewmen followed him through each step, ready to address any anomaly he found. Hernandez completed his inspection as if on autopilot, and once he was again at the ladder, he gave his aide his wedding ring and took his St. Christopher's medallion from around his neck. The somber ground crew knew the meaning of his actions, but they were unwilling and unable to stop him. Hernandez reached into his vest and pulled out his parachute shroud cutter. He reached up to his forehead, grabbed a length of dark, wavy hair, and cut it. He then placed the hair inside his garrison cap emblazoned with the insignia of a *Mayor General* of the *Fuerza Aérea Venezolana* and handed it to the shaken capitán.

"*Señor—*"

Hernandez silenced him with a look, and turned to salute the crew who once again had formed into a rank next to the jet. Whatever the AMV lacked in capability, these men made up for in spirit. Despite failing them, Hernandez had been proud to lead them.

Hernandez finished strapping in as the plane captain descended the ladder in tears, and he soon signaled to start. The huffer air inflated the hose with a rigid *whoosh,* and the engine cranked over and soon reached a piercing whine. Hernandez lowered the canopy.

The men did their normal checks, and Hernandez signaled to pull chocks. The crew saluted as the F-16 taxied past them. The solemn pilot returned their salutes and turned right to the taxiway, cycling the controls as if to wave goodbye.

With lights out, Hernandez took the taxiway and lined up. His radios were off. He had no need to talk to anyone, ever again.

Hernandez roared down the taxiway and got airborne. The dazzling white-hot burner cone illuminated the jet against the darkness as those on the ground watched. Pulling out of burner, Hernandez rolled right at 100 feet and held the jet just above the treetops as he set a course to the northwest. As the booming rumble of his engine receded, he disappeared behind the trees, and after three minutes, his men could no longer hear it.

Hernandez flew past Río Salta and over the channel, still at 100 feet and now 420 knots. With the dark outline of Paria on the horizon, he aimed at Daniel's compound on the ridge and stayed low on the water, lower than he had ever been at night. As the peninsula loomed up, he climbed so he could pass over it in near level flight and not break the radar horizon. The *American* radar horizon, not his own.

Hernandez accelerated, pushing past "the number" just as he approached Daniel's mountaintop retreat. He didn't know if Daniel was there or not, but he concentrated in order to stay level and out of the trees. The crest of the mountain and a palatial *hacienda* flashed underneath as he rocketed past, and a man outside on the grounds blinked in disbelief as he saw a silent apparition approach at incredible speed. It *exploded* above him, and the sonic boom knocked him to the ground and shattered large panes of glass throughout the house.

Over the waters of the Caribbean, Hernandez transitioned from supersonic to transonic flight. Although held by the straps, Hernandez slid forward in his seat and felt as if he had hit an invisible wall. His intelligence officers thought the American carrier was another 200 miles ahead, so he would keep his emissions under control until he passed by Grenada. He would then energize his radar and *hope* to dash his jet into the American control tower and take their admiral with him to Valhalla. But, first, he had to find the carrier and selected a fuel efficient engine setting as he again descended to the deck.

Hernandez was taking the easy way—what some would call the coward's way—but was it "cowardly" to man a fighter jet and dash it into the side of a ship? *At night?* No, the AMV was no match against the Americans. Everyone knew it. But if he could sacrifice his life to bloody the Americans where it hurt them most—their damned floating airfields— he would do it. That should dissuade them from further action against his beloved Venezuela. He had grown up learning that taking one's life was a mortal sin. As he concentrated on maintaining altitude, he knew that he had crossed the mortal sin threshold long ago. How could God ever forgive him his many sins? Hernandez knew he would be dead within the hour, probably sooner. He could no longer live with shame and dishonor and could no longer face anyone, even himself. *It is in God's hands now*, Hernandez thought as he continued north. He then dismissed that thought, unable even to face the thought of a merciful God. Considering the vastness of eternity, this was the most courageous thing he had ever done.

After twelve minutes he saw on his inertial navigation moving map that Grenada was fifty miles to his right. He also saw a dark ship with running lights to his left and avoided it. Once clear, he energized the radar and kept his eyes scanning for a large, flat silhouette, the moon providing a satisfactory level of light. He didn't have enough fuel now to return to his homeland—he *would* die over the Caribbean. Indifferent to it all, he noted the stars and silent clouds above him,

Ten more minutes passed, and Hernandez saw nothing but water. *Where are they?* His radar warning receiver picked up an emission at his one o'clock, and he deflected the side-stick to center it. He bumped up his speed to 540 ground, nine miles per minute. Then at forty miles his radar picked up a large and sharp return, with a smaller return next to it. Several miles away was another slash. *Ships!* And the big return must be the carrier. He eased left to center it. Thirty miles.

Hernandez selected mid-range burner and increased speed to over 600 knots, edging up to supersonic. Two thousand pounds of fuel left. *Plenty. The carrier is right there!* He had never seen one before, but now, inside ten miles, he had no doubt that was it. Ahead of him was a long object, a little square with yellowish lights resting on it...lights that suddenly extinguished! His threat receiver had multiple indications, and sensing the wave tops as they glistened below him in the faint crescent moonlight, he got down to fifty feet, concentrating as never before on maintaining altitude with his radar altimeter.

The hulking shape was heading west, and Hernandez pushed the throttle all the way up. He heard the engine rumble increase and felt the aircraft buck from the airspeed. Inside five miles, he saw a bright light shoot from his target and observed small lights coming from one end. He thought he saw a flash from a ship on the horizon, followed by another, but he put the images out of his mind. The carrier was turning away from him, and he saw lights again flash from the back of it and then whip over his canopy. *Bullets!*

Unseen by Edgar Hernandez, an SM-2 Standard missile launched from the vertical launch tubes of USS *Gettysburg* four miles away and exploded its proximity-fused warhead over him, shredding his fuselage and pushing his nose up. Hernandez gasped at the sudden ten g's on his chest and saw he was climbing. He would get another ch—

His *Viper* tore itself apart as the relative force of 700-knot air molecules gushed into the jagged holes that appeared on the smooth airframe skin, the supersonic aluminum dashing itself headlong into the transonic "wall." A Rolling Airframe Missile launched from the carrier entered the maelstrom of metal and detonated, while CIWS 20mm bullets finished the job on unrecognizable masses of hurtling debris, chopping them up further as they plummeted into the sea off *Coral Sea's* fantail. The *Viper's* engine, still in burner as the fuselage was ripped away from it, devoured the last bit of fuel in the flaming lines and arced over *Coral Sea* with wild fiery oscillations, seeking something to control it, *someone* to *command* it. It's hot turbine blades exploded into spray and steam once they met the cool surface of the dark Caribbean swells on the other side of the carrier.

What was left of Mayor General Edgar Hernandez also splashed into the sea, his final resting place unmarked.

CHAPTER 80

A dazed Wilson felt 610 enter a hover. He sensed the rotors and engines change pitch and felt the floor beneath him twitch as the pilots maneuvered the *Sierra* over the embassy landing pad at Port of Spain.

When the gunners opened the side doors, he wasn't sure where he was but noted a tree and a building through one of the openings. The Marines, Garcia and Smith, and Doc Woodruff got out, as did Jill, who was now ambulatory. They each, in turn, reached down to where he sat on the floor and patted him on his good shoulder. Wilson returned a weak smile. When Monique got out, Sackheim held her arm so she would not stray into trouble beneath the rotors of the still turning helicopter. While Sackheim waited for Father Dan so that he could escort them both inside, a barrel of aviation gasoline was wheeled over to the helo. An embassy employee helped Petty Officer Souza pump the helo with fuel sufficient to get to *Coral Sea* over 200 miles away.

Father Dan scooted past Wilson to the door and grabbed Wilson's right hand. "Good luck, lad," he shouted. "I hope you are reunited with your family soon."

"Father," Wilson spoke over the din.

"Yes?"

"Thank you," Wilson croaked. "*Thank you...*"

The priest made a sign of the cross over Wilson and brought his hands together in a blessing. "Now go and spread the good news of the Lord!" he shouted.

Wilson nodded, and Father Dan swung his legs over and hopped down to the ground to join Monique. Sackheim took them both forward of the nose and away to safety.

"Father?" Wilson called out, but the priest was gone.

Within minutes the refueling was complete, and the gunners jumped inside and closed the doors as the helo lifted. Wilson gazed at the lights of the city until they receded from view, replaced by the black Caribbean waters. The vibration of the machine lulled the cabin passengers to sleep, and the SEALs dozed head down on their gear during the long transit to the ship.

Wilson stared at the darkened cabin overhead. Its wire bundles and bare frames, exposed as in all military aircraft, were bathed in the faint green glow of the cockpit lighting. *Alive.* He was alive...against all odds. How did he get out over San Ramón? How did he survive the terror of the thunderstorm, the broken limbs as he crawled through the jungle, the firefights with cartel thugs and the Venezuelan Army? He had shot several men—and killed two. In his *Hornet* cockpit he was seldom sure if he had killed. Today he was.

He thought of all those who had rescued him. Jill, Doc, and the Marines. The SEALs dozing next to him, men he had never met. People on the ship, no doubt, like Annie and CAG and Admiral Davies. They hadn't abandoned him but had ordered these men and this *Rustler* crew to risk their lives. And Wilson knew they had done so willingly, eager to risk all to save him—even though none of them had a personal relationship with him. Wilson was an American fighting man. That was good enough for them.

He thought of Father Dan. The priest had saved him, fed him, bathed him, defended him, and ministered to him. Harboring Wilson was a sure risk, and the arrival of the drug thugs had confirmed it. Father Dan was only a missionary serving the inhabitants of The Devil's Woodyard. *Until I showed up,* Wilson thought. He knew he would contact the priest somehow once he could write. Maryknoll. They could get him a letter. Wilson would return one day, too, once things with Venezuela got back to normal.

Wilson saw lights far to the east, an island. He motioned to a crewman to ask what it was. The petty officer keyed his ICS to ask the pilots. A few seconds later, he spoke near Wilson's ear. "Grenada, sir."

They droned on, and Wilson saw another *Sierra* in formation with them. He looked at his combat watch. It had stopped. *No matter,* he thought. *We'll get there when we get there.*

Wilson then thought of Mary. He wanted to be next to her, to hold her, to forgive her—and to ask her to forgive the fact he had ignored her with his preoccupation with command—even when ashore. Derrick. He needed a dad to care for him, a dad who was just there listening, not smothering. They all needed balance.

His leg was killing him.

Another 30 minutes passed, and Wilson sensed the descent of the helo. The SEALs did, too, and by the activity of the swimmers, he knew the ship must be near. They entered a turn, followed by another one, and Wilson could make out the ship a mile abeam. A *Hornet* was crossing the ramp; they were in the middle of a recovery.

More turns followed, and Wilson watched through the window when he could. He caught sight of an E-2 rolling out in the landing area and knew they would be given a signal to land next. They flew aft of the ship and turned right to final, the aircraft jerking and twitching as the pilots maneuvered it on the ball. One of the swimmers opened the right door as the pilot lifted the nose higher, and Wilson saw *Hornets* parked on the starboard shelf. The *Sierra* slowed along the landing area, past the island, to its landing spot at the edge of the angle. Wilson saw a medical team on the foul line and spied CAG in among them. After the aircraft weight transitioned from the rotor blades to the landing gear tires, the swimmers hopped out. Blue shirts then scrambled to the *Sierra* with wheel chocks as squadron personnel followed with tie-down chains.

Wilson was home. Safe. *Alive.*

Medical personnel helped him out of the aircraft as CAG pushed through them. "We missed you, Flip!" he shouted over the noise as he extended his hand. Wilson took it and smiled back. Behind him were Stretch and Olive. Grateful to see him, they all helped him to El 2 so he could bypass the multiple ladders leading down to sick bay. Once the alarm rang, the elevator descended to the hangar bay as warm Caribbean salt air cascaded down the hull.

They put him on a stretcher and carried him to an ammo elevator while dozens of sailors observed. As the hangar bay crew rigged the safety lines, Olive and Stretch stood back and watched. Wilson turned his head and caught their attention. "Where's Annie? Flying?" he asked.

Wilson saw their faces fall just as the elevator lowered him down. He knew. He was still trying to process the blow when the elevator door opened next to him, and the medical response team lifted him out to the florescent world of the forward mess decks. Numb, Wilson stared up at the overhead as they carried him down the port passageway to sick bay.

The 1MC sounded: "T-*weeeet*... Now stand by for the evening prayer."

Daniel recoiled from a shower of salt spray as the boat bucked on the swells between Paria and Trinidad. Lights out, they passed the darkened shape of Isla de Patos to the south, the halfway point on their thirty-minute transit to Trinidad, and safety. A G5 awaited him at the airport, but the timing was going to be close. Everything depended on Daniel's men paying off key men at critical points. Right now, they had to get past the Coast Guard station in order to dock at the coastal village of La Retraite where a car awaited to take them to the airport.

Once in the car, it took, even in the wee hours, over an hour to get through Port of Spain. Needing a shave, Daniel wore a Washington Nationals baseball cap and sat in the passenger seat of a used Honda Civic, hiding in plain sight. His three other loyal thugs followed in a beat-up Opel. *Stay calm and look bored....* He had done this before.

Daniel knew that Ramos would soon grab Annibel and the kids, raping his wife and terrorizing the girls to exact his revenge. Daniel felt bad and tried to blot it from his mind. They wouldn't have to suffer long—Ramos would kill them.

The group made it to the airport and stepped aboard the G5 without any luggage, and, as the door was closed, the pilots started the engines. Greasing the palms of linesmen and two air traffic controllers was easy, and the aircraft taxied for takeoff within minutes. In the cabin, two female flight attendants, dressed appropriately, served as the in-flight entertainment for Daniel and his men.

Daniel was dozing as they made their final approach to Madeira. Then, after spreading more cash, they were airborne again, this time for Minorca. He thought of the traitor Edgar, and thought about the wife and family he had left behind for Daniel to brutalize. He wouldn't mind raping his daughter, Daniel thought, but it was too late for that now. One day, he vowed, he *would* have Edgar's son killed.

It was late afternoon when the *Gulfstream* landed at the quiet 8,500-foot strip, and another car took them to a safe house at Cap d'en Font. They ate a quick meal before scrambling down to the beach to a waiting launch that allowed them to clear the jagged coastline as the sun sank into the Mediterranean. The fifty-mile crossing to Mallorca required three hours of pounding across moderate seas. Although Daniel was able to avoid the spray and stay dry in the cabin, he became seasick. His mood improved as he saw Mallorca draw near, and he hoped he could rally for a little nightlife, banking that what little Catalan Spanish he knew would suffice. And he planned to buy everyone a round of drinks before retiring to his room. *The whole bar! The whole town!* His boys had done well. They would own this little town tonight, and tomorrow they would begin building his empire anew, this time in southern Europe. This, too, he had done before. Daniel noted the clouds above were backlit by a waxing moon, and they reminded him of the puffy clouds about Paria. He could get to like this place.

The engine stopped, and a puzzled Daniel turned to the coxswain. His second, Alphonse, who had been loyal to him for twelve years—since Colombia days—drew a pistol and pointed it at him. *"Esta la hora, mí amigo."*

Hurt, Daniel looked at him in shock as the boat rocked on the waves. *Why?* he thought.

The others watched, unconcerned. Daniel then surprised himself with a slight grin and nodded his acceptance. *I let my guard down.* Familiar with the routine, Daniel did not resist as the men grabbed him, tied his hands behind his back, and attached dive weights to his ankles. They took his valuables, including the switchblade he had used to save Alphonse's life that night in Medellin so long ago, and led him to the stern. Daniel had a final request.

"I was good to you, Alphonse. May I go with a bullet? Like a man?"

In the shadows Daniel saw Alphonse acquiesce with a gentleman's nod. *"Certainly, my friend."*

Daniel looked in turn at the others, what passed for his friends, as he accepted his fate. He knelt on the transom, surprised he had the urge to pray. He had not said a prayer in years, not since his boyhood in Buenaventura.

"Padre Nuestro..." he whispered.

The bullet tore off the top of Daniel's head, and his limp body fell overboard. The weights caught up in the gunwale and left Daniel hanging upside down until one of the men freed the weights so they could lead Daniel's dead body 200 feet below the channel.

The torch had been passed, and Alphonse motioned to the coxswain to continue toward the city. He saw blood on the transom and motioned to another to hose it off as he turned to look west at the lights of Mallorca, their new home—where he would begin the first day of *his* new empire.

CHAPTER 80

(USS *Coral Sea*, Central Caribbean)

The following day, *Coral Sea* turned her bow north.

Venezuela's military had suffered days of crippling blows from the Americans. Its message delivered, the United States withdrew to maintain strategic stability in the region, hoping for a revolution of moderate reformers who would return the country to a liberal free-market democracy. With NATO alerted and surface and air units arrayed from the Denmark Strait to the North Cape, the Russians stood down, having watched with amusement as NATO, and especially the United States, had spun up for nothing. Knowing the Americans would exhaust themselves for years to come, the Russians prepared for a too brief summer on the Kola Peninsula and husbanded their resources for the next time they could make Washington jump.

Likewise, the Cubans withdrew most—but not all—of their forces from along the fence line at Guantanamo. In smug satisfaction they believed that, true to form, the Americans would concentrate their forces in and around the southeastern tip of Cuba, which would open the rest of the Caribbean to cartel traffic as before. The waters off Venezuela and the West Indies would continue to be a future deployment theater for carrier strike groups as a sign of Washington's interest, despite the fact it pulled needed resources from the Middle East and the Mediterranean, which was becoming a rough neighborhood again, the likes of which the U.S. Navy had not seen since the long-ago days of the Barbary Pirates.

Indeed, the Venezuelans had been taught a lesson—with the AMV half destroyed and its Army aviation losing significant frontline capability. The Bolivarian Republic had kept their Navy in port to spare it, and the Army remained all but intact, calming nerves in Foggy Bottom where stability was sought above all else. To Washington, all of Latin America had been taught a lesson about American power and resolve—a lesson that was lost on Latin America. Countries in the region saw that Venezuela, which enjoyed poking Uncle Sam in the eye, had paid a relatively small price for doing so, and they knew, after a while, the United States would lose

431

interest. The Bolivarian Republic could then resume their previous activities, whether aboveboard or underground, confident that the Yankees would not soon return. Venezuela had not been defeated, which itself was a win, and plans went ahead to erect a statue of the Mayor General Edgar Hernandez. The gallant hero had led the AMV into battle against superior American forces and had given his life while saving South American soil from invasion and humiliating subjugation.

In the end, the United States settled for containment, and the region could be managed at the price of the drug trade and limiting for now the small beachheads of bad actors like Russia and an increasingly muscular China.

The United States could *hope* for stability...a national pastime in Washington.

In places like Miami, Norfolk, and the Pentagon, staff officers pored over the effectiveness reports of CENTURY RATCHET and analyzed the air campaign over Venezuela. Negotiations began for the Americans to clear the mines dropped off Río Salta so Venezuela's "legal" energy industry could once again resume shipments of crude—and smuggled narcotics—to customers worldwide, the largest market being the American northeast.

Wilson wished to remain aboard *Coral Sea* and in command of his squadron, but his injuries made the act of traversing the distance from his stateroom to the wardroom a daunting challenge. After he had clogged passageways too many times, he chose a self-imposed exile, accepting visitors in his stateroom most of the time. With Weed's assistance, he was able to preside over Annie's memorial service on the flight deck. When he learned from Macho and other witnesses of her courageous sacrifice, he first wrote Mike Schofield a heartfelt letter and then, with CAG's strong approval, drafted a citation and recommendation for Annie to be awarded the Medal of Honor.

Whenever he was alone with his thoughts, Wilson thought of Mary—and of Father Dan. He said prayers of thanksgiving and pulled his Bible off the shelf—where it had lain available but unopened for many months. With help from Billy and Weed, he boarded the COD and flew to Roosevelt Roads, and then to Norfolk, to begin his rehabilitation. *Coral Sea* and the *Firebirds* returned to Norfolk two weeks later.

Monique was getting her life back after the nightmare of the cabin. She helped Father Dan find an apartment in town, which he hated, but it was much closer for her. Why she put up with him, after their near-death experience with the Americans, was beyond her. She decided it was because of his friendly, good nature. He didn't worry, he *trusted* come-what-may, and she knew whatever protests she came up with would be overcome by his impish grin. So far, though, she was having her way on one matter—no more cabins in the Woodyard.

At least she had a "new" car. The parish had replaced the old one, being full of bullet holes, with a newer used vehicle that had air conditioning. Yes, she was happy to serve Father Dan, which allowed *him* to serve the parish, and her simple life had meaning. Thirty-five and single. Everyone asked her why she didn't marry, and she had suitors who told her she was beautiful. She didn't mind men, but she didn't want the aggravation of married life. "So become a nun," they said.

Maybe she would.

As she drove up to her small house and stepped out of the car, she noted an unfamiliar car coming down the single lane road. As she watched it, she wondered which neighbor was expecting visitors. The glare on the windshield concealed those inside as flashes and loud sounds erupted from the passenger's side.

Monique was on the ground, unable to move, unable to speak. She concentrated on the blades of grass in front of her eyes. She had never seen them so clearly but remembered placing her head like this against the ground when she was a child. She became fascinated by a lady bug climbing one of the blades: red-and-black wings, innocent, beautiful, peaceful....

She bled to death before any neighbors could help her.

At the same moment, Father Dan walked along the Edward Trace enjoying the fresh air and sunshine. How he missed the cabin and his daily exercise. He swung his arms in vigorous full motion as he walked, an occasional car his only company.

He appreciated the letter he had received from Jim Wilson, now safe with his family in Virginia. *A good lad,* he thought, *just a bit misguided.* But his heart was in the right place, and it was good to hear from him. *What an adventure that day in the cabin was! Right out of the movies!* But at what cost? He still couldn't believe he had lived it—and survived it. He prayed for the dead and for an end to war, and he gave thanks he and Monique had been spared and could continue a life of service. *What makes men behave this way?* he thought as he ruminated on a homily for the weekend mass. Attendance was way down since the incident, and Father Dan sensed some were nervous to be around him. He chalked it up to his vivid imagination and settled on "Selfless Service" as the topic of this week's talk.

The quiet. He missed it more than anything else, and, looking around, he realized he was alone on the road. Smiling, he thought of a ditty he could bellow out here. *Free.* Free to enjoy the glory of God's creation. He extended his arms and took a deep breath.

Oh, it's no...nay...never...!

No nay never, no more!

Something popped him hard, and, collapsing to his knees, he grabbed his chest in surprise. *What happened?* He felt a warm fluid flowing down his right side and a sharp pain. He had difficulty breathing. He looked down and saw a tear in his jacket. "*What?*"

The second bullet exploded into his sternum, killing him before his back hit the asphalt. He lay there for five minutes before a motorist passed by—and didn't see him. His body was discovered after two more minutes by one of his parishioners coming from the other direction.

Three days later, Father Dan and Monique shared a funeral mass given by a visiting priest. The nervous townspeople paid their respects and buried them side by side in the small cemetery along the Trace. One of his fellow missionaries flew down from Maryknoll to be present. No one from the American Embassy was there. They did not know of the deaths of these two locals who had given great assistance to the United States of America, and who had led one American citizen to a deeper relationship with God.

And the people prayed God would have mercy on their souls.

EPILOGUE

Macho gazed out the window of her commuter turboprop as the city of Washington loomed larger. The aircraft snaked down the Potomac on its visual approach to Reagan National, and she noted the National Cathedral, the football stadium at Georgetown, and the Kennedy Center. She could also make out the White House, and, in the distance, the Capitol Building that dominated the city.

Below, she saw racing sculls on the river and people walking along the green shoreline near the Lincoln Memorial. The Potomac was calm, showing barely a ripple as the aircraft descended closer to the water. This was a viewpoint she had never had in her dozens of carrier landings, which required complete focus on the glide slope and the line-up in front of her. Out there, she was surrounded by water yet had never really "seen" it during any of her landings, and at night it didn't matter as all was black nothingness.

Macho watched the water come closer and closer as the pilots maneuvered the aircraft for landing. With the LSOs screaming for power and the wave off lights warning them of impending disaster, it seemed as if they were going to ditch the aircraft in the river. The waves came closer. *Death* came closer, a death she deserved and would welcome, if only it could be her and not the other 30 passengers, innocent and oblivious to what Macho knew about herself. The water was *right there*, seconds from impact. Macho wondered for an instant if they were going to hit the carriers' ramp, and then the airport shoreline popped into view and the pilots performed a gentle flare over the runway. They floated above it for a few moments before the wheels kissed the concrete and they were down. *Alive.*

The turboprops dug into the air with a *WHAAAA* as the pilots put them into reverse, and the aircraft slowed and turned off on the nearest taxiway. As the passengers gathered their belongings and started texting on the way to the gate, Macho kept her gaze outside, lost in her thoughts. *Betrayal.* She knew it well. She was drenched in it, was *swimming* in it. She lolled

435

the bitter bile of it around her tongue, knowing it would be forever hers. She could not escape it.

On the flight from Norfolk, she had had time to think about what she was planning to do. She still didn't have a clue about how she would be received, but each step brought her closer to the dreaded reckoning. She deserved humiliation, in public, screaming invective aimed at her for what she had done, deliberately and with malice. A black eye, scars, broken bones.... She had earned them, and she would stand still to receive them.

It was a pleasant day in Washington as she stepped off the aircraft and onto the bus that took the passengers to the terminal. Macho gave a polite nod to the linesman as he directed her to stay well clear of the stationary prop. He must have taken her for a young woman naïve about the ways of airplanes, he being her protector on this dangerous ground. But that was a flight deck lesson Macho could teach *him: Never walk through a prop arc, and you'll never get hit by a prop.*

Once inside the terminal, Macho followed the directions to the Metro station, fumbling through the ticket machine for a pass before boarding the Yellow Line to Metro Center. She took a seat in the front car and watched commuters get on and off as they dove into the Crystal City underground. At the Pentagon, a commander wearing khakis got on the train and stood as it departed the station. Macho stole glances at his rows of uniform ribbons; he was a surface warfare officer, with a pin signifying command at sea, and ribbons denoting the number of deployments, their locations, command and personal awards, the everyone-gets-a-trophy end-of-tour recognition the senior officers wore on their chests to validate themselves to each other and to the public. No doubt this passed for *street cred* here in the Pentagon, and if she stayed for a career, she too would have a nice "rack" of *been there-done that* ribbons.

A nice rack. That's all Coach and Trench had seen in Shane.

Macho's eyes then met those of the officer who had caught her eying him, and she looked away. She now knew a great deal about him by his ribbons and devices, but he knew nothing about her—and would never suspect that Macho had a Silver Star.

A career. Annie had stayed for a career.

The train burst out of the underground tunnel and onto the 14th Street Bridge trestle. The water made her think of the ship again. On the ship was the last time she had seen Shane. Her face—a blended image of hurt and bitter contempt toward Macho for what Macho had caused her to lose: her dignity and sense of belonging and her trust in her squadronmates, current and future—would remain an indelible image in Macho's memory.

In less than a minute, the metro dove again, now under the district streets, as Macho stared out the window at the darkness of the tunnel wall, similar to the darkness she had brought to herself and to another human being who personified light and love of life. Macho had won, but was it worth it to destroy the trust of one —and her own soul—in the process?

At Gallery Place-Chinatown she switched to the Red Line, and a crowd of midday riders pushed in. After a few stops, Macho took a seat, and, with her hair caressing the shoulders of her sleeveless teal dress, she looked like any other young professional woman in Washington taking a break for lunch. She gazed out the window into the empty black subway wall as the train moved from stop to stop, careful not to make eye contact with a scruffy older man who was staring at her in the same way Trench and Coach looked at women. And she had made them pay—at great cost and with significant collateral damage. The "no-load" eyeing her now wasn't qualified to carry her helmet bag, but he was a man and men looked.

Although she was wearing Sketchers on her feet, the dress, the hair, and the spray of perfume all made a *statement*. And she could not turn it off for this man and then turn it back on for a professional man her age whose attention she might welcome.

But none of that today…. She was on a mission, and she had to remain focused. There was only one man she had to talk to today before she returned to the airport to catch the flight back to Norfolk.

Crossing into Maryland, the creep got off the train, and Macho relaxed. She kept her professional face expressionless, though, like the other bored young professionals who stared at nothing or were lost in their cell phones. *They should be happy*, she thought, *living in this incredible city, partying all night in Georgetown and getting up the next morning to do it all again*. She studied the jaded expressions of the twenty-something girls and their expensive suits, perfect make-up, and killer shoes. She was embarrassed to be caught in her clunky sneakers, despite the comfort. The young men in their wrinkled, ill-fitting suits needed haircuts and seemed unsure of themselves around the girls and around each other. *Screw them*, she thought. They were up here making policy on Capitol Hill that she and the Skipper and Big Jake and Olive had to execute, that Annie had given her life for. None of the girls looked like down-to-earth girlfriend material, and for a moment Macho judged them in contemptuous superiority—until she realized she had *proven* to herself and to Shane that she was not down-to-earth girlfriend material either.

At the Medical Center station, Macho got off the train and climbed the broken escalator into the humid air scented with the fresh cut grass workmen had blown off the sidewalks. The maple and oak trees were still green—though the fall change was only days away—and the sunshine felt good. She walked to the crosswalk at Rockville Pike and crossed with the crowd to the long semicircular driveway of the Walter Reed National Military Medical Center, the former Bethesda Naval Hospital. After showing her ID to security, Macho found a ladies' room and changed into the black pumps she carried in her tote bag. She also freshened her makeup and looked at her reflection, scowling at the image that scowled back at her, nervous at what was about to happen. *You earned this,* she told herself.

Alone in the elevator, Macho's heart raced as her clammy hands pushed the "4" button. When the doors opened on the ward, she stepped to the desk. A young nurse, an ensign by her collar device, lifted her head.

"Lieutenant James? May I visit him?" Macho asked.

"Yes, he's in Room 412," the nurse replied. Macho turned and smiled to herself as she walked away. No doubt Trench had this girl's attention, as well as that of a *harem* of nurses who had bought into his program. Then she reminded herself that, yes, he was wounded in combat, undeclared or not.

Macho's heels echoed as she walked to the end of the corridor and turned left. She slowed her pace when she saw that the door to Room 412 was open. She leaned forward to peer inside and saw someone in stocking feet and blue jeans on the bed.

"Trench?" she called in a soft tone.

The body flinched, and Trench said, "Who's that!"

Macho walked in. "It's me, Macho."

Trench looked up with wide eyes, not *at* Macho but away from her, out of the corner of his left eye. His opened his mouth in shock at this unforeseen visit—from the last person he would have ever expected. He soon recovered, and his face went blank.

"Hey."

Macho stepped to the foot of the bed, and as she did, Trench turned away from her. His wide eyes stared off into space.

"Hey. How are you doing?" she asked him.

"Okay. What brings you here?" His terse answers didn't make it easy for Macho.

"I came to visit my shipmate."

Trench closed his eyes and exhaled. "Why?"

"Because I sinned. And since I can't make it up to the person I betrayed, I'm trying to make it up to you."

Trench chuckled. "So, Wonder Woman won't talk to you? Can't say I blame her."

"And *you*? Have you talked to her since she left the ship?"

"No, but I've heard she doesn't blame me. It's you and Coach…. mostly you."

Absorbing the blow she deserved, Macho looked down to gather her thoughts. She tried a new tack.

"Can you see at all?"

"Yeah, but only with my peripheral vision. It's like I always have a big black circle in front of me, like I'm holding my fist in front of my nose. I can tell you're wearing a green dress and your hair is down, but I can't focus on any details. 100% disability. Soon to be Lieutenant, U.S. Navy, retired."

"Teal."

"Wha…?" Trench asked, turning his ear.

"Teal. The color of my dress."

"Oh, yes, of course, my apologies. *Teal*. Please forgive my Neanderthal ignorance. Not really a word common to the ready room as I recall. Maybe not even a color found in nature, but *you are right*. It *is* important to always be right."

Macho berated herself. *You stupid bitch!* Trench had his shields up. *Teal. Green. It doesn't matter. He* was the one who was blind, and Macho knew her personality could be grating, always having the last word, always having to be *respected*. She had to stay in control of her emotions.

"Heh, no, you're right. It's green. Chicks know things like *teal*. Can't help it."

"Matches your eyes," Trench said. Macho, stunned that Trench had ever noticed her eyes, didn't know how to react.

"Tell me about the XO," he added.

"She led a strike against their anti-ship missile launch facility. I was with Annie on that one. One of the sweepers was shot down—Lemur in VFA-62. He was about 15 miles off the coast, and the Venezuelans sent all kinds of small craft out to get him. Annie got us some gas and took us back as On-Scene Commander. We were shooting '*Winders* at them, strafing, but they just kept coming. The *Flintlocks* found Lemur and were hoisting him up as Woody and I were off chasing a *Flanker*. Annie was by herself, and she was making cold runs…. She even pickled her drop tanks on them, anything to hold them off. She was flying through small arms, got hit, lost an engine and was on fire, and *still* she came back to unload her last drop tank. She was slow in her dive and took a hit by a *Grail*. She corkscrewed in and didn't get out. I saw it."

"Did they put her in for a medal?"

"*Medal of Honor.* Skipper wrote the citation."

"Wow. They should name a ship after her. Annie was a good XO. I always liked her husband."

"It got downgraded," Macho sighed. "SOUTHCOM weenies wanted to downplay the military action and not spin up the region by recognizing someone—*a woman especially*—with a high-profile award like that. She's getting a Silver Star—same as me—and all I did was shoot a guy in the face with a bigger missile. Never really saw him. She was down there among them, taking fire the whole time, giving *everything* to keep them off Lemur. I'll never forget her."

Trench let it sink in, the *unfairness* of the decision by guys who were miles away in headquarters and whose biggest risk was the evening commute. *Fuck 'em,* he thought, knowing they weren't qualified to shine Annie's shoes. "And the Skipper?" he asked.

"He came back to us after spending three days on the ground in frickin' Trinidad. The *Flintlocks* got him, too, after they and the *Hunters* shot down something like ten helos—*Hind* gunships and shit. *At night.* Skipper was holed up with a priest and holding off drug guys and Venezuelan soldiers. I guess it was like the OK Corral. Skipper was beat up bad, but he took out some bad guys. Shot one point-blank with his .45."

"Holy shit." Trench shook his head in amazement as he absorbed her account.

They spent a few more minutes catching up on everyone, and then the small talk seemed to dry up. Macho wasn't sure how to proceed, so Trench did it for her.

"No more bullshit, Macho. Why did you come here?"

She took a breath. "I had to reconcile with you. I *hated* you, and I'm done with hate."

Trench thought for a moment before he spoke. "Why did you hate me?"

"Because you embodied everything I hate about guys. The frat-boy culture, the porn stash, the catcalls, the hook-ups...."

"So that justified your holier-than-thou condescension, the bitchy sermonizing?" Trench added.

Macho recoiled at his cutting remark but nodded to herself. *He's right.*

"Great then. You've seen me in a fucking hospital ward, broken, depending on the chicks out there to bring me food, and with a bright future at Lighthouse for the Blind. You *won*, Macho. Coach and I are out of the *Firebirds*. You got what you fucking wanted. Now *leave*."

"Please forgive me!"

Trench looked up, his way of observing what he could of her. His anger melted, but he was puzzled. "Why? What did you do to me?"

"I used Shane to set you up."

"I know.... Why do you come here and apologize to me instead of her?"

Macho gathered her thoughts.

"I want to get it off my chest, to let go. To put it behind us and move on."

"Fine. Thanks for coming. Safe trip to wherever Shane is," Trench muttered as he turned away from her.

Macho pursed her lips and swallowed. She had hoped it would go better, but Trench wasn't going to make it easy on her. Still, she had done what she came to do, and, resigned, she gathered her bag and stepped toward the door. Her heels echoed in the chasm of bitterness between them.

When she got to the door, Trench spoke in a low tone, "*Tiffany*."

Macho turned and saw Trench standing by the bed, looking away, but his hand was stretched out to her.

She walked back to him and placed her hand in his.

"I'm sorry, too," he whispered. "I'm sorry.... *I'm sorry*."

They stood there, sworn enemies, considering the uncertain futures that lay ahead. Fighting back the tears of guilt they felt about the lives they had devastated in their combat with each other, they remained still and held each other's hands for a moment in silence, two squadronmates forged in battle.

Both broken. Both forgiven.

The End

ABOUT THE AUTHOR

Captain Kevin Miller, a 24-year veteran of the U.S. Navy, is a former tactical naval aviator and has flown the A-7E *Corsair II* and FA-18C *Hornet* operationally. He commanded a carrier-based strike-fighter squadron, and, during his career, logged over 1,000 carrier-arrested landings, made possible as he served alongside outstanding men and women as part of a winning team. Captain Miller lives and writes in Pensacola, Florida.

DECLARED HOSTILE is the second novel in his Flip Wilson series.

Contact the author at **kevin@kevinmillerauthor.com**.

HIGH OCTANE AERIAL COMBAT

KEVIN MILLER

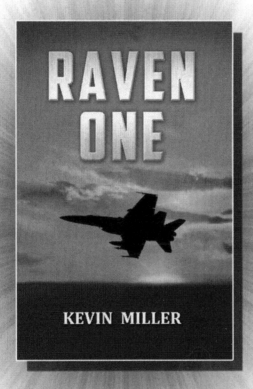

Unarmed over hostile territory...

www.StealthBooks.Com

CUTTING-EDGE NAVAL THRILLERS
BY
JEFF EDWARDS

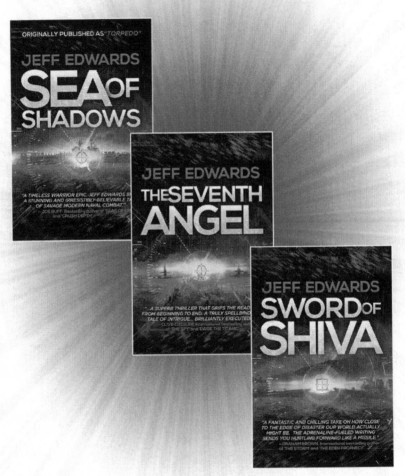

WHITE-HOT SUBMARINE WARFARE
BY

JOHN R. MONTEITH

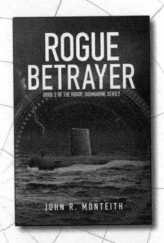

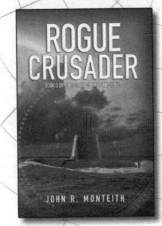

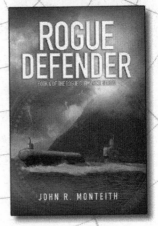

www.StealthBooks.Com

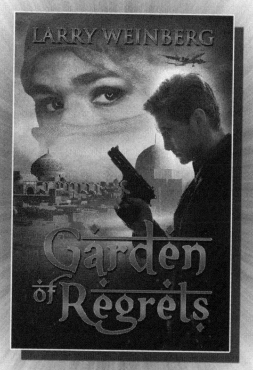

36078389R00275